HISTORICAL LOVECRAFT

TALES OF HORROR THROUGH TIME

Edited by
Silvia Moreno-Garcia and Paula R. Stiles

Library and Archives Canada Cataloguing in Publication

Historical Lovecraft : tales of horror through
time / edited by Silvia Moreno-Garcia and Paula R. Stiles.

Issued also in electronic format.
ISBN 978-0-9866864-0-5

1. Horror tales, American. 2. Horror tales. I. Stiles,
Paula R. (Paula Regina), 1967- II. Moreno-Garcia, Silvia

PS648.H6H57 2011 813'.0873808 C2011-901092-5

Published by Innsmouth Free Press, April 2011.
Visit www.innsmouthfreepress.com

CONTENTS

Introduction   7

ANCIENT HISTORY   9

The God Lurking in Stone   11
  Andrew Dombalagian

The Seeder From the Stars   21
  Julio Toro San Martin

Deus ex Machina   33
  Nathaniel Katz

If Only to Taste Her Again   37
  E. Catherine Tobler

Shadows of the Darkest Jade   43
  Sarah Hans

The Chronicle of Aliyat Son of Aliyat   53
  Alter S. Reiss

MIDDLE AGES   59

Silently, Without Cease   61
  Daniel Mills

The Good Bishop Pays the Price   69
  Martha Hubbard

The Saga of Hilde Ansgardóttir   87
  Jesse Bullington

An Interrupted Sacrifice   99
Mae Empson

Pralaya: The Disaster   107
Y.W. Purnomosidhi

The City of Ropes   115
Albert Tucher

MODERN ERA   127

Inquisitor   129
William Meikle

The Far Deep   137
Joshua Reynolds

City of Witches   151
Regina Allen

Ahuizotl   159
Nelly Geraldine García-Rosas

An Idol for Emiko   163
Travis Heermann

The Infernal History of the Ivybridge Twins   173
Molly Tanzer

Black Leaves   195
Mason Ian Bundschuh

The Second Theft of Alhazred's Manuscript   201
Bradley H. Sinor

Ngiri's Catch   215
Aaron Polson

What Hides and What Returns   223
Bryan Thao Worra

Black Hill   239
Orrin Gray

Amundsen's Last Run   247
Nathalie Boisard-Beudin

Red Star, Yellow Sign   253
Leigh Kimmel

Found in a Trunk from Extremadura   265
Meddy Ligner

INTRODUCTION

T HE INSPIRATION FOR this anthology came to us easily. We have an
interest in history and historical fiction. One of us has completed a PhD
in Medieval History on the Knights Templar (Paula) and the other spends a
vast amount of time reading about Prehispanic Mexico and the Tudor period
(Silvia). And history, of course, is an important element in Lovecraft's stories,
whether it comes in the shape of the *Necronomicon's* false provenance or allu-
sions to New England's 17th-century witchcrazes. To Lovecraft, a tainted past
is the rotten core from which present-day horror germinates.

Lovecraft comes from a long line of New England writers of dark fiction,
both before and after him, including the likes of Nathaniel Hawthorne,
Edgar Allan Poe, Shirley Jackson, and Stephen King. New England of his
time possessed a sinister history full of paranoid Puritans, hatchet-wielding
daughters, dour and isolated farmers, and Cape Verdean whalers with
connections extending across the seven seas (hence his obsession with the
ocean). Lovecraft was also fascinated by the "long view" of weird fiction
that was popular in his time, extrapolating frightening pasts for humanity
that extended back to the Paleolithic and even further.

In this volume, we decided to take that interest in history, in the past,
which Lovecraft's stories show, but to jump back in time instead of anchoring
the tales in the present.

We received vast amounts of tales set in Victorian England, because that
seemed the setting *de rigueur,* and at one point, despaired that we might have
to change the title of this volume to *'Cthulhu With a Cravat and a Top Hat'.*
Soon, however, stories with other locations and time periods began to trickle
in. Eventually, we assembled 26 stories, two of them translations from French
and Spanish, set in ancient Egypt, Prehispanic Peru, Stalin's Russia, and
many more places, and ranging from the Neolithic to the early 20th century.

The result is a collection of stories that span the world and the centuries, and which we hope Lovecraft and historical fiction enthusiasts alike will find as unique and exciting as we do. Enter our eldritch time machine … if you dare.

— Silvia Moreno-Garcia and Paula R. Stiles

ANCIENT HISTORY

THE GOD LURKING IN STONE

ANDREW DOMBALAGIAN

WHEN I FOUND him, flies were buzzing across Marduk's vacant face. He sat without shade by the river's bank. He stared down at the sand around him. Already, the hot morning had begun to bake his back into a reddish sore. My brother would not know to move out of the heat, even if his skin began to blister.

Marduk did not twitch a single muscle until I stood right next to him. He turned his dim, grey eyes towards me. After slow, grinding thought within his head permitted him to remember who I was, he cracked a simpleton's grin. When his mouth opened, two gadflies flew out, freed from their toothy prison.

"Tigranes, look. Look what I make."

He pointed to the squat heap of silt and clay before him. I could not recall anything that had ever excited Marduk as much as the terraced hill built at his feet.

"Mother was worried that wild dogs had eaten you, her idiot son, and here you are, playing in the sand like a child."

"From my dreams, Tigranes. Gods showed me. Showed me big villages. Full of temples. Like this. This one."

"Why would the gods bring visions to a fool who burns his eyes by staring at Utu's radiance in the sky? You could not see a serpent crawling towards you, much less visions from the gods."

"The shapes. Gods show me shapes. Can't make them. Hard. Hard to make. I can't copy. They look scary. Have you seen, brother? Do gods show you? Do you see cities?"

"What are you babbling about now, Marduk?"

"I belong to gods. Oonana says that. She says I belong to gods. That why they show me. They show me 'cause I am theirs."

The crazed crone had spread more nonsense to his feeble mind. The gods had allowed Oonana to live to eat the bread of forty-and-two harvests. Our neighbours claimed that her withered body stored the grain of wisdom. All of her ravings were inane and fit only for an unfit mind.

The truly wise ones were the ones who had abandoned Marduk in the rugged uplands. Father should never have brought Marduk into our home. He should have left him on the hillside for the dogs and vultures.

Mother always commanded me to bring him along when I guarded Father's flocks with sling and staff. I would leave Marduk on the grassy hill and tell him to brain any wild dogs that came near. I told Marduk that the wild dogs were brown and that father's hounds were grey. No matter how many times I told him, his thick head would not remember. Marduk had once smashed the skull of father's favourite she-hound.

"Come on, now. We need to get to the square."

I hauled Marduk to his stumbling feet and set him walking home. As he shambled up the verdant hill rising from the river, I looked down at his trivial construction on the bank. Marduk had piled and shaped the clay into a series of heaped squares. Each level was smaller than the last, creating a series of tiers that escalated to the pinnacle. At the top was perched a mockery of our village altar, left empty of its rightful shrine.

From the top of the hill, Marduk called out for me. He did not see that my foot had trampled his temple into nothingness.

THE NOMADIC TRADERS had come early from the cedar forests to the west. Traditionally, our village would have reaped the harvest before the traders' arrival. There would be stores of grain, animal skins, dried meat, and pots of fermenting beer to offer. In exchange, we would get tools of sharp stone and exotic woods, preserved fruits, and goods that had seen the distant sea.

But harvest was still days away. There was little to barter with and everyone was in a rush to amend this plight. Alongside our neighbours, my entire family was hurrying in the fields to reap, slaughter and store so we could trade before the caravan departed. With our family so busy, we were sent to market to barter for a few important things.

My eldest sister, Ishara, admired herself in the polished surface of the obsidian mirror held by one of the nomadic traders. She turned and posed, coaxing the string of blue stones around her neck to look their most appealing. The cloth she knelt upon cradled nothing but useless adornments and trinkets.

"These are not the things our family needs."

"Tigranes, I have already gotten the flint blades, dried figs and salt that father asked for. I finished my tasks, even with Oonana bothering me."

"What did that hag want?"

"She was casting warnings about a man travelling with the caravan. She claims he is a wicked sorcerer from far to the south. He carries a long blade that brightly shines, but it is not made from flint or obsidian. Oonana says he walks with wild beasts that kneel before him and lick his feet like servants."

"Sounds like the sort of muck that Marduk might believe. No wonder he hangs around the old woman with the other tiny children. It would be fitting, if only he weren't twice their size and with half their cunning."

"Don't you ever tire of abusing him? No wonder he disappears from you all the time."

"Where did he go this time? He was just here."

"I wish you fortune finding him again."

"Don't waste your wishes. I'm not going to waste my effort on Marduk again. If the gods want him, I will leave him to them."

ISHARA AND I brought home the goods Mother and Father wanted before harvest. No one raised an eyebrow at Marduk's absence. Our parents, siblings, cousins, and other relations had supper without even noting that my supposed-brother was missing. Everyone felt burdened to have him beneath our roof. I was merely the one with the daring to admit this disgust.

I was awakened that night by whisperings that flittered down from above. I did not want to confront what was waiting for me, but if I did not attend to my troublesome duties, everyone would wake up and be furious. Our family did not care about what Marduk did as long as I kept him from bringing shame to our house.

Marduk had raised the ladder reaching up from the common room through the exit in the roof. Climbing up after him, there on the roof, I found my useless sibling sitting under the soft, pale glow of Nanna's throne. His body swayed like a brittle reed in the dry wind. He was speaking in hushed tones, even though there was not another body to be seen.

My reaction was baffling. On a normal night, I would have tossed a pebble at his head to break Marduk from his dullard's trance. This night, however, I crept closer to listen in on his mutterings. His voice was thicker, and his words were not those of a man with the addled mind of a child.

"One thousand pillars will rise from the southern sands. They will glitter with gold and jewels for centuries before they are swallowed by the merciless deserts of oblivion. Why should Irem's fate be other than that fallen city with no name? The reptile and serpent men no longer crawl and slide through those narrow halls and arcades of nameless antiquity.

"This servant race will know the destructive touch of ages before all is through. Cyclopean megaliths beyond their comprehension have already crumbled or sunk into strange eons. These primitives' mud bricks and reeds cannot even survive the paltry river floods that are outside of their pitiful strength to control. The ziggurats and pyramids that will awe their mewling descendants have not even germinated in the dreamy minds of their artists, yet the decay of those low wonders is already written.

"These clans bicker over rocks and stones to fashion into tools. Cults and armies have already danced in the tallest mountains and deepest forests with blades of iron and stranger metals, calling for the glory of their Old Ones. These people scratch and claw at the dirt and sand like the beasts they have hardly risen from. They have only begun to label the heavens with their meaningless words, ignorant of the true names of the beings chained to those damned spheres."

Here, in Marduk's incessant, unnatural ranting, I found myself peering over his shoulder. He sat much like he did that morning on the river's bank. However, rather than a childish construction of clay, an oddly-shaped hunk of smooth stone sat before him.

The stone was large, larger than Marduk should have been able to carry onto the roof. Of its shape, I cannot say anything for certain. My first impression was one of a stout spire of cut stone, standing straight in the air with its peak reaching the level of my seated brother's seared eyes. With each tilt of my head, however, it seemed to bow and sway. One moment, it appeared to bend outward, only to deceive me with the appearance of its five sides curving inward on themselves.

The lines, dots, and curls carved into those smooth surfaces were a puzzle. Oonana had often spoken of painted etchings in distant caves. But while the crazed miller woman had described images of men and beasts, these designs mimicked nothing but their own irrelevant forms. I would have believed Marduk himself might have carved this stone from his own senseless imagination, but where would he have found the tools and presence of mind to do so?

My idiot brother seemed to share some secret, not just with this stone, but with luminescent Nanna on high. When the light of Nanna's pearly glow caught on the contours of those carvings, I suspected that they moved and flowed like river water, creating new designs and patterns. In these shifting shapes, hints of colour twinkled in my eyes. The colours of twilight, rush fronds, goat's blood, dried barley, and others I could not name, shimmered like illusions along the edges of those graven lines.

Suddenly, I realized that Marduk was pulling on my arm. He was frenetically trying to seize my attention. In shock and disgust, I shoved him away, sending him sprawling like a turtle on its back.

"Brother. I called you. You stared at rock. You did not hear. I called you."

His witless speech had reasserted dominance over his empty mind. Had I really been staring for so long at that stone? Perhaps demons of night had been playing a jest on my mind, filling it with false sensations. I resolved that

my brother's bizarre speech and the oddities of this stone were all products
of my weary thoughts.

"Why did you bring that rock onto our roof?"

"My rock. I got from market."

"You actually traded something of value for this useless hunk of rock?"

"No. Gave to me."

"Who gave it to you?"

"Trader from South. Oonana talk about him. He had big knife. It was
shiny. I could see faces in it. Oonana say he has magic. She say he has many
faces. She call him 'faceless'. What she mean? How he be faceless? I saw his
face. Only one face. I see no wings. Oonana say he flies. At night, he flies.
But no wings. She call him 'Pharaoh'. Oonana say means 'king'. Black Pharaoh. Black King from South. Why king be trader?"

"You are the only fool in town who listens to her lies. Now help me push
this rock off of our house. Father will be mad if he finds it on his way to the
fields in the morning."

"Don't push! My rock! Black Pharaoh gave me! Don't break!"

"Keep your voice down. Everyone will be furious if we raise a commotion.
Fine. You can stay up here with your rock. I am bringing the ladder down after me. You can stay up here all night with your rock and that crazy woman's
stories. If your rock tells you to fly like that trader, go ahead. Just jump off the
roof, flap your arms like a hawk, and you will fly away from me."

WHEN UTU RECLAIMED the sky throne from Nanna, Marduk was not to
be found. When we all climbed out to finish bringing in the harvest, my idiot
brother and his rock were both gone from the roof. I did not see him sitting
on any of the neighbouring roofs adjoining our house and none of the other
families climbing out from their homes noticed anything amiss.

I peered down the front of our house. It was the only wall bordering
on the lane and was adorned with only narrow, high-set windows. Father
lowered the outside ladder to the ground. There was no trace of a rock, or a
rock-head, having fallen to the earth.

Father and our uncles led the flocks out of the town walls. The he-beasts
among them would be slaughtered. Their skins would be scraped clean then
stretched out on the roof, pinned down by heavy stones, and left in Utu's light
to dry. We would not be able to tool the bones and horns into anything useful
before the traders left. We would have to make do with what we could get for
the hides and meat.

Mother, Ishara, and I marched out into the fields alongside our cousins.
We carried long knives and sickles made from new flint to cut down the
wheat and barley. We worked until Utu's throne sat at its baking zenith before

resting. A cousin brought forth a basket of brown bread and a goatskin bag filled with fresh milk.

While we ate in the shade of uncut stalks, Oonana approached. She ignored the tides of sweat running down her frail body. Her violent raving could not be abated by heat or hunger.

"The Southern Trader has gone. He left in the night. He flies south to the land of the great river. Beneath the sandstone gaze of a man-lion, in bright robes, he is worshipped by cults that proclaim him their dark god. He leaves behind his vile curse! Where he walks, madness and destruction follow! Even if every knee bent in honour at the town altar, no respite of the gods would protect us!"

Interrupting her wild gesticulations, Oonana looked squarely at me. A twisting, terrifying fire danced in her eyes. The crone rushed forward, charging like an enraged beast. She kicked me to the ground and flailed at my chest with clawing hands. Amid shrieks and curses, her fingers tore at my skin. With her savagery, Oonana sent every heron and toad into flight from the scene of chaos.

Mother and Ishara tried to pull the old woman from me, but with uncanny strength, the hag pushed them into the barley. I grabbed the flint sickle beside me and swung in a powerful arc. The freshly sharpened blade sank deeply into her flank. Stunned by the wound, Oonana staggered away.

Onlookers had collected, drawn by the sounds of the skirmish. Oonana shoved her way through the crowd, casting aside everyone that offered her a hand. She ran to the river and tumbled down the grassy banks into the rich waters.

The beast had been lying in wait for this meal. When Oonana fell splashing into the dark water, a great, toothy reptile rose up to claim her. The monster snapped its jaws down upon the doomed old woman and dragged her into the wide depths.

I rubbed the sickle blade on the soil to remove the blood. Everyone returned to their plots of land. The gods had elected to protect Oonana no longer. Whether by beasts, flood, or famine, those doomed to die would meet their fate. They would be spirited into the Lightless World to drink ash and eat clay.

"TIGRANES, ARE YOU sure you are not hurt?"

"Oonana was feeble, even in her fury. I am fine, Ishara."

"Perhaps she had the same evil dreams, as well. Maybe her aged mind could not handle the burden and that is why she broke into this fit."

"What evil dreams?"

"Mother confided in me that she and Father had terrible visions last night. Our uncles, aunts and cousins had them, too. But their impressions

were all just vague feelings of misery and unease. They had lingering sensations of doom, accompanied by the music of demons. My evil dreams were
far more vivid."

"What did you see?"

When Marduk would pour the disjointed memories of his dreams into
my ear, they mostly fell uselessly to the ground. My sister, on the other
hand, even if prone to flights of fancy, was a hard worker and a level mind.
When Ishara spoke of such slumbering hallucinations, I was more apt to
lend credence and listened intently to her story.

"At first I saw only a wide, black emptiness. I could hear the same music
as our family in their nightmares – the cruel beating of drums and the inhar-
monious wailing of flutes. Lights, like bright torches, flickered in the vastness,
yet all remained dark. I had a grim impression, as though I were walking
through an endless graveyard. Those multitudes of light hanging in the null
vastness were as dead as a field of men slaughtered by heartless raiders.

"A towering temple suddenly emerged, bubbling up from the viscous
plume of the audient void. It was made of massive bricks of dried mud. They
were so big that I imagine an entire riverbank of clay and mud would need to
be dredged just to mold one brick for this monstrous house of the gods. Tier
upon tier was heaped to great heights. Four steep pathways cut with steps
led up to the pinnacle at its immeasurable peak. From every doorway issued
moans of agony and shrieks of maddened laughter.

"Then I saw Marduk. He marched down from the pinnacle of the temple in
triumph. His face was set in hard, fierce determination. There was a cunning in
his eyes and a malice that I have never seen anywhere before. Tigranes, please
tell me what Marduk has been doing? You watch over him. Where is he?"

"I do not know. I do not care to know."

THAT NIGHT, MY fists clenched in sleepless furor because, anew, my
brother's shapeless words haunted the roof of our house. His distorted
speech merely kept me in irate wakefulness, but did not initially wake me.
What stirred me from sleep was the heavy, pulsing sound of wind, as though
the air were disturbed by the beating of large wings.

When I climbed to the roof, I brought Father's obsidian knife with me. I
concealed the blade, but would not hesitate in resorting to it if needed. I had
already freed the world from one mad mind that day.

Marduk was again staring at that rock, chanting phrases of veiled meaning. He did not hush his voice, or perhaps the night air amplified his words
just for my ears. His fevered thoughts were of an even stranger bent tonight.
It seemed that Oonana's wild ramblings, denied entrance into the Lightless
World, had been passed along to my brother.

"The old woman has taken into oblivion the secrets of her lineage. Flowing through her blood was an ancestral memory of the flesh digested in her fore-bears' stomachs. Those were not the bones of deer and mammoth left behind in long-forgotten caverns before the Great Thaw. They picked those femurs and fibulae clean of flesh and marrow, but those tiny bones covered in supple flesh, harvested fresh from the young livestock, were the true delight.

"Now they have all fled to distant Leng. Only that festering old woman remained to pick apart at humanity, although she preferred to feast on their minds and sanity, leaving the meat to rot on the living bones. Nevertheless, the banquet of ghouls shall be rejoined. Already, on a rain-sodden isle of blight far to the north and west, the Great Mother has sounded the call for her children to devour the scratching, squealing bipedal beasts who believe themselves sentient."

Marduk had been a revolting vermin in our house since the day Father rescued him from the barren hillside. His vacuous face and abbreviated thoughts nagged me like a swarm of gadflies. He had brought embarrass-ment to our family and vulgar frustration to my life.

Never before, though, had I felt him so intrinsically repellent. Deep within his heinous, cryptically shocking words, lurked something alien in his nature that made his very existence abhorrent to my eyes. The godless words that had slithered foully from his lips confirmed that I would be purging twin abominations from the world this day.

I protected my eyes from even fleeting glances at that shining rock of shifting form and unimaginable mental horror. I lunged at my fiendish brother when he turned his own eyes to meet me. The milky veil was lifted from his eyes and in their depths, I saw forbidden secrets, waiting without patience to emerge. In my haste to extinguish those secrets forever, I tack-led Marduk and wrestled him into submission.

I held his throat against the precipice of the roof, leaving his head sus-pended above the dusty lane below. Nanna's light danced on the notched surfaces of the obsidian knife. The glassy, black blade glimmered against Marduk's neck. His eyes, almost rolling back into his skull, turned up to look at me one final time.

In that instant, I saw the weakened eyes of my idiot brother, containing his old, harmless, imbecile spirit. Beside his face, having rolled along the roof in the scuffle, lay the menacing, multicoloured shimmer of that horrendously enlightening stone. My sight betrayed me and my eyes became affixed to the leering secrets that danced across its etched surfaces.

The unbearable truths of Time and Space wriggled their way into my brain to fester like maggots bloating themselves on a ripened corpse. That stone opened doors for me, revealing the expanse of worlds that should not exist. I bore witness to darkened stars that consumed the light of the heavens to feed their captive masters. In caverns vast enough to swallow all the rivers in the land, I observed writhing hordes of contorting bodies clinging to the walls of the Inner Earth. Those beasts waited for the summons into wakefulness that would herald the new age of the hunt. All the while, these tormenting insights were chorused by a cacophony of pipes and drums from the ends of eternity.

When my fractured mind returned to my family's roof from those far-flung abysses, I found myself alone in the cold wind. Marduk and the stone both lay broken on the ground below. Kneeling in stunned shock, I could still feel the sting where my hand had gripped that wicked rock as a weapon against my brother. The insanity of wisdom would not let me spare him.

Amongst the fragments of bone and stone littering the ground, my uneasy senses beheld movement, but not from my brother. An amorphous creature, resembling the abnormal spawn of a slug and serpent, slid across the dirt towards Marduk's body. In grotesque shades of black and green, the thing was a faintly luminescent amalgam of bubbles and eyes that stared everywhere, but saw nothing.

Leaving a viscous trail of slime, and unleashing an odour that wafted up the height of a tall tree to assault my nose, the fluid beast crawled onto Marduk. It flattened itself out and inched towards his face. Morbid curiosity and an undying familial connection compelled me to slide down the exterior ladder to inspect my brother.

The wound I had dealt him made it impossible, yet my brother was rising to his feet again. He ignored me, at first, and he focused his attention on the rubble of his precious stone. From the remnants, he selected one shard – a stone of many faces and angles that shone with a light other than that of Nanna on high. Marduk tightened his fist around the stone and would not expose it for the duration of this, our last confrontation.

The blood was still fresh on his brow, but the gash I left on his skull with the ignoble stone had healed with unnatural celerity. His bones, assuredly snapped and smashed in the fall, had all knitted back into cohesion. His eyes were cold and knowing. The madness from the raw magic of the stone was diminished from his aura, but from his bearing, it was clear that a vastly different person was inhabiting Marduk.

"The Trapezohedron is still imperfect, but there are whole epochs left to correct that."

"What are you that has stolen my brother?"

"Suddenly, you care for the animal you spent a lifetime cursing? He will harass you no more and yet, you are not joyous. The buffoon has served his purpose and his destiny has reached its end. Marduk the ascending god has been born. My eyes see centuries forward and back. I shall grow this stagnant collection of farms into a mighty city and force your race into a civilization. My temple will be built from their mud, wood and bones. From the pinnacle, the prayers of the worthy will reach out into the spheres as a beacon to the Great Old Ones."

I searched the ground desperately for Father's knife. With growing despair, I realized the obsidian tool lay back on the roof. Marduk smiled in defiant victory, sensing my fear.

"Do not hope to kill me. It cannot be. Your bloodline will not know the glorious burden of my yoke. You will march north and abandon the fertile lands of the flood. In the bitter rock of the highlands, you will lay the foundations of your ill-fated progeny. The weight of ceaseless subjugation will weigh on your people and they will never know triumph in their bitter knowledge."

Against the hypnotic might of his command, I could muster no defense. In accordance with his whims, my feet carried me down the lane and out from the town walls. The comforting safety of drudging toil was left behind. In the be-nighted world stretching out in all directions before me, I marched north into the crushing liberty of the unknown.

For all the disappointing promises that lay sequestered in those distant peaks, the crushing pressure of the secrets relayed to me ensured that the world would never again look as bright. Long after the names of our gods had fallen into the grave of eons, there would forever be a pall cast over the whole of existence. In a doomed universe, where ever-hungry ghouls lurk in the shadows, and blithering idiots are reborn as tyrannical gods, how may hope survive the rise and fall of empires in the sand and stone?

Andrew Dombalagian lives, writes and dreams in Havertown, Pennsylvania. He works as a writing tutor at his university: Penn State Brandywine. His fiction and poetry have appeared in the collegiate publications, *Crimson & Grey* and *Penn in Hand*. "The God Lurking in Stone" is his first professionally published story and he is thankful for the support of his fiancée, Ellen.

The author speaks: Ancient history has always been a fascination of mine, so I thought it would be fun to surpass the historical and take my story into prehistoric realms. Set in Neolithic Mesopotamia, "The God Lurking in Stone" was born out of a curious idea to explore how Lovecraftian elements, such as Nyarlathotep, may have shaped the gods and mythologies of ancient civilizations. I also wanted to offer a possible origin for the Shining Trapezohedron featured in Lovecraft's "The Haunter of the Dark".

THE SEEDER FROM THE STARS

JULIO TORO SAN MARTIN

ALWAYS, THE HIGH Priestess communed with her Lady, Inanna. We lived in the great temple ziggurat and out of all her servants and retainers, I alone can boast that I was the closest to her in her detached affections. My Mistress was the *En*-Priestess of the Moon God, Nanna, but his daughter, Inanna, was the deity most dear to her heart.

I served her in the high place closest to the stars, charting the heavens and their revolutions. I saw from above the great city – clearly, the vast buildings, houses, orchards and agricultural lands. My name is Smenkhkare.

Always, she'd say strange things to frighten me, and that I didn't understand. I knew she was possessed of the divine and that I, a mere commoner, could never know of such things. But I was proud to be the friend of such a mighty princess and serve her, body and soul, in the Temple of Ur.

Because my Mistress was a member of the Royal House of Akkad and *En*-Priestess of the Moon, her decrees were unquestioned. She handed out many secret prohibitions, such as: never peer behind the curtains of the Holiest Room.

The years rolled unnoticed in the Temple of Nanna, in the now-far city of Ur, and great were those early times. Great was the drink of youth we enjoyed. Great, especially, were the hymns of my Mistress, Enheduanna. If I praise her too much, it's because I can do no else and if I speak of myself but little, it's because I am not important.

ISHME ARRIVED FROM the ruined city-state of Kazalla, from west of the Euphrates River, in the seventh year of my Mistress' *En*-Ship. Without father or mother and orphaned to the world. He'd been found amid toppled blocks of burnt mud, clothed in filthy rags, and eating dirt and crawling bugs. I was assigned to tutor him in the duties of the temple, but early on, he showed promise of greater things. Secret rumours spread that one day, Ishme would outgrow the temple and leave to be a great administrator. Because I was the boy's principal teacher, he was moved to call me 'Father'. I was pleased with this.

My Mistress took an early interest in the boy, also. She taught him much of her secret wisdom, but of the hidden thing of darkness that was whispered to live behind the curtains in the Room of Nanna, she remained quiet.

When sometimes, because of the rashness of his youth, he'd say something untoward towards the noblewoman, I'd scold him severely. "Do you think of him as our son, perhaps, Smenkhkare?" she'd insinuate and laugh.

Oh, never let it be imputed to me that I, Smenkhkare, ever harboured any sacrilegious thought towards the Holy One of Nanna!

One day, as the three of us walked the lonely corridors of the dark temple together, a crazed man approached and attacked my Mistress with a sword. Ishme jumped in front of her. Quickly, the rest of the temple household, having heard our commotion, arrived and subdued the man.

ALL NIGHT, MY Mistress knelt by the bedside of Ishme, praying her beautiful poems under the stars. Her poems had power to soothe the Gods, had power to change their wills, or could summon screeching Ereshkigal from the nether hells. But this day, the High Gods remained silent.

I knelt beside her. I looked at her eyes and saw, for the first time – the second would be many years later – that they were watery. I reached out and touched her shoulder, covered by her woolen robe. I touched her just this once and she didn't stop me.

"Why did the boy do such a thing? I could have protected myself," I heard her say. We both wept together.

Then she arose and left the room.

Hours later, after the temple physicians told me the boy's health was worsening, I went to look for my Mistress and found her behind the curtains. Strange now were her songs, strange yet beautiful, sung in a language I didn't understand and that disturbed me deeply. I let her finish.

When she emerged, I looked at one of her hands and saw she carried something. I could not make it out.

Entering the boy's room, she ordered everyone out, except for myself. Then she placed the thing in Ishme's wound.

I heard the boy cough.

I looked and saw the boy's wound was healed. The child looked at us, perplexed. Then he turned to Enheduanna, opened his arms, and hugged her tightly.

SHORTLY AFTER MY Mistress' assassination attempt, great anticipation engulfed the temple. Sargon, her father, was coming to Ur. From atop the stony girths of the temple, Ishme and I watched, engrossed, as the Great King with his hundreds of military men, carrying weapons of flaring bronze and sturdy bows, marched in ordered phalanx into the celebratory city. Later in the day, a small band of mercenary men arrived and encamped on the outskirts of Ur. We knew they were hostile towards my Mistress and her father.

He conferred with his daughter and counselors in the temple, instead of in the customary palace of the ancient kings of Ur.

"The whole of the city-states of Sumer," I recall the Great King saying, "are not pleased being ruled by just one city. They want their autonomy back. It isn't safe here, anymore."

"I have sung to the Gods," my Mistress said, while braiding a lock of hair dispassionately, "and will sing again. They are always pleased with my offerings."

"It isn't only the Gods that keep you safe, daughter, but also the sharp edge of my battle-axe. When I go to the distant north, what great army will stop the rest of the Sumerians, as now Uruk and Lagash do, from rising against you? Your death and dethronement from the High Place of Nanna would be a great blow to my ambitions. Come with me and be safe."

My Mistress laughed fearlessly and showed those terrible eyes, while saying, "My Lady, Inanna, loves me as she loved you long ago, when you were taken from a basket and placed as the Cup-bearer to the King of Kish. She helped you usurp that dreamer, Ur-Zababa, and now helps you in this empire that you create for Akkad. But she helps me, also. She's given me a pet. With this pet, I'll strike such a fear into the traitors' hearts that they will cower like defenseless babes and dare not rise against me."

"Do this, then," Sargon said, with a ferocious look. "Show this beast tonight. But if, by tomorrow morning," he warned, "the forces of our enemies are still encamped, I'll flay them alive and then you'll come with me to the far north, where already great hosts of my armies march."

He left immediately. We were left speechless at what we'd heard pass between them.

A MIST-ENSHROUDED EVENING came.

That night, as the High Priestess sang her songs in the Inner Sanctum, Ishme and I went to one of the higher places of the storied temple. It was especially dark that night and the strong fog, which was heavier in some places and sparser in others, made visibility a jest. Yet, still, we tried to see what we could across the teeming land. From our vantage point, we could barely make out, dim in the foggy distance, the vast, sprawling campfires of the enemy. Ishme, who at eight years old, barely reached my waist, held my hand with a full and nervous anticipation.

Suddenly, a slow wind began to pick up, gnawingly cold, and in its rising crescendo, through the darkness and the fog, we felt the rudiments of some-

thing huge awakening high above. Ishme pointed deliriously up. We heard
a loud scream and saw, vaguely, a black presence, broad-winged above us,
in the night sky. The wind blew terribly and the scream grew louder, and a
rising panic began to overpower my senses. Ishme hugged my legs in fright.
Now totally terrified, I grabbed the boy in my arms and rushed quickly into
the safe womb of the temple. From inside, I could hear the frenetic shrieks
grow dimmer, as it flew away, and then, after a small interval of silence, began
the desperately mad screams of the encamped men.

In the clear morning, Ishme and I returned to the spot where we'd stood
that night and noticed the enemy was gone. Ishme pulled at my tunic, and
pointed excitedly at the spot and yelled. I could tell the boy was proud.

Later that day, I went into the city to gather news. What I learned I
gathered from several citizens in beer halls, who were intimate with some of
Sargon's spies. These spies, it was rumoured, later went mad and the king
put them to death.

I learned that once the creature, with thunder-loud shrieks, had appeared
over the enemy, they hastily sought to arm themselves for war. In this confusion, overtaken by this nightmare wraith, the men saw from the bedeviled
skies spores of luminous matter fall. These spores, wherever they fell, grew
astronomically fast into frenzied monstrosities of chaotic life. All that was
heard was a babel of screams, from beasts and dying men, and then, as if for
the climax of some grand cacophony of sounds, the Seeder from the Stars
itself dipped into the pith of those unfortunate men, wildly tearing and raven-
ing with abandon.

Sargon left that very day to continue his conquests in the far north. When
he left, I could tell he was deathly afraid and in great awe of his daughter.

LAZILY, THE YEARS unwound afterwards. Ishme continued to improve in
favour and it was certain one day he would leave to become a well-respected
Ensis of the empire. I trembled to think of this, for after all, was he not ours?

During this time, I began to be plagued with inexplicable dreams of an
archaic Nile, that long, meandering river being the place from which I'd
originally come. In my dreams, I was no longer Smenkhkare, but another,
who couriered secret messages and who fought alongside King Scorpion
to subdue the red, sceptered crown of Lower Egypt. I lived and relived this
troubled man's life, yet if he ever existed, it would have been centuries before
my time.

I also began to notice a gradual change come over Ishme's behaviour. He
became detached, less welcome in his affections. At first, I thought this was
because he was becoming a man. In time, however, this episode passed.

When the day arrived for him to leave the temple and continue as an administrative assistant, he told me to follow him to the Holiest Room of Nanna. Already, the stub of manhood was thick on his face. I remember him looking at me and saying, "I'll never leave to be a governor of this empire. I'll never serve it in that capacity."

His refusal was incomprehensible to me. I knew the old ghost that troubled him before was now resurfacing. I decided to confront him. I said, "Ishme, Sargon didn't mean to hurt you when he killed your parents and caused your people to suffer, when he razed your old city of Kazalla to the ground. It was done as policy. He wanted to unify and they refused. It is the way of this world. Did not his daughter, with Sargon's blessing, take you in? And see, today, you leave to be a great man in his empire. You cannot hate him, or more especially, she who is like your mother?"

Ishme looked at me with the eyes of a son; they softened. But suddenly, another thought struck him and they hardened to stone. He said, "It isn't so simple. It isn't so simple, Smenkhkare."

I tried to reason with him, "If there is something else bothering you, Ishme, tell me. I will help."

"I can't!" he yelled at me. "You love her too much!"

"It is so," I answered. "I am loyal to Akkad and always will be."

"If you love me, come with me behind the curtains of Nanna. Let us see what lies behind them."

The boy was now extremely agitated and spoke madness. I refused to entertain his wish.

He said, "What lies behind the curtains, Smenkhkare? Haven't you ever wondered? Let me pass!"

Then he made a great effort to pass the curtains. I grasped him and would not let him go. As we fought, he yelled angrily, "She and her father – they are murderers and usurpers! She is a sorceress, a witch, and a devil! Can't you see, Smenkhkare? She is a devil!"

Hearing his insinuations, I grew furious and threw him hard to the floor. It's then that I said what I now most regret in life. It would be the last lie I ever told the boy. It was then that I angrily told him that I would never speak to him again.

He rushed from the room.

We desperately searched for Ishme, first throughout the temple, and then throughout the entire city and empire. He didn't want to be found. We could only hope our beloved boy was safe.

MY OWN AND Enheduanna's thoughts never strayed far from memories of Ishme. In time, we heard from a potter in Nippur that he'd gone to the

Zagros Mountains, many years before. We shuddered when he told us. Tales of distant travelers, and traders in lapis lazuli and other treasures, spoke of the far-off Zagros Mountains and of a mist-enshrouded kingdom on ghastly peaks, over-seen by what was only whispered of as 'the Monstrosity on the Throne': a king of evil learning, who worshiped Gods of strange names. The tales were vague, however, and never an exact route was divulged in these rumours. We prayed Ishme had not found it.

As for me, my unwanted dreams continued and became more baffling and bizarre. I dreamt I was a man leading a group of ragged humans out of Africa; a fisherman in a village on a frosty continent; a king in Serannian; a pauper in Girsu; the coiled serpent that talked with dimly-remembered Gilgamesh; a lute musician in the glorious palace of Olathoë, in doom-laden Lomar.

One day, the Princess came to me, with the libation baskets and wearing her Crown of *En*-Ship, from under which I noticed long strands of grey hair falling, almost obscured by the rich black, around a face still young and pretty. She looked at me sadly and said, "Why do you never age, Smenkhkare? Were you, too, chosen for your role, as I was, by the Gods? A duty you cannot shirk?"

I didn't know what she meant. I was only Smenkhkare and when I died, I would be nothing.

She smiled and continued, after a pause, "We are all offspring of it, Smenkhkare. Some of us are more closely linked to it." She then looked at me with a look of new recognition, which made me shiver. "It came from the emptiness of space and brought its secrets with it, a terrible and distant God, unlike the fickle and stern Gods of Earth. Earth's Gods, who have forgotten the touch of cold stars and love high mountains, seas and virgin forests, who dance on misty mountaintops, they forbid us to come to them and yet, at times, will come and kiss us tenderly in our sleep. It is gone now, the Seeder from the Stars. I haven't seen it in many years and my Lady, Inanna, who wears the Laws of Civilization tied around her waist, does not acknowledge or speak of it, anymore."

She finished and left to continue her work.

With the passage of time, Sargon died, a mortal death, and passed into legend. The Kingship of Sargon then devolved to his heirs: first, Rimush then Manishtushu and then the so-called God-King, Naram-Sin.

DURING THE REIGN of Naram-Sin, the nephew of Enheduanna, shattering revolts broke out throughout the whole of the civilized lands of Sumer and Akkad. Shortly before this, I'd been warned in hushed tones by my Mistress that the Gods of Sumer and Akkad were in strife and preparing for battle. I was terrified and shook in awe of this coming apocalypse.

It began when Lugal-Anne, vassal King of Ur, turned against us. Having no respect for the semi-divine being my Mistress now was, he cast her Crown of *En*-Ship off, bid her commit suicide, and then smashed the holy and adored things of the temple. On a day when fire began falling from the sky, we fled with the temple household and our meager possessions, and wept on the hills, tearing our hair and scratching our eyes in grief.

During a blinding storm, on the road to Uruk, I experienced my first vision of Earth's Gods. I saw mysterious Lady Tiamat, towering in the clouds, engendering disorder and flames and coaxing Lotan, the vile serpentine dragon of many heads from the sea, to hinder our escape with hell-winds, upthrown by his foul, membranous wings.

Weather-beaten, tired and near collapse, we managed to make our escape to Uruk and find exile in the temple of An.

Soon, messengers arrived and said a great army was marching from the Zagros Mountains. Where the army stepped, they informed us, the *mes*, the very Laws that governed in order our cosmos, dissolved. Darkness heaved and took on distorting, palpable form. Once it crossed the Tigres River, Lugal-Anne was seen to join them.

My Mistress, hearing this, was worried.

She'd put up curtains in the Sacred Room of An and, upon hearing the news, she immediately rushed behind them, to pray for the *mes,* that our order might not completely break.

I remember dimly the elaborate words she spoke, but my weak, scribal hands will still attempt to transcribe, albeit poorly, the magnificence I heard. She prayed, "Lady Inanna, hear me, you whose shield is the moon and whose star is Venus. You, whose least simple command cannonades like a streak of gold across the fervent atmosphere. I kneel before you, to pray for the *mes* of this sphere and their continuance, for the harmony, alignment and form they bring. Without them, what will become of the strong, well-built cities? Cities of architectural symmetry and splendour, great altitudinous towers and sylvan gardens, founded under Order and the Laws of Civilization, by the black-haired people so many years ago. People of art and music, workers in words, in metals and gold. These are your people, who built mighty ships and when the ships sailed out, they returned with cargo, laden from remote, mystical lands, for your greater pleasure. Do not let the good people perish, or does my Lady now favour strife over love, darkness over light, unworked rock, chaos, lawlessness, enmity, and discordant sounds? Is this what you want, my Lady? Shall I also break what you brought with your ordering presence?"

She sang all night and, emerging in the morning, she stood before me disheveled and tired-eyed. Moving towards me, she slowly said, "Smenkhkare, it's Ishme who is coming."

CHAOS REIGNED AT that time.

The King of the Four Quarters of the Earth, Naram-Sin, couldn't protect us, since he was embroiled in deadly battle with Iphur-Kisi of Kish.

The King of Uruk, Amar-Girida, went to Enheduanna, to supplicate her to sing her beautiful hymns to the Gods, to help Uruk and fight Lugal-Anne and the dread King from the Mountains, Ishme, whom all men called the 'Creature'. He begged her to summon the Seeder, as she'd once done.

"It's impossible," she said.

FROM A HIGH place, I saw the advance of Lugal-Anne and Ishme's army. In their march, tremours hit the earth, buildings shook and the sky became dark, bilious and smoky. The army came in spastic motion, coiling and pulsing out of existence. I recall hearing an old priest, holding a bronze sword, yell at the sight, "Now, at the end of all things, let none seek to stop me, as I break free from the Lords of Creation!" Then, running into the temple, he killed himself. Many followed his example. Prescient with defeat and fear, King Amar-Girida let their armies enter the city.

"You are weak and you bring this on us," the King said. "I will now fight alongside Ur and Kish."

The city was spared, but we weren't. Lugal-Anne wouldn't stop until he'd destroyed the *En*-Priestess and her nephew.

Once the black armies entered, soldiers loyal to my Mistress fought to protect the Temple of An, which was also our fortress. Against the combined might of Ur, Uruk, and the shadow kingdom, however, they were no match. The enemy advanced easily.

Screams of dying men assailed our ears, from all corners, amplified a thousand-fold throughout the enclosed corridors. I carried on me a sword to protect my Mistress. When I entered the Room of An, she looked at me strangely. "It is back, Smenkhkare," she said. "The Seeder is back." And then she walked behind the curtains.

As this happened, a soldier hurriedly broke into the room. He implored us to flee. He said the Creature was coming. Realizing his pleadings were useless, he resolved to stay with us to the bitter end.

We stood a few paces from the entrance. Unholy noises of dying men continued to sound the depths of our despair. I stared at the opening, into the dark hallway. Seconds passed, agonizingly slow. Confused war-cries bellowed and I felt every fibre, nerve, and tissue in my body ache. The blackness of the open entrance took on the illusion of a solid tableau, the more I looked at it, and then, out of the blackness, a darker outline began to emerge.

As I saw a cyclopean shape grab the soldier, I was blinded by the man's viscera and blood, meat and limbs, which sprayed the room. My hand grasped the hilt of my sword tightly, as if to break it, but before I could make a mad, desperate swing, I was on the floor, weaponless. The air itself heaved and swayed to and fro like a beast in the room. The soldier was a grotesquery of pieces and I a hopeless wretch, lying before the towering arc of Ishme.

He stood a monumental shape, hooded and in a long cloak of black, a cloak which seemed to embody more negation, an absence of all light, rather than colour. It twined and slithered around the contours of his body and from its bottom, where legs should have been, instead swirled and twisted outwards massively pink, tentacular limbs, coiling and writhing purposely like heavy pythons. Under the darkness of his hood, I discerned – oh, but how can I explain to you the sadness and horrified wonder I experienced when I saw those large, grey, abnormal lips and engorged, abscessed tongue, or the small, blinkless, couchant, yellow eyes? Hands, swollen and cracked like crevices of grey stone, or the foulness of his smell, which was as if worms were inside, gnawing on his innards?

Carrying a ponderous sword, he proceeded to walk, or glide, fluidly, towards the curtains, his awkward and distended robe flowing and his tentacles leading and searching. As he did this, the hulking shape said, in a voice hoarse and deep, yet, in a manner of articulation recognizably like Ishme's, "Do not try to stop me, Smenkhkare. I know who and what you are, even if you don't."

When he was near the curtains, Enheduanna stepped out and stood defiantly in front of him. "Do not do this thing," she warned.

Like a wounded animal, Ishme gave a sudden, long-winded moan then, lowering his face, he eased it towards hers. He passed it in her view, so she could scrutinize it. Upset, I saw her contract and then compose herself. Staring at her, he asked, "Am I hideous to you? Is your work hideous to you?"

Perplexed and saddened, she answered, "What do you mean, Ishme?"

He gave another bellow and yelled angrily, "It's because of what you put in me! You should have let me die, rather than live and suffer this shame!" Then, looking at me, he said, "When I ran away, Smenkhkare, hidden in Nippur, I began to change. A hideous thing, I remained hidden. Ashamed, scorned of men, I fled to the Zagros Mountains and there met a man, who explained to me secret lore passed down from ancient times. He divined that my transformation, because I possessed a part of it, was caused by the Seeder. I killed the man and began my kingdom on the mountains."

He then turned towards my Mistress. "What lies behind the curtains? If my first cure came from there, then whatever is there can cure me again; isn't it so? I must see the beast. Then I'll be a man, again."

He pushed my Mistress and she struggled to hold him back, saying, "No, Ishme, it can't be trusted!"

Breaking free of her grasp, he entered the room and, in distress, she followed him.

All this while, I'd tried to help, but I couldn't. I was paralyzed. I trembled with fear for them both. I exerted and worked myself into a frenzy to move, but it was as if my body were a foreign entity and I an unbodied mite trapped within. I lay on the floor and, after they passed behind the curtains, I willed myself even more desperately to move but to no avail.

"Do not go there, Ishme!" I heard her yell.

He thundered, "Get away from me, sorceress! Move! It's your fault all that's happened to me!"

"No, Ishme – do not say that! How could I have known?"

Fumbling noises I heard, a loud bang, and then a body fall. After which, Ishme hollered triumphantly, "There you are! What manner of thing are you? I only want to be human! Speak to me! I'll make you with my sword!"

Commotion followed after and I heard a great noise A blinding light pierced the curtains. The temple rumbled. I felt a strong wind and then, only Ishme's voice, growing dimmer and dimmer, roaring, "By Yog-Saduk, the Keeper of the Gates, and Aniburu, the Fearsome Planet, I order you to help me!"

A silence ensued and I started weeping uncontrollably. I couldn't imagine what had happened behind the curtains. Then my Mistress appeared, bloody and with tears in her eyes, and lowly whispered, "A fissure cracked through space. I saw the cavernous void. Ishme is no more. It has taken him." Then she collapsed.

MY CHRONICLE ENDS here and, even though there is more I could say, with Ishme's passing, the story is finished. My Mistress was eventually restored to her temple in Ur and, at long last, she joined Inanna and the Gods in Heaven. When she changed and her eyes became like spindles of flaming fires, and her form in expanse as huge as gigantic cedar trees, I heard her voice filling earth and sky, saying, "Do not fear, Smenkhkare. If there is fear, it's only in you. I'll go and look for Ishme and if he still lives, I'll come and tell you – but the spaces beyond are much vaster than I had imagined."

Once she left, I never saw her again. By my reckoning, that was over seven hundred years ago.

Whenever I tell my story, men call me mad and a liar, saying no man from Kemet on the Nile can serve in a foreign land, but they don't know that I wasn't always known as 'Smenkhkare', for I've had many different names and sometimes, I confuse them. For I know now more of my mystery. Every one hundred years, I must go to steamy swamps and shed my skin. I make strange, sibilant sounds and, once the process is finished, I emerge a new creature.

I remember in dreams the ancient Lady once saying, "We are all a part of it." I've come to believe I am more so. The mystery of my beginnings I still search out, though I've partly convinced myself that I am one of the unwilling eyes of the Seeder from the Stars.

I've left Crete and, after centuries of other lives, I'm finally returning to the Land of Two Rivers. Sumer and Akkad are dust and gone, and I travel as a merchant to Babylon. I'll bury this papyrus scroll. If, in the aeons to come, I don't forget, I'll dig it up again when the time is right and remember.

I'll remember Ishme, poor Ishme, and the God-Woman, and what mysteries happened, what mysteries I lived and what mysteries lay behind the forbidden curtains. What really happened? I believe only two on earth have ever known – and one is dead.

Julio Toro San Martin lives and was raised in Toronto, Canada, but was born in Chile. His only other short story published to date was in *Innsmouth Free Press* Issue #5. He hopes, barring his slow writing, to eventually write (and get published) in every conceivable short story genre and subgenre before embarking on writing a novel … or maybe not. Maybe he'll write a play instead.

The author speaks: Reading about the Sumerians and Akkadians in the "cradle of civilization", I became interested in their idea of order, or the *mes*, and how, if these things fell apart, for them I imagined it implied there would be chaos. What can be more Lovecraftian than that? And Enheduanna, daughter of Sargon the Great and one of the first writers (if not the first) known by name, can there be anything for a writer more interesting than her as a subject for a story?

Lovecraft's short story "The Other Gods" was one of his first stories I ever read. I wrote my story as a sort of companion piece to it, since, much as I've been able to tell, as an influence on other writers, it lies pretty much like the wastes of Kadath, cold and alone. I didn't strive for 100 percent consistency between the two, though, and also, Enheduanna, beloved of Earth's Gods, is more fortunate in her story than Barzai the Wise is in his. Another influence may be a certain story by Clark Ashton Smith, which may contain a hint as to who or what The Seeder from the Stars really is. But maybe not. And perhaps Smenkhkare is the same as that mysterious pharaoh from Egypt's Eighteenth Dynasty. But maybe not. I wrote this story in a cloud of agnosticism and unreliability. Borges was also an influence.

DEUS EX MACHINA

NATHANIEL KATZ

E VERY RELIGION, NO matter how supposedly beneficent, has exclusion at its heart. Did you think Dionysus an exception? Are you that naive, brothers? Every one of our secret society was an outcast of Dionysus. We were not wanted by your gods, but we refused to be playthings, compliantly knocked aside at our masters' whims.

Don't bother trying to apportion individual measures of guilt. All the members did their part. We all read and critiqued the script; we all helped compose the rituals and invocations. We all disseminated those occult texts so frowned upon by your jealous gods. We were roles, instruments, nothing more. The Playwright wrote our drama, wrote what became your Tragedy. The Merchant funded us. The –

Me? You want to know who *I* was? I was the Actor. But you knew that, already.

We were one of the last in the festival, that celebration of accursed Dionysus, and we were well aware of the public's expectations. In addition to being blasphemers, we were also talented men of the stage, you see, and we sat in that open-air theater and looked upon the others as the crowd whispered our names. Watched satyrs, summoned, prancing upon the platform. Saw those gods that we'd sworn against appear and descend to the stage, the mortal plain, from that great, behind-the-scenes machine, that Crane, towering so close to us.

The clay eyes of the gods were terrible. To look upon them and plot such things ....

But we persevered. We stared into their masked faces and we did not look away.

The Traitor was not in attendance and you will not find her. She slipped through Dionysus's clutching fingers, so what hope have you mortals? She used to be one of those maenad followers of Dionysus, a member of that most revered circle of that most sacred cult.

Or did you think those followers of Dionysus, those maenads, willing? They are *deceived* and *bound,* fellow citizens! Open your eyes! You have

allowed the gods to shape your perceptions, to shape your thoughts and your
world. And now you try to claim that you follow them freely. How blinkered
you are, my brothers. Those maenads, those *raving ones*, as you call them,
are attached to Dionysus, pleasure and instinctual abandon their chains, even
as their will is put to the sword by that god's base nature.

But enough of the Traitor. She escaped, she helped us, and that is all you
will ever know of her. Torture me, if you must. Torture all of us. We can tell
you no more because we know no more.

The play that we produced would have been the crown of any other life.
You leaned forward to see better; you watched, rapt, as we strode upon the
stage. Our dialogue shaped your reality. Seduced from your sacrosanct paths,
you were plunged into our drama.

Do you know what I hate about the customs of our drama, fellow citizens,
judging public? I hate the endings of our plays. We have managed to make
life into *art,* to render our own souls upon the stage, and learn from our flaws
and virtues. And then, time after time, we ruin it.

I have wept at the creations of Euripides. And then, as his plays draw to
a close, he deprives us of resolution. He turns away from the humanity that
he has created and, instead of finding mortal solutions to mortal problems,
invokes the divine.

It is *delusion*; can't you see that? The gods do not intervene! The gods do
not care! The gods merely *dissemble*.

Time after time, they appear on stage, force-feed us those *damned* lies,
try to comfort us by their presence, and tie those messy strings of life into a
pretty bow with which to adorn their wretched amorality.

It disgusts me.

When I descended to the stage, lowered by the Crane, did you think I was
one of them? A god as all the other actors had so briefly become?

I remember little of what followed: of striding forward, hands outstretched; of our Chorus' suicide, of their sacrifice; of the words spoken as
they drove those daggers into their hearts.

I remember little of it, but the evidence is all around me in the toppled
altars, the burned buildings, the slain priests.

We made a deal with an Entity. It has no name. We do not know what it is.

We released a hunter among the flock.

We killed your gods, fellow citizens. That Being that rode my flesh like the
driver steers the carriage; that Being that strode to masked Dionysus watching our plays and drove a blade through his neck to see that all-too-mortal
blood pour out; *that Being* was our prayers given physical shape, a god-killer
born of invocation and drama on holy ground.

It is not gone, that Being that we summoned. I woke up, as you all know, memory-less and dying in the midst of the carnage, but it did not go back to sleep. It has been released.

It will not sleep again until the gods are dead, the world changed forever.

We have liberated you, even if you are too faith-smitten to see it.

Mortals – we give you the reigns to your world!

Do with us what you will.

Nathaniel Katz blogs about genre fiction at The Hat Rack (evilhat.blogspot. com). This is his first published work of fiction.

The author speaks: In Ancient Greece, the gods were like regular people – just stronger, faster, smarter, braver, more beautiful, and long-lasting. During plays, performed as rituals during the Celebration of Dionysus, the gods were thought to actually walk the stage in the body of the actor. The actors-cum-deities would be mechanically lowered into the scene and resolve the characters' dilemmas – the literal origins of the term *'Deus ex Machina'*. Which, for a Lovecraft-themed anthology, begs the question: what else might be coming down?

IF ONLY TO TASTE HER AGAIN

E. CATHERINE TOBLER

THE WINDS WERE blowing low and remained warm when our five boats returned across the wine-dark waters of the Red Sea. It was late in the season – the winds should have begun to cool by then, for it was later than any of us planned, but the Queen of Punt had been exceptionally generous in her welcome of us. The days spent in her kingdom seemed longer than an age, the nights filled with wine, figs and the attention of slim, young boys. The Queen spared us no expense, so that we might return to Djeser-Djeseru with riches none expected; so that she might receive the grand favours of Hatshepsut, the King's Great Wife, the Lady of the Two Lands.

Our boats came into port with great fanfare. Though it was late into the night, Hatshepsut had roused a great portion of her court to bid us welcome home. Torches burned bright like stars to illuminate a path across the water for us and musicians sounded their rattles and bone clappers the nearer we drew. The oarsmen caught the rhythm and drew us closer to our homeland.

As it would slowly become known, these attendants and musicians had lived in the port for some weeks now, rotating their shifts so that some would be prepared when we appeared. From Punt, there had been little reasonable way to send word when our return was delayed. Did Hatshepsut believe the Queen of Punt had eaten us? She was a beautifully round queen, to be certain, but we had not witnessed such behaviours during our stay with her.

These attendants who welcomed us were weary-eyed. My own brother stood among the musicians and tucked his bone clapper away, to slip his hand around my arm and help me from the boat. The land seemed to rock under my feet, even with his support. He was tall, my brother; I would always remember him as such, even when the horror took him.

He made only one comment as to our late return, but there was no reproach in his low voice. Perhaps there was concern, but I said nothing of it, only nodding as the men I had traveled with these long weeks began to unload the cargo from the ships. Five boats, each packed to brimming with boxes of stone and baskets of reed; tall trees of myrrh and frankincense with their roots bound and kept wet during our journey, so that we might plant them for the Lady of the Two Lands. Lapis and silver, panther skins and elephant tusks. Beautiful lengths of cassia were tied in fat bundles; soon, the cassia would perfume the halls of the court, wending its way into my own rooms.

Hatshepsut welcomed us at the palace, when, at last, we had made our long way there. She stood at the end of the long stairs which led to the temple. I could see only pride in her stance, the still-warm wind that carried us home now caressing the Queen's fine linen gown. Her dark hair was tightly wrapped, gleaming with oils. When she drew me into her arms, to whisper a welcome into my ear, I could smell these oils. Warmed by her body, they smelled of lotus and olive. I pressed my own lips against her cheek, tasting a trace of those oils. They tasted of home.

The world would speak of this journey and triumphant return for lifetimes to come, she told me, as the offerings were carried up the terraced walkways and situated so that Hatshepsut might explore each at her leisure. She stepped from my side to do just that, opening one reed basket to trail her hands through the grain inside. There came then a low whisper – perhaps from the grain as it slipped through her fingers – but later, I would have cause to doubt that. She opened the boxes and baskets at random, the air seeming to warm around us as she did. A shiver still skated over my skin, and I felt strangely sick, as Hatshepsut kneeled before a box wrought from gold and opened its chained lid.

The scent of myrrh lifted into the warm air, the box packed with gleaming globules of incense. It was perhaps the fatigue that gnawed at me; it was the length of the journey and the stresses encountered therein. These things combined to assault me then, to make my vision darken and fade. There was that low whisper, again – *Grain through the Pharaoh's fingers*, I told myself – but that sound rolled across my shoulders, down my spine, and then reached for Hatshepsut.

Perhaps she felt nothing, for Hatshepsut moved away without comment. It was easy to tell myself then that I was exhausted and fully believe it. Yet, I stayed by my Pharaoh's side as she moved down the line of baskets, as she reached a hand up to stroke a low-hanging branch of myrrh on one of the many trees. She began calling out then, orders to her men to see the trees planted in straight lines along the colonnades, by the pools of water. It was my brother who came then, drawing his hand around my arm to pull me gently away. He walked us back toward that golden box and, though I tried to pull myself up short, I was too tired.

Beside that damnable box we stood. Too long, too long, my brother spoke of things that felt inconsequential when compared to the box at our feet. The box seemed to radiate a heat, a presence, a *something* which reached for me again and teased the hair at the nape of my neck. It was unholy and dark, this thing, and could my brother not feel it? He laughed low as he spoke of events that had transpired in my absence. I cared for none of them, wanted only to get away from the box.

When I could break free, it seemed too late. I felt somehow dirty and hopeless, my throat closed tightly. Nausea wrapped itself around my belly, sinking claws into my hips. I fairly ran for my rooms, brushing past concerned friends. Water, I wanted water and cried that everyone stay away, leave me be, give me only silence! Yet, once within my rooms, I found no sanctuary there. The walls seemed largely foreign, the floor uneven, and the fire sparked when I walked too near its warmth. I clawed at the linen which seemed keen on strangling me. Finally, bare of its treachery, I lunged for the pool of water at the room's far end. It looked nothing like water, then – it looked like liquid galena, black and thick, and I sank into it, onto my knees, wholly under the cool embrace.

There, I somehow slept.

In my slumber, the warm stroke of brush and fingers seemed to weave a complex lattice around my body. Strands of light and vein wrapped me and held me down. Small, strong hands pressed me into the tile at the bottom of the pool, but it didn't occur to me to struggle against these restraints. *Let me come through you,* a voice seemed to say. This voice sounded like everyone I had ever loved, something dark and terrible, with a weight I could not fathom.

There was a sense of emptiness when I woke at the edge of the pool, hours later. The fire had burned to embers, the sky full-dark beyond the balcony. I rolled onto my back and stared at the ceiling, at its interlocking patterns of lotus and stars, and breathed. The fatigue of the journey seemed to have left me and so, too, the strange sensation I'd had upon seeing that golden box.

The rooms were heavy with the scent of myrrh, which made me vaguely nauseated until, at last, I regained my feet and stood. I found fresh clothing, the cool linen a comfort over my skin, and painted my eyes with the darkest galena before I left my rooms. The halls were quiet yet, but I felt assured in my path. When I thought of the night before, there were strange absences in my memories, but I brushed these aside and focused instead on the tall form of my brother as he lay in his bed, breathing low like the warm wind outside.

Warm wind, warm water and the incessant whisper of grain through fingers. I reached for my brother with arms that seemed no longer like my own. My fingers wriggled and elongated, curled around his arm and his throat until the tapered ends vanished into his ebony hair. He was sweet – I could taste him through my fingers – sweet like roasted figs and dripping mango, and some buried part of me drank its fill, until this sweetness burst apart and the shell of my brother shattered. Terrible fingers pasted him back together, blackened tongue sealing the seams until one could never tell what horror lurked within.

Amber sunlight spilled into the Pharaoh's rooms and over her shoulders by the time my brother approached her side. He had spent the morning making the brightest music for her, while she sorted through the gems and other stones the Queen of Punt had sent. She found great pleasure in everything that glittered with a hint of blue. She wanted to polish every bit of lapis and cover her body in a coat of it.

How beautiful she would look, my brother told her, which drew her darkening gaze. How dare he? The Pharaoh waved him off – foolish musician – but he came onward, bare feet silent against the floor. That old whisper tickled the back of my neck, ran down my arms and slithered against my belly the closer my brother came, though, when his hand befell the Pharaoh, the whisper fell silent. There seemed some strange fulfillment at only that touch.

The Pharaoh shrieked; my brother had begun to dissolve before her eyes. Those seams came apart and a thing that none of us could imagine broke out of him. A creature that seemed made of wine-dark water clawed its way up and out, discarding my brother as one might a robe of linen. My brother pooled against the floor, blood and water washing over the Pharaoh's feet, while this monstrosity lunged for our beloved Hatshepsut.

She pushed backward from the thing, her chair toppling. The Pharaoh's guards stepped forward, but they seemed baffled as to where they might attack the creature without harming Hatsheput in the fray. The thing spilled her into the bounty of treasure from Punt, into baskets and boxes, into linens and incense. Crying, she crawled through the fortune and, all the while, the living horror stalked over her, reeking of the deepest Nile, black with fertile revulsion. Purple-black water oozed around them, soaking the Pharaoh's linen gown until she looked bruised. Many-limbed arms (Oh, they were the arms beneath the water of my pool, pressing with small, warm hands) latched onto her legs and pulled hard, bringing her back from the treasures, the gems and daggers and dishes. But, in her shaking hands, Hatshepsut held a broken ivory dish and she slashed its ragged edge against the grim ovoid head of the thing upon her.

The creature fell apart with a cry that felt to me like that voice, that dark and terrible voice. That scream seemed to reach deep inside of me, to curl around my heart and pull. As the creature flailed, still trying to reach the Pharaoh in its death, I crumpled to the floor. Now the guards rushed forward to Hatshepsut, hacking at each long, watery arm as it whipped free from her body. These arms came apart, splattering everyone within reach with a thick liquid that smelled to me like the stars. Clear, cold, stinging. Vast and empty.

The silence afterward was peculiar. The women in the room had leaped away from Hatshepsut, but now they moved forward; the drenched guards stepped warily back and made to secure the entries to the chamber. But it was too late, I thought, watching from narrowed eyes. Those small, warm hands pressed against my heart and that voice ... that fathomless voice ... whispered its plea in my ear. *Let me come through you.*

My gaze focused on the discarded skin of my brother, on the bloody footprints near the edge of the table. My tall and beautiful brother, with his hands that could make music. That blood called me as much as the voice did; that blood anchored me as much as those small hands. And my Pharaoh ... the Lady of the Two Lands ... struggling to her feet, unable to rise because her legs shook so terribly ... I ached for her, for the lotus and olive taste of her. It was that ache which became the seam, the seam which broke me apart with a scream that tried to shatter the heavens. *Let me come through you.*

I let it come, if only to taste her again.

— For Joseph

E. Catherine Tobler lives and writes in Colorado – strange how that works out. Among others, her fiction has appeared in *Sci Fiction*, *Fantasy Magazine*, *Realms of Fantasy*, *Talebones*, and *Lady Churchill's Rosebud Wristlet*. She is an active member of SFWA and the fiction editor at *Shimmer Magazine*. For more, visit www.ecatherine.com.

The author speaks: I've always had a soft spot for Egypt and I'm not sure why. I wish I could retrace the steps that got my brain to thinking, "Oh, wow" about the place for the first time, but that is, alas, lost. Still, all those ruins that were once not ruins were absolutely fascinating. In doing research for a novel, I came across the Pharaoh Hatshepsut and my interest deepened. A female pharaoh? How could that be? Her image largely destroyed after her reign? Why in the world ...? One intriguing part of Hatshepsut's reign was the ships she sent to Punt, which returned with Many Fabulous Things. In some accounts, the fish that came back could be identified down to their very species from ancient drawings ... Fish from strange lands? *O, what other marvels might have come back with them?* I wondered and therein found this story.

SHADOWS OF THE DARKEST JADE

SARAH HANS

WHEN THE GURU asked me to explain the horrors Satindra and I had witnessed, I found that I could make no words to explain what had occurred. When he asked me write the words I still could not explain. Only now, as I lie dying at last, am I able to write, but even so, there are parts of the tale that must remain known only to me. There are things that weigh on a man's soul that simply should not be shared.

We followed the Silk Road out of Gandhara and down into the plains of the Empire of Han, surrounded by merchants and travelers. The people we met along the Indus River, even many miles beyond prosperous Gandhara, recognized our saffron robes and gave generously to our alms bowls. We sat at their fires night after night, welcomed guests. In exchange for food and a warm place to sleep, Satindra told them of the *dharma*, mediated their disputes, and blessed them with his quiet strength. I knew, as I sat listening to him retell the tales I had heard a hundred times, that the Guru had chosen wisely when he sent Satindra among the Han, for he had the calm charisma and sagely demeanor that befit a true disciple of Amitabha Buddha.

As we journeyed, the number of other travelers on the road began to dwindle. Eventually, we left the great Silk Road and walked into unknown territory. The road narrowed and wound its way through expanses of rice paddies, where stoop-shouldered peasants laboured in the hot sun.

Unfortunately, the people of the Han Empire had rarely seen monks and, even more rarely, begging monks, and did not know what to make of us, especially as one of us was a foreigner and the other was barely a man, then unable to grow a beard. When we brought out our alms bowls, they scoffed, made offensive remarks about beggars, and some even spat on the ground at our feet. We ran out of our carefully preserved rice ration within a few days of leaving the Silk Road, and were so hungry our steps began to falter.

"Brother Satindra," I said reluctantly, as we trudged through another hot, dusty day, "we must find food." I meant to imply that we should steal what we could not beg, though I could not bring myself to suggest it outright.

Satindra nodded. "Amitabha will provide," he said, with perfect faith, never indicating whether he understood my hidden meaning. "The Guru sent us here to bring the *dharma*; Amitabha will provide."

I am ashamed to say that I lost faith, but Satindra never stopped believing. Even as we staggered up to a small, bamboo-and-mud hut, so exhausted we could barely stand, he drew his alms bowl from his robes and said the traditional words of blessing in a voice weak with hunger. The smell of the evening meal drifted out to us, a scent so tantalizing that I moaned aloud.

The girl who came to the door of the hut could have been my sister. She was small and golden-skinned, her jet-black hair tied modestly at the nape of her neck. She wore the simple, cotton garments of all the Han peasants. Her narrow eyes – so like mine! – grew wide, and she turned and ran back into the house, calling to her elders in the local dialect.

I groaned again, this time sure of defeat, certain that we would be turned away and meet our deaths on the dusty road. Satindra turned and looked at me, a small smile curving his chapped lips, and said "Have faith, Little Brother."

The girl returned with a hugely pregnant woman in tow and behind her followed a little elderly woman with a round, plump face. Both women immediately ushered us into the hut, without any questions or explanations, and just like that, we were saved and Satindra's faith was proven.

The girl's name was Jun. The pregnant woman was her mother Bao-Yu and the elderly woman was Jun's grandmother, Grandmother Mei. The men of the household were off drinking rice wine and gambling, Grandmother Mei explained, so the women could do what they liked, including feeding wandering monks. She explained all this while we eagerly devoured rice and what I can honestly say was the most delicious hot soup I have ever eaten. Grandmother Mei chattered throughout the meal, gesturing with her small, shriveled hands, squinting at us with her beady, black eyes and smiling a toothless grin. Unfamiliar with the local dialect, I only understood about half of what she said and poor Satindra, who spoke only the scholarly language of the Han and none of the rough dialects of the peasants, understood nothing, but we nodded enthusiastically and tried to be a good audience.

Finally, when our appetites were sated, Grandmother Mei asked us to tell our story.

"You will have to excuse Brother Satindra," I said. "He only speaks the scholar's tongue."

"Your accent is strange," Grandmother Mei said, squinting at me over her plum-like cheeks.

"I was raised in a village near here," I said, "but I have been away for many years. I remember very little."

She nodded, sitting back on her pillow, and repeated her request for our story.

I obliged as best I could, using words from the scholar's tongue and the dialect of my village interchangeably. This seemed surprisingly effective.

"We are monks from a monastery in the nation of Gandhara," I told her. "Satindra is gifted with languages and I was born in Han, so our Guru thought it would be wise to send us to spread the word of the *dharma* here. We have walked a long time, seeking the village where I was born. I do not remember the way, because I was very young when I left home."

Grandmother Mei snorted. "Why did your parents send you away? A healthy, strapping young boy?"

I shrugged. "I was told later, when I was older, that I was sent away because my family was so large my parents were unable to feed all of us."

The old woman nodded sagely, her head bobbing on her neck. "A few years ago, there was drought. I remember well, there were many families whose children starved." She clucked her tongue at the misfortune of it all. "Your parents were farmers, then?"

"Yes. My father and mother both worked in the rice fields. I remember four brothers and one sister, but there may be others, who were sent away like me, or who were born since I left," I said.

"You should be grateful that your mother sent you to live with the monks," Grandmother Mei chided me, perhaps hearing some sorrow in my voice when I spoke of my family. "She saved you from a life of backbreaking work, toil and sorrow. Instead, you have learned to read and write, haven't you? And now you travel the world!" She snorted. "It is a lucky thing for you. I only wish that little Jun were a boy so we could send her with you, away from this life."

I looked at Jun, who blushed and looked away. "Some say that the Amitabha Buddha's most dedicated disciples were his wife and consorts," Satindra volunteered, speaking slowly in the scholarly language of the Han nobles.

Grandmother Mei guffawed her skepticism. "The day women are allowed to become monks will be the day we learn to piss standing up," she declared and then laughed wildly, slapping her small hand against her thigh. Bao-Yun and Jun looked uncomfortable, but smiled obediently at the old woman's coarse joke. Wheezing with laughter, Grandmother Mei requested tea and little Jun hopped up and began preparing tea for all of us.

"Tell me more about your Amitabha," Grandmother Mei demanded and, while Jun ground tea leaves and boiled water, Satindra and I – Satindra speaking in the scholar's tongue and I translating some of the unfamiliar concepts into a more familiar dialect – did our best to explain the *dharma*.

While we talked, Jun placed an earthenware bowl of tea in her grandmother's little hands, and the old woman sipped and made appreciative sounds.

"It's too bad neither of you needs a wife; little Jun is an expert tea-maker, already, and she is barely ten years old! Think what a woman she will be in just a few years!"

Satindra and I blushed and looked at the floor. Some orders of Ambitabha's followers took consorts, but ours did not; we were humble monks dedicated to poverty and chastity. Grandmother Mei chuckled at our modest reaction to her words and said, "Did your mother make tea like this, Little Brother?"

"You should call me 'Wen', Grandmother Mei," I replied. "And yes, she did. I remember the scent of it." And it was true: the scent of the mint leaves crushed with the tea leaves brought back memories of my childhood and the bamboo house where I had slept chest-to-back with my brothers.

"Then the village of your birth is near here, Brother Wen. You will always know what part of the Han Empire you are in by the taste of the tea, because the leaves taste differently and are prepared differently wherever you go." She took another sip and sighed contentedly.

My memories stirred as Jun placed a bowl of tea in my own hands. The minty scent and warmth of the pottery clasped in my hands brought me back to that dark, warm bamboo hut with my family. "I don't remember much about the village, not even the name," I said softly. "But I do remember a festival, where we burned offerings of tea leaves like this ... the festival of the Jade Crane."

Grandmother Mei threw up her hands so quickly her tea bowl dropped to the floor, spilling hot liquid across the dirt floor. She shrieked something unintelligible and the eyes that she turned to me were no longer sparkling with kindness and amusement, but rather were full of fear and loathing. Her toothless mouth opened, a black maw, and she made a loud keening sound that raised the hairs on my arms. The change was so abrupt that I had no time to react; no one did. We all just stared at Grandmother Mei for a moment, baffled.

Then the little girl and her mother took action. Bao-Yun put her arms around her mother and began speaking calmly to her, so that gradually, the keening subsided to a low moan. It was still a terrible sound, like the squalling of an infant. Jun, meanwhile, collected the tea bowls from me and Satindra, and began hustling us out of the house.

"What did you say?" Satindra asked, as Jun pushed us from the hut.

"I only said that there was a festival in my village," I replied. "The festival of the Jade –"

I could not finish this thought, because Grandmother Mei began to shriek again, and little Jun pressed one small hand against my mouth. She shook her head fervently, her narrow eyes so wide that I could see the whites all around her black irises. She pushed us both out of the hut and down the road a little ways, and then ran back into the house.

Satindra and I stood in the dark road for a few minutes, listening to Grandmother Mei's terrified wailing. It had all happened so quickly that I did not know what to make of it. We stared at each other numbly, then placed our alms bowls back into our robes and began to move down the road, away from the house.

Eventually, the wailing stopped and we heard the sound of footsteps. We turned to see Jun running toward us, a small bag of uncooked rice in her arms. Wordlessly, she pressed the bag into my hands. Her eyes were full of fear, but also compassion, and I thanked her for the generous donation. Then I said, "What did your grandmother say when I mentioned ... the bird?" I asked, careful to avoid using the phrase that had so upset Grandmother Mei.

Jun frowned, licked her lips, and glanced back at the hut, where the firelight spilled out of the open doorway and onto the road. "'Cursed'," she said, in a whisper, and the wind seemed to steal the word from her mouth, so that it did not linger, but was whisked away into the night, so that it almost seemed unreal. I wanted her to repeat it, so that I could be sure of what she had said, but instead, she turned and ran back to the house.

"'Cursed'?" Satindra repeated in the Han dialect. "Does that mean what I think it means?"

"Yes," I replied.

To my surprise, Satindra laughed, drawing one arm around my shoulders and patting my back. "Don't let a superstitious old woman frighten you, Little Brother. Cursed. Ha! If anything, we are blessed. Let's find a field where we can spend the night."

We slept under the stars that night and, though I glowered, Satindra remained in high spirits. He detailed the reasons we were lucky: before her fit, Grandmother Mei had blessed us with a generous meal and a chance to share the *dharma*; the evening was a pleasant temperature, and no storm clouds threatened to interrupt our sleep with rain; we had not been robbed or set upon by criminals; and we knew that soon, we would arrive in the village of my birth, and perhaps even find my family. Two wandering monks could hardly want for more, he said, as we bedded down in a cow field.

The following day, I was melancholic, having slept fitfully. Our morning meditation, where we chanted a mantra as we walked, brought me no comfort. During the hottest part of the day, we rested. Satindra cooked a little of the rice Jun had given us and we ate it slowly, savouring every grain. It tasted of mint and the flavor brought me a confusing jumble of memories.

As we had walked on the Silk Road, we had passed many shrines to local gods. Some of the richest had been statues carved of jade or ivory, housed in pagodas and tended by priests. Travelers had laid offerings of milk, honey, rice, and even meat at these shrines. As we had left the main road, the size of the altars had become less impressive. Every day or so, we passed one of these little shrines, with a tiny, crude stone likeness of some god or another, or simply a collection of pebbles meant to be a marker. There were usually the remains of meager offerings at these smaller shrines, or no offerings at all, because so few travelers passed them.

Now, as we walked farther from the Silk Road and Grandmother Mei's house, the character of these shrines changed. Though we had ignored the altars previously, I now felt compelled to look at the small statues. The other shrines along this country road had been simple cairns or had little hand-carved animals made of a common stone or wood, something that would have no value to thieves. But the afternoon after our encounter with Grand-mother Mei, we passed a shrine with a statuette, carved with great detail, out of what appeared to be some kind of jade.

I crouched in front of the shrine, staring at the dark statuette it housed in what might have been half of a huge, stone bowl, turned on its side. The little statue was black, and mostly in shadow, but when the sunlight hit it just right, it looked green, like the darkest jade. The details of the statue were difficult to discern because it was so dark, but the shape was not human, nor that of any animal I had seen before. I got the impression of bulbous eyes and an elongated head and many arms, like the Hindu goddess Kali, but no mat-ter how I squinted, I could not determine the exact features of the statue. Fi-nally, thinking that perhaps my fingers could make sense of what perplexed my eyes, I reached out and ran my fingers over the stone.

I expected the cool hardness of jade, but instead, the stone was warm, perhaps from the sunlight, and the texture was wet and slippery. I jerked my hand away and looked at my fingers, expecting them to be wet; they were dry, though the sensation of the oily stone remained. I did not want to touch the thing again and could not stand looking at it, so I backed away from the shrine and hurried to catch up to Satindra, who squatted further down the road, waiting for me.

"What's wrong, Little Brother?" he asked as I joined him, still staring at my fingers. They felt tainted, somehow, as if I had touched something unclean. I had the urge to wipe them on my robes, though they were not actually dirty.

"There is something wrong with the statue in that shrine," I told him, scowling.

Satindra chuckled. "I think that today, you are determined to find some-thing wrong with everything," he replied. Thinking that perhaps he was correct, I sighed and resigned myself to our daily trudge.

We walked for several days more, each day passing more of the shrines with the black-green soapstone idols. The road became increasingly pitted and overgrown with weeds, narrowing down to almost nothing, but the shrines seemed only to grow larger, each statue taller than the last.

Even stranger, the number of people we saw along the road dwindled as the idols to the local god grew larger. The fields once full of workers were now empty, the rice overgrown and unkempt, as if the crops had simply been forgotten. The fields that had gone on forever now ended in forest, and the forest was reclaiming those fields.

Eventually, we came upon some simple bamboo huts much like Grandmother Mei's, but these were empty and beyond them, the forest was dark and forbidding. The remains of cooking fires were still smoldering, in some cases, and half-finished cups of tea sat beside dirty rice bowls that swarmed with ants. After investigating one of these houses, I turned to Satindra and said, "It's as if everyone has just disappeared. This is unnatural. I don't like it."

Satindra tried to laugh off my fears with his usual grace, but failed. His laughter sounded hollow and misplaced in the silent, empty village. "Don't worry, Brother Wen. I'm sure there is some explanation. We should find a place to sleep."

Though we were not superstitious men, Satindra and I did not sleep in the village. We ate the last of our rice in a field nearby, where we could to see the huts without being too close to them.

Every night since Grandmother Mei's, I had slept poorly, my dreams fraught with screaming old women and huge black birds with sharply curved beaks. Now the birds dripped oil and opened their mouths to shriek with Grandmother Mei's raspy voice, "Cursed! Cursed!" I woke in the night, sweating and tangled in my robes. I looked about for Satindra and found him crouched beside me, awake and alert despite the late hour. His eyes were so wide that I could see the whites even in the darkness that shrouded us.

I followed his gaze to the abandoned village. There were lights moving among the previously empty huts. I started to say something to him, to suggest that we go speak with the villagers, but he silenced me with a hand squeezing my arm. Never had I seen him like this, with every nerve taut and straining, so I bit my tongue. After some time, the lights moved away and Satindra turned to me.

His eyes looked doubly huge with his face so dark. The night around us was eerily silent, not even the wind stirring the fallow rice fields. "I don't think those were people," he whispered.

"What do you mean?" I replied, squatting beside him in the dirt so that we were almost at eye-level.

"I saw their faces. They didn't look right." He shook his head emphatically.

"What did you see?"

Satindra swallowed hard, as if something large and ill-tasting were caught in his throat. His huge eyes remained fixed on my face, unblinking and intense. "*Dakini*."

Dakini is an ancient word that refers to an otherworldly, inhuman being: a god or a demon.

"We should go," I said.

To my horror, Satindra shook his head. "No," he said firmly. Though his hands were shaking, he stood, his eyes still fixed unswervingly on me. "This is why we were sent here, Brother Wen. Your people need to hear the *dharma*. The Guru sent us here to free your people."

I shook my head and stood up, too. Satindra was a full head taller than I, so I still stared up at him. "No, Brother Satindra! The Guru could not have foreseen this! We cannot go alone; it's too dangerous. We should return to the monastery ...."

He interrupted me by gripping my arms hard and giving me a little shake, as one would a hysterical woman. "You would dare to question the enlightened Guru?" He released me abruptly and I staggered back.

Satindra whirled away from me and began walking resolutely toward the village.

I watched him for a few moments, debating what to do. The night air seemed to rush into the space left by Satindra's quick departure, enveloping me in dark, cool silence. And then, beyond the quiet of the abandoned village and the overgrown fields, I heard a sound, faint but persistent. At first, I could not identify it. Then I thought it was the buzzing of insects. Finally, I realized that it was human voices, chanting a repetitive mantra.

I ran after Satindra.

The tracks of the *dakini* were easy to spot; they had not bothered to hide their movements, and we followed their trail of muddy footprints and broken branches deep into the dark, dense forest, where trees and bushes tugged at our robes and we tripped over huge roots. Here, we lost the trail, because the darkness was too omnipresent, but now we could hear the chanting and the high-pitched, frantic notes of a zither.

The people were in the center of a clearing, where they sang in the darkness without benefit of a fire. I couldn't see the zither player in the darkness, but I knew he was off to the right somewhere, because I could hear the slithering, off-key notes. He played no tune, just as the chant seemed to have no rhythm. I had thought that perhaps, upon approaching the chanters, we would be able to discern their words, but I realized, as we approached, that the words were gibberish, meaningless, though they repeated them with conviction.

In the dim moonlight, we could see that the villagers were mostly naked, though a few still wore shreds of clothing. They were turned away from us, kneeling on the ground, facing something at the center of the clearing. I had to peek around Satindra's bulk to get a glimpse of them – it was impossible to walk two abreast in the close forest – but I could see that a few were dancing ecstatically to the tuneless music. The din was horrible and I covered my ears to drown out what I could. It made me feel confused and hopeless, as if the veil between sanity and insanity could be breached by this combination of sounds.

There was a stench that made my eyes water. It smelled like rotten meat, sour milk, feces, and blood all together. I fought the urge to vomit.

Satindra stopped in front of me and I ran into his back. I clawed at him, trying to make him move so that I could look at the people in the clearing, but he was frozen in place. Standing on my toes, gripping his shoulder, I was able to see a little around him, where the moonlight illuminated the dancers. For a moment, I glimpsed with terrible clarity the twisted bodies, arms and limbs akimbo in unnatural positions, scattered on the ground. Among them were the tiny feet of children and the gnarled hands of the arthritic elderly. The dancers moved around and on top of these motionless forms, seemingly unaware of them, naked bodies gyrating horribly, eyes wide and mouths distorted.

Beyond the dancers was the thing they worshiped. It was so tall that it blotted out the stars behind it, dwarfing the huge trees, and I squinted to make out its features. Was that a long, crane-like neck or arms? Was that a deformed head or a stooped back? Like the statues in the altars along the road, it was a thing that could not be seen completely, as if it undulated without moving.

Suddenly, Satindra turned and wrapped his arms around me, crushing me to his chest. His hand held my head against his shoulder. He mumbled something as he held me hard against his robes. I didn't struggle at first, thinking that perhaps he was frightened and hugging me against him in fear, but soon, I ran out of breath. Crushed against his chest, I could not inhale, so I fought him. Taller and stronger than I, Satindra won easily and, as I thrashed against him, he chanted softly in my ear, "Don't look, Little Brother. Don't look at it!"

I awoke some time later back in the village. Satindra sat beside me, guarding me from the possessed villagers lest they return, his eyes wide and unblinking as he stared into the darkness. When I asked him how long I had been unconscious, whether we should go back to the monastery, whether we had any food, his only reply was to repeat his bleak chant: "Don't look, Little Brother. Don't look at it!"

These were the only words Satindra spoke throughout our journey back to the monastery in Gandhara. The trek was dismal. Satindra was no longer an inspirational young monk, but instead, a mad, sorrowful man who sometimes screamed at strangers and other times wept uncontrollably for hours. The weather turned foul and we trudged through mud up to our calves. We both grew pathetically scrawny, bones showing through our skin, but the other travelers shunned us because Satindra still moaned his disturbing mantra. We survived on will alone and the rare, meager donations of those truly generous followers of Amitabha who knew their duty, even if the monks to whom they gave alms were dirty and mad.

We arrived on the Guru's doorstep shells of our former selves. The Guru could get nothing sensible out of Satindra, of course, so eventually, he came to me to ask what had befallen us in the terrible wilds of the Empire of Han. I could make no words in reply.

Now, knowing that death awaits me soon, at last, I can write about the events that occurred, though they seem so much like a dream after so many years. Even now, however, there are parts of the story that I cannot reveal, which I will take to the funeral pyre. These horrors destroyed poor Brother Satindra, who died muttering his cursed phrase to the last, mere days after our arrival in Gandhara. He left me alone to carry the burden of the horror and now, at last, I will be free of it, for perhaps in death, I will at last no longer see the jade crane when I close my eyes, blotting out the stars with its vastness, or hear the chanting of the mad acolytes dancing naked at its feet. There was a time when I sought the peace of enlightenment, but now I seek only the silence of death, where these terrors may be obliterated in nothingness.

Sarah Hans is a resident of the Airship Archon, currently docked in Columbus, Ohio, though on the weekends, she can be found at science fiction conventions across the Midwest. She primarily writes horror and steampunk stories, and you can follow her convention schedule, or read more about her work, at www.sarahhans.com.

The author speaks: Many of Lovecraft's stories explore the idea of outsiders from a more-civilized realm, often Men of Science, exploring a more primitive, less-enlightened world, where they find themselves doomed by ancient and unfathomable gods. I used Buddhist monks because I am, myself, a Buddhist and I rarely have the opportunity to write about Buddhism in a horror/science fiction/fantasy setting. Inescapable insanity is my favourite of the horror themes Lovecraft mastered and this story was born as an attempt to combine all these elements.

THE CHRONICLE OF ALIYAT SON OF ALIYAT

ALTER S. REISS

IT WAS IN the fifteenth year of the reign of Aliyat son of Aliyat son of Obe-dagon, of the line of Callioth, that a stranger came to the city of Ashdod, an exile from the kingdom of Judah in the hills.

The guards at the gate made a mockery of this man, for he was a stranger and he wore a cloth over his face, that none might see him. Then the stranger unhooked the cloth from one of his ears, that they might see the corner of his face.

When the guards saw the corner of his face, they could not speak, so great was their fear, and they fell down upon their faces.

Word of this was brought before the King and he commanded that the stranger be brought before him. "Who are you, Judean?" said the King, "that you come into the city with a cloth before your face, that none might see you, and before whom the guards at the gate have bowed in fright?"

"Hear me, O King of Ashdod," said the stranger and he spoke in the old tongue of Ashdod. "Judah in the hills is like a stick that is rotten in its heart. They drove me forth, so I have given their king over to leprosy and their people to the slaughter. I have come before you, Aliyat son of Aliyat, to offer you a precious gift that will see your enemies driven before you and will see the walls of your city rise up, even to the heavens."

At this, the nobles who were in the court made mock, saying, "Who is this that comes to the court of Ashdod, who speaks in the old tongue of Ashdod? Let him go back to Judah in the hills, where he can follow sheep with unshod feet, and drink young wine." And indeed, the stranger's feet were unshod and the fringes of his coat were covered in the dust of the road.

"Well that you mock, O children of Ashdod," said the stranger. "And well that you laugh, O sons of Callioth. Judah has laid waste to your land and built cities in it, even to the plain of Gaza. In the North, Assyria grows strong and proud and her armories grow fat with arrows, which thirst for your blood. Well that you mock and well that you laugh."

But Aliyat son of Aliyat, of the line of Callioth, did not laugh and did not make mock. "Show us, then," he said, "a proof of the gifts that you offer."

"Certainly, O King of Ashdod," said the stranger. "Have them bring before me a male slave and a female slave."

The slaves were brought before him and he extended a finger toward them. The slaves were struck with leprosy, so that their faces became white with it, and they fell to the ground. "Thus I have done," said the stranger, "to Uzziah son of Amaziah, when I was cast from Judah of the hills. He who was a mighty king now sits outside the city, in a separate hall, and even the slaves of his people will not enter there to be defiled by him. Thus shall I do to all the enemies of Ashdod and to those who conspire against it."

The men of the court were amazed as they looked upon the male slave and the female slave that had been struck with leprosy, so that their faces had become white with it, and that they fell upon the ground and the men of the court grew fearful of the stranger. "What would you have from us," said Aliyat son of Aliyat, "that you will do these things on our behalf?"

"Build for me a temple, fifty cubits in length by fifty cubits in width, with a roof of strong timbers, so that I may conduct the worship of my god, where none shall see and desecrate the rites of my god."

The workers of Aliyat son of Aliyat built a temple for the stranger, of fine cut stone, fifty cubits in length, and fifty cubits in width. It was decorated on the outside with gold and precious jewels, and none but the stranger would enter the precincts of the temple. There were brought bullocks and great-bellied sows for sacrifices, and male slaves and female slaves. Soon, the stranger did as he had promised and delivered gifts unto Aliyat the son of Aliyat.

For a time, the stranger talked with the priests of Ashdod, sharing with them his lesser secrets. Many things he told them, which they had known and then forgotten, and which sorely troubled them. Gabridagon of no father, High Priest of Moloch, who conducted the awful rites of Moloch and who guarded the secrets of Moloch's temple, spoke for a time with this stranger. Then he was seized with a great fear, so that he fled the city of Ashdod and the lands of the Philistines, and he was never again seen in the lands of man.

When he saw that his wisdom was not wanted, the stranger gave to the people gifts. Gold and silver he gave and fine old wine, and poppy juice for their delight. Male slaves and female slaves he gave also, comely in form, who spoke not and who worked tirelessly. Fine horses and cattle, powerful in their work, and the storehouses of grain were filled without the work of the harvestmen.

The gifts the stranger gave to the king of Ashdod were greater than these. The enemies of Aliyat son of Aliyat among the nobles and among the priests were stricken with plagues, or were seized by fits so they died, or were found on dry land with their bellies filled with water, as though they had drowned. Ashkelon bowed its neck to the king of Ashdod and even the prince of Gaza sent him tribute, because the power of Ashdod grew great in the land.

As the gifts the stranger gave waxed and grew large, so too did the price he demanded. Animals of every sort were brought to his temple, to feed the hunger of his god, and slaves in their hundreds. Not even the blood of offerings left his temple and the smoke of his sacrifices did not rise to the sky.

In his youth, Aliyat had heard the voice of the people, but as his power grew in the land, he heard not the voice of the people, or of the priests of the gods of Ashdod, or of the noble families of Ashdod. When an enemy of the king was killed, Aliyat would send the sons and the daughters of that man to this stranger, so that they went into the temple and were never seen again.

In those days, the priest of Dagon in the high temple of Ashdod was Melichibal son of Abedizevuv son of Amnon the Israelite. He was struck with a plague of the kidneys and he died in the temple, while making the morning offerings. The people were sorely afraid, for Melichibal was beloved and he had spoken ill of the nameless priest of the hidden god.

Ishbal, son of Melichibal, tore his hair when he heard tell of the death of his father and cut his flesh with a knife, but he did it in a secret place, so that none might know his grief, and he wore rich clothing, with his sackcloth beneath. "When the king hears that I do not mourn my father," said Ishbal in his heart, "he shall make me priest of Dagon in the high temple of Ashdod in my father's stead. And when the king comes to bring the royal offerings on the festival of the dying moon, I shall strike him with my mace of office and he shall die. Thus shall the blood of my father be avenged." For Ishbal knew that his father's death came from the King.

And so, it happened that Aliyat son of Aliyat made Ishbal son of Melichibal priest in his father's stead and when it came time for the festival of the dying moon, when Aliyat son of Aliyat brought his royal offerings, Ishbal son of Melichibal struck him with the mace of office, so that the blood flowed freely from the head of the King and he died.

When they saw what Ishbal son of Melichibal had done, some of the mighty men of the King, who were his guard, pierced Ishbal with their swords in the thigh and in the breast, and Ishbal died upon the altar of Dagon. But the hearts of the multitude who were in the temple for the festival were not with the King and they took up burning staves from the fire on the altar of Dagon. They beat the mighty men of the King with them so that they died. Then they went out into the streets of Ashdod.

Many men had lost their fathers to the temple of the stranger who had been cast out of Judah. Many had lost their sons, or their daughters, and had seen their land given to the stranger, so that they no longer loved the rule of Aliyat son of Aliyat. They went up to his palace and they cast down the stones of it, and they killed all the servants of his body and all the officers of the court. Yanshuf his royal wife and Reuma his concubine, and also the sons of Aliyat they killed, so that the royal line of Calioth was utterly extinguished.

From the ruins of the palace, the people came to the temple of the stranger, into which he had fled when he heard the news of the death of the King.

The doors of the temple were of brass, ten cubits in height, and bound up with iron. When the people came upon the gates of this temple, they did not know what to do, for the doors were too strong for them to force open.

Then Zarikash son of Balnatan, of the mighty men of the King, took up an axe and hewed down a sycamore that had stood in the outer courtyard of the temple. The people made it into a ram to force open the gates of the temple.

The first time the ram touched the door, a voice was heard from within. "Hear, O people of Ashdod and listen, sons of the Philistines. You have killed a king on this day and spilled the blood of princes. Return to your houses and repent your crimes, lest you assuredly be destroyed." And on the moment the ram first touched the door, the gold and the silver that the stranger had given turned to slime and decay.

The second time the ram touched the door, a voice was heard from within. "Hear, O people of Ashdod and listen, sons of the Philistines. Baal will not protect you, and Dagon has turned his face from you. Ashtoreth hides in her weeping and Zevuv has departed from your lands. Return to your houses, lest the last of the gods of this land depart from you." And on the moment the ram touched the door for the second time, the grain that the stranger had given turned to slime and decay in the storehouses.

The third time the ram touched the door, a voice from heard from within. "Hear, O people of Ashdod and listen, sons of the Philistines. Judah grows proud in the hills and Edom grows numerous in the desert. In the north, the armies of Assyria grow ever larger and they lay in provisions for the conquest of your land. Only through strength will Ashdod stand and if you strike at me, you will lose a third portion of your strength." And on the moment the ram touched the door for the third time, the slaves and the female slaves, and the horses and cattle that the stranger had given turned to nameless, shapeless things that rent the flesh of those who owned them.

The fourth time the ram touched the door, the doors burst open and a spirit of corruption emanated from the temple. Many were struck dead by that spirit of corruption and many others were sickened so that they never recovered. But still, the people pushed forward and would have entered the precincts of the temple, when a thing came forth, the like of which was never seen before and the like of which should never be seen again.

The hidden god of the temple seemed to some like an octopus of the seas and to others, like a great frog, but all who saw it knew it as an abomination and they fled from it, or covered their faces so that they saw it not. All the men who had battered at the gates of the temple fled from the monster, except Zarikash, son of Balnatan, who took up his sword, and struck at the monster. It availed him not. When his sword struck the monster, his arm was withered and he was struck senseless where he stood.

The temple of Dagon the monster destroyed, and the temples of the Baalim the abomination laid to waste. The trees of Ashtoreth were uprooted, the statues of the gods were humbled, and their servants were stricken with madness or slain. The gates of Ashdod were like open wounds and the people fled the city like blood.

Stones cracked where the abomination that came from the temple stood and the water beneath the earth recoiled. Finally, the mouth of the earth open and a chasm opened up which swallowed the monster and the temple, and the stranger who had been cast out from Judah in the hills, and many of the houses and the people of Ashdod.

Then the earth spoke and it said, "Woe unto me that such a one is taken into my hidden depths." And there was a great earthquake, even unto Moab and the furthest borders of Egypt. Upon the altar of the stranger, ten thousand died and from the earthquake, ten thousand myriads. And Athishuf son of Menelegar, who had been among the men who carried the ram at the temple gates, sang this song:

> The towers of Ashdod are broken
> The pride of Gaza is reduced.
> The line of Calioth is extinguished
> The crown of the Philistines is lost.

> Woe unto us, the children of Dagon.
> Let us grieve, who followed Calioth from the West.
> Woe unto our sons, who will be sold as slaves.
> Woe unto our daughters, who will be sold as female slaves.

> The towers of Jerusalem are broken.
> The pride of Samaria is reduced.
> Not one stone stands on another in Lachish.
> Gezer is an utter ruin.

Who shall aid us, when the Assyrian comes?
Who shall protect us from the sword of the North?
Aram is conquered and Egypt is a pit of decay
And all of our strength has been lost.

When the monster was swallowed up into the earth, some of those who had been struck with diseases were cured and some of those who had been struck senseless were able again to stand. None of those men would ever speak of what they had seen, when they lay in stupor, but they were all seized with great fear when they looked too long upon the waters of the sea, or when they gazed upon the light of the stars.

Zarikash son of Balnatan ruled in Ashdod after Aliyat son of Aliyat. The right arm of Zarikash was palsied from the time that he struck the monster and he suffered from terrors. It happened in the twentieth year of the reign of Zarikash, during that time of year when the influence of the dog star is strongest, certain strange fish were brought forth from the ocean. When he saw these things, Zarikash threw himself from the highest place of his palace and none could say why.

Baldad son of Zarikash of the line of Balnatan ruled in Ashdod for seven years. Then he was stricken with a fever of the blood, so that he died, and Athishuf son of Baldad of the line of Balnatan ruled in his place. In the thirty-second year of his reign, Athishuf son of Baldad was taken captive to Assyria and he and all his line died in their exile beyond the Euphrates.

Alter S. Reiss is a field archaeologist and scientific editor who lives in Jerusalem, Israel, with his wife Naomi and their son Uriel. His stories have appeared in *Abyss & Apex, Daily Science Fiction*, and elsewhere.

The author speaks: I've excavated at two important Philistine sites: Ashkelon and Tel es-Safi, which is identified as Gath of the Philistines. "The Chronicle of Aliyat son of Aliyat" is informed by my experiences there and my interest in early texts. I've taken some liberties with the history. The earthquake of 760 BCE is generally thought to have happened before the leprosy of Uzziah of Judah, for instance, and is generally considered to have been a matter of geology, rather than theology.

MIDDLE
AGES

SILENTLY, WITHOUT CEASE

DANIEL MILLS

HE OPENS HIS eyes, roused by the twitch of a curtain, the rustle of fabric on the tiled floor. The sound is deafening, magnified by the silence of the chamber. It slashes through the haze of dream and fever, restoring him to the agonies of his failing body. The room is dark. He cannot tell the hour.

The curtains withdraw from the doorway, admitting a veiled shape, the scents of saffron and jasmine. *Theodora.* He closes his eyes as the Empress glides across the chamber. Her slippers make no din, her approach discernible only by a faint increase in the strength of her perfume. Her steps carry her to the side of Justinian's sickbed, where she stands for a time, saying nothing.

He pretends to sleep. Her shadow covers him like another blanket, darkening the space beneath his eyelids. She has brought no candle and, for this, he is grateful. He cannot bear to be seen. In these last hours, his mind resembles a twilit desert, a night sky lit solely by the shimmering specks of his fading vision. His time is not long. The carbuncle in his groin is the size of a closed fist, its crown beginning to darken with the soft threads of infection.

She leans in across him. Her veil slides down over his nose and forehead, his blackened lips. Easing his head from the pillow, she cradles it against her breast, holding him close though he has begged her to stay away. The smell of saffron fills his sinuses, erasing the odours of fever and incense, the powders they burn to ward off the miasma. He exhales.

She will not leave him. He raised her out of the brothel and she has stood beside him through his reign, even when the City itself rose against him. Days of torment, days of fire – rioters besieged the Imperial Palace. He wanted to run, to take to the water and escape the roaring mob, but she would not go with him. She told him she would gladly die there. Her robes, she said, would make a fine burial shroud. What, then, could he do but stand and fight beside her? Tens of thousands had died on his command, slaughtered within the confines of the Hippodrome, but what small sacrifice that had been when Theodora had lived.

Now she rules the City in his absence, though they will soon be separated, banished to their respective sufferings, the loneliness of the grave. He holds no hope of Heaven. Alone with the night, he has even prayed, entrusting his soul to the hands of the dark, since no god will come near. The Horsemen are abroad, the Last Days upon him, as they are upon his city.

The plague is now in its second year. It came from the south, from Egypt, appearing in the most distant provinces during the previous spring. From there, it spread from village to village, from city to port city, receding as the cold set in, only to reappear on the fringes of his empire with the warmth of spring. In April, the first cases were reported in the harbour of the City.

The physicians despair. They have never seen its like. First, chills. The victim takes ill and descends into delirium. A few cough up blood and suc-cumb to a swift end, but the others are not so fortunate. Too weak to rise, they can only wait for the carbuncles to appear: egg-sized, sprouting like mushrooms from the groin and armpits. In time, the buboes blacken and crumble, and the infection seeps into the bloodstream, where it pours like fire through the body's channels, driving the victim to a screaming death. Many curse God with their final breaths, mouths open and foaming, even as the darkness swirls like oil into their eyes.

The sickness spares few. Those who survive its ravages are those with lumps that rupture and suppurate, but Justinian doubts their life is worth the price of future suffering. For the survivors are inevitably scarred – cripples with ruined faces and muscles that twitch constantly, so that they sometimes cannot stand.

Within days of its appearance in Constantinople, the sickness had spread to all quarters and Justinian determined to take action against it. One of his advisors – a man of unusual ideas and temperament, who disdained astrology and the advice of physicians – recommended that the city gates be shut, halt-ing all traffic. Justinian assented. Later, he bid his men collect the bodies of the fallen and bury them outside of the city. When the pits overflowed – and the labourers fell lifeless in the graves they had dug – he ordered the dead to be dissolved.

A tower was set aside for this purpose. The floors were chopped out with axes and the bodies of the fallen hefted into this makeshift silo from above. Lye was poured down into the hole so that the corpses liquefied and ran together, the resulting stench like the fumes of Hell, a noxious cloud to hang over the city like a pall, a shroud for the empire whose end it presaged.

Theodora stirs behind him. She murmurs a brief prayer before lowering his head to the pillow. Gently, so gently. His brow burns in the absence of her touch. She steps away – pauses – then turns back to the sickbed. She touches her lips to his forehead.

He does not open his eyes. He cannot look at her – not even when she unbends herself and retreats toward the curtains, lingering long enough only to wish him farewell.

"Rest, my love," she whispers. "Soon, your suffering will be at an end."

Then she is gone. Her footsteps withdraw down the corridor, the last hints of her perfume smothered by the odours of incense.

The room is empty. He is alone.

AGAIN, THE CURTAINS rustle.

The shadows wink into existence, followed by the inevitable onrush of agony – throbbing buboes, the blinding heat of fever. There is someone in the room.

His eyes roll to the corners, seeking out the far side of the chamber. He dare not rotate his neck. The carbuncle at his throat has grown so large and inflamed that even the slightest motion can cause him to lose consciousness. A ripple moves through the curtains, stirring them as with a faint breeze, though the air remains stagnant, stifling.

"Yes?" he croaks, unable to lift his voice above a whisper.

No response.

The curtains part slightly, causing the shadows beyond to shift, curling inward, splintering to jagged pieces. A visible darkness leaches into the room, eddying like smoke from the part in the curtains, darker than the deepest shadow. It traverses the chamber, advancing silently, without cease, approaching the bedside with the inexorable slowness of a world-circling ocean, the tides that swallow even the mountains, given time.

At the foot of the bed, the darkness takes on definite form, coalescing into the outline of a thin figure: hairless, attired in rags, taller than the tallest of warriors. It inclines its head as though in deference. A voice seeps from it, a murmur like the creak of cedars in a storm.

"Your Majesty," it says.

"You have come at last," Justinian whispers. He is resigned, relieved. For days, he has awaited this final visitor to his sickbed.

"It is true that I have come," it says. "And that my visit has been long-delayed. But I fear I am not whom you imagine."

"Not ... Death?"

It shakes its head. "I am but one face of the dark, Your Majesty. The small death that is always with you: the end that you carry, as do all men, like a secret in your body. One that can never be confided or shared – not even with a woman."

"Who, then ...?"

"I am a newcomer to your realm," it says. "For centuries, I dwelt in Egypt, among the pyramids and shifting sands. Some called me a pharaoh. I was vested with power, resplendent in terror, but my hunger was … insatiable.

"Your present agony is considerable. I know this. Nevertheless, you cannot know what it is like to bear a hunger for a thousand years, a yearning that can never be sated. And so, I journeyed north, arriving in your lands last spring."

Comprehension dawns. "You are the Fourth Horseman? Pestilence?"

The darkness shrugs, or seems to. One shoulder detaches itself for a moment, hanging in the air like a wisp of smoke before rejoining its body.

"It is true that some have called me that. To others, I am simply the Black Man. To you, I must appear a thing of shadow, as death does to all who fear its coming. In truth, I am corporeal by nature – indeed, no different than yourself. While you are made of blood and bone, my body is formed from a million rats, a billion insects – all gathered together in me, concentrated into a shadow deeper than any shade.

"This April, I stowed away on a ship bound for your city. When it arrived, I waited for nightfall and then slipped down the galley ropes into the harbour. Since then, my labours have been tireless. But my hunger has not faded and I grow … so … *weary*."

Here, its voice cracks – a cedar splitting, sheared by a heavy wind.

Silence falls.

"I do not understand," Justinian manages. "If it is my time… then please, take me and be done with it. Prolong my suffering no longer."

The darkness sighs. "Again, you misunderstand my purpose in coming here," it says. "I come to you, not as a king – though some have called me such – but as a supplicant."

To Justinian's surprise, the figure folds in on itself, buckling inward from the legs so that it is suddenly kneeling, its featureless skull rising above the piled blankets. "Your Majesty, I come here to beg – to ask of you a favour and to offer a proposition."

Justinian closes his eyes. The room spins, the ceiling descending. He doubts himself, doubts everything. When he opens his eyes, the darkness has not stirred. It kneels before him with head bowed, a subject awaiting his decree.

"What … favour … can I grant you?" Justinian whispers. "You, who have such power over me. Over whom no emperor can rule."

"I am dying," it says. "You have defeated me – or nearly so. My hunger grows even as my strength fails me. It is true that men die in the streets every day, but you have trapped me here in this city. There are other nations to which I have longed to travel, empires I have read about that I shall never see. I shall die here, Your Majesty – but I will not die alone."

"No," Justinian agrees. All down his body, the buboes throb – pulsing, poisonous – aching to spread their fire through his blood.

"Your time is indeed near," it says. "In a matter of hours, you will cough your last breath and pass beyond the veil to whatever lies beyond. Can you not picture it? You will lie here some time before they find you. Naturally, they will call for the Empress: the wife you have loved so dearly, whom you raised from a harlot to be your equal. And she will mourn you. She will kiss your cooling lips and lie beside you through the night. And this –"

The darkness sighs again, its breath like the rustling of distant branches. Its tone communicates genuine regret, a sadness deeper than any Justinian has ever known.

"And this will be her final mistake."

The last words hang in the air between them, joining with the smoke that curls from the braziers, further obscuring the figure at the foot of the bed.

Justinian struggles to raise himself onto his elbows. The agony is too great. His mind clouds over, permitting one thought, one word, a name.

He asks, "Is there nothing to be done?"

"Indeed, Your Majesty – there is always something. I come to you on bended knee, but with my hand extended." A protuberance emerges from its body, thrusting forward and unfurling to reveal five elongated fingers. "We are both dying men," it says. "Dying kings, after our own fashion. But we need not die. And neither must your empress."

"What are you proposing?"

"Give me dominion over your empire," it says. "Make of me an ally and I shall be a friend – the truest that you have ever known. The sickness that eats at you shall be healed. The Empress, too, will live to die, but it shall be in her time."

"Go on."

"The plague pits are nearly full. Let them overflow. And for those who die in the streets – alone, unloved and unknown – I ask only that you allow them to go unburied. Let them rot. Let the air grow clotted and foul. In the ensuing chaos, let but one wagon go free of the city walls. I shall be upon it."

"What, then? What will you do?"

The darkness spreads its hands, its long fingers streaming like candle flames. "I will feed," it says. "I am ... hungry. So hungry."

Justinian clenches his eyes shut. The future presents itself to him with the clarity of revelation, a vision birthed from the fires of nightmare. From Thrace to Nicomedia, the pestilence will spread, a poison in the blood of Empire, laying waste to one city then another, leading the East to desolation and ruin. His wars, so carefully planned, will come to nothing. The West will revert to its Gothic barbarism and the dream of Rome will die forever, never to be resurrected.

He opens his mouth to speak.

The darkness holds up its hand. "Please," it says. "You must think this over. Carefully."

Carefully.

His mind spins as in the orgies of dance. In the smoke of that stifling chamber, he recalls his first sight of Theodora: the sweat that beaded on her brow, the shape of her body as she whirled in the glow of a dozen candles, light following shadow across her churning hips. The flash from her brown eyes, as sharp as polished flints. The squalour of her surroundings. Some men stood and cheered, crying out for more. Others stood ashamed, watching from the shadows of the overhang as she spun with the light, changing shape, taking on one face then another before disappearing into the dark at dance's end.

He attempts to swallow. His throat is too dry.

He can only nod. "Let it be done," he croaks.

The smoke wavers, rippled by a sudden wind. The darkness unfolds itself, standing to its full height so that its head nearly scrapes the stone ceiling.

A square of parchment is pressed into Justinian's hand. It is a writ of passage, permitting the bearer to pass through the city gates. The darkness produces Justinian's signet ring and holds it out for him to take. The metal scorches his fingertips. He presses the ring to the wax, marking the document with his seal before collapsing, exhausted, onto his back.

"You have made a wise choice," the darkness whispers. "And I think you will find me the worthiest of allies. I may gorge myself on the fruits of your land, but in eight centuries, I will return to savage your enemies, to avenge your name on the destroyers of your city."

It leans in across him.

"But a bargain is a bargain," it says. "And now you shall be healed."

There is something in its hand, something thin and pointed. Justinian had not noticed it before. The darkness lifts the object above its head, where it catches the faint light. He sees that it is a long needle, more than a foot in length.

"Wait – no," Justinian manages, the words catching in his throat.

The needle flashes toward him. It punctures the flesh of his neck, lancing the bubo. A stream of warm fluid pours out, washing down his bare chest. He screams – or tries to – but illness has robbed him of his voice and the emerging shriek is no louder than a death rattle.

The darkness takes aim at his arm pits, rupturing one carbuncle and then the other, driving in the lance with practiced ease. Blood and pus bubble from the wounds and stain the blankets. The world blinks white before him. The breath streams out of his chest. He gasps and pants, his vision fading as he lapses toward unconsciousness.

His visitor flicks back the blankets with the needle-tip, revealing Justinian's bed-wasted body. The final bubo sits like a tumour in his groin, red and swollen, pulsing with heat. His eyes roll back into his skull. They find a place on the ceiling, even as the darkness grins and lifts its lance to deliver the final blow.

HE WAKES TO a chamber awash in morning sunlight. Cries echo from a distant street – howls of the dying, the damned. Days have passed. His sickness has departed, but it has not left him unscarred. The buboes have crusted over, forming ugly cysts that will never heal. His skin is pocked and ashen, his cheeks sunken, the bones protruding. He is disfigured, horribly so, transfigured by darkness as Christ was in light.

Theodora sits at his side. Veiled in purple, her hands folded in her lap. His blood surges at the sight of her, racing to his throat, though he cannot breathe to speak. His hands tremble uncontrollably. With the last of his strength, he lifts a wasted hand from the blankets and reaches out to her, his fingers settling on her knee.

She flinches. She lowers her gaze to her lap, repositioning herself so that he cannot reach her. He whispers her name. She will not meet his eyes.

THE PLAGUE OF Justinian – as it is known to history – ravaged the Byzantine Empire for more than two centuries. The Empire entered its final decline during the High Middle Ages, with Justinian's city falling to Frankish crusaders in 1204.

Years later, a lone traveler, dressed in rags, disembarked from a ship in Sicily. His appearance occasioned some comment, as he was unusually tall and possessed a voice like wind-swept trees, the groan of masts in a winter gale.

He was later heard securing passage to Marseille. He admitted himself fascinated by the West and hoped his visit there might prove an interesting one.

Daniel Mills is a young writer and lifelong resident of Vermont. His first novel, entitled *Revenants: A Dream of New England*, is available from Chômu Press. He is a graduate of the University of Vermont.

The author speaks: "Silently, Without Cease" is set in the plague-stricken city of Constantinople in 542 CE. It attempts to recreate the suffering of the

Byzantine Emperor Justinian I, whose dreams of reuniting the Roman Empire died with the catastrophic outbreak of bubonic plague known as the 'Plague of Justinian'. The disease first appeared in Egypt, where it was widely believed to have originated. For generations, the plague ravaged the Mediterranean Basin, resulting in general chaos and massive depopulation. The connection to Nyarlathotep – especially the pharaoh-like herald of apocalypse described by Lovecraft's early prose poem – came all-too-easily. While much of the story has its basis in fact, the quarantine of the city is my own invention.

THE GOOD BISHOP PAYS THE PRICE

MARTHA HUBBARD

THE BISHOP OF Celestia stood on the roof-top of his residence, watching the bulging carts: exhausted, wheeled elephants creaking down to the harbour, taking their places by the imperial triremes waiting to be loaded. "Timos, that's the last one. How many were there in all?"

"Thirty-three, my Lord."

"Only! Do you think it's enough?"

Timos raised his eyebrows, in that eternal gesture of negation mastered at birth by all bureaucrats. He was only a secretary – and a slave, at that; what did he know of the workings of the Emperor's court? His master was a bishop, spiritual leader of the dusty flock clustered around the Church of the Holy Martyrs on the eastern shore of the Euxine Sea. It was the Bishop's responsibility to 'know' what was required to persuade the Court of Theodosius that their claim to the disputed relic was just, fair, indisputably correct – that the blasted thing should be returned to its former resting place in the Chapel of Saint Nicholas of Heraclitus.

Bishop Probus scratched his magnificent nose. Then, because it was July and stiflingly hot, he lifted his hat and scratched thoughtfully at the greying tangled nest wound up on his head. He sometimes felt that one of the most difficult aspects of being a bishop was carrying around this itchy mass under his mitre.

"Tell me again. What did we send?"

"Everything?"

"Well, no, maybe just the most important items."

With the universal sigh of martyred civil servants, Timos took up the first of 100 scrolls and considered where to begin. He wished Probus would read them for himself, but he couldn't read. Although, as a boy, he had failed to master any language beyond his native Armenian, his father, General Marcus Probus, had managed, through assiduous use of family connections, to secure this sinecure in remote Eastern Anatolia for his only son.

"Six bales of red-and-azure Phrygian silk, 100 lengths of purple-dyed wool-stuffs suitable for winter cloaks, ten gold-and-silver embroidered altar cloths for which five holy sisters from the Convent of Saint Eulalia forfeited their eye-sight, three caskets of saffron – hand-picked locally by children under three, especially selected for their tiny fingers, 20 prepared hides of unborn spring lamb – suitable for inscriptions, four caskets of whole black peppercorns, two caskets of cinnamon, two of whole cloves, and one of ground; in a separate vessel, two barrels of smoked sturgeon roe and three of salted carp ...."

As Timos recited the list of treasures prepared to entice the Emperor to order the return of the precious stolen relic, Probus drifted into dreams. He imagined the Abbot's outrage when the Caesarean Guard, come especially from Constantinople for the job, would escort him and his congregation up the mountainside to that accursed monastery. That brigand's lair wouldn't protect the thieving Abbot and his scurrilous band, then. What Caesar declared would be effected.

It wasn't as if it were just any old relic: not a supposed feather from the Archngel Gabriel's wings – there were hundreds of those around – or one of the coals Diocletian had used to roast poor old Laurentious (God keep his soul), or a beaker of dust stirred up when Giorgios of Konya slaughtered the dragon. Oh, no, this was an authenticated pouch belonging to the Holy Nicholas of Myrna, which had contained gold pieces used as dowry for an impoverished young woman. It *belonged* in the church recently renamed in his honour. And blast those monks, anyway, for thinking they could just carry off one of his Bishopric's finest, holiest treasures without so much as a 'by-your-leave' – as if he, Probus, would have consented to such a thing, anyway.

Probus drifted on cushions of reverie. It had been a hectic and expensive few weeks, ordering and assembling all those luxuries for the Emperor – even if Timos had done most of the work. When he awoke, half an hour later, Timos was just coming to the end of the 99th scroll and the ships sailing for the Holy City of the Emperors were tiny specks on the horizon. "Are you finished? I've just had such a wonderful dream."

"Have you? Before you tell me, perhaps I should get some of the yellow wine we brought in last week ...."

"Some olives would go nicely with the wine. How kind you are to me."

MOST OF THE time, this far from the upheavals and intrigues of New Rome, life in Celestia, a Byzantine seaport city in the middle of the fifth century after the birth of Jesus Christ, was quiet and orderly. Bishop Probus had been flung into a niche that perfectly suited his talents and abilities. Possessing neither strong political nor passionate religious convictions, his genial tolerance of the swirling multiplicity of cultures and populations that called

Celestia home had won him the overwhelming affection and support of his congregants.

In this, he was assisted by Timos, his clerk, scribe, friend and – ah ... er ... slave. Many years before, Probus' father, the General, recognising his son's limitations, had conscripted a Bulgarian village boy – grabbed him by the scruff of the neck, in fact – and brought him back to Constantinople to be young Probus' companion, bodyguard and helpmate. Timos, possibly too smart for his own good, had attended and benefited from all the classes through which Probus slept and dreamed such pleasing dreams.

But, as some wit would one day write, the times they were a-changing. After years of regency by his sister Pulcheria, the Emperor Theodosius, now in his full majesty, had commissioned:

"... a full and proper compilation of all laws promulgated since the assertion of Christianity as the one true religion by the blessed Emperor Constantine ...."

Timos, wishing, not for the first or thousandth time – the ponderous language made his teeth hurt – that the Bishop could read for himself, was interrupted.

"Damn! Why has he wanted to go and do that?" Bishop Probus, disappointed that the missive just arrived did not contain the confirmation of his claim to the purloined relic, expressed his irritation with emperors, overlords and bureaucracy, in general.

"What's wrong with trying to bring order to the snakes' nest of rules and regulations that every half-wit emperor has dumped on the empire since Diocletion?"

"Careful whom you're calling a 'half-wit' – one of them was my namesake."

"I rest my case. But what's wrong with trying to bring order out of chaos?"

"It's not the ordering I object to; it's the imposing of that order, afterwards, that's going to cause the problems."

"What problems?"

"Wait and see. This will not end well."

"What's happened? You're not usually so pessimistic."

"I had a very bad dream last night."

"Oh ...."

Probus' dreams were as good a barometer of portentous events as eagle droppings or the appearance of two-headed mice in the marketplace.

"I dreamt the Emperor had sent us a proclamation confirming our right to Saint Nicholas's pouch. As we processed up the mountain to the monastery, I heard a noise like waves breaking over the seawall. Rocks, sand, great pink-and-ochre boulders began to tumble down, rumbling, bouncing and cracking. I jumped out of their path and hid in a cave ...."

"... that appeared conveniently."

"Don't jest! This is serious. Once the avalanche ended, a quarter of our town was buried under fallen stone."

"That does sound ominous. Was there anything else in the dream?"

"No. I woke myself up at that point."

"There's nothing more in this missive. The Emperor has compiled his new Codex and wants you to announce his achievement from the pulpit this Sunday. That doesn't sound so bad."

"Don't count on it. Great disasters are oft-times born from grains of sand."

AS THE BISHOP had predicted, the unpleasant codicil was not long in arriving. A scant month after the announcement of the Codex, a phalanx of soldiers in austere trappings marched through the Porta Hesperia and clanked down the Strada Memoriam to present a papyrus signed by the emperor's sister:

In gratified cognisance of the magnificent work created by our beloved brother, the Emperor Theodosius, Second of that name, and out of our great and abiding love for the Basileus, we, the Honourable Pulcheria, Bride of our Lord Jesus Christ ….

"Dear saints and little chickens, she goes on worse than her brother. Skip the preamble and get to the point – if there is one."

"Let me see if I can find it. Ah … here: *I command you to search out, and consign to cleansing holy flame, all pagan, heretical or otherwise impious writings which have heretofore despoiled the minds and hearts of our innocent subjects ….*"

"I told you. We're to organise a book burning. How long before she turns that vicious mind to putting people to the 'cleansing flame'?"

GUIDED BY DEFINITIONS in the new law code, the *'what'* of the task was clear. Any scroll, papyrus or text, any scrap of writing not sanctioned by this code, was to be seized and burned. The *'how'* of it was another matter.

Celestia, a metropolis, of more than eight thousand souls – give or take a slave or two – had created itself down the side of a mountain, a cascade of fading rose, ochre and sienna limpets stuck fast to a crumbling hillside of low bushes, pines and olive trees, that tumbled, without form or reason, to a curve of harbour far below. Houses carved from the soft *tufa*, in many cases fronted cave dwellings burrowing far back into the mountain. Streets were vertical, better suited to donkeys than heavily armed soldiers. In a few places, *fora*, essential places of assembly, had been carved and levelled out of the rock.

At least, thought Timos, *we won't have to carry the debris all the way down to the harbour for burning. We can dispose of it on-site. Scouring each neigh-*

bourhood for proscribed material and wrenching it from protesting owners would be a despicable job. This damned project would waste days.

Muttering to himself, stepping over Pulcheria's scroll as if it were a dead viper, Timos exited the Bishop's study without saying goodbye.

Watching Timos' departing back, Probus thought, *I hate being right. This is going to be a nightmare.*

On Sunday, Timos read Pulcheria's proclamation from the pulpit. Notices were posted throughout the town, giving the times on which, and locations to which, proscribed materials were to be delivered. On Monday, Timos and a small guard arrived at the first location, Plaka Ilonia. The fire materials had been prepared, but remained unlit. To one side, the commune elder, Antonios, stood with a small collection of scripts from the community center, ragged, scribbled over by many hands. He pointed to them. "Take and destroy these, if you must. It is all we have."

"I thank you, Kyrios Antonios. This is a good beginning, but I fear it is not all. I am sorry; we must now search each home to verify that all banned texts have been sanitised."

"Sanitised? Is this how you describe destroying the knowledge of centuries?"

"Kyrios Antonios, I don't make the laws. I only obey them – just as you must."

Without another word, the old man spat in the dust in front of Timos and stalked out of the plaza.

"Leave him." Timos restrained the soldiers. "Dispose of these. Then we can begin our search."

When the fire was burning bravely, the soldiers struggled to gather up the discarded documents and carry them to the flames. The papyri ripped, slipping from their fingers; wind pushed fragments into the air. The soldiers chasing them tripped and fell. Frustrated and embarrassed, they determined to gather up and burn every scrap. Faster and faster, angry soldiers fed resisting papers onto the fire, only to hear them moan and grumble as the flames took them. These bits were old and tired. Soon, the last fragment gave a strangled whimper and died.

"All right, then. Let's get on with our search."

By afternoon's end, a larger pile of papyri, velum sheets and tablets had been assembled. Timos ordered the firing of these. The soldiers hung back, eyeing the pile of books and the silent crowd of sullen faces. "Maybe we could do this in the morning ...." the Captain suggested.

Timos gestured to the angry townsmen gathered at the edge of the square. "By morning, that lot will have disappeared everything into the mountains. We don't go down until this is ash."

With dragging feet and downcast eyes, weary men began the task of carrying the scripts to the leaping flames. This was not the debacle of the morning; it was worse – much worse. The texts struggled and squealed, fighting the soldiers like desperate children as they were dragged toward the pyre. On the fire, their howls of pain and anguish seemed endless, rising on choking smoke as the books gave up their lives to the flames. By the time they had finished, and the last papyrus screamed and gasped to its death, night had fallen. An ugly darkness blocked out the stars and the moon.

"That's it for today." Timos relieved his exhausted troops. "Tomorrow, we rotate. No one will do this more than one day in a row." *Except me,* he thought to himself.

"Put a guard on all roads leading out of the city. Now the community knows we mean to do this, they will try to protect the most precious pages by hiding them in the caves above. Bring anything you recover to me."

As Timos staggered slowly towards the Bishop's Palace, every step was a nightmare, his hips frozen with the effort of dragging his protesting body forward.

Dismissing the house servants, he retired to his chamber. He was too exhausted to give Probus an account of the day. An hour later, when Timos had not appeared for dinner – the quiet time they spent together, sharing food, good wine and the day's gossip, at the end of each day, was the Bishop's favourite – Probus ordered a servant to bring a light supper to his friend's room and went, sighing, to bed.

Timos, who had been sitting in his darkened room too tired to think or call for assistance, watched the man set out the plates and glasses. The smell from the steaming bowl made him want to retch. He watched the slave set a full flagon of wine on the table, light the candle and depart.

"Thank you, Oscar," Timos whispered to the closing door. He reached for the flagon, filled the cup to the brim and drank it off in one swallow. Again and again, he repeated this desperate gesture until the flagon was empty. Falling onto his bed, pulling the light coverlet over his head, he mouthed a silent 'thank you' for his friend's generosity. Darkness claimed him instantly.

IN THE MORNING, Timos rose and bathed before presenting himself to the Bishop. Somehow, a report would have to be delivered. And there would be tea.

The Bishop turned from contemplating the rising sun. "That bad, was it?"

"You have no idea. It was like burning babies; they cried like children."

"That's awful. Perhaps we should stop."

"How can we? Pulcheria'd have us on the pyre next, if we didn't finish."

"True, sadly. Maybe you could take a day off and continue tomorrow?"

"No. The sooner I get this finished, the sooner I can forget about it."

MAKING HIS WAY to the guards' quarters, Timos looked up at the sky. Fat Sol, climbing relentlessly over the horizon, had dissipated any residual evening coolness. This day was promising to be hotter than the previous.

In the guards' office, Captain Ochrid, grizzled veteran of too many years fighting the Barbarians, was waiting for him. He looked as tired as Timos. "So, did you catch anything?"

"Yes, sir, a few items. Pretty ordinary, except for …."

"Except for what?"

"Well, there was … is a book."

"A book? What kind of book?"

"A book kind of book. Sheets of vellum, bound with leather."

"Okay, what's in it?"

"I don't know, sir. I … the soldiers were afraid to open it. It's over there."

Timos looked around. "Where is it?"

"Over there, behind the desk. We covered it with a blanket."

In the darkness of the far corner, barricaded by the commandant's desk, several chairs and a battered campaign chest, was a striped wool cloak with a bulge in its middle. It might have been a sleeping foot-soldier – or a body. Timos strode to it and reached to pull the cover off.

"Be careful, sir."

"Why, does it bite?" Curious now, he continued. Even in the gloom of the corner, the book glowed and rippled with violet light. Timos knelt to open the cover.

"Sir, I think we should wrap it up and burn it – right away."

"You may be right, Ochrid," Timos said, stroking the smooth, soft leather. "But this will take too long to be consumed. If we burn it now, we waste half the morning."

"You are right, of course. But we don't want to leave it here – do we? Something might happen to us – to it."

"Exactly. You go ahead and start searching. I'll deposit this safely in the palace. We can dispose of it later."

Ochrid hurried off like a man pursued by wolves. Reverently, Timos rewrapped the book in a clean linen towel and tucked it into his satchel. The book clucked softly, warm against his back, as he strode back down to the palace.

Mid-morning, no one was about to question his presence or offer assistance. He passed straight to his chambers, noting with satisfaction that Oscar had been in to tidy up and remove the empty cup and flagon. No one else

would enter now. Placing the parcel on his desk, Timos removed the linen
to reveal a work of undulating beauty. The air around the book rippled and
gleamed, inviting him to reach out and stroke ... to open the cover – just an
inch ....

Come here; you know you want to, it whispered, the voice musical, soft
seductive ... Timos was not bound to celibacy. He had heard voices like that
before. Those experiences, while infrequent, had usually been pleasurable.
"Not now," he said. "We'll get better acquainted when I return tonight."

Offended by his rejection, the marvellous violet light snapped out.

"Don't be like that. I'll see you tonight." The book remained dull, an inani-
mate, brown-leather lump.

Leaving the Residence, Timos walked towards the *plaka* of the ward that
was to be cleansed today. Sol, now well-advanced in the sky, bounced burning
swords off his head. Timos was not a spiritual or superstitious man, leaving
that to the Bishop. Just now, he felt that the entire natural world was assault-
ing his frail, skinny body.

In the center of the *plaka*, Ochrid had just set fire to a mound of brush
and boards. To one side, a large pile of tablets and documents waited to be
burned. The soldiers standing guard eyed them with suspicion. They had
been fully and gruesomely apprised of the previous day's experiences.

"Is that it?"

"We think so," said Ochrid. "Our citizens seem to have realised that the
dictates of the Emperor's sister must be obeyed."

"I hope you're right."

"Me, too. You – men! Get that stuff disposed of straight away."

The troops set to work, pushing, pulling and dragging the struggling
manuscripts to the licking flames. As tongues of fire reached out to claim
them, the doomed texts cursed and groaned, spitting angry imprecations at
the fire and their tormentors. By the time all had been reduced to a pile of
smouldering ashes, the detachment, mostly boys, conscripts away from home
for the first time, were dizzy and pale, tears streaming down their cheeks, a
few vomiting onto the dying embers.

"I think that's it, then. Do you want us to continue searching? Maybe we
missed something."

Timos was about to agree when the sweet scent of lilacs filled his nostrils.
A sinuous, velvety melody began to weave through his head. "Ah ... no, I
think that's enough for today. The *miles* are clearly exhausted."

"That's very considerate, sir."

"Also, I'm starving – aren't you?"

"I think we could all do with a meal and a rest."

Leaving Ochrid to complete cleaning the plaza, Timos headed out of the square. Head held high, steps precise and measured, he presented the very image of dignity and decorum. Once out of the *plaka*, beyond the eyes of his men, he began to run, skipping, jumping, tumbling down the steep staircases that led to the main city below. Head burning under the sun, sweat flying from flailing limbs, Timos felt none of it – only a deep craving to be inside the cool privacy of his room and the beautiful book that lay there waiting for him.

Passing into the cloistered courtyard, he checked the sundial. Half an hour before the call to dinner. Time to spend with the creature.

Only half an hour, a voice in his head complained.

Inside his chamber, Timos stopped. "How can I touch such a being with filthy hands? Forgive me, I must wash. I cannot sully your loveliness with these." *Yes, do. Only, hurry.*

Five minutes later, cleansed and in a fresh tunic, Timos stood before the book and reached out to stroke its cover. The leather seemed softer, more sensuous than before. *Open me,* it begged.

Hands trembling, he lifted the heavy cover. Marvellous violet light filled the room, dazzling him. Flowers and animals never seen on this earth twined around strange symbols, challenging him to parse out their meanings. He traced their shapes with his finger. Fire, feeling, desire flashed up into his brain. New knowledge, unintelligible concepts, startled his senses. "It will take a lifetime to know you, to understand you." *Oh, yes …,* it whispered.

At that very inopportune instant, Oscar rapped on his door. "Master Timos, please, the Bishop is waiting for you to dine with him. What shall I say?"

"Tell him … tell him, I am coming immediately."

As Timos closed the book's cover, he heard sobbing. *How cruel you are to leave me so.*

"I must. Bishop Probus is my master."

At those words, the violet light flared out; the cover snapped firmly shut. Timos fell back onto his bed, so painful was his sense of loss. Nonetheless, after a few moments to straighten his clothes and his senses, he made his way to the *loggia*, where the Bishop was waiting.

"I was afraid I was going to have to eat alone, again."

"No, Your Excellency. The day has been long, the sun fierce. I felt the need to bathe before joining you."

"That was considerate. Are you all right? You look pale."

"Just tired, sir. This is not the easiest task you have ever asked of me."

"I can see that. Perhaps you would like me to relieve you for a few days."

"No … I think I should see it through to the end."

"All right. But if you look this distraught tomorrow night, I shall set Ochrid to finishing it."

"I wouldn't. He looks worse than I – if you can believe it. Come, let's have some of this cool Candian wine."

"That should help."

Dinner progressed, more or less as normal. Probus wanted a detailed account of the troops' activities. At first, Timos was reluctant to describe the way the texts had screamed and cursed. But, as always, bit-by-bit, the full picture was pulled out of him. The Bishop, hands folded over a replete tummy, had an uncanny knack for pouncing on the odd aspect, using it to pull down another fact and another, until a complete story had been assembled.

"That sounds horrific. Perhaps I should order a cask of good wine sent round – what do you think?"

"I think the boys would appreciate it. But from the look of them, the only thing that would make them feel better is their mothers."

"Poor lads, they really are so young, aren't they?"

Timos shrugged. "That's the system. A man doesn't become a citizen, *polities*, until he's done his duty to the state – as it was, so shall it ever be."

"I know. Still doesn't feel right."

Shortly after this, Timos returned to his chambers. There, he spent a fruitless hour trying to persuade his book to open her cover. Pleadings, begging, imprecations – nothing worked. At last, angry and frustrated, he gulped down the flagon of wine Probus had sent along with him and fell again into an inebriated sleep.

THE NEXT DAY was worse than the previous – if that was possible. By noon, Timos was so ill – from sun, wine-sickness, from frustration and anger – that Ochrid took charge, ordering his captain back to his quarters.

"Yes, yes, you're right. What I need is some rest. I'll be fine tomorrow."

"I'm sure of it Sir. Don't you be worrying. I'll see everything gets done properly."

"There'll be extra *solidii* in your pay packet – for all of you. I promise."

Once again, released from the book burning, Timos was a beardless youth skipping to a rendezvous. He wondered if the texts they were destroying had been friends of his book.

What if she hadn't – wouldn't – forgive him for abandoning her last night? Nearing his room, he slowed, heart pounding in his chest. Ahead, emanating from the edges of the doorframe, the glorious violet light welcomed him back.

Locking the door carefully behind him, Timos regarded the beautiful creature reclining on her bed of white linen, glowing softly. The air was filled with glorious perfume: lilacs and violet, hyacinth and tuber-rose. Heavy, musky, it made him dizzy. Falling to his knees before his beloved, he wrapped his arms around her and rubbed his cheek against her soft leather cover. "I'm sorry," he whispered.

It's all right. You came back. I forgive you. Now open me.

Timos obeyed, turning pages filled with remarkable beauty, glowing pictures of demons and maidens, of far-away cities never seen – only imagined – of calligraphy with strange shapes – not Greek or Latin – and runic-like inscriptions .... What could it all mean?

Hours passed. Timos felt neither hunger nor thirst. Diving deeply into the wonders on the pages, he barely heard Oscar knock, again and again. More time passed. Timos was certain that all the mysteries of the universe were contained in this extraordinary volume – if only he were strong enough, brave enough, to master them.

His Beloved led him on, her voice now not always so sweet. When he begged for a rest, she hissed that he was a weakling.

A DAY AND night had passed. Timos had not left his room or answered any attempts to summon him. The Bishop was worried, more than worried. He knew something was very wrong. First, he questioned Ochrid, who had just completed the odious task of searching out and destroying the proscribed texts. Probus felt much pity for him, but his dinner would have to wait until he reported what he knew of Timos' situation. The story of the book came out immediately.

"... and you say he took it with him to our residence? Did you ever see it burnt?"

"No, Your Excellency, I never saw it again."

"That means it must be with Timos. Thank you, my good man. Go now to your justly-earned rest. Before you retire, however, send me four fresh, seasoned soldiers. We need to have a look at this book. I'm afraid Timos may need some persuading to allow access to his treasure."

"I'll arrange it immediately."

WHILE HE WAITED for the troops, Probus pondered his next move. Rising to dress, he took out the royal purple chasuble embroidered with jet. It was worn during the darkest hours after the death of the Lord Jesus. Probus contemplated the symbolism of this. Then, placing it back into its coffer, he put on the glorious green, white and gold of Resurrection Morning. *If I am to fight the Devil, I need a magic stronger than Death to defeat him.*

As Probus had suspected, Timos didn't answer his knock; only a low moaning issued through the door. "Break down the door," he ordered the servants. "Stay out unless I call."

Inside, he found Timos curled into a ball, gibbering, on the floor. By his side, an old book hissed and vibrated a rainbow of obscene colours. With courage available only to the truly innocent, Probus moved to the book and began to examine the strange texts.

"What are you doing?" Timos cried, "You can't read."

"Maybe not. But I can understand this ... abomination"

"Yes!" Timos howled. "It is that. Can you help me?"

"Possibly. We must journey together, to a place no man in this world has ever seen."

"Where we will die," moaned Timos.

"That is to be determined. Where are the herbs given you by that northern shaman you met years ago?"

Timos raised a limp hand, indicating a shelf above the desk.

"Come on, now. Get hold of yourself; help me. I can't do this alone."

Timos lit a fire in the brazier and passed the shaman's scroll to Probus, who studied the diagram indicated by Timos and began to assemble a collection of noxious herbs in the brazier. During this, the book hissed and muttered at the two men. When all was ready – Timos protesting weakly – Probus lit the pile of aromatic plants.

Taking Timos' hand in his, the Bishop pulled the trembling man with him to lean over the smoking fire. Together, they inhaled the bitter smoke from the herbs. The air around them grew dim; the room began to spin, faster and faster, until the evil book rose into the air and took flight, leading them towards a cave, laughing as a powerful wind pushed them into a yawning cavern. Deep below, spirits cackled from bubbling and seething flames. They were falling, helplessly, eternally falling.

THE BISHOP LANDED with a crunch on his backside. Falling back against a wall of the cave, he cracked his head. All around him, dazzling and swirling, a myriad of images shifted from shape to shape – some too vague to parse, others sickeningly clear. A dragon breathing flames of blood, with blazing wings, each feather ending in a claw, clutched the book. There were snakes – hundreds, writhing and hissing – and scorpions, rats, lizards; giant orange-and-black-striped spiders – all fearsome and poisonous, crawling towards him.

While Probus stood there, gasping, drawing ragged breaths, willing his heart to stop thudding in his chest, a monstrosity before him coalesced into a luminous purple blob with tentacles.

"Enough!" he screamed. "What do you want?"

"It is I who should be asking that of you; you have invaded my sanctuary."

"Who are you? What are you?"

"Don't you know it's rude to answer one question with another? Who I am is not pertinent to this discussion. The relevant question is, I believe: 'What do you want?'"

"I can't answer that until I know if you are the per ... er ... entity that can satisfy my request?"

"Clever answer. Let me assure you that I am the only being that can satisfy the pilgrims who find their way here."

"If that is true, where is Timos?"

"Your unfortunate slave?"

"My companion and friend."

"Ah ... look to your left."

"Timos, Timos ...." Probus tried to rush to his friend struggling on the floor of the cave.

Timos yelped and gurgled.

An unseen force more powerful than Probus's will to aid Timos held him fast in place.

"You cannot touch him, now. He journeys to another realm," the monster said.

Drawing a knife hidden under his *dalmatica*, the Bishop leaped at the monster, "You fiend. Let him go!" He sliced off a tentacle before the blade was wrenched from his hand.

"That wasn't polite," the creature said, licking the bleeding stump of the severed tentacle.

"Release my friend, you beast – you monster!"

"My, my. Does he mean that much to you?"

"He is the kindest, most decent, thoughtful, caring person in my life. Without him, I would be nothing."

Lying in the dirt by the wall. Timos' eyes, round with surprise, showed that he understood every word.

"And this is really so?"

"I swear to it on this cross that has never left my body since the day I was baptized." Raising the heavy gold cross, Probus kissed it and held it out towards the demon.

"Ahem, we don't think much of crosses here," it said, backing away. "You may put it back into its nest on your chest."

"How else may I convince you of my sincerity?"

"I believe you. You argue very convincingly for an illiterate churchman. However, I cannot be expected to give up my prize without receiving something of equal value in return," the monster purred.

His insides turning to jelly, his belly twisting and cramping, Probus did not feel very convincing or very brave. He wanted to be home in his study, drinking camomile tea and discussing the latest madness from the *Polis* with Timos.

"What would you have of me?"

"Well-spoken, my good man – only that which is most precious to you."

What an odd question, Probus thought. "The thing I hold most dear – that which sustains me through every trial and pain – my faith in the Almighty God?"

The waving tentacles shrivelled, shrinking back from the sound of those two words. "Give up your faith? You would do that to save your friend?"

"Gurgle, gurgle …," Timos protested.

The Bishop ignored him. "For Timos, yes. I would ... try."

"So, tell me about your faith; how would you be experiencing that, then?"

"I see God in everything. Once, when I was a lad, I saw His face in the knot of a tree trunk."

"You didn't tell your father that, I'll wager."

"Er ... no. He sees the face of God in a glittering helmet, carrying the Roman *fascia*."

"Is that bad?"

"No, it makes him happy."

"But not you?"

"People are different." The Bishop shrugged.

"You really are a Holy Innocent."

"There's no need to be insulting. I have refrained from commenting on those ridiculous tentacles you are waving in my face."

"Argh …!" squealed Timos.

"You don't like them? Excuse me; I'll change."

The air around Probus vanished; a flash of light blinded him and a stink, far worse than sulphur, rose from the floor of the cave. When he could see again, before him slithered a snake – grown to monstrous size and smirking at him.

"That's worse than the tentacles. Couldn't you change back?"

"Sorry, you hurt its feelings. It's gone all shy; I don't think I can persuade that *persona* to return."

"That's too bad. This *persona* is really, *really* ugly."

"Are you certain you want me to switch again? You only get three chances. What if my next face is worse than the first two?"

Probus hated and was more afraid of snakes than anything. He was even more afraid of them than he was of his father. Ordered by the General to kill a snake that had frightened his horse, the young Probus had picked up his sword to decapitate the beast. It had raised its sleek, green head, gold eyes glittering within iridescent scales, pink tongue flicking in and out of its mouth, and smiled. Probus had fainted. More than any other dereliction, that disaster had convinced his father that his son would never have the readies to become a soldier.

Probus clenched his sphincter muscles and stared directly at the monster, willing himself not to faint.

"Where were we?" it said. "Oh yes, you were going to give me your faith in exchange for restoring your friend's sanity."

"I could try, but I don't think I'd succeed. Thing is, it's too deeply in-grained in every part of me – not only in my mind but in all the fibres of my body, even the soles of my feet – all belong to God." He lifted his hat. "It's even in every strand of my hair."

"Ew! Put that back. It's disgusting."

The Bishop returned his cap to his head, methodically tucking all the greasy strands under its edges. The corners of his lips curved, a tiny bit, like a new crescent moon.

"You may be right. We haven't had much joy of faith-renouncers. If their beliefs are strong enough to make them worth having, the pesky things always seem to find a way to sneak back to their original owners."

"There must be something else of mine worth having. I'm not a rich man, but my father … you seem to know my father."

"Bah, earthly riches mean nothing to us. Now that I look at you more closely, I see … There is something else, something you value and depend upon so much that you've stopped thinking about it."

"What is that?"

"Arrrrrrrrr!" screamed Timos, writhing in the corner, his inchoate mouthings ever more desperate.

"Your dreams."

The demand was so unexpected, Probus swayed, dizzy from trying to contain his fear and understand the game the monster was playing.

"Maybe you do need a less threatening *persona* to deal with. I can't negoti-ate with an unconscious supplicant," the beast said, before shifting once again. Before Probus now stood a singular, ancient man. His skin was jaun-diced; bruised purple bags hung below each goiterous eye. What remained of his hair – grey-white, unwashed and smelling of mould – was plastered across the top of his ash-grey scalp. He stank of decay and resentment – like the deepest pit of a neglected cistern.

"That's better, '" the apparition croaked.

"Marginally."

"So, your dreams, your ability to have and remember the lands you tra-verse when asleep … Are you willing to part with them to save your friend?"

"If that's what is required to reclaim Timos from this nightmare, I will do it."

"So be it." The ancient creature reached out a horrible, slime-yellow hand, wet and slick like a dying man's sputum. It plucked at his hair and caressed his cheek.

Determined not to disgrace himself, Probus held his breath and his body rigid, eyes fixed on Timos against the wall, while the monster explored the crevices of his face and head, alighting at last in his ears. Probus felt the tentacle fingers probing his ear canals, pushing deeper into his brain. The pain of it increased and increased, but he found himself powerless to move or scream, as a burning fluid washed out of him and into a jar the demon was holding. *What a pretty shade of azure*, he thought, just before he fainted.

HE WOKE – if you would call tumbling around in a maelstrom of whirling dust, shrieking ghouls and giant, cawing, glittering black birds – wakefulness. Falling through the murk, he was aware of Timos clutching his arm, like a drowning man determined to not lose the life-saving ring he had caught. The wretched, evil birds dove and slashed at their eyes and faces, howling and spitting. Probus knew that if he let go of Timos' hand, his friend would be lost to him forever.

"Hold tighter, Timos. We can do this."

"I'm trying, I'm trying," a hoarse cry came back to him.

A part of his mind registered that if Timos could speak, he must be improving. Filling his lungs with air, Aaron Probus, drawing on courage he never knew he possessed, shouted with all his strength at the birds and the whirling clouds, "Damn you all to Hell! You will not take my friend."

The cyclone revolved faster and faster; an inferno of dust, flying branches, rocks, stones, sand, and bits of dying sea creatures pushed them forward. The howling voices began to recede; the bombarding birds gave up pursuit, until he and Timos were expelled in a heap on the floor of Timos' chamber.

"You look better," Probus said, picking himself off a floor for the second time that day.

"Thanks to you. How are you?" asked Timos, regarding the Bishop as if he were afraid the good man would dissolve into a pile of ash at the slightest breeze.

"All right, I think. Do you remember where we have been and the promise I made?" Probus said, shaking his head.

"I remember everything. You shouldn't have done that – you know – agreed to give up your dreams."

"What good would my dreams be to me if I didn't have you to tell them to?"

Timos made a face. Sometimes, there was no arguing with the Bishop's logic. "So, how are you, really?"

"I don't know. I'm not sure – lighter, I think," Probus said, tapping his head. "Ask me in the morning."

Note: The city of Celestia no longer exists – if, indeed, it ever did. The descriptions and geographical errata are consistent with the Eastern shore of the Black Sea, in the area now known as the Republic of Georgia.

Martha Hubbard left New York City in the early 80s and spent nearly twenty years roaming around Europe. In 1997, she washed up on an island off the north coast of Estonia, where she has been teaching English to Culinary and Service students ever since. She has written a first novel, which was rubbish. The Good Bishop stories will be the second novel.

The author speaks: The middle of the fifth century was a time of powerful and far-reaching transitions. Christianity had 'won' its battle with the pagans. The Roman Empire in the West was a shambles, supplanted in the East by the glittering metropolis, Constantinople. Far from the intrigues of the capitol, on the Eastern shore of the Euxine Sea, Bishop Probus and his scribe, Timos, explore what it means to be human, to be a friend and to live a life infused by faith – even if not one sanctioned by the authorities.

The Saga of Hilde Ansgardóttir

JESSE BULLINGTON

1

ANSGAR GRÍMSSON WAS a man of many great deeds, a warrior and a
hunter and an explorer, and he earned his place as a *jarl* in the realm
of Garðar, on the island of Grænland. Ansgar was long-descended from that
noble hero Leif the Lucky and so, Ansgar ruled at Brattahlíð on Eiriksfjord,
just as his ancestors had done since Eirik Thorvaldsson first tamed that savage place. Ansgar was as strong of mind as he was of arm, and fair in his dealings, and so, when it was decided that a council should be held after some
time without one, the other rulers of that land agreed that Brattahlíð was a
worthy place to hold the Althing. Men came from Hvalsey and Vatnahverfi
and even Herjolfnes, and among them were kingly men with kingly gifts, but
also among them came Volund Deep-Friend, slinking up the steep slope of
Brattahlíð like a lean wolf looking to steal from a camp of men.

Volund Deep-Friend was not trusted, for he had named the island he
settled on the western coast 'Hymirbjarg', claiming it was the point from
whence the giant Hymir launched his boat to fish for the World Serpent with
the old god Thor. It was not only Volund's talk of old gods that earned him
scorn and hatred, for it is fine to tell stories of the old times, but there was
rumour that Volund still held such things sacred, that he had not taken to
the true Lord, but still bowed before heathen altars. Worst of all, those who
steered their boats near Hymirbjarg, as dusk fell on those cold waters, told
of hearing strange bells in the mist, and chants echoing down from the high
crags, that called out not to the old gods of men but to other things, not gods
nor giants, but names forgotten or never known by good Christians.

No word had been sent to Volund inviting him to the council, for no more
than twenty men and half as many women dwelt at Hymirbjarg, and so, few
would call him *jarl*, but Volund heard and Volund came, and the true men of
Grænland cursed to see him approach. Ansgar was proud, as well as strong
and clever, and would have no whisper spoken that he was afraid to council
with Volund, and so welcomed him into the hall. Ansgar poured ale and bid
his prettiest daughter Hilde deliver it to Volund, but when he pulled back his

cape and revealed himself to be a man changed by the sea, she dropped the tankard, spilling it on Volund's feet.

More than one man turned his eye to the weapons cache at the doorway, where he had surrendered sword and spear before entering the hall, and more than one who called himself a man turned his eye into his ale or up to the rafters rather than looking a moment longer at the visage of the Deep-Friend. He had no hair nor beard, and long, thin scars looped and wrapped around his face, as if a whip of fire had scourged him. These scars were black, instead of white, and pitted with yellowing circles. He paid no mind to the slight of the spilled ale, instead reaching into his cloak and drawing out a sparkling chain, which he held out to the girl.

She turned to her father rather than accepting it, which cheered the assembled men as surely as it irked Volund. Pushing past her, he went to the honour seat and sat opposite Ansgar as though he were welcomed to it. Other men protested and Ansgar might have cast Volund out if his eyes were not captured by the necklace the Deep-Friend pushed across the table to his host, a necklace unlike any seen by the men of Grænland, and Ansgar quieted the council with a wave of his hand as he took up the jewelry.

The chain was of a metal neither gold nor iron but somewhere betwixt them, the necklace shining like seafoam at sunset in the firelight. At its center hooked a tiny tusk inlaid with such scrimshaw work that in all his years of horde-gathering and wealth-trading, Ansgar had never seen its equal. When he peered at the imagery, it fairly swam across the ivory and that great man, who knew not fear when the battle raged, nor when waves ate the capsized longboat, nor when the hunt went long and no choice remained but to find game or die in the wilds, that great man Ansgar Grímsson became afraid to his very bones and knew not why. When he looked up from the necklace, he saw Volund Deep-Friend smiling and, casting the jewelry back at the interloper, Ansgar spoke:

> Volund, who men call Deep-Friend,
> You come here with fine gifts
> And take your place at the honour seat
> Yet, in all the years I have lived,
> I have never before seen your face.
> What cause have you to join us now
> And claim such an honour as the throne you take?

Volund Deep-Friend was no longer smiling and spoke with none of the courtesy he owed his host:

I come as I choose, as is my right.
For I am lord of this island.
None may question this
And the time has come at last
To return to the true ways,
The old ways,
The ways that once were
And will be again.

Now at this the council of men raised voices and cries, each eager to be
the one to challenge this scoundrel to a duel and end his disrespect, his heresy, his madness. Again, Ansgar silenced them, though a wave of his noble
hand did no longer suffice. Instead, he stood and bellowed for silence then
turned to Volund, a smile now creasing his bearded face:

Volund, who is friend of the Deep
But no friend of mine, nor my Althing,
I see you are as mad as they tell
And a great boaster beside.
What say you to meeting me
On the island of the shield-sea,
Where we shall prove who is lord of this place
And Lord of the heavens.
For it is not your giant Hymnir,
Nor the Midgard Serpent Jörmungandr.
The true Lord God rules above
And in his name, I shall teach you
Who rules this land.

Volund shook his head, as if it pained him to say this next, and spoke as if
to a child:

This is not a quarrel you may win
And you prove your folly yet again.
For his name is not 'Jörmungandr'
But something like what your priests call 'the Dragon',
In the tongue *they* call old.
A name you're not fit to hear
And even He is not most low beneath the waves.
You will bow, or this place shall fall
And I –

But none could hear the end of Volund's boast, for Hilde, prettiest of
Ansgar's daughters, struck Volund a blow with the tankard she held. She was
a wild girl when angered, fearless as her father, but given to the old ways –
unbeknownst to all those wise, assembled men, she herself bowed low before
heathen altars, but not those favoured by Volund and his people. She was a
seeress and, in an earlier age, should have been heeded for her second sight
instead of considered only for the bride-price her beauty would command.
She spat on Volund, who crouched low where he had been knocked from the
honour seat and, as the council roared with laughter and approval to see this
villain struck down, and by a girl at that, she spoke harsh truths to Volund:

> 'Deep-Friend' they call you,
> But who should desire such friendship?
> You are a coward and a devil,
> You who blaspheme all gods.
> Long have you been laughed at
> And short will you live in our memories.
> You and your wretched island-dwellers,
> Living in sea-caves like rooks,
> All so horrid of visage that children,
> When they seek to quarrel, tell each other
> *That one has the Hymirbjarg look.*

Volund spoke something else, then, but not in a tongue of men, and
before he could be properly taken to task for it, he fled and the thingman
who tried to stop him fell, with his neck running red. At this, the council
realized Volund had brought a weapon into the hall and, if for nothing else,
they leapt up as one and followed him in pursuit, each man thinking to be
the one to bring the captured wretch before Ansgar, and Ansgar thinking
to strike down Volund himself. Under the light of the full moon, they saw
Volund rushing down the path to the fjord and gave chase as one. Yet, for all
their speed and rage, Volund was too quick and gained the beach. He had
no boat awaiting him, instead plunging into the chill cove as if it were the
Sun month and not Hay-time. A few men swore there were other shapes in
the water with Volund Deep-Friend as he swam out into the night, but none
were willing to paddle after and find out.

2

THE DOOM THAT came to Grænland was fast in coming, and cruel when it came, for not a fish was landed from Cape Farewell all the way to Dyrnes Church after the night Volund Deep-Friend was chased from Ansgar's hall. It was as if the sea-crop had quit those waters altogether. The only walrus that was caught from Hay-time to Slaughtering month was a terrible black brute that had human teeth in its mouth and writhing cuttlefish arms instead of tusks. It killed Biôrnólfr Snorrason, the man who speared it, and those hunters who came close enough to slay the walrus in turn swore it cried like a child as they cut it down. The meat was black and oily and rank as its hide, and it was agreed upon that no good would come of keeping it. They returned its corpse to the sea and rowed home, and no more walrus hunts were raised.

After Volund Deep-Friend had invaded Ansgar Grímsson's Althing, Ansgar and his council waited only so long as the dictates of custom required before suiting up for war and rowing to Hymirbjarg. Yet, when they arrived, they found the coward Volund and all his fellows absent, their longboats flipped and fled, the island abandoned save for heaps of waste and countless bones, many of which were the skulls of men. When they departed, Snorri Ketilsson, a friend of Ansgar's from childhood, discovered what appeared to be altars nestled down in the flood pools, but even at that low tide, the carven stone statuary was too deep beneath the icy water to extract and demolish.

One pool in particular seemed to give way to a cave and, squatting down for a look, Ansgar clearly saw a great wooden door set into the side of the tidepool. This door was carved with runes and icons that seemed to shimmer and move like the scrimshawed necklace Volund had shown him. Vowing to return in the Lamb-fold-time when there was heat enough in the water to dive down and explore the sunken mystery, Ansgar returned home to Brattahlíð.

The news of Volund Deep-Friend and his people fleeing their island cheered all, save Hilde Ansgardóttir, who thought more and more that it boded ill. She was clever as her father, no slouch himself, and more than he, she knew the danger of scoffing at the old ways, for her mother and her mother's mother and her mother's mother's mother, and so on, had been seeresses of no small renown, before they were forced to hide their talents, and of no small prowess, both before and after their husbands forbade them from sitting on graves and praying at crossroads for hints of the future. Hilde did not assume Volund had come to the council and then fled with his men simply out of folly or madness. As it became clear that the sea would provide no provender that winter, she wondered more and more at what secrets the Deep-Friend knew and what counsel he kept.

Hilde could find no answer in the scudding grey clouds, or the murder of ravens that sometimes hung above her like a small thunderhead as she wandered the high places, and she sat at each crossroad without answer. When she served the ale for her father one night, she heard him and Snorri Ketilsson discuss returning to the old countries if the fish and walrus did not return. To hear them speak of the sea-roads gave her such pause that she almost spilled the drink. Knowing what must be done, she waited until the morn and then instructed her most trusted slave to keep word of her departure hidden from her father as long as possible. She then set out in a small boat, pausing on the cold, stony shore only long enough to smear herself with seal fat, lest she tumble into the water, for there was talk that the sea was rougher than it had ever been.

She rowed out the length of Eiriksfjord, which should have taken some time indeed, yet a current took her and she scarcely needed to dip wood in water to propel herself along the wide, rocky canal. As the sun set, she saw the bay yielded to the emptiness and so, moored herself on a spit of rock long anchored against for that purpose. She ate dried reindeer and drank from her waterskin, and slept on the cold, wet floor of her boat. That night, sights came to her. She knew even in her fear that she was right to seek the crossroads of the flood and surf.

A man was sitting above her on the seat of the rowboat when she opened her eyes, the year-counter full and casting its wan light upon the fishing ground. She did not know him at once, for without his scars, the Deep-Friend seemed as any man, hale and fierce-bearded. Then he bared his teeth at her as he spoke. Seeing the white saw-blades of the mackerel shark shining behind his lips in the lune-light, she knew him for Volund.

> You slandered me, child
> And called me mad.
> Yet, here you sit amidst the tempest,
> Alone upon the Engulfer.
> I should accept this sacrifice,
> If that was your father's purpose
> In letting you come.
> Yet, I am gone from this place
> And while I walk the sea-roads,
> Instead of sailing them,
> And walk the dream-roads
> Like my Lord Beneath,
> I find you beyond the cut of my teeth.

At this, Hilde grew bold, for she had long trafficked in the sleeping places and knew she could not be harmed by such as he while she slept. Thinking to have her answer, she demanded then of Volund,

> Where have you fled, fiend
> And why, if you be so kingly,
> Do you run
> Instead of making the Raven god's sport
> With my father and his men?
> You chose a quarrel at the Althing
> And now, the sea-fields lie fallow.
> How might this curse be lifted?
> Heed my word, oh grey sea-beast,
> Watcher from the tarn heath,
> And answer, or risk my wrath.

The laugh of Volund Deep-Friend was the sound of a cog scraping its belly on a gravel shoal. He winked at Hilde as he stood, revealing his nakedness.

> I am bound by your weird
> To answer, it is true.
> And so know, O daughter of Christmen
> And Giant-bane alike,
> That I sailed for the Markland.
> When you and your father would not hear me,
> I sought to save this place.
> But only through peace could I stave off
> The Encircler of All Lands.
> And now He shall have his due.
> Unless you row further, look deeper,
> The last hope of dying Grænland
> Dies along with you.

3

HILDE ANSGARDÓTTIR AWOKE to see the day-star already hoisted to the top of the fjord and wasted no time in unhitching the rope lashing her to the mooring stone. She looked from the ever-lying fluid-and-expanse before her to the mouth of Eiriksfjord behind her, and set her mind on a course. She had seen many sights and felt many portents, but never before had she found

herself so sure that she was indeed a seeress and not a madwoman. If any
hope at all was to be found for her homeland, she must take it, no matter the
risk. Even still, braving the sea-fences in a rowboat was folly and she knew it.
She offered prayers to Æsir and Ægir, wondering if they could hear her, even
as she rowed into the sea-fences.

Almost at once, she found herself swept along on some current and, try
as she might to steer her little vessel, the current ignored her. She almost
lost an oar trying to slow herself. Soon, the sea was widening around her and
the land falling away to her back and she became truly concerned. Then, as
quickly as it had taken her, the current slowed and released her. The waves
calmed and vanished, until no sea-fence rose as far as she could see and the
whole of the ocean was as flat as a frozen pond.

Here she knew must be the intersection of the sea-roads. She sat in her
boat and closed her eyes and did as she had so often done in the crossroads
of Grænland, letting her mind go where it might. In her hand she held the
necklace Volund had brought and left on her father's table, the jewelry she
had taken while the council pursued Volund away from the hall. She sat and
she waited. Soon enough, it came to her, the vision making her boat rock and
spray drench her. She did not flinch, transfixed by what she saw.

She again beheld Volund Deep-Friend. He was in the Markland, that
western realm Hilde's ancestors had inspected and found wanting before
returning to Grænland. There Volund and his men were waging battle in a
dark forest, their enemy a strange people who resembled the northmen the
Grænlanders sometimes traded with for white bear pelts. These beardless
foes of Volund carried no swords, but fought like berserkers. Hilde somehow knew these foreign men worshiped some hungry thing in the sky, of
the sky, and they hated Volund and his deep god. Before she could see who
would conquer, she was rushing back across the waves, under the waves,
and then she saw the bottom of a little boat bobbing in an endless black sea.
She came back to herself with the dread certainty that something watched
her from below.

Her boat began to move again, but Hilde did not open her eyes, for she
knew to do so would be to lose herself forever – the sound of much water sloughing off in the cold air was sign that something greater than any
horse-whale had surfaced. She had seen enough that taxed her mind without
adding to the iron weight of madness that already pressed down upon her
skull, seeking to leave a crack wherever it could. Her boat moved quicker and
quicker, until it skipped over the breakers like a giant-cast stone, but still she
would not look. Then she heard the sound of water parting, as if to accept a
falling ice floe. A pause, a silence, and then the nose of her boat dipped down,
its bed scratching and sticking on something hard. She felt her stomach

churn as she fell forward and, much as she wanted to keep blind, her eyes fluttered open.

It was sunset. A great island of rock reared up before her. Her boat was beached on the edge of a large tidepool, the rear of the craft bobbing in the air, the nose angled down into the water. Peering closer, she saw there was a cave in the rear of the pool. To her confusion, a door seemed to be set in the rock. Upon this door were images that she could clearly see, despite the depth and distance. What she saw there chilled her marrow, more than any night visit or second sight, and she would have turned away were she a child of lesser blood.

She had little time to wonder at her delivery to such a place, for the door suddenly opened inward, pulling the water with it in one greedy gulp. Before she could scream in fear or bellow in challenge, Hilde's boat rocked forward, tipped fully into the pool, and shot downward like a leaf rushing along a mill sluice. The boat skidded again onto something hard and dry as she passed through the doorway. She only had time to marvel that it was so much brighter on the other side of the door before it slammed shut behind her.

4

ANSGAR GRÍMSSON MOURNED his daughter when she did not return, and had the slave who had seen her row out that fateful morning hanged for not reporting it sooner, though such punishments were rarely doled out in that learned age save for murder. Ansgar grieved as few fathers have, for some part of him suspected that he was to blame for her disappearance. Even in a good year, that winter would have been grim for her passing, but as the sea raged ever rougher and the game grew ever scarcer, all upon the island felt the pinch of a father's sorrow for the failing of his family. Then the dead of winter arrived and there in the Ram month, Hilde Ansgardóttir returned to her father's hall at Brattahlíð.

There are two tales told of what fate Hilde brought with her for the people of Grænland, but both accounts agree she came, not from the sea as a corpse, nor from the sky as an angel, but instead from the very rock of the fjord, like a dwarf in the old songs. Upon her breast and back, a byrnie of lustrous green mail shone even in the dark of the night. A helm of similar make sat heavy upon her golden brow. In her hand, she held a sword unlike any seen since the time of legend, a great, end-scored blood-waker emblazoned with runes as black and twisting as the fresh scars striping round her arms and legs. Quitting the cave she had sprung from, she went straight to her father's hall, but would not place her worm-borer in the weapons cache, a dangerous, golden

glint to her eye when the thingmen made to take it from her. It is here that
the tales spring in twain. We shall follow that daughter of necklace-throwers
to the worthy end the song-singers grant her, with this boast given to the
thingmen of Brattahlíð:

> I have cut my way through Hells beyond ken
> And walked where I ought to have swum.
> I have seen the dark of the Deep
> And that which Volund calls 'Friend'.
> To tarry enough to council is to tarry too long,
> For They come, both by the caves I wandered
> And the sea that has betrayed us.
> To arms, to armour, to row and tumult.
> To the snowfall of bows
> And the spear's vicious thrust.

Ansgar Grímsson and his friend from childhood, Snorri Ketilsson, took
Hilde at her word, for woman or no, the battle fire in her face and the scars
scoring armour and flesh alike bespoke a great champion. So, they readied
for the fray as best they could. The moon, that hastener in the sky, would
not be still, however, and the Enemy had moved faster through the waves
than Hilde had through the tunnels under the sea. Thus the men of Brattahlíð were warned and ready when the slippery horde came forth from the
sea, yet there was no time to warn Hvalsey or Vatnahverfi or Herjolfnes. In
those places, no trace was left of hall nor ship. What bits of men and children
remained strewn upon the battle-places would not be touched by eagle nor
wolf even in that hungry season.

In Brattahlíð, the steel torrent did not slack, even as night became day
and then night again. The men who could not stand the sight of their foes
were the first to fall as they sought shelter in flight or prayer, long bristly
stingers of the Enemy sprouting from chest and back in dark mockery of
the spears of men. Bench-mates made hero and corpse before one another's
eyes. The tide of foes would not recede or break, but pushed ever up the
steep slope of Brattahlíð. One by one, the men of Grænland failed as the
Deep rose up to take that place. In the end, Hilde and Ansgar fought shoulder to shoulder, then back to back, atop a mountain of their fallen kith and
kin, slave and landed man equal in that cruel night as the moon again sank.
The only light came from Hilde's sword and armor, and the green irons of
the Enemy.

Yet, against all odds, the second dawn found the strife-and-clamour
failing. By midday, daughter and father had fought the Enemy back to the

sea-cliffs. As night fell, the last of the things that were not men, nor trolls, nor even elves, had fled back into their deep lairs. At this, Ansgar at last dropped to the earth, bleeding from twenty dozen wounds. He begged his daughter to take what food she could and flee into the high places before the Enemy could issue forth another campaign. Instead, Hilde Ansgardóttir laid her father and all the men of Brattahlíð upon a pyre. As the third night's gloaming fell, the last living Grænlander descended back into the cave from whence she had so recently risen, intent on bringing doom to that sunken temple of the Deep. None remained to tell if she ever returned.

5

ANOTHER PEOPLE SING another song of Hilde Ansgardóttir. It is not one to know, except that, by its telling, you may know the Enemy despite his human face, his golden hair. The Enemy tells that Hilde had different words for the guards of her father's hall, when she came with edge-sharp green sword held in hand:

> Once this hall has failed,
> And I shall not allow it to fail again,
> We shall take the paths of the sea.
> And the first to step against me
> Shall fall without breath to wail.
>
> I have wandered through heavens beyond ken
> And walked where I ought to have swum.
> I have seen the dark of the Deep.
> And beyond that great circling son, lies a father,
> The dreaming Lord,
> Who shapes the world in His sleep.

The first man to step against her was Ansgar, himself, and she cut down her own father with her strange blade. The thingmen brought scrap to her then, but though the odds were grim, she fought them all and won. So fierce was her visage that none in that place dared question her anew. Brattahlíð fell first but not the quickest. By the Lamb-fold-time, all of Grænland had bled out or bowed down; the single longship that escaped Hvalsey before her coming could not crest the sea-fences, that suddenly rose as tall as fjords, and was wasted against the rocks. Those who remained congregated upon the sea-cliffs with babes held close to breast. When all was made ready, they burned lamps of man-fat under a summer moon and followed Hilde Ansgardóttir down into the sea-caves from whence she had come. None remained above to see if they ever returned.

Jesse Bullington spent the bulk of his formative years in rural Pennsylvania, the Netherlands and Tallahassee, Florida. He is the author of the novels *The Sad Tale of the Brothers Grossbart* and *The Enterprise of Death*. His short fiction and articles have appeared in numerous magazines, anthologies and websites. He currently resides in Colorado and can be found online at www.jessebullington.com.

The author speaks: "The Saga of Hilde Ansgardottir" springs from my longstanding desire to tap into the rich style of the Icelandic sagas, which I was introduced to as a child by my Norwegian grandmother. Fusing elements of distinct folklores into something fresh was obviously a tactic Lovecraft himself was fond of. So, mingling his Mythos with Norse beliefs seemed a fun way of approaching the project. In terms of the specifics, I wanted to write something that incorporated Lovecraft's favourite themes (the degeneration and fall of individuals/societies/civilizations, the insignificance of humanity in the greater universe, the inability of humans to comprehend reality without going mad, etc.) while still giving the old boy a few good kicks to the coffin (Gasp! A woman! Gibber! A woman *with agency*!). While the abandonment of Greenland's Eastern Settlement at the dawn of the 15th century was likely due to more mundane causes than the one presented here, one can always dream.

AN INTERRUPTED SACRIFICE

MAE EMPSON

TODAY, THE GODS of sea, land and sky demanded that Featherhair sacrifice her lover. His hands, so sure and clever in painting vessels and tattooing flesh, had turned clumsy in the warrior's rite.

Featherhair had made the trip from their coastal city at the mouth of the Moche River, to conduct the island sacrificial rites, every moon since her mother died and she was chosen as the new Sky Priestess. They knew Bat-Winged God favoured her because he had sent a true seeing of her mother's death.

Featherhair was still screaming from the image of how the gods had punished her mother's body as the tribe whispered that she now had the gift from The One Who Sees With Eyes of Spirit, dressed her in her mother's blood-stained robes, and began to braid her feather-soft black hair.

Wrinkle Face – the old man chosen to speak for Spider Decapitator God, for land and mountain – told Featherhair that her mother had shamed the gods by failing to conduct a ritual properly. The gods had punished her mother, as she had seen. And, worse, Bat-Winged God, Lord of the Sky, now withheld his rains as punishment to all, even as Spider Decapitator, the Mountain Lord, withheld the mountain runoff. The irrigation canals and ditches offered only dust and sand. Wrinkle Face did not remember a drought like this, old as he was, in all of his seeing, and he had lived more than six cycles of seven-harvests, and been the Mountain Priest for more than two seven-harvests.

For ten moons, Featherhair conducted the island rites with the goal of ensuring that the gods' gifts continued and the gift of water returned. But the rain did not come. She knew they whispered that she could not clear her mother's taint, being of her blood. Had the sky not been particularly generous of late with its other gift of bird-and-bat *huano*, she suspected she would have been replaced.

The reed bullrush boat in which she traveled to the island held herself, the three who would die, and three empty vessels for gathering the *huano* that would lie feet thick in the bed between the three altars in the sacred place where sky, sea and land met: Huano Island. Featherhair had gathered the reeds for the boat herself. Wrinkle Face oversaw their weaving into seven, tightly-bound sections and the binding of those sections into the shape of a boat, since weaving and binding was spider work. But only her hands provided the blessing of air that filled the reeds so that the boat floated across the surface of the water and did not sink, though the sea water seeped up through the gaps in the bound bundles of reeds and wet their feet.

The two other sacrificial victims knelt on the floor of the boat and willingly paddled. Skinpainter stood at the front of the boat, spear in hand, to defend them against the creatures of the sea, should any attack. Featherhair did not think they were at much risk. Crab-Armoured Warrior Priest – the priest of the sea, its creatures, and Octopus Lion God – maintained his own set of rites to assure that the sea creatures were calm, that the harvest of anchovies was rich, and that the sea did not flood. Wrinkle Face had warned them both of times in his seeing when the sea had flooded their coastal desert valley. Many had died and all of the crops failed. The mud-brick *huacas* built before the flood had washed away.

Octopus Lion God would receive the skins of the three men, and the bones of their arms and hands, just as Bat-Winged God would receive their still-living eyes, and Spider Decapitator God would receive their blood and skulls.

And this was the root of the idea that fluttered in Featherhair's heart like a bat in a cage. Octopus Lion God with his sea lion face and mane of eight tentacles, each lined with suckers and teeth, and with mouths at the end, had no need of additional arms. He was all face and tentacles, sun-shaped. But his servants, the demon fish, had the heads and bodies of large fish, and the feet of men. They longed for arms and used the skins of men to come ashore and walk among the people, assuring in secret that rites were followed and that the people's finest goldwork – masks, ear spools, nose ornaments, and necklaces – were offered equally to the sea, sky and land.

So, Featherhair imagined that a demon fish would soon walk secretly among the people, wrapped in Skinpainter's skin and using his clever hands. She would see him again. His skin would be easy to recognize, painted as it was to demonstrate his skill. She would know him if he came to her in the city, in the shadow of the mud-brick platform mounds of Huaca del Sol or Huaca de la Luna, or to this island, where he knew she came once a moon.

She had not shared this dream with Skinpainter. He was defeated and therefore, near-dead. She could not speak to him in this state. But she studied his bare back above his loincloth, as he stared out across the water, and memorized the lines of his tattoos – interwoven spiders, crab, octopi, cormorants, and bats – over and over. She would know him, fish-ridden.

But would he know her?

On a mad impulse, she knelt at the side of the boat and cut open her right palm with her ceremonial *tumi*. She placed her bleeding palm down beneath the surface of the water. Salt water was like blood. She sang a prayer of her own sudden invention, a new prayer: "Octopus Lion God, taste my blood. Share it with the demon fish who will wear Skinpainter's skin, so he will know my blood-scent, my blood-taste, and how to find me again."

She knew Skinpainter and the other two defeated had heard her new prayer. Skinpainter turned and glanced at her, his expression concerned, and then returned to his role. She could see that he gripped the spear more tightly and stood in a more alert posture, as if expecting some attack.

It was dangerous to feed blood to the sea.

But she felt emboldened. Could Skinpainter not see that she did this for love of him? She deliberately cut her second palm and let it also bleed into the sea, repeating her prayer song. "If you do this for me, Octopus Lion God," she added, "I will love you and your demon fish as I love this man. As no woman has ever loved a man."

A bird, a red-legged cormorant, screamed overhead and veered towards the island, which grew larger and larger on the horizon. Featherhair told herself that this was a sound birds often made, signifying nothing, but she could hear the anger in it. Blood was for Spider Decapitator, not for Octopus Lion or Bat-Winged. This was known. Her act might have angered all three of them.

She wondered briefly if her mother had felt like this before she died – giddy and awful and newly afraid.

AS THEY REACHED the shore of the island, Featherhair convinced herself that she could make up any perceived slight by executing the island rites perfectly, without the slightest hesitation or error.

They climbed up the ramp that led to the top of the earthen mound on the island – a mountain her tribe had made for this purpose. The top of the mound was cupped like an empty lake bed, hollowed out, with altars at three points along the rim of the mound. She could see a rich, silver harvest of *huano* in the cup of the mound, but would wait to gather it until the sacrifice was complete according to their custom.

The men lined up with their backs against the tall stone of the sky altar, lifting their arms above their heads for ease of her closing the manacled chains around their wrists without touching their near-dead flesh. They faced towards her, towards the center of the island mound.

Featherhair began singing the song that would bring the giant birds, shaking a bone rattle and dancing the steps. "Bat-Winged God who rules the sky, accept the offering of these still-living eyes and with them, see our plight. See how thirsty we are, and send your rain. Thank you for the *huano* that makes the land fertile and rain it down on us when we mate in the rite of fertility, that our numbers – for your service – will also grow."

It could take hours, in her experience, for the birds to come. She would sing until she was hoarse, if it took that long.

The men tried not to blink or flinch. It was the open eye that called to the sky.

THE BRIGHTEST MOON had fled the sky to sleep. The golden sun beat down on her back. She'd never called this long without a response. She dared not stop her chanting and dancing, though her voice cracked and squeaked. Sweat marred her braids – the thick, insect-wing-shaped, wrapped loops at the center of her back that marked her as the sky priestess. Insects were the lowest of all things that fly, befitting the sky's humble servant.

She heard footsteps coming up the ramp. She chided herself to not break her steps, no matter what came into sight. She imagined a demon fish, called by her blood.

BUT IT WAS Wrinkle Face and Crab-Armoured Warrior Priest, who she knew was one of his many sons, who appeared at the top of the ramp. Behind them stood Llama-Tall Woman, an attractive girl of about Featherhair's age.

Wrinkle Face looked at Featherhair. "Last night, Bat-Winged God sent a vision to Llama-Tall Woman. You know the gift is rare and what it signifies. We are here to see if it was a true seeing."

Crab-Armoured Warrior Priest grabbed Featherhair's wrists and jerked her to a halt, interrupting her dance and chant. He lifted her palms for the others to see.

"A true seeing," Wrinkle Face whispered.

Crab-Armoured Warrior Priest dragged Featherhair away from her position in front of the altar and she saw, seeing Llama-Tall Woman in profile for the first time, that the young woman had her hair arranged in the insect wing braids at her mid-back.

Llama-Tall Woman stepped into Featherhair's footprints and resumed the rite, mid-step and mid-syllable. Featherhair knew that someone had to have been training her for many moons for her to do it so flawlessly. Featherhair had not trained her. This has been some time in the planning, she realized.

Crab-Armoured Warrior Priest dragged Featherhair closer to the sky altar. "You are defeated," he chanted to her, as he had chanted to Skinpainter at the conclusion of the warrior's rite. "You are defeated by one who is your better and claims your place."

Defeated. Featherhair could no longer speak to them or touch them. She was near-dead, like the other sacrificial victims. She tried to catch Skinpainter's eyes, suddenly united with him in fate, but he would not look at her. He stared at the sky, watching for the birds to come to take his eyes.

Wrinkle Face tilted his head towards the sky altar stone where there were silver chains enough to bind several additional sacrifices.

Featherhair knew what was expected of her, the steps that her own victims had followed so willingly and eagerly, moon after moon. But she hesitated. What would it feel like to have her still-living eyes plucked from her face and to feel herself lifted and dropped to her death, comforted only by the inability to know how quickly the ground was rushing towards her falling body?

"Please, child," Wrinkle Face said quietly. "We cannot survive more than one or two moons more of this drought. Something had to be done. I know you have served as well as you could."

Skinpainter faced the rite bravely and willingly. Could she do less? She remembered her pride in his calm acceptance, knowing that he was a good and gods-fearing man. She could give him the last thought that she had been worthy of the touch of his clever hands. She could do this.

Featherhair leaned back against the sky altar and reached for the chains.

THE TWO GIANT birds came. The same birds, or others like them, had always come previously to her call, but came now at Llama-Tall Woman's bidding. They were big as llamas, themselves.

She watched them take Skinpainter's eyes, carefully, one eye in each beak. His face bled. The birds bent and clawed at his silver manacles, finding the catch that triggered their release. Then they lifted him between them and flew high up into the sky before dropping him into the *huano* bed. His body folded into impossible angles, but no bone pierced his skin – a sign of the god's approval of his sacrifice that would be credited as much to Llama-Tall Woman's worthiness as to his own.

The birds took a second man's eyes, opened his manacles, and lifted and dropped his body, as well. Then, they took the third man. Three mangled bodies with three sets of unbroken skin. A good omen.

They were coming for her next. She would not shut her eyes.

And then, abruptly, there was a deafening roar, as a wave of water tall as the island mountain crashed over the back side of the sky altar stone and drenched them all in a spray of salt water.

Chained to the sky altar stone, Featherhair faced into the *huano* bed, away from the direction of that tidal wave. But she saw the faces of the ones who could see behind her, beyond the stone altar. She saw Wrinkle Face, Crab-Armoured Warrior Priest and Llama-Tall Woman, and their face-twisting terror. They all stood in shadow. Something rose behind her, large enough to block the sun. Even the giant birds, warrior-priests of the sky, fled up into the safety of the clouds.

A huge tentacle crashed down in front of her. It was taller than she was and blocked her sight in all directions, encircling the rock to which she was chained. Teeth as long as arms protruded between its round suckers. She choked from the overwhelming smell of brine and rotting fish. She expected the tentacle to contract around her and crush her against the rock, piercing her with its teeth, but it did not.

She heard the others screaming.

After several minutes, the tentacle lifted and disappeared back over her head. She saw Wrinkle Face and Llama-Tall Woman kneeling in prayer, their faces pressed to the earth. Crab-Armoured Warrior Priest stood with his back to her and seemed to be fumbling to remove his armour. As he staggered, his profile came into her sight and she realized that the birds had taken his eyes. Blood poured down his cheeks from his empty eye sockets.

Wrinkle Face rose to his feet. She caught the moment when he realized that she was unharmed and the mask of his face shifted from surprise to relief. He crossed to Crab-Armoured Warrior Priest and helped him to continue to remove his armour. "My son," he said sadly, "was it your error and not her mother's that brought the drought? Have you poured poison in my ear all this time?"

Crab-Armoured Warrior Priest moaned wordlessly and she thought perhaps his tongue had been taken as well, but then he gave answer: "We did wrong together, in this very place. I knew she would be conducting the island rite, and I interrupted her chant and dance to take her into my arms. We lay together in the way that is forbidden separate from rite. The fault was ours, but I let the blame be hers."

"You and my mother?" Featherhair asked. He was not much older than she was. And to lie together in the way that could produce a child, separate from the rites of procreation with its full ceremony, was a terrible crime indeed.

Crab-Armoured Warrior Priest turned towards the sound of her voice. "He spared you. Spared you and claimed you." He sank to his knees. "I am defeated by one who is my better and claims my place."

Llama-Tall Woman began to sing the words that called the birds, but she wove into the chant this new truth: "Come for the one whose unfitness was visible only to your sight, Bat-Winged God, who sees all with eyes of spirit. We praise you for revealing that which has been hidden and for making peace with Octopus Lion God by this gesture."

The giant birds lifted the man who had been Crab-Armoured Warrior Priest and carried him high into the sky before dropping him. White bone thrust up through the skin of his mangled limbs, marking him clearly as unfit for service, even in death, to Octopus Lion God. *His skin will rot on his bones,* Featherhair thought, which was the worst of fates.

Wrinkle Face brought her the crab armour. It sat strangely on a woman's body, but she realized that the tidal wave had also washed up an offering of spondylus shells – best gift of the sea – and that the treasured, pink, thorny shells, smaller than the giant crab-shell pieces, could be integrated to make something new and glorious.

"My son failed in his service to Octopus Lion God, not in his rash act of desire, for desire is of the sea," Wrinkle Face reasoned. "He failed in the moons that followed as he hid the truth with cold, calculating lies. Remember his lesson, Featherhair. Octopus Lion God feeds on strong feeling and folly."

"Even my own," she acknowledged and held out her scarred palms, which now seemed sacred and right. "Call me 'Crab-and-Shell Priestess'," she pronounced. Feathers were of the sky.

Llama-Tall Woman continued to dance for the sky, asking once more for Bat-Winged God to return the rains, now that all was restored to a new rightness.

Crab-and-Shell Priestess looked at the sky and thought, without jealousy, that Llama-Tall Woman might finally bring the rains for which she had begged so many moons. There seemed to be more clouds than she could recall ever seeing over this island.

But this was no longer her concern.

She turned her eyes to the sea, and tried to imagine her master's mountain-sized face and tentacled mane, somewhere deep beneath the dark waters. When she'd promised to love him, she had not imagined his monstrous immensity. When she closed her eyes, she could see herself surrounded by that section of sharp-toothed tentacle on all sides, taller than her. This was like a small strip of a man's wrist in comparison to the length of the arm.

She loved him, already. For protecting her. For choosing her. He had driven even Skinpainter from her fickle heart.

The others had seen his face. She had not. She would tie a dozen diving weights to her skirts and let herself sink to the deepest place and try to see him where he slept. He'd like that.

She knew now what even Wrinkle Face did not know in all his long seeing. Octopus Lion God slept out of the desire to be awakened. And the alarm that roused him best was the rare, strident, dizzying, blood-flavoured call of a mad act, a foolish gesture, or a breaking mind. Like hers.

An open eye called to the sky.

The blood of man called to the land.

A mind broken free – insanity – called to the sea.

Mae Empson began selling fantasy and horror short fiction to magazines
and anthologies in July 2010. Her first Lovecraft-inspired story was in the
anthology *Cthulhurotica* (December 2010). She is a member of the Horror
Writers Association and of HorrorPNW – the Pacific Northwest chapter
of HWA. She lives in Seattle, WA. Read Mae's blog at: http://maeempson.
wordpress.com.

The author speaks: "An Interrupted Sacrifice" was inspired by my research
into the Moche people of Precolumbian Peru. I first encountered the Moche
while researching a story about modern graduate students and a newly-
discovered Moche tomb for the anthology *In Situ* (April 2011). I've been
fascinated to see how many Lovecraftian elements are incorporated into their
art and rituals – from tentacled gods to blood-drinking priests and human
sacrifices. The two stories that I have written about this culture use the same
set of historical facts to describe very different explanations for their beliefs
and pantheon.

PRALAYA: THE DISASTER

Y.W. PURNOMOSIDHI

IN THE NINTH century, in the central area of Java Island, after a sheep-wool-like heat cloud covered some villages near Mount Merapi peak, the Medhang Mataram kingdom sent Arya Sotya to lead the team of soldiers and medicine men who would aid the survivors. Joko was in that team as an *Acaraki*, a medicine man.

Everything was grey. The flying dust in the wind was a memory of death. It was hard to breathe.

Joko saw that some men plundered the villagers' properties. They took advantage of the injured.

"How could you?" Joko shouted.

"They will die and their properties belong to us now," said a plunderer.

"This does not belong to you."

"We don't need your advice. Don't be a hero!" the villains replied.

"They suffer. You are supposed to help them," Joko said.

They mocked him. "A hero like you will die here."

The men drew their blades and attacked Joko. Joko drew his *kris*, the Javanese traditional wavy, doubled-bladed dagger. It was not only a weapon but also an amulet. Joko moved, nimble as a snake, defending from and attacking his opponents. Suddenly, an arrow hit a plunderer.

"Freeze! We are the kingdom's soldiers!" Arya shouted.

Six soldiers readied to attack the plunderers with spears and *kris* daggers. Growing pale, the plunderers stopped their attack and ran away.

Joko and other medicine men treated the injured villagers with herbal medicine. To spare them the next disaster, they evacuated the people of the slope villages of Mount Merapi to a safer place in Prambanan. Quakes rumbled seven times and people feared nature.

"Look! That's Prambanan," a villager cried, happily pointing his finger at the complex of beautiful Hindu temples.

From the high land, they saw the complex. It housed three main temples, Shiva Temple, Brahma Temple, and Vishnu Temple, with small temples surrounding them.

On the way to the temples, some strangers blocked their way. An old man moved forward, towards the refugees. "My name is Ki Atur," said the old stranger, holding a stick in his right hand.

"This disaster happenned because of their sin. God punished the people of the slope of Mount Merapi. Mount Merapi is angry. If these sinful people stay here, the punishment will come to us. So, you must take them back."

"These people need help. They do not need your judgment," Joko said.

"Young man, you do not understand God. If you are against God's will, you fall into the heresy of worshiping older gods," Ki Atur replied.

"God's will is a mystery. I am neither a wise nor a smart person. I just follow my heart to help people. I do something for people and pray to God to lead my way into Thy way. However, you are not God. You add another disaster by judging people. We must go now," Joko said.

"Ask your people to disperse! If you block our way, you are an enemy of the kingdom," Arya shouted, drawing his dagger.

Holding weapons, Ki Atur and his people were ready to fight and so were Arya's soldiers. "Stop!"

Soldiers with kingdom banners and symbols came to them. A nobleman with golden arm bracelets and medals was standing gallantly. He was Pu Sindok, the King Wawa's son-in-law. When people saw Pu Sindok, they put their blades into their sheaths and knelt.

An old man in white, who accompanied Pu Sindok, walked to Ki Atur and hugged him. "Ki Atur, my brother," said the old man, smiling at Ki Atur.

"Romo Giri, why do you come without first sending word?" Ki Atur asked the old man.

Romo Giri was one of the spiritual leaders in the Medhang Mataram kingdom. 'Romo' means 'father'. His real name was 'Giri'. People called him 'Romo' because they considered him their spiritual father.

"I see wild animals running away to the south and east," Romo Giri said. "There will be *Pralaya* here. There will be a big disaster. Mount Merapi is going to erupt. Nobody is perfect, but this disaster is not about our sin. We live on the island with many mountains. Through the mountains, the Guardian Spirit of Merapi gives us a prosperous and fertile land, beautiful green country, fresh water, sand and stones, and she always requires a price. People give offering of flowers and food to the Guardian Spirit of Merapi to calm her explosive anger. However, disaster is also the price of this plenty and beauty. There is a time for the mountain to erupt and the earth to quake. Today, Mount Merapi is going to share her prosperity through the eruptions and take back her tithe from us. If it is the end of days, let's make our last days become the time to share love and help people. It would be a great honour if you joined us and helped people. We are going to evacuate them."

Ki Atur frowned. He thought of what Romo Giri had said.

"Ki Atur, all people should go to the east. Don't lead your people into death. We will try to go to a safe place," said Pu Sindok.

"Sir, we will follow you," Ki Atur said, respectfully greeting Pu Sindok with palms together, fingertips upward and touching his nose.

"My brothers and my sisters, *Pralaya* will come. We must leave this land! We will go for a new life!" Ki Atur told his people.

Ki Atur and his people joined the refugees. Pu Sindok and his soldiers led them to the square near Prambanan's temples.

The twilight in Prambanan was beautiful, but fear made people unaware of the beauty. Medicine men healed the injured refugees with herbs and magical powders. Some religious leaders and followers prayed for gratitude and safety at the temples. The women from Prambanan and Kalasan distributed food and water to the refugees.

"Do you want fresh water?" a beautiful, dark skinned girl asked Joko.

Joko took an earthenware flask from her and drank the fresh water from it.

"Thank you, Sri!" Joko smiled at her.

"You should eat enough food. You should take care of yourself," said Sri.

"Don't worry! Your smile can raise my spirit." Joko said.

Sri's face was flushed. She smiled and bent down her head shyly.

Joko and Sri ate rice and vegetables, wrapped with a banana leaf. While enjoying his meal, Joko saw ten villagers quarrelingwith Arya Sotya. Joko left his meal and Sri's side. He went to Arya, to see if there was something he could do to help.

"Sir, I have a local belief," a vilager said. "I don't want to depend on help from people of other religions. I don't want to be deeply indebted. I don't want them to convert our belief."

"To take advantage of people's helplessness as opportunity to win converts is exploitation. Who has asked you to convert?" Arya asked.

"They haven't, yet, but they will."

"So, it's just your prejudice. It's time to unite for our nation."

They did not listen to Arya's words. They meant to leave, but Arya and the soldiers stopped them.

"Use your head! You don't want to let your family die, do you?" Arya said.

"Sir, I have a different reason. I don't want to receive help from Sanjaya's people," said another villager.

The villager explained to Arya about an old local dispute. Many years ago, there had been conflict between Sanjaya and Saylendra's families. Those two families had great influence in the Mid-Java. The conflict had only made innocent people suffer. Then, both families had united with the marriage of Princess Pramudawardhani and King Rakai Pikatan. Borobudur temple, a pyramid temple with many *stupas*, was built in the middle of the lake as a monument of peace. However, there were some people who were still not satisfied with the situation and wanted to return to the old ways.

"I don't want to live with Sanjaya's people. I want to move to the northwest," the villager explained.

"Northwest? Do you want Mount Merapi or invaders to kill your family? Listen to me! Now, our soldiers are blocking any attack by invaders, who call themselves 'brave enemy-killers'. They are the allied forces of the Emperor who conquers the sea and worships older gods. Go there if you wish death!" Arya said.

"My friends, no matter who you are and what you believe, we are equal here," Joko said. "We should help each other. We are in a complicated situation. Enemies attack us and we face disaster. It's not the time for internal conflict. Conflict only creates additional disaster. If you love your family, please come with us to a better place."

The villagers, who did not like Sanjaya's family, were thinking.

"Let's see whether we may live together," one of them said.

"But we have different beliefs. I don't want to be with them," another villager said.

"You feel the heat of prejudice in this cold night, don't you?" Someone behind Joko and Arya said.

Joko and Arya turned around and saw Romo Giri.

"My sons, look at Mount Merapi!" Romo Giri said. "There are so many ways to the peak of the mountain. You can go there on the south path, west path, or other paths. It's your choice. You can choose the path that you love. Beliefs or religions are like the paths. The peak is unity with heaven or God, or Hyang Widhi, and the religion is the way to the peak. Choose your path and respect the others. I respect yours. Don't worry about the difference."

The villagers were silent. They bent their heads.

"Arya, don't force them. If they want to go, let them go," Romo Giri said.

Romo Giri smiled and touched a villager's shoulder.

"Arya has given you his explanation. Now, it's up to you. You can join us or not."

He turned around and left them. Joko and Arya accompanied the villagers back to the refuge.

People at the refuge took a rest. Warnings and ancient prophecies of great disaster were on the tip of every tongue in the Medhang Mataram kingdom.

MEANWHILE, IN THE northwest area, Medhang Mataram kingdom soldiers countered the attack from the invaders, who called themselves the 'brave enemy-killers'. The tension was horrible. Both parties fought hard.

Arrows flew. Soldiers screamed and shouted on the battlefield. Blood and blades decorated the scene. The brave enemy-killers were experienced men of war, but they were unable to penetrate the power of the Medhang Mataram soldiers. The invaders were aware of the great disaster that might come from Mount Merapi. There were two possibilities of death. They might be killed by their enemies or by natural disaster.

Mount Merapi shook her body again and again. A dark cloud emerged from her crater. The earth quaked. People moved away from the palace, temples and other big buildings to avoid the falling stones of the buildings. King Wawa, the ruler of Medhang Mataram, sent couriers to give information to the commanders and lower kings, including his men on the battlefield, that they should prepare for evacuation in face of the great disaster.

At noon, King Wawa instructed Pu Sindok, the king's son-in-law, to lead the people to the east, but there was something that weighed on Pu Sindok's mind.

"Your majesty, you don't need to go to the northwest. Give me an order and I will go there," said Pu Sindok.

"I command you to bring your family and lead the people to the east," King Wawa replied. "I should go to the northwest to save the villagers. I am the king of mountain and to save my people is my responsibility. My son, you can start a new life in East Java."

King Wawa put off his golden sandals, which were the symbol of the King's existence, and gave them to Pu Sindok. Golden sandals symbolized the King's steps on the land under his power. To give the golden sandals might be interpreted as to pass on his power to continue his kingdom.

"Your majesty, it's not the time for me to receive it," said Pu Sindok, distressed.

"Yes, it's the time. If this is the last time I see you, you must continue my kingdom and lead my people," said King Wawa.

"Why don't you just go with us?" Pu Sindok asked.

"I love my people. I love this place. I love this mountain. I know you also love this place, but you must bring the people to safety. The end, the *Pralaya*, will come, but I am sure it's not the end of everything. It is just the end of the old for the beginning of the new."

"Father, come with us," said Pu Sindok, his eyes bathed in tears.

"Sindok, this is an order from me!" King Wawa turned away.

THE GREEN COUNTRY turned grey. Grey dust was flying everywhere. Pu Sindok could not stop his father's strong will. King Wawa, his soldiers, and some medicine men moved to the northwest.

Pu Sindok gave an order to his men to announce to the people that it was the time for journey to the east. Following his advisors' advice, he led his people to the south to put distance between them and Mount Merapi. People brought what belongings they could, to join the exodus. The leaders, soldiers and medicine men helped in the process of evacuation.

A mud rain fell – rainwater mixed with volcanic ash.

When the people got to the riverside, some brought their goats, bulls and pigs to the river to drink. Suddenly, they heard a thundering from the north. Goats, bulls, pigs, and other animals screamed in panic.

"Run! Run! Run!" the soldiers cried.

People ran away in panic when they saw the big brown flashflood, which brought dead trees. They pulled their animals to higher places, but the flood was too swift and washed some of them away. Even if they had ever learned to swim, it was too hard to swim in volcanic mudflow. Women screamed and children cried. The soldiers threw ropes to help people. They saved some, but others disappeared forever.

A man tried as hard as he could to drag his horse to safety, but it was swept away by the mudflow. The mud's power was stronger than his and it began to pull him down int the flow.

He wouldn't give up. "It's my expensive horse. I must get it!" he cried.

Joko hugged the man and tried to drag him to a higher place.

"Idiot! Don't stop me! I don't want to lose my horse," shouted the man, trying to release himself from Joko's hug.

"Fool! You'll kill yourself!" Arya shouted, forcing the man to release his horse.

"Let it go, sir!" Joko shouted.

The man wept. "I don't have anything left," he mourned.

PU SINDOK DID not want to wait for the death of his people, so they continued their journey. They marched with worried faces, avoiding the mudflow and hiking to the southern highlands. Mount Merapi thundered and Mother Earth quaked. Everything was dark-grey when they looked to the north. Their minds and bodies were tired. Sadness and sickness killed some of them. They believed that it was the end of days.

Mount Merapi erupted, throwing stones and covering the area around her with dark cloud. The green land became grey stony desert. Buildings collapsed. Soil and stones buried Borobudur temple and the lake around it, as well as the other temples and most of the villages near Merapi.

Day by day, through the track to the southern highlands, the Medhang Mataram refugees marched east. It was an exodus to a new hope.

One day, they saw a beautiful sunrise in the east. They arrived in a safe place between Mount Semeru and Mount Wilis in East Java. It was their new land for a new hope. They united to build their new country.

Two years later, people had a more normal life. In East Java, they built temples and homes. Joko married Sri and they had two children. Arya Sotya was promoted. Romo Giri chose to live in the highlands with his disciples.

The hell near Mount Merapi turned back into a green, wild paradise. With no worshipers to torment, the old gods faded away. Wildlife came back and natural beauty appeared. Overgrown vegetation claimed the ruined temples. Buried, the temples lay, unseen and forgotten, under the green land. With no word from his father since the eruption, Pu Sindok became King and founded a new dynasty, called 'Isyana Dynasty' in East Java, to continue his father's kingdom. *Pralaya* was the death of the past and rebirth for the future. Pralaya was the process from dissolution of old form to recreation of new form. Pralaya was the end of the old things and the beginning of new life. With hope and spirit, the end became a new beauty, though ever mindful of the next time the Guardian Spirit of the Mountain would require her price.

To this day, Mount Merapi is still one of the most active volcanoes in the world.

Y.W. Purnomosidhi resides in Indonesia, where he works on the staff of a human resource service company. He loves to learn about art, culture and spirituality. Since 1995, he has studied *silat,* a traditional martial art from Java Island. In his free time, he writes short fables for journals like *Authspot, Wikinut, and Etos Tabloid,* and articles for *Triond.*

The author speaks: *"Pralaya:* The Disaster*"* was inspired by a mysterious ninth-century history of the end of the Medhang Mataram kingdom in Central Java and Yogyakarta, Indonesia. In the ninth century, the kingdom was moved from Central Java to East Java by Pu Sindok, who established the Isyana Dynasty to continue King Wawa's kingdom. According to experts, the exact cause of the exodus is still uncertain, whether it was caused by Mount Merapi's eruption or invasion by another kingdom. The history says that there was a disaster in the Medhang Mataram kingdom, that was popularly known as *'Pralaya Mataram'* or the 'Death of Mataram'. Several ancient temples were buried and ruined. Some temples, such as Borobudur and Prambanan temple, were only rediscovered in the 18th century. The last eruption of Mount Merapi made me interested in exploring the last day of this kingdom in Central Java and the struggle of people to survive. I have added some fictional characters – such as Arya Sotya, Roma Giri, and Joko – to this story, but Pu Sindok and King Wawa were historical kings of ancient Java.

THE CITY OF ROPES

ALBERT TUCHER

"SHE MIGHT NOT be dead."

"So go in and look," I said. "Either way, he'll want to know."

In the torchlight, Anastasius looked unhappy. "But if she isn't, somebody else will be. Namely, me. They say she has powers."

"Then why has she spent four years in a dark cell?"

"Send Theodore in. She hasn't hurt him, yet."

"It's no good sending Theodore in. He can't tell us anything. He's deaf and dumb."

I said the words as if explaining to an idiot. Deaf Theodore was her caretaker because she could not trick him into communicating with her – at least, not in the dark. He had come to us with wild grunts and gestures. Since the Senatrix Marozia was his only responsibility, his problem had to concern her.

Theodore stood with us in the spiral corridor of Castle of the Angel Saint. In the flickering light, it would have been easy to mistake him for a moss-covered stump, until he moved. Anastasius shooed him back into the cell. He came back out in seconds.

"I guess she hasn't miraculously recovered," I said. "That would be too much to hope for."

I took a deep breath. I would need it. However foul the air was in the corridor of the fortress prison, in the cell it would be worse. I took the key from my sleeve and turned it in the lock. The door groaned as I stepped inside.

"Torch," I said to Anastasius behind me. I could see nothing.

Anastasius passed me the torch, which guttered and nearly went out. There on the floor, almost concealed by rotting straw, lay the woman who had once ruled Rome.

"Marozia, daughter of Theophylact and Theodora, are you living or dead?"

My words brought no response. If she was dead, I almost envied her. Having spoken, I now needed breath. The air in the cell almost sent me to my knees. The decaying straw and the smell of human excrement were only the beginning. All of the world's corruption seemed concentrated here.

The torch dimmed again. We had used most of it getting to the cell.

As the light faded, Marozia opened her eyes. In the near darkness, they seemed to give off a light of their own that sliced into my eyes. I admit that I screamed.

"What?"

Anastasius barked manfully, but I could not help noticing that he stayed outside.

"She's alive."

Terror had turned my voice to a whisper.

The torch died and the darkness became complete. I could feel the absence of any life but my own.

"Never mind."

My voice returned, but my eyes felt as if someone had singed them with hot coals. I groped my way out of the cell into the corridor. When I saw Anastasius in the light of his torch, relief weakened my legs. I realized that I had expected to find myself blinded.

"We have to tell the Prince," I said. "And we need to get out of here. That's our last torch."

I touched Theodore's shoulder and pointed, but he shook his head. He would stay with the body. Anastasius and I began to descend the inclined corridor. We emerged from the base of the Castle into the slightly-less-fetid air that blew from the Tiber. We crossed the moat and climbed stairs. In the intermittent moonlight, we found our armed militia men, who waited near the bridge that crossed the river.

I counted more men than I had brought. Another party of six had joined us.

"Change of plan," said one of them. "The Prince wants us at the Lateran Palace."

"That's quite a slog," I said.

"We can cut out some of it."

He had a rope coiled over one shoulder.

We marched halfway across the bridge and found two more of our men keeping watch over our escape route. I stepped between them and looked over the parapet. The black shape of a boat was barely visible against the dark surface of the river.

The man with the rope tied one end to the parapet and dropped the coil toward the river.

"The Prince has forbidden having a rope this close to the city walls," I told him. Anyone who left a rope dangling could let our enemies into the city.

"You want to walk all the way to the Lateran?"

"No."

"We're the Prince's men. We can do what we want."

One after another, several of our men climbed over the parapet and slid down to the boat.

"Wait," said Anastasius.

He pulled the rope up and fashioned a loop in the free end. I appreciated the thought. I could still climb but no longer as easily as a young man. Nor could Anastasius.

The men still on the bridge lowered me to the boat. I looked around. It was a fishing vessel, one of the larger ones that worked the Tiber.

The fisherman grumbled, until I opened the cloth purse folded over my belt. Silver glinted in the moonlight.

"There's a coin here for you and you'll still make it back in time to fish."

The rope went up and brought Anastasius down. Then the rest of our men used the rope, one by one.

Traveling by water, we would avoid a great deal of mud and many possible ambushes. In the daylight, the Romans would recognize us as the Prince's men, but darkness made us nothing more than prey.

We passed under the third bridge, where the river veered outside the city walls. Anastasius called out a password to the guards as we slid under them. To our right, campfires dotted the plains and hillsides that surrounded the city, but the points of light offered no reassurance. They meant that the Burgundian forces of King Hugh of Arles were besieging the city, as usual.

The fisherman and his three sons manned their oars and started guiding us downstream. To our left, we saw nothing but darkness, but we knew that more militia men kept watch on the ramparts of the walls.

The King had certainly posted his own sentries, but not to guard against us. Their task was to watch for marauding Hungarians, who also surrounded the city. The mounted archers from the east could ride silently among the campfires, slit a few Burgundian throats, and disappear.

We knew what they could do if they ever got inside the city.

Before the Hungarians came, we had played unwilling hosts to the Arabs, but their heyday was history. It was always something.

We maintained complete darkness. If we showed a light, the Hungarian archers would make quick work of us.

Ahead of us I heard a thud, a groan and a splash in the river. Another paid assassin had earned his fee. By the time we reached the spot, any trace of the transaction had disappeared.

We came to the Island. The best fishing areas clustered around it and numerous families slept on their boats near their livelihoods. Our fisherman grumbled again.

"You'll make it back by dawn," I whispered to him.

"Someone will take my spot."

He knew it was unlikely. The Prince enforced fishing claims strictly. The man simply liked to complain.

The river cut back behind the wall. Soon, the Aventine Hill loomed huge and black to our left. Our fisherman steered toward the bank. He probably knew the currents as well as any Roman knew the streets of the city. The boat scraped on the shallow bottom. I paid the fisherman. Our men began to jump out into the mud.

I sent several men ahead in a protective formation. Anastasius and I then disembarked.

I am no longer a young man and the hour was very late. Floundering through the mud cost me, but I had no choice. The winter weather had turned just cold enough to make my feet ache. We reached the Lateran palace. The commander led me to the Prince, who had occupied the innermost apartment of his brother John, the Bishop of Rome.

Prince Alberic sat, hearing reports. Men his age need little sleep. His fair hair held no grey, and his face no lines.

He favoured tunics and boots that would have suited commoners, which meant that his nobles also had to wear plebian garb, no matter how embarrassing we found it. The Roman mob loved Alberic for the gesture. They had favoured him for four years now, but it proved little. No one knew better than Alberic that the Romans might stop loving him in a moment.

I waited through three recitations from his spies. They kept their voices low and I heard nothing. The Prince spoke a few words to an Arab slave, who began clearing the hall. I knew it was time to approach.

"So?" he said.

"Prince, your mother is dead."

He nodded. "Tell my brother," he said. "And my sisters."

I looked around the empty hall.

"Are you sure, Prince? We can keep the secret."

"Not this kind of secret," said Alberic.

"Yes, Prince. Will your brother say a Requiem mass tomorrow?"

"No. Tomorrow, we'll have a trial."

At the age of nearly fifty, I had seen much. I knew what he meant, as few Romans could.

Anastasius and I spent the next day directing the militia men, as they cajoled, threatened and flogged the citizens to the Lateran Basilica. Now we walked up the northernmost aisle toward the sanctuary and surveyed our work. We passed the Romans, all who could cram themselves into the rear of the nave. Next came the foreign communities: the Saxons, Franks, Greeks, Lombards, and others. All wore their national dress, although many were the grandchildren of pilgrims who had come to Rome and stayed. They no longer spoke their ancestral languages.

We had allowed them closer to the sanctuary, because they kept better order, and because they had always supported the Prince. He trusted them to stand between him and the mob, if necessary.

Alberic sat facing the high altar on his wooden throne from his palace in the Via Lata. I saw no signal, but ranks of monks standing at both sides of the altar began to chant. I hated the sound. I have no ear, but even I could tell that their Latin was vile and their modes off.

John the Bishop of Rome, eleventh of that name, approached from the north, where he had a protected walkway between his palace and the basilica. He wore a petulant expression and I knew why. He had just learned that he would not say the Requiem mass for his mother. I doubt he cared much for her, but he cared a great deal for his privileges and rituals.

He took a seat prepared for him next to the Prince. Neither brother acknowledged the other.

From the same direction came the Prince's two sisters, surrounded by a formation of nuns.

My gaze inched up toward the ceiling, with its ancient fresco. Men and women, in their strange white draperies, did things that I could not quite understand. It did not help that crucial parts of the painting had faded badly.

Somehow, the monks knew when to stop chanting. They may simply have become bored. The Romans, never silent even during the most solemn occasions, raised their usual din of quarrelling and bargaining.

Anastasius fought his way through the ranks of nobles and churchmen behind the Prince and his siblings. He faced the Romans.

"Quiet!" he bellowed. "We have come to do justice and justice will be done."

I turned to watch. Men at arms blocked the exit from the nave. More waded through the sea of Romans, and kicked and clubbed those who refused to pay attention.

"Good," said Anastasius. His voice carried through the huge space. "Bring the accused."

I still watched behind me. Light appeared at the far end of the basilica, as the doors opened. Then I saw a party of a half-dozen rough commoners, the kind of men who spend their lives hauling things for others. Their burden did not seem to bother them.

It was another wooden throne. I knew what weighed it down.

So did the Prince. He did not turn to look. He waited until the men had detoured around him and deposited their burden in front of the high altar.

Anastasius spoke into my ear. I started. I had not seen his approach, which was a bad omen.

"You're elected."

"Why?"

"You were here for the last one. You know how it goes."

"I know that. I mean, why is he doing this?"

"You can figure that out."

Indeed, I could. The Prince had not wanted to try his mother while she lived and could defend herself. Now he wanted to poison her memory and cement his supremacy among the Romans.

For a moment, I sat without moving, but I had no choice. I stood and approached the chair under the altar. As I looked, memory assailed me. The similarities were too great to miss.

I saw myself as a young boy again. By staying low and keeping quiet, I had just reached the front of the crowd in the same basilica. I had evaded the kicks and cuffs of dozens of churchmen. My goal was to get a closer look at Formosus, the former Bishop of Rome. He wore the robes of his office, but he had looked better.

More than a year in his tomb had seen to that.

His cheeks had sunk into his bones and pulled away from his teeth. His skin had turned a grey that matched pale granite. He smelled cold, as if he carried the chill of the tomb with him. For days afterward, I could not get warm, no matter how close I sat to the fire.

Dead, Formosus would hold still for the vengeance he had parried in his nimbler days. Now his enemies saw nothing to fear. Bishop Stephen led the attack, howling and spitting accusations. A young deacon stood by to offer the dead Pope's defenses. The young man trembled too much to speak, but that did not matter. The proceedings required nothing from him but the appearance of justice.

Someone jostled my young self. I looked to my right and saw that a small girl had joined me. I had seen few noble girls in my short life. As a rule, they did not leave their homes.

This one had. She watched the trial of a dead man as if she had seen worse.

Our eyes met. Mine burned.

Forty years after the trial of Formosus, I looked at the body of the young girl I had met that day. She had become a woman celebrated for her beauty, or perhaps it was her power, or both. I had never again come close enough to exchange looks with her.

Her face had swollen, and her skin had mottled red and purple. Where Formosus had chilled me, she reeked of hot corruption.

I knew my job. The dead woman was entitled to an advocate. A stupid advocate would do his job zealously. I did not intend to be stupid. The young deacon who had failed to defend Formosus had shown me the prudent course.

"Marozia, daughter of Theophylact," Anastasius began, "how many husbands have you had?"

I looked again at the corpse. No one had closed the eyelids. No one had shown even that much respect for a dead Christian. For the third and last time, I looked into those eyes. It could not have been tears that stung my own eyes. I had given up grief with other childish things.

"Three husbands," I said.

"Three? A pious woman has just one. What were their names?"

"Alberic, Guy and Hugh."

"Alberic the Elder was the father of our beloved Prince."

Anastasius looked sideways at the Prince, who ignored the flattery.

"But Hugh of Arles – is he not the enemy of Rome? Is he not the same Hugh who besieges our city, as we speak?"

"The same," I said.

"And why did you marry Hugh of Arles?"

"My ambition misled me," I said. "Hugh is a descendant of Charlemagne."

"Who died over a hundred years ago!"

"Nonetheless, Hugh had a claim to the highest office. With my help, and the help of my son the Bishop of Rome, he seemed destined to become Emperor. I truly repent my error."

"Repentance is good, but first, let us get the whole truth. Was there conflict between Hugh and our Prince before he became Prince?"

"Hugh planned to kill my son. The King wanted me to have no male heir when I became his empress."

"And you were willing to let this happen?"

"I was, to my shame."

"Our Prince inspired the Romans to rebel and chase Hugh from the city. Your son imprisoned you. But you never gave up your ambition, even in prison. And now, Hugh prevents anyone from entering or leaving our city."

"Correct me if I'm wrong, but has your Prince not sealed the gates?" The words had come from my mouth. What was I doing? "And has your Prince not threatened with death anyone caught near the walls with a rope?"

Anastasius gaped at me, but I was not finished.

"What I did, I did for Rome, to restore our greatness. We could have been the seat of emperors, again."

"Did you not sneak out of the city by night to meet with the Hungarians?"

"That would be treason."

I noticed that my words fell short of denial. Now I looked straight at the Prince and raised my voice.

"Romans, do you want to restore your glory?"

Here is the thing about the Romans. They bore easily. Anyone can sway them with a speech. Alberic had done it when he inspired the Romans to overthrow Hugh. They had hounded the King to the walls of the city and down a rope to the outside world. Alberic had ruled us for four years. Now it was time for us to forget the whoring and murdering of the mother, and turn against the son.

That explained the reeking shout that rose from every mouth full of rotting teeth in the vast basilica.

Alberic stood and faced the mob.

"Romans! Romans, listen to me! Have you forgotten? This woman tried to raise up a Burgundian over you. A Burgundian whose place should be on his knees lacing your boots. Four years ago, I asked for your help to protect your ancient rights. You answered me with deeds. You chased Hugh the Burgundian over the wall and out of the city like a thief. You threw this woman into prison, where she belonged."

It was working. The bellowing and jeering subsided. Alberic seemed about to finish this sordid business in the strengthened position that he sought.

"Romans!" said another voice – my voice.

"Romans! Look at this son of mine. His throne looks modest, but it has cost you much – not in treasure but in blood. Each of you knows of someone murdered on this man's orders. Only when it came to his mother did he shrink from shedding blood. But not from murder. He murdered his mother slowly and in stealth, through starvation and neglect. And for what? For daring to survive as a woman in a man's world. I call upon you all to absolve me."

The Romans bellowed their approval.

"This Prince stole your ancient liberties. Remove him. Chase him, hound him, kill him. Is this not your birthright as Romans?"

They were very close to the words Alberic had used against his mother and her husband Hugh at their wedding, the moment that should have been their triumph.

The strange hold released me and just in time. Alberic made a gesture and his men at arms charged into the mass of Romans with clubs swinging. The foreign communities joined them. If the Prince felt relief when they obeyed, he gave no sign.

I had no doubt that he would deal with me, but at the moment, the mob was his most urgent problem. I turned in a circle, unsure of what to do. I came face to face with Anastasius.

"What the hell were you up to there?!" He shouted just inches from my face, but I could barely hear his words.

"That wasn't me!" I shouted back. "She made me do it."

"She made you. Brilliant. Get going."

"Get going where?"

"Do I have to explain everything?"

He did not. I had to run and no place in the city would be safe from Alberic. I would have to go to Hugh of Arles. I only hoped that I had something to offer him.

I thought this as I ran for the vestibule, dodging Alberic's men and kicking and punching men, women and probably children, for all I know, who got in my way.

The nearest section of wall was directly to the south of the Lateran. If I could reach it ahead of my pursuers, I could hope to pay silver for a rope and a boost over the wall. I churned a great deal of mud getting there. I could not believe that the militia men had beaten me there, but they had. They thought they had hidden themselves well enough to lure me into a trap. But I saw their tracks on the wall where they had climbed to the battlements.

I turned and headed north. Maybe the most distant point would be the most unexpected. But the journey was long and exhausting, and as dusk began to gather, I looked for a place to hide overnight.

By the time full darkness had come, I had become lost somewhere in the heart of the city. I had never left Rome, but I still knew how to get lost. I staggered through the streets as blindly as if Alberic's torturers had put my eyes out. I had slipped in the mud and stumbled over blocks of stone embedded in the ground, or newly fallen from ancient buildings.

Then I came to a stone fence that, to my questioning hands, felt like something built on a human scale and maintained by living men. With the last of my strength, I climbed over the fence and collapsed against it.

I expected to sleep like a dead man, but exhaustion kept me awake. I kept seeing Marozia, several days dead, then as a child, then as a child several days dead. That last vision made me whimper and my snivelling brought a response. It sounded at once human and bestial, and it came closer to me. One voice became several and then more than I could have counted, even had I not covered the sounds with my own shrieks.

With my back to the stone fence, I kicked out and encountered solid flesh. By the sound of them, my attackers retreated briefly, but then they came at me again. I screamed, "No, you devils! Don't take me to Hell! I only followed my orders!"

Light came from somewhere, first dimly then with more strength. The light became a torch that bobbed mundanely and reassured me. The bearer was human.

"Caught myself a pig thief, have I?"

The bearer of the torch illuminated his own face as he guided himself. I did not know him, but I had seen him among the butchers at the meat market.

"No, Cola, I am not a pig thief."

Half of the butchers in Rome are named Cola, but I saw that I had succeeded in impressing him.

"Do I know you?" he said.

That one was easy. "One time when you were drunk. I spoke with the militia and they didn't beat you."

"I must have been very drunk. I don't ever remember them not beating me." He hauled me to my feet. "Mustn't sit here. Pigs will eat you."

I believed him. From what I could see in the torchlight, Cola's pigs looked more than half-wild.

"Come. I have a better place for you to sleep."

"Why would you help me?"

"You spoke up for the Senatrix."

Cola had undoubtedly cheered her overthrow four years earlier, but I decided not to remind him. If it was Alberic's turn to fall from the Romans' favour, that was his fault.

We climbed his stone fence, again, and he led me to his hovel. I ducked to enter and encountered odours almost as vile as those in Marozia's cell, beginning with his smoky fire. I did not want to consider what Cola burned for fuel.

He extinguished the torch. In the dim light from his fire, he pointed me toward a straw pallet.

"My wife's. She died."

He looked me over by torchlight. "You look like man who needs a rope."

For a moment, I misunderstood. Did he intend to strangle me and present my body to Alberic?

"To leave the city," he said.

"I've never been out of the city."

"Same with most of us. The Senatrix was different, though. She feared nothing and no one."

"Did she really visit the Hungarians?" It would be interesting to find out what he believed of her.

"I once saw her coming back. At night, yet. She climbed up the wall without a rope. Like a bat, she looked, in the moonlight."

A day ago, I would have ridiculed him, but now I needed him.

"Friend of mine up north will help you," said Cola. "I'll take you if there's a coin in it for me."

"There will be. When I'm on the wall with the rope in my hand."

"Fair enough."

Cola sprawled on his own pallet and in moments, started snoring. I stretched out on his wife's straw and stared into the darkness.

His hovel did not improve in the daylight. Wordlessly, we shared some bread, chickpeas and sour wine.

"Might want to look more like one of us," he told me. He threw me a tunic that was more holes than fabric, but his point was sound. I needed to look more like a plebian and less like myself. I stripped off my better tunic.

We headed north. I lacked the time for furtiveness and the most direct route took us past the Pile, the largest building in Rome. A good part of the population lived in it, or did business in it, or buried their dead in it, while others dismantled it for building materials. It was large enough to accommodate all of these uses.

The ancients seemed to have sat in it and watched spectacles, but we no longer knew what they had seen.

In my borrowed tunic I strode boldly up the Via Lata with my new friend. Soon, we reached the People's Gate at the northern rim of the city.

I looked and thought, *I can die now.*

The gate stood open. I had seen an open gate once before. It was my earliest memory. I had watched Formosus greeting an emissary from Constantinople.

Prince Alberic rode a horse, the finest in his stable. On another fine mount, a man in a warrior's leathers faced him. Even at a distance, their smiles looked like the leers of false friendship.

I had not survived the past forty years in Rome without learning something about powerful men. Alberic no longer trusted the Romans and he had turned to another source of strength. He would make an alliance with Hugh of Arles, besieger of the city, last husband of Marozia, and Alberic's enemy until now. Young Alberic had chased Hugh from the city. Alberic the ruler had invited him back.

"That," said Cola, "leaves you the Hungarians. I hope you can learn to ride a pony."

"Possibly. I doubt I can learn to shoot one of their bows."

Cola shrugged.

"Now, about that coin."

"Several. Here's the first."

Cola kept his word, which no one assumes of any Roman. He and his friend lowered me to the plain outside the walls. Until dusk, I cowered in the shadows, where the watch would not see me. Then I set out on foot. I had no destination, but I needed none. I wanted only to make myself visible.

Sinewy men on wiry ponies surrounded me. The silence of their sudden appearance would have terrified the old me.

"A Roman," said a man who acted as their leader. "We kill Romans. Why shouldn't we kill you?"

"You would lose an opportunity," I said.

The words tasted unfamiliar as I said them. They emerged in a language that I did not speak.

"What kind of opportunity?"

"You want to plunder Rome," I said. "I want to rule Rome."

Poor Rome, I thought.

"You sound like someone we used to know," he said.

"Imagine that."

"Let's talk."

Albert Tucher's hardboiled crime fiction has appeared in numerous print and online publications. He is the creator of suburban prostitute Diana Andrews, who figures in five unpublished novels and thirty published short stories, one of which appears in *The Best American Mystery Stories 2010.* For years, he has been trying to use the bizarre and fascinating Rome of the tenth century AD in fiction. At last, success!

The author speaks: Few historical periods are as obscure as the early tenth century in the city of Rome. Literacy was rare and sources are sparse, but it seems clear the city had closed its gates figuratively, if not literally. Where a half-million-to-a-million people had once crowded within the city walls, perhaps twenty thousand now lurked among the ancient ruins. One family ruled the city as a private domain and betrayal was their way of life.

MODERN
ERA

INQUISITOR

WILLIAM MEIKLE

From the journal of Father Fernando. 16ᵗʰ August 1535.

THE TIME HAS come. It arrived yesterday from the New World in the hold of the *Santa Angelo* and it has been brought to the castle. The Inquisitor General has tasked me with discovering the true nature of the abomination, to make a full and careful examination, and ascertain what manner of *Inquisition* might be made. It is a great honour and one which I will fulfill with all the diligence the good Lord hands to me.

There is a certain doubt in my mind, a cloud that has hung over the proceedings since I read Juan Santoro's journal last night. A dark evil is detailed in those pages and although the Inquisitor General teaches us that all things are powerless before the truth of our Lord, I have grave misgivings about the thing I am about to see for the first time

I have prayed for strength, but still, my knees feel like water and there is a cold pit in my belly that nothing can assuage.

However, my duty is clear.

It is time for the questioning to begin.

From the journal of Juan Santoro, Captain of the Santa Angelo. 3ʳᵈ April 1535.

If there is a hell on Earth, then surely it is in this place here. No god-fearing man should have to face the horrors I have led my crew through on this day. I give thanks that I have brought us all back safely to the ship, and I am much afeared with the thought of the return voyage, for the cargo is most foul and ungodly. But I would be remiss in my duty to the Church if I did not report on the things that plague this new land. If the Crown wishes, as I have been told, to colonize this place, then we must know what manner of things lay claim on it at present.

In truth, I know not what we have found. The natives died bravely defending it and for most of the day, we bethought that we had stumbled on a great treasure. We fought through their defenses, hacking and slashing our way through the savages to the centre of that dark temple.

As I have said, we expected treasure. What we found was beyond our ken. I have had it sealed in a lead casket and will take it back to Seville.

But the journey will be long, for already, it whispers in my mind and I fear my dreams will be dark indeed during the long months at sea ahead.

From the journal of Father Fernando. 16th August 1535.

"ALREADY, IT WHISPERS in my mind."

I had given no thought to that phrase, believing it to be the product of a sailor's superstition. But now, having seen my new opponent, I know better.

When we opened the casket that had been brought to the chamber where the questioning was to take place, I originally bethought that we had been played false and that trickery was at work. At first glance, the lead box seemed empty, its bottom a dark shadow. But, as Brother Ferrer leaned over it, something *surged* within and he was forced to step back, so suddenly that he knocked over a brazier and sent coals skittering on the flagstones. The blackness that rose from the casket, a thick liquid which had the consistency of pitch, seemed to rear back at that, giving me time to slam the lid closed on the obscenity.

And that is when it happened.

There was a *tugging* in my mind, a probing of an intelligence. I knew immediately what it was doing, as it is my own profession also. Even as I sought to ascertain the form of my opponent, at the same time, it was questioning me.

I am not the only inquisitor here.

And there was something else, something I am loathe to relate here lest it is discovered and my sanity is brought into question. I only caught but a fleeting glimpse, just as the lid of the lead casket dropped back into place, but it was unmistakable. As the black thing *oozed* to the bottom of the box, a single eye, pale and smooth as a duck's egg, opened ... and blinked.

From the journal of Juan Santoro, Captain of the Santa Angelo. 29th May 1535.

CALAMITY HAS OVERTAKEN us, as I feared it might.

The thing has plagued our dreams since the start, and the crew has been without sleep for many days. There have been mutterings of mutiny since the beginning of the month and last night, matters came to a head. Three crewmen took it upon themselves to rid us of our tormentor.

At least, they tried.

Their screams in the dark alerted me to their plight and I was first to enter the hold. It is hard to describe the fear that gripped me as I saw the carnage the thing had wrought on my men. It was obvious that they had lifted the casket, probably intending to throw it overboard. But someone had dropped his end – that much is also obvious from the dent in the left-most edge. I can only surmise that the jolt opened the casket – and let the beast out.

What did not need conjecture was the fate of the men after that.

The black ooze lay over the bodies like a wet blanket – one that seethed and roiled as if boiling all across the surface. Pustules burst with obscene wet *pops* and flesh melted from bone, even as the men screamed and writhed in agony.

Their pain did not last long. All too soon, the blackness seeped in and through them until even their very bones were liquified and, with the most hideous moist *sucking,* drunk up by the beast, which was now three times larger than previously. It opened itself out, like a black crow spreading its wings, the tips touching each side of the hold walls.

All along the inside surface of the *wings*, wet mouths opened and the air echoed with a plaintive, high whistling, in which words might be heard if you had the imagination to listen.

Tekeli-Li. Tekeli-Li.

My every instinct told me to turn and flee. But there was nowhere to escape to except the sea itself and that was a choice no sailor would make. Instead, I stood my ground while Massa, stout coxswain that he is, brought forth some firebrands. Only then did the thing seem to cower and retreat, and only then did I remember the circles of burning oil which we had crossed on entering the black temple in the jungle.

I called for a barrel of pitch and tried to hold the beast at bay with a brand until aid might arrive. My adversary had ideas of its own. Now that it was free of the casket, its powers had increased. It probed at my mind, searching for my weaknesses, taunting me with my dreams. I saw things no man should have to see as I was shown the atrocities that had been committed in this thing's name by the savages in the temple.

The grip on my mind grew stronger.

I saw vast plains of snow and ice, where black things *slumped* amid tumbled ruins of long dead cities.

My head swam, and the walls of the hold melted and ran. The firebrand in my hand seemed to recede into a great distance, until it was little more than a pinpoint of light in a blanket of darkness and I was alone, in a vast cathedral of emptiness.

A tide took me, a swell that lifted and transported me, faster than thought, to the green twilight of ocean depths far distant.

I realised I was not alone. We floated, mere shadows now, scores – nay, tens of scores of us – in that cold silent sea. I was aware that other sailors were nearby, but I had no thought for aught but the rhythm, the dance. Far below us, cyclopean ruins shone dimly in a luminescent haze. Columns and rock faces tumbled in a non-Euclidean geometry that confused the eye and brooked no close inspection. And something deep in those ruins knew we were there.

We dreamed, of vast empty spaces, of giant clouds of gas that engulfed the stars, of blackness where there was nothing but endless dark, endless quiet. And while our slumbering god dreamed, we danced for him, there in the twilight, danced to the rhythm.

We were at peace.

A flaring pain jolted me back to sanity. I smelled burning skin, but took several seconds to note that it was my own hand that had seared. The coxswain, stout man that he is, had broken the hold on me by touching his firebrand to my skin.

I had no time to thank him, for the beast had encroached closer to me while I dreamed and even now, threatened to engulf me.

Once again I held the firebrand ahead of me and, with the aid of the coxswain, I held the beast at bay, struggling to keep its grip from settling on my mind. Indeed, if the barrel of pitch had not been brought, I might have succumbed.

Burning the pitch enabled the recapture of the beast to proceed more rapidly. The heat from the flames threatened to set fire to the deck of the hold itself, but I refused to allow the men to put it out until we had driven the beast back into the casket.

I have ensured that the box is sealed completely and it is now stored at the furthermost end of the hold. All I can do is keep the crew as far away from it as is possible on this small vessel.

That, and hope that in our dreams, we do not fall again under its spell.

But it is hard. For every time I close my eyes, I dream of vast empty spaces, of giant clouds of gas that engulf the stars, of blackness where there is nothing but endless dark, endless quiet. And while my slumbering god dreams, I dance for him, there in the twilight, dance to the rhythm.

In dreams, I am at peace.

From the journal of Father Fernando. 17ᵗʰ August 1535.

CAPTAIN SANTORO'S JOURNAL has at least given me a place to start. I already knew that *strapado* would not be an option for this particular miscreant. Nor would I be able to utilise the rack or the maiden. But fire would be more than sufficient for my purposes. It took little work to prepare the cell for *Inquisition*, as matters are already set up amply for the ordeal. I ensured that the lead casket was placed inside concentric circles of oil, such that they could be lit immediately in the event of an attempt to escape. I also had a brazier full of coals at hand to my right side and three needle-pokers burning white-hot in a small oven to my left.

Even before I opened the casket, I felt the *tickle* in my mind, but I pushed it away. My God is stronger than any heathen devil. I mouthed the *Pater Noster* as I lifted the lid.

Once again, the black ooze surged and the tickle in my mind turned into an insistent probing. Memories rose unbidden in my thoughts: of summer days in warm meadows, of lessons learned in cold monastery halls, of penance paid for sins.

I was under questioning.

That I could not allow. I am master of this *inquisition*. Several wet mouths opened in the black ooze. Using a pair of pliers, I plucked a hot coal from the brazier and, as another mouth formed, I let the coal drop inside.

The grip on my mind released immediately, replaced by a formless scream, which quickly became a chant that echoed around the cell. I knew the words. I had read them in the Captain's journal.

Tekeli-Li. Tekeli-Li.

A long tendril reached from the lead box, coming towards me. I took a poker from the oven and, with one smooth strike, thrust it through the black material. The ooze retreated, shrinking back as far into the corner of the lead casket as it could get.

I leaned forward, a fresh poker in my hand.

"Are you guilty?" I asked, and stabbed down hard.

The *Inquisition* proper has begun.

From the journal of Juan Santoro, Captain of the Santa Angelo. 17ᵗʰ July 1535.

WILL THIS NIGHTMARE never end?

The beast, despite its incarceration, has steadily increased its hold on us since we forced it back into the casket. We cannot allow ourselves to sleep, for when we do, we are trapped in its spell, lost in the dream somewhere above the cyclopean ruins.

In truth, the dream is seductive, even more so than drinking endless flagons of wine or constant inhalation of the weed that the natives smoke in the New World. Three of the crew have succumbed, falling into a deep slumber from which they cannot be awakened. They breathe and their eyes are open, but I cannot get them to eat and they are already close to starving. I fear they will be long lost afore we reach port.

Some days, I almost feel like joining them. I am kept awake by a suffusion made from a roasted bean, a drink we discovered among the native tribes where we landed in the New World.

Would that were all we discovered.

Some of the crew have reported that the beast is also reaching into their minds during waking hours. Many of them have had the same compulsion – to go down into the hold and open the casket, releasing the thing to roam the decks. No one has yet given in to the demands, but it is another reason to make for port with all speed.

I know not how much longer we can hold.

From the journal of Father Fernando. 25th August 1535.

IT HAS TAKEN more than a week, and sorely tested the Inquisitor General's patience, but finally, after I have burned away more than nine-tenths of its matter, it has weakened. I have found that the mind-grip works both ways. If I concentrate hard, I can catch glimpses of what the beast is thinking and feel its fear.

I have put it to the *inquisition*, and it has answered me.

As shocking as it seems, the beast has no conception of our Lord. Indeed, it seems never to have encountered a single Christian, despite the fact that it is possibly the oldest living thing on the face of the earth. That revelation came as something of a shock to me. The creature has memories going back to a time when ice covered the face of the earth. Its first encounter with Man shows a savage race clothed in furs, with only rudimentary speech, and I am at a loss to know how such a thing can be reconciled from what I know from my study of the biblical texts. I must seek guidance from the Inquisitor General, for my thoughts are troubled and dark.

This beast I have under my ministrations is devious and subtle. It works constantly at me, testing my belief with scenes of lust and debauchery: maidens in states of undress displaying themselves wantonly for my pleasure, hot blood flowing to feed my growth. I have to see these things, and endure, for in the seeing, I also learn more about the beast's drives and passions, which are mightily strong.

I had almost come to believe that this might be the most ancient of evils, the Great Deceiver himself. But the thing has memories even older than the time of ice, memories of a time when it was but a servant of something vast and strange ... memories of a *creator* that I do not recognise as being anything resembling my Lord. I am at a loss to know what to think of this new information and must question the beast further.

I have learned one other thing. The *creators* gave it a name, a moniker by which it recognises itself. It is known as *Shoggoth*.

From the journal of Juan Santoro, Captain of the Santa Angelo. 14th August 1535.

WE WILL MAKE port on the morrow. It matters little, for the dream is with us now in every waking hour and no distance from the beast will make any difference. It has passed on to us so completely that we will never be free from it. Nor would we wish anything other. Indeed, I am not the only one who has found himself standing over the lead casket, just to be closer to the blessed, drifting peace it offers.

There is no pain in the dream, no fear, no hunger, just the sweet forever of the dead god beneath.

I have talked to the crew. We will do our duty and take our captive to the castle. But we will no longer work for the Church after this task is done. I intend to set sail again as soon as night falls. There is a spot in the South Seas where a dead god lies dreaming.

We will find him and join him there.

From the journal of Father Fernando. 25th August 1535.

I WISH NOW that I had read Santoro's journal a mere hour sooner, for then I might have been able to prevent the *Santa Angelo* slipping out of port under cover of night and I might have been able to question the crew as to the nature of the malady that so sore afflicted them.

For I, too, have been dreaming.

I am not alone. We float, mere shadows, scores – nay, tens of scores of us – in a cold, silent sea. I am aware that others are near to me, but I have no thought for aught but the rhythm, the dance. Far below me, cyclopean ruins shine dimly in a luminescent haze. Columns and rock faces tumble in a non-Euclidean geometry that confuses the eye and brooks no close inspection.

And something deep in those ruins knows I am there.

But it is of no matter. The beast is now in my thrall and its secrets shall be mine before the day is out. They will have to be, for I fear I have been lax in my *inquisitions*. Even as I have been burning my will into the beast's flesh, so it has been leaving its mark on me. This morning, at my ablutions, I discovered a fleck of blackness betwixt thumb and finger that no amount of scraping will shift. It has now covered most of my left hand, forcing me to wear a glove lest it is discovered. For, if the Inquisitor General were to find out I am *tainted*, my questioning would be brought to an abrupt end and that I cannot allow.

The beast *will* reveal its secrets.

I will begin again as soon as the irons are hot.

By order of the Inquisitor General, 28th August 1535.

IT IS OUR command, on this day of our Lord the twenty and eighth of August, that such parts of Father Juan Fernando that can be safely transported shall be taken to the place of the *Auto de-fé* and burned at the stake, alongside the blasphemy which has afflicted him with its heresy.

It is further commanded that, if the *Santa Angelo* is found in Spanish waters, it should be set aflame and sunk with all hands, and that no man is to touch any part of it under pain of himself being subjected to ordeal by fire.

Any persons found spreading the sedition of the *Dreaming God* shall be subjected to the full force of the *Inquisition*.

Let this be the end of the matter.

The Lord wills it.

William Meikle is a Scottish writer with ten novels published in the genre press and over 200 short story credits in thirteen countries. He is the author of the ongoing Midnight Eye series, among others, and his work appears in a number of professional anthologies. He lives in a remote corner of Newfoundland, with icebergs, whales and bald eagles for company. In the winters, he gets warm vicariously through the lives of others in cyberspace, so please check him out at williammeikle.com.

The author speaks: I've always been fascinated by the concept of the Spanish Inquisition and Man's inhumanity to Man in the name of religion. I've been searching for awhile for the right concept to introduce them into a story, and when I had a dream about Conquistadors finding something in a temple in the jungle, something with questions of its own, I just had to write it.

THE FAR DEEP

JOSHUA REYNOLDS

IT WAS THE Year of Our Lord 1571 and John of Austria was dancing a gal-liard on the gun platform of the *Real*. Men crowded the decks of the vessels – Italian, Spanish and corsair alike – that made up the Grand Fleet of the Holy League to watch as their admiral succumbed to youthful enthusiasm for the coming battle.

On the far flank, aboard the Maltese galley *St. Elmo*, Francisco Felluci, Knight Hospitaller, late of Venice, said, "He is dancing." His much-battered, ornate armour creaked in sympathy with the rigging overhead as he turned to glance at his man-at-arms, Agostino. "Dancing."

"Who?" Agostino was a bulky Sicilian, with one good eye and a cleft cheek, through which yellow teeth were visible. He rubbed absently at the crude patch that covered the memory of the Turkish bullet that had taken his eye at the battle of St. Elmo.

Felluci had been there as well, in those mad final hours, locked sword-to-sword with the Janissaries pouring over the walls, until a bullet had shattered his ribs and sent him into the water. It was Agostino who had helped him swim to safety after stripping him of his armor, beneath the thunder of Turkish guns.

"The Austrian whelp, who else?" Felluci said, sighing. "This is a farce."

"I thought it was a fleet," Agostino said. Felluci fixed him with a glare, but the one-eyed man took no notice.

"A farce," Felluci said again, teeth bared. "Why are we even here?"

"To sink the ambitions of the Turk?" Agostino said innocently.

"Ha!" Felluci tore off his peaked helmet and ran a hand through his sweat-soaked hair. "Stop that, or I'll put you down with the galley slaves."

Agostino shuddered. "I'd rather kiss the Sultan's rear."

"Hrm," Felluci said, replacing his helmet. "You might get the opportunity, at that. This is going to be bad."

"They always are." Agostino hefted his arquebus and sighted down the barrel. "Still, no call to mope. God will provide."

"Whose God? Ours or theirs?"

"Does it matter?" Agostino shrugged. "Religion is a cloak. Wear it, or another, as you see fit, sir."

"Blasphemy," Felluci murmured, staring out at the coastline of Lepanto. The Sicilian was right, of course. Many was the Knight who had been a Janissary, or vice-versa. One master or another, one god or the next, when it came down to the sword-edge, it seemed to matter not at all. He sighed again and set a boot on the rail. Resting his forearms across his knee, he turned from the spectacle of a Christian admiral dancing like a madman and towards the approaching fleet of the House of Osman.

The great emerald banner of Islam, shot through with golden thread, flapped in the sun over the red-hulled ship carrying the admiral of the Turkish fleet. A low thudding, as deep as the ocean's heart, rang out, accompanied by the blaring cacophony of *zornas* and cymbals from the ships of the enemy fleet. Distant figures clad in extraordinary colours stalked the decks of the swift-moving galleys surging forth from Lepanto, calling out the twenty-nine thousand names of God and shouting verses from the Koran.

On the vessels of the Holy League, it was much the same. The sky-blue banner blessed by the Pope, himself, was unfurled from the mast of the *Real*. Men roared imprecations in Spanish and Italian, and trumpets warred with the drums of the timekeepers. The sun caught the polished breastplates and helmets of the troops, creating a blinding sheen of brightness that threatened the eyes of any who looked too closely.

One fleet coming to challenge the other's control of the Middle Sea and the center of the world. It was a sight to stir the blood.

Felluci, who preferred his blood unstirred and safely in his veins, made a sound of disgust. "Farce," he said again.

"You said that about St. Elmo, as well," someone said. Felluci winced and turned as Henri Argustier, the commander of the galley, strode towards them. "And look how that turned out."

"A bloody massacre?" Felluci said. Argustier, a stern French knight with a disapproving countenance, frowned.

"A God-sent triumph," he corrected.

"St. Elmo fell," Felluci said. "If that's your idea of triumph, I'd hate to see a defeat."

"Your cynicism verges on defeatism, *Venetian*," Argustier said, emphasizing the last word. "But then, your people never had the stomach for battle, did they?"

"I prefer to eat tastier fare," Felluci said. "Did you strike the slaves' shackles?"

Argustier snorted, showing what he thought of that idea. The general order to free all slaves of Christian bent was being tacitly ignored by several commanders – including Argustier, apparently. Felluci frowned.

"We were ordered–"

"The Austrian can spit, for all I care," the French knight said. "We serve only the Order."

"And the Pope," Agostino said quietly. Argustier shot him a withering glare, but nodded brusquely.

"And the Holy Father. Of course."

"Amen," Felluci said. He drew his sword. "I'll go free them, then." Slavery – whether the victim was Christian, Muslim, Jewish, or pagan – was a fact of life in the Middle Sea. Galleys needed crews and volunteers were in short supply. Felluci found the entire concept detestable, but was far too practical to protest openly. He had no slaves of his own, not even before he'd lost his estates to the Doge's whim. And after he'd joined the Order, he'd kept that practice. Agostino was his only servant and one servant like Agostino was often one too many.

"You'll do nothing but man your post," Argustier barked. "The last thing we need is galley revolt. They'll stay chained until I say otherwise. And that fisherman we took earlier, as well."

"Of course," Felluci said, after a moment, glancing at the mast. The fisher-man was a Cypriot Greek, small and wiry. He looked more tired than fright-ened, even tied to the mast as he was. A number of fishing boats had been taken by the fleet, both to prevent any possible warning to the Turks and to learn what could be known about the disposition of the enemy fleet.

So far, any useful information had been less than forthcoming. The Greek was unlettered, unkempt and pig-ignorant. He knew next to nothing, save that the Turk was there and the Holy League was here and the fishermen on this section of coast were trying to be anywhere other than in-between them.

Sensible enough, Felluci supposed. He sheathed his sword with a flourish and bowed his head to Argustier. "Forgive me my presumption, Brother-Commander."

Argustier made a noise, but turned away, apparently satisfied. He looked at the fisherman. "Filthy pagan. Should burn him here; let the Moslems see what awaits them at the end of the day."

"Probably not worth setting our boat on fire," Felluci said. Argustier turned back.

"I see you set to looting early," he said, smiling crookedly. Felluci started and looked down at the small golden ornament hanging from his sword-belt. It was an ugly thing: chunky but gold through and through.

The Cypriot had been carrying a number of such trinkets. Primitive iconry, wrapped in burlap and hidden beneath his catch, wet with salt and covered in fish scales. The priest onboard, a phlegmatic Genoese who was more interested in drink than judgment, had shrugged when they were revealed, saying that the men of the Ionian Sea were heretics and pagans, and often threw things – foodstuffs, mostly – into the water to placate their heathen gods.

Felluci had thought the bauble too valuable to feel the sea's embrace and had, along with a dozen other sailors, swiped his share from the lot, pitiful as it was.

The Greek hadn't protested, beyond an initial panic. Either he wasn't a man of strong faith, or he was easily resigned. Now, he stared at the water beyond the deck rails, his eyes following the movement of the waves.

Felluci shuddered, though he couldn't say why. Maybe it was the way the man looked to the sea, with a longing that wasn't quite right. Like a saint approaching the pyre.

"Well, when the battle starts, take him down to the rowing benches. We'll need extra men before long," Argustier said.

"Of course." Felluci looked at the fisherman and felt a stab of pity mingle with the disgust. He was a stupid brute, by his look, closer to the fish he caught in nature than the men around him. Pop-eyed and wide-mouthed, his skin had been turned rough by the sun and weather. If he survived the battle, he was destined for a life chained to an oar.

Something about the man's face, though, pulled at Felluci's attention. Something familiar. On impulse, he looked down at the icon. He gave a grunt of realization.

It was a bad likeness of anything living, but if it could be said to resemble anything, it was the fisherman. He blinked, wondering what to make of the unusual coincidence.

As if aware of Felluci's attentions, the Cypriot looked up, his dull eyes fastening on the stolen trinket. Felluci brushed it with his fingers and the man's eyes lit up. He opened his mouth, displaying snaggle teeth. The expression reminded Felluci of a shark's grin and he felt his blood curdle. He turned to Agostino. "Stay beside me. When the battle starts, I mean."

"Never fear, sir. I'll guard your back."

"It's not my back I'm worried about. Stand to my front, if you please. Be sure to absorb as many shots as you can. Any slacking and I'll pitch you overboard."

"My master is kind."

"Yes. Any other knight would have swept your truculent head from your shoulders by now." Felluci watched the Turkish fleet draw closer. He looked back at the fisherman. The Greek hung from his bonds, head bowed, apparently dozing, now. "Hnh," Felluci grunted. "How anyone can sleep –"

Agostino chuckled. "When you're poor, you catch sleep where you can."

"Before a battle?"

"He's probably slept through storms." Agostino looked over the side. "Speaking of which … the waters here are dark," Agostino said. "Ever seen them so dark, sir?"

Felluci glanced at the water. Silvery shapes cut through its dim reaches. Fish, he thought, scattering out of the path of the two fleets. Much like the men who sought to net them. It wasn't as funny as it should have been. He shivered as the shapes darted to and fro, just out of easy sight. "No. But considering the noise we're making, I have no doubt we've stirred up the ocean bottom something fierce."

"Or something fierce from the ocean bottom," Agostino said. "I knew a fisherman once, who used to use a gong rather than a net. He used to sound it just over the deep water and things'd swim upwards to investigate. 'Bigger the gong,' he said, 'bigger the catch.'"

"If we lose the battle, maybe we can make our money selling the catch, then," Felluci said, smiling. Agostino shook his head, but said nothing. "So, what happened to him?" Felluci said.

"Caught something he couldn't handle," Agostino grunted. Before he could say more, the ocean heaved and screamed and the battle started, so swiftly that they almost missed it. The first Felluci knew of it was a series of bright flashes, as if someone were throwing jewelry into the sea. For a moment, Felluci was reminded of the baubles hidden on the Cypriot's boat, wet and filthy. And then came the roar.

It was as if some great titan had awoken, angered and in pain. A vast, sweeping bellow of sound, a sheer wall of noise that rocked Felluci to his core. Then came the shriek of splintering wood and the screams of dying men, as iron balls shredded the decks of the opposing fleets. Galleys burst asunder, as Felluci watched, literally exploding up into the air and dropping back into the water as huddled masses of wreckage.

Black smoke coiled on the wind as the Venetian galleasses ranging ahead of the fleet raked the Turkish formation with a withering cannonade at one hundred and fifty yards. The warships were armoured so heavily that they rode low on the water and, with every belch of cannon fire, they rocked back a little.

Felluci, overcome with a sudden nationalistic fervor, pounded the rail with his gauntlet, shouting "St. Mark! St. Mark!" The feeling passed soon enough, washed away by the sheer carnage being meted out.

The sea was soon covered in bodies, yardarms, water casks, powder barrels, and jetsam of all kinds as ships clashed in a nightmare of smoke and fire. Cannons gave vent to pent-up fury as ships swung around each other in a mad dance.

While the roar settled into a thunderous, omnipresent growl, Felluci steadied himself on the writhing deck and happened to glance towards the mast and the Cypriot. The Greek was awake now, mouth gaping in what might have been either a scream or a song.

"What is that heathen shrieking about?" Argustier snapped, turning from the battle, his cloak flapping. "Someone quiet him!"

"One more scream in this won't make a difference," Felluci said, though not loudly. No sense straining his voice, not when his brother-knight wasn't actually listening. And, for his part, he didn't want to get any closer to the fisherman than he had to.

Something about that scream, about the way it seemed to ride the roar of the ocean and turn back in on itself, made Felluci's spine quiver. It wasn't a cry of fear, or anger. Not entirely, at least.

"God almighty," Agostino mumbled, visibly resisting the desire to fire his arquebus into the bound man. "He sounds like – ah …."

"What?" Felluci said, but Agostino simply hunched in on himself, shaking his head. The crew began to mutter among themselves. War-hardened men, yet the screams of a fisherman were setting their nerves at odds.

The Cypriot continued to scream, tongue waggling behind his teeth like a fish trapped in a reef. He strained at his bonds and jerked back and forth, stomping his foot rhythmically on the deck. For a moment, just a moment, Felluci thought that he could hear an answering sound to the mad wail emerging from the fisherman's throat.

Almost as if something were knocking on the wooden hull of the galley in response. His fingers found the bauble. It felt so cold that it was almost warm. He could feel it through the stiff leather of his gauntlet. Like something that had been buried in the silt for so long that it had absorbed something of the chill of the ocean bottom. Felluci yanked his hand away, but couldn't lose the chill. It climbed his arm and settled in his head.

The scream went on and its weird echo was lost in the storm of battle. And then, Argustier's sword was sliding across the Cypriot's throat and the scream was drowned in blood.

"Filthy creature," the Frenchman grunted. Felluci looked away as the body sagged in its bonds. He tried to push aside the memory of the scream and concentrate on the battle swirling around him. Covered in the powder smoke that hung over the galley's deck, he rested on his sword, waiting for the inevitable collision. Artillery was all well and good, but it always came down to sword-work in the end.

"They saw falling stars the other night," Agostino said, looking at the dead Cypriot, his good eye narrowed to a slit. "Like clawmarks in the sky."

"Who saw?"

"Them. The fishermen and the priests and the sailors. All of them," Agostino said. He spat over the side. "Bad omen, that, no matter what the God-botherers say. On the coast, they say the fishermen make their offerings then. To the masters of the far deep and wide dark."

"Who says?"

"Them." Agostino fixed him with his good eye. "Cypriots. Maltese. All of them. You should toss it, sir. Get rid of it," he said, gesturing to the bauble.

"I'll have you know this will be paying your wages for the next year."

Agostino grunted. "Mark my words, sir. It's an omen."

"'Clawmarks in the sky,'" Felluci repeated, shaking his head. "Any other omens I should know about?"

"Crows," the Sicilian said.

"Crows?"

"Crows," Agostino repeated. "Ottomans scared them up when they set sail. Flock as deep and wide as Hell. Saw them myself."

"Crows," Felluci said again. "Stars and crows and deep fish following the sound of battle. As omens go, I admit those don't sound auspicious."

Agostino grunted and settled down to wait. Felluci watched him for a moment then turned back to the battle before his eyes could be lured back to the fisherman's body. It wasn't that he was squeamish. He had done his share of God's cruel work on the Earth. It was simply the way the body hung, jerking in its final throes.

The fisherman jerked and twitched for all the world like a fish that had been caught in a net. He thought of what Agostino had said. *The masters of the far deep.*

He'd had a classical education. He knew the names of the gods of antiquity, including those for whom the sea was their domain. The far deep, down where the light wouldn't reach and the warmth couldn't penetrate.

Felluci stared at the dark water and fancied, just for a moment, that he could see something staring back.

At dusk, the flagships met in the center of the maelstrom, trading hammer-blows with frenzied abandon. Similar collisions occurred up and down the battle line. Ships spun lazily, driven off-kilter by lucky shots, and bows connected with sterns, the crunch of wood meeting wood mingling with the snapping of hundreds of oars and the serpentine hiss of arrows, all echoing up into the darkening sky. Everything became a tangled mass of thrashing ships, individual vessels obscured by the smoke.

Aboard the *St. Elmo*, Argustier barked orders and men set to building barricades at the mast stations, making ready to face boarders. Those nearest the mast where the fisherman hung did their best to avoid even looking at the body. As one of the handful of knights aboard the galley, Felluci was free of such scut-work and able to concentrate on the approaching Ottoman flank. The ships were moving fast. Sleek Algerian galleys that cut the water like knives. He heard Agostino hiss and glanced at him.

"What?"

Agostino pointed wordlessly. Felluci looked and gave a groan. "Oh, bloody hell." He knew Argustier had seen the same thing he had when he heard the other knight give a bellow of frustration.

The line was in disarray. Somewhere, someone had given the wrong order and now, what had once been a proper battle line was an absolute mess. The whole flank was collapsing in on itself as ships peeled away and headed in every direction, save the one the enemy occupied.

Felluci knew what was coming next. It was as inevitable as the dawn. He tensed as a storm of bullets and arrows fell on the *St. Elmo* like the first snow of winter, plucking men from their stations and washing the decks in blood. Felluci staggered as arrows plucked at his armor. A bullet spanged from his breastplate, leaving a dent and knocking the wind out of him. Leaning against the rail, he tried to catch his breath.

"They're coming!" Agostino barked. He took aim with his arquebus and fired. A few yards away, a Turk was punched backwards and the Sicilian gave a snarl of triumph. Felluci rose back to his feet, sword in hand, just as the ships crashed together.

Janissaries and marines hurled themselves over the rails, eager to get to grips with the men wearing the crimson-and-white of Malta. Felluci gripped his blade in two hands and swung it in short, brutal arcs, chopping through flesh and bone with desperate abandon.

Again, he heard the scream, the fisherman's cry, but knew it was just a dying man. There were so many screams and to become distracted by one was a guarantee of adding his own to the chorus.

He sent a head tumbling from a pair of shoulders and whirled as the deck beneath his feet trembled. The *St. Elmo* listed like a drunkard, its guts shorn through by a lucky shot. He could feel the shaped boards of the deck curl beneath his feet like flayed skin.

"Sir!"

Felluci turned back, just in time to block a halberd blow that would have split his head like a melon. He sheared through the haft of the weapon and spitted its wielder. Kicking the body free, he stumbled on the bloody deck as the ship gave a groan. Algerians in leopard skin and silvery mail pounced on him, trying to bring him down.

Agostino was there, firing his weapon again, then using the heavy stock of the arquebus to beat about him. Felluci kept his feet and soon, he and his man-servant were back to back, turning in a circle, surrounded by blades. He struck and struck again.

The air was thick with black smoke and Felluci could taste the tang of fire on the air. Somewhere, a powder magazine went up, taking a ship with it. Turkish war-cries split the air. The other ships that weren't sinking were crowded with the soldiers of the enemy, who hacked and thrust at any living thing.

The flank of the fleet of the Holy League was gone. In an hour, it had been reduced to a memory. The battle itself wasn't lost, but this side of it was.

"Damn it. We're sunk," Felluci said. The last of the Algerians was down, gasping out his life on the rough wood of the deck, but the galley was almost on its side. It was taking on water quickly and would soon sink. He could hear the cries of men flailing in the water beside the ship and the men trapped in the hold.

The thought chilled him. He'd been in sea battles before, and storms. He knew what happened to chained men when a ship rolled or sank. He'd seen the bloated bodies, floating trapped. It was no way for a man to die. Even a Turk.

His eyes found the fisherman's corpse, still tied to the mast, head bobbing, bulging eyes staring at the water creeping over the deck.

Then the sounds again. A thudding against the wood. It had to be the water, didn't it? Just the water lapping at the hull. The icon was cold against his hip, so cold it burned through his jerkin and mail.

Argustier rushed past, covered in blood, sword in hand. Beard bristling, he shouted oaths in his native tongue. Felluci grabbed his arm. "We're sunk, Argustier! We need to get the crew overboard – get them to strike out for shore or one of the other ships!"

"We have no crew!" Argustier growled, slapping his hand away. "That last broadside scythed the useless bastards like wheat. It's just us!"

"What about those in the hold? The slaves? We can at least give them a fighting chance!" Felluci snapped back.

"Do what you want," Argustier said. "I'm for whatever ship I can reach. I –"

His head disappeared in a spray of blood and bone and gunpowder stink, most of which splattered across Felluci's cuirass. Argustier's body tumbled down into the hold. Felluci, pale-faced and trembling, stepped back. A Turkish ship loomed out of the darkness, guns firing. Arrows peppered the deck.

"The water, sir! Just like St. Elmo!" Agostino said, grabbing for his sleeve. Felluci shrugged him off with a sudden, berserk frenzy.

"You go, Agostino. I'm for below."

"Sir?"

"The slaves, man. Isn't Christian to leave them to drown, even if half of them are Turks." Felluci descended into the hold without waiting for a reply.

He couldn't leave them. Not like this. He was not a good man, but some touch of pity was blazing into being, now that the end was here. Maybe a few less lives on his tally would set the scales even.

In the darkness, men were howling for mercy. The lanterns, what few remained lit after the broadside that had cracked open the hull, showed a scene out of some poet's dream of Hell. Dead men floated in pieces, still chained to the living. The ocean surged through the cavernous hole and more than half the surviving slaves were up to their necks in water.

The wood of the hull shuddered as something heavy crashed against it. A repetitive cycle of blows. Men shrank back as far as their chains would allow.

It was the water. Just the ocean. That was frightening enough. In his mind's eye, he saw silvery shapes thrusting through the darkness, in pursuit of the galley.

Cursing, Felluci shoved the thought aside and waded towards those closest to drowning. He swung his sword, chopping through the chains with a grunt. Men began to swim. Someone began to scream. Felluci turned and saw a chained slave slip under the water, his knuckles white on the oar. He surfaced in a rush, his screams peeling out again, as he clung to the oar as if his life depended on it. The water boiled around him when he went down again.

"Jesus," Felluci said as he watched the dark water go red. And then he heard it.

The scream.

The icon hanging from his belt felt heavy, suddenly. As if it carried the weight of a dead man with bulging eyes. The cold shot through him and he froze. Something silvery and sharp came out of the water, lamp-like eyes staring into his as claws scored the wood of the hull and it lunged with supple swiftness towards him.

Remembering that he still clutched his sword, he raised it, though only half-heartedly, as the deep-mud stench of whatever it was rolled over him.

Then came a different stink, and a yowl of gunfire, and whatever it was was gone, flipping back into the water like a fish released from a line.

"Sir?" Agostino said, clinging to the ladder into the hold. "Sir, are you –"

"Still breathing, yes." Felluci whirled, panic lending him speed, and swung his blade down, chopping through more and more chains, conscious of the crawling water and the silvery glint that came with it. It was still out there, still swimming. What was it? What was it?

Maybe the Cypriot would have known. Or Agostino's apocryphal fisherman. Men waged war on the surface of the sea without giving thought to what watched from below. What was it? Men grabbed at his arms, babbling prayers and plea. He shrugged them off.

"What was it?" he said, shouting. "Agostino! What was it?"

"I …." Agostino shook his head and awkwardly tried to reload his arquebus. "I didn't see it!"

"Damn your eyes; you did!" Felluci gestured with his sword. "Up! Up and swim, if you value your lives!" Agostino climbed quickly back up. The slaves crawled out of the hold after him.

Felluci turned as he heard the sound of something sharp digging into wood. Claws? His heart sped up. He wasn't frightened. Not really. He didn't know what it was and a man like Felluci could not be afraid of the unknown.

At least, that was what he told himself. It was getting harder and harder to hold to it as he stood in the rising water, amidst the floating dead, and tightened his grip on his notched sword.

The chains clinked. Something crept among the bodies of the drowned. It was just beneath the surface. Like moonlight, only, not a reflection.

He backed away, towards the ladder, sword extended. The fisherman's bauble seemed to anchor him in place, making him move slowly. Then the smell again. Wet and clammy and foul.

It rose slowly this time, as if it had all the time in the world. Pale eyes fixed on him and followed his progress as he tried to back up the ladder. It was more fish than anything, lacking the smooth dichotomy evident in the woodcuts of tritons, mermen and monkfish. It was ape, frog, fish, squid, and all things far and deep. Webbed paws reached for him.

No. Not him.

Felluci's hand slapped against the bauble and he spun, scrambling the rest of the way up. The thing screamed and followed, not bothering with the ladder, just digging its claws into the wood and hauling itself up.

On the deck, Felluci found himself face-to-face with a dozen Janissaries. One stepped forward, mustaches bristling as he leveled his arquebus and barked an order in Turkish.

Agostino lay nearby, face slack, dazed by a blow to the skull. Several of the slaves were dead, the others huddled behind the Turks, already enslaved again after only a few moments of freedom.

Felluci didn't drop his sword. He didn't dare. He turned and backed away, ignoring the Turks, as the great frog-shape of the thing heaved itself up out of the hold, dripping water. It screeched and the cry was answered from the water by a dozen eerily similar sounds. Arquebuses barked and foul smoke spread as a half-dozen bullets struck the creature and flung it down, oozing whatever passed for blood. It sprawled on the deck, long arms reaching towards the feet of the dead fisherman. It wheezed like a drowning fish.

Had it come for him? Or for its due? He recalled the way it had looked at the bauble he wore, then tensed, waiting for the bullet that would do the same to him. Instead, the ship rocked. Dark shapes clambered aboard, pale-moon eyes gleaming out of silvery skulls. The Turks turned, some trying to reload, others drawing their curved swords. Then the things were upon them in a rush, croaking and screeching.

Felluci wanted to laugh at the spectacle, but instead, he grabbed Agostino and hauled him out of the way, slicing his sword out at anything – man or beast – that got too close. Shouts of alarm came from the Turkish vessels pressing close as the men aboard got a look at what awaited them on the *St. Elmo*.

"S-sir?" Agostino coughed. Felluci hunkered down beside him, trying to ignore the sounds of butchery rolling down the deck.

"Can you swim?" he said harshly.

"I …." Agostino's eyes focused on the golden icon hanging from Felluci's belt. "Get rid of it!" he screeched, clawing for the thing.

Cannons thundered then, cracking the ship in two. The Turkish response to things that disturbed them, swift and brutal. Agostino and Felluci were flung into the water. The latter lost sight of his manservant as he slipped beneath the waves.

While he sank down into the black waters, he fumbled with the snaps and catches of his armour, stripping it from his body. His lungs began to burn, the weight dragging him down. Above, a distant orange haze marked the burning ruin of the ship, like the light at the end of a tunnel.

A shape swam towards him and – for a brief, hopeful moment – he thought it was Agostino.

It wasn't.

Webbed paws seized his face and held him close. Alien eyes stared into his. Black eyes, like marbles or perhaps the spaces between stars. They were eyes that had seen the golden offerings of generations of Greeks, of Persians, of Phoenicians and older, forgotten peoples, stretching back into dim mists. Eyes that had witnessed the beginning of some ancient covenant between Man and the sea, a covenant that could not be broken by something as ephemeral as warring empires.

Felluci stared into those eyes and saw the whole of history unfold. He knew that the darkness was full of them, quicksilver shapes that swam back and forth, just out of the edge of his blurring vision. Hundreds, thousands.

The masters of the far deep.

Claws cut into his cheeks and it blinked, mouth tendrils flaring. He couldn't breathe. He knew what he had to do. Agostino had been right. Black spots dancing in front of his eyes, he wrenched the golden icon off of his belt and let it sink.

A scaly arm snapped out, catching it. Felluci was released and he shot to the surface as quickly as possible, his chest on fire. He surfaced with a gasp, reaching out to grip a chunk of scorched wood.

Down below, the silver shapes circled, withdrawing deeper and deeper into the depths. Felluci watched them, half-waiting for a clawed hand to seize his ankle.

Instead, it seized his shoulder. He screamed and turned, splashing. Agostino looked at him blearily.

"Sir? Did you get rid of it? Do you live?"

Felluci stared at him then looked around at the wrecked hulks that floated on the water, the ships that were still locked in combat for the fate of a world that was, perhaps, not even really theirs.

And down below, what? Something brushed gently across his legs and he shuddered, not from the water but from a last, sudden knowledge.

It hadn't been a mercy. Merely a stay of execution. As long as Man crossed the sea, they would wait for their tithe.

"Sir?" Agostino said again, as he clung to a floating powder barrel. Felluci looked at him then closed his eyes.

"For now, Agostino. For now."

Joshua M. Reynolds is a freelance writer of moderate skill and exceptional confidence. He has written a bit and some of it was even published. For money. By real people. His work has appeared in anthologies such as *Cthulhu Unbound 2* and in periodicals such as *Innsmouth Free Press*. Feel free to stop by his blog, http://joshuamreynolds.blogspot.com, and cast aspersions on his character.

The author speaks: I've always found the history of the Mediterranean fascinating, especially the all-too-frequent clashes between the (theoretically) allied Hapsburg Empires of Europe and the Ottoman Empire. And let's not even get into the independent operators like the Barbary Pirates or the Knights of Malta (or, in the case of my story, "The Far Deep", the Deep Ones!), who made life tough for everybody, regardless of faith or faction. The Battle of Lepanto, during which I set "The Far Deep", was one of the last great naval battles of this period and one of the largest head-to-head conflicts between the faiths of Catholicism and Islam (and Cthulhuism, I suppose). In the end, that's why I set the "The Far Deep" where and when I did. At a point where faith and fury collide, it's only natural that you'd find a few monsters.

CITY OF WITCHES

REGINA ALLEN

HOT METAL WHIZZED past his ear. Warm air filled Iyapo's aching lungs as he fled the white slaver. The shackles around his neck, hands and ankles fought his limbs, but he pushed against the stiff, unyielding metal that swelled his wrists so they resembled bloated wildebeests.

"Catch him!" came the cries of men following his tracks.

Birds, startled from the sound, shrieked alarm. The waving canopy sent brisk breezes to Iyapo's strained muscles. Sweat ran down his temples, blinding him. He stumbled, lost his footing and rolled like a pebble until his body smashed against cool stone.

Coarse sand stuck in his throat. Ignoring the pain, Iyapo jumped to his feet. He saw crumbled, decayed huts with malnourished trees, bent and twisted. They heralded a ruinous city of basalt, diseased with rot and tropical growth along crooked walls and cavernous windows.

As a boy, Iyapo had remembered his father's stories about ancient cities, cities of the *afiti* – the witches – where poor souls were taken and given to their gods.

Gunshots interrupted his thoughts. Iyapo, a confused antelope, ran to and fro until he found two large worm-eaten wooden gates open just enough to allow him passage. His brain screamed *Don't enter!* But fear of the alternative overruled and he slipped inside, just as a bullet nicked the hinge of the gate.

The sand burned his calloused feet. He winced at the sharp pain stabbing his left temple. No songbirds or insects chorused; no flowers or festive colours paraded in windows or doorsteps. The round, whitewashed huts, with gaping doorways and two black sockets for windows, billowed the stench of decayed flesh into his nostrils. Iyapo flinched, covered his nose and made quick searches of the huts for a weapon – any weapon – he could use against the white men.

Iyapo ventured deeper into the city. Hut after hut lay barren, save for bones and smashed skulls scattered on the floor. He didn't want to think about how they had died, didn't want to see in his mind's eye the gruesome dinners held in this city. He just wanted to find a weapon and get out of there.

In the distance, Iyapo saw a dark, towering structure, a termite hill above ant mounds. The sun shone brightly, but the structure absorbed light so it neither reflected nor bathed in the sun's warmth. *This must be a temple or great oba's palace,* Iyapo thought. If so, there should be a cache of weapons, and maybe a few gourds of water, stashed somewhere in the palace rooms. If there was any hope of defending himself, of getting out of here and somehow back home, his answers lay in whatever that structure held.

As Iyapo neared, he noted the palace was composed of basalt like the city's walls. An oba wouldn't construct a basalt palace and one with corners. The roof should be round as well as the palace. *This is an* afiti*'s palace,* he realized. Yet, he hoped to find something to use as a weapon against the relentless white slavers and break the shackles from his limbs.

A dark-grey current of smoke snaked from the structure's mouth to slither under his feet. He suddenly felt lightheaded and couldn't focus his vision. The current licked his feet until he felt a slight tug, as if it wanted to carry him forward, toward the palace. A *feeler,* Iyapo realized. It meant *afiti* still lived in the city. They knew he was here.

Carefully, so as not to create ripples in the grey skein of smoke, Iyapo slipped out of the current. Any sudden movement in the smoke would alert *afiti* to his presence. More grey tendrils flowed from the palace in all directions, searching for more humans within its walls. Iyapo, worried that an *afiti* would swoop from the skies and spring from the dead huts, strode toward what he now knew to be an *afiti* temple.

Gems flashed a kaleidoscope of colours that danced along the walls. Spears, javelins, swords – so much weaponry to choose from. Never had he seen such riches in his life! Many weapons he did not recognize. Many foreign headdresses adorned the place. One metal headdress caught his attention. Its faded plume waved like cotton burdened with shoots. There were many shields from the Ashanti, the Fullah and the Bambara. Others were strange. Faces of white men with short hair and crested helmets adorned metal shields. The shields were different shapes: some were round and had strange animals painted on them, while others were long and rectangular, painted red with gold trim. Perhaps these white tribes searched for the ancient city of Kultar.

Kultar was a place of great knowledge, wisdom and riches. *Griots* told stories of the ancient city along an old caravan route that led to the Northern Kingdom where lions were revered and worshiped. Knowledge was a commodity, and Kultar and the Northern Kingdom exchanged ideas. The *griots* also told of Kultar's demise when a traveler from the North brought with him an ancient scroll. The traveler read the scroll aloud to the citizens who, when they heard the words, tore out their hair, wailed and shredded their clothes.

Over time, Kultar's greatness faded; its wisdom dimmed as it decayed into depravity. Its inhabitants forgot the old ways and began to worship gods older than the known gods. The inhabitants soon developed a taste for human flesh. Many poor travelers ended up as cuts of meat in their markets. The Northern Kingdom cut off all ties and alerted other cities of Kultar's evil. It was the Chezwe, Bringers of Knowledge, who drove them out, drove them away from the cities of men. In the forests, the swamps and caves, the remnants of Kultar worshiped their gods.

Iyapo wondered if this was the ancient city Kultar.

"CAPTAIN, WILLIAM, HIS tracks lead to those ruins in front of us," a tall, lanky man, with blond hair plastered to his neck, pointed toward the ancient city.

Captain William Marsh appeared from the brush and let out a low whistle as he surveyed the city. Finding the Negro in the ruins complicated things. "I'll cover this section of the city and you take that, John. We'll meet toward the center where that black structure is," the Captain said.

John sighed. "All this for one Negro? Ain't we got enough to take back?"

William spat on the ground. "I never leave with half my cargo. It's all or nothing."

John and William walked toward the city, rifles cocked and ready in case the Negro should ambush them. John blinked several times; his vision was out of focus. He felt dizzy, caught his breath because it felt as if he were pulled under water. The dark-grey smoke snaked through a set of gates to curl like a pet dog around his feet. He absently kicked at it, watched it dissipate, only to swiftly reform and continue its journey.

"Hmm, William, see this smoke. Ain't it strange?"

William never looked down. "Just means he's here. C'mon, we've got him now."

Though William scouted the city, John's eyes locked on the tall black structure in the city's center. There must be gold – more gold then he could ever amass in all his voyages to this cursed land for slaves. Besides, half the cargo died in the Middle Passage, so the risk of capturing all the black heathens couldn't stem the overwhelming debt he'd accrued back in New Orleans. Being brother of the captain didn't translate to instant wealth. It just meant he got scraps, was all, and he wanted more – much more.

John strode, then ran, toward the temple involuntarily, yet anxious because he hoped to find treasure, treasure that would pay off his gambling debt, buy his own plantation and provide an easy life.

IYAPO'S EYES DRANK in all the treasures so openly draped in and around the temple. He stepped closer to the altar; dried bloodstains and tufts of hair stuck at the rim. He didn't want to think about the men, women and children offered upon that gruesome table. He needed a weapon, anything to defend himself against the whites and break the confining chains off his limbs.

He heard the careless footsteps of someone running toward the temple. From the mound of gold and jewels, Iyapo snatched a purple robe and draped it over himself. He found a dark corner behind the altar and pressed his body against the wall until he blended with the shadows.

John followed the trail of gold, silver and gems, stuffing what he could into his boots and shirt. At the altar, he saw a large, golden shield. "Will, come look. You won't believe –"

He never finished his sentence. A bronze spear lodged in his abdomen. He dropped his rifle and collapsed.

"John? John!" William, more cautious than his brother, stepped slowly toward the altar. The sun's journey across the sky would end soon and what light the temple held, diminished. William looked down at the great wealth strewn about and knew it was a trap. Poor John lay dead somewhere inside. Stupid fool. The Negro was smart, had spirit. He'd break his spirit so thoroughly he'd have that Negro licking his boots before the end of the voyage. William cocked his rifle. He wasn't going to be the Negro's second casualty.

AN INVISIBLE HAND dragged away the dead man's body. Iyapo's heart thundered. The blackness melted his silhouette into its fleshy folds. *Who or what took the white man's corpse?*

He heard a gun cock outside the temple. Iyapo's eyes widened. Trembling, he clutched his spear tighter. A shot fired. The bullet hit its mark. A surge of burning metal ripped into Iyapo's left shoulder followed by a river of pain that rushed down his side. He saw the barrel of the gun floating and, just as quickly as it appeared, the barrel disappeared. Shots shattered the silence, followed by a human cry. Animal and inhuman grunts drowned out the white man's strangled cries.

A cold finger traced down Iyapo's spine as a monolithic figure filled the doorway, blocking all light. Cold talons snatched Iyapo's spear. Lightheaded and feverish, Iyapo consigned himself to his fate. He stumbled to the floor and fainted.

The creature fell upon him like a vulture on carrion.

IYAPO AWOKE TO find himself tied to a stake. The slaver beside him was also bound. The moon lurked in the shadows of the forest. Lit torches lined the huts and the temple's entrance. A creature that resembled a black hyena

loped toward the altar and dropped the dead man's naked body onto the
stone slab. Every bone in Iyapo's body shook at the sight. The white man
whimpered and cried. He glared at Iyapo with dread and hate.

"John didn't think you were worth tracking. Now, John's dead. You damn
black heathens!"

A laugh, deep and hollow, froze Iyapo's blood. He struggled fiercely cran-
ing his neck to see an *afiti*.

The *afiti*, taller than Iyapo, had a nose more vulture than human and a
crocodilian grin. He wrapped his muscular body in a black hyena hide.

"You damn – you led us into a trap!"

The *afiti* turned his head to the white man and approached him until
their faces were within a hair's breath. "Address me as 'Lumo, *afiti* to the
Most Exalted'."

"What the hell are you?" William's voice now wavered.

"*Afiti!*" Iyapo shouted.

"'Witch', in the white man's language."

At that, William's muscles went slack. "That's it? A witch doctor? Hah!
When I get back to the ship, I'll send more men to hunt you down and kill
you for killing John."

Lumo smiled. "Greed led you to my city. This was your undoing."

William spat in Lumo's face.

In the same stern tone, Lumo said, "You whites believe yourselves the
supreme masters of our land. There are things of this earth you do not
understand."

"Well, I do know that, one way or another, I'm getting out of here."

"Perhaps you are right. One way or another, you shall leave."

Lumo raised an arm, and then let it fall to his side. The drums spoke
shadow talk, an ancient and strange language that provoked an involuntary
shudder from Iyapo. The talking drums awakened the dead. The skies blackened with *afiti* on the backs of emaciated owls with membranous wings. They
came from the forest; phantoms with insipid hyena laughs shambled toward
the temple. Lumo approached the altar. He called for an attendant, who
handed him a large, curved knife that caught the glint of firelight. He uttered
strange words that Iyapo knew were older than any human language.

Arms outstretched, Lumo cried, "Tonight, our god, the Ancient One, will
grace us with his appearance!"

Lumo carved up the body. He placed the pieces in a bowl and passed it
around to the crowd. Some ate the meat raw, while others skewered their
piece and roasted it over the fires near the huts.

An *afiti* larger than Lumo strode through the crowd and ascended the
steps, swinging an axe. He stood over the dead man and, in one swing,

decapitated the corpse. The crowd cheered. Lumo lifted the severed head for all to see. Then he faced the temple with outstretched arms, chanting, calling again the name of his god. The ground quaked from the thing that came from earth's bowels. Two glowing orbs peered from the blackened temple. Iyapo saw a flash of white, dagger teeth set in a reptilian snout. A tendril snatched the severed head and disappeared back into the temple.

The crowd, lazy from their feast, savoured every scrap and morsel of their first meal in centuries. Then the drums sounded and *afiti*, beast and human, rose up to dance.

Lumo came to Iyapo. "You are next."

Iyapo struggled fiercely against the ropes, despite the intensifying pain in his shoulder. William whimpered and cried. He said this was no way for a white man to die. Iyapo stared at him. And this was okay for him?

Lumo laughed as he untied Iyapo. As soon as he was unshackled, Iyapo swung his good arm and struck Lumo across the face with his chain. Lumo staggered from the blow, touched his face and looked at his fingers wet with blood. Iyapo didn't wait, but struck him repeatedly, keeping Lumo unbalanced until he fell beneath the altar, stunned. Frantically, Iyapo searched for a rifle and saw one of the attendants running towards him with one. The attendant cocked and fired, jerking back several paces from its recoil. No time. He had to flee.

He ran past the slaver and then stopped. The revelers became aware of what had occurred and shouted their alarm. He hated himself for this but ….

Another shot fired. Iyapo ducked from the whizzing bullet as he desperately untied William from the stake. With two people to catch, the *afiti* would have to split into two hunting parties. A slim chance but a chance, nonetheless. He wasn't releasing the white man out of sympathy.

William slapped Iyapo on the back. "Let's get out of here before they roast us, too."

Both slaver and Iyapo ran through the throng of *afiti*. William grabbed a javelin and used it to cut a small swath for himself and Iyapo. Iyapo swung his chains overhead, keeping the swooping owls away from them. As soon as they entered the forest, they separated, followed no more by *afiti* because their god rumbled angrily in the temple. Unbound by Lumo's words, their god arose from the temple and punished its worshipers.

Iyapo heard strangled cries from the City of Witches. He ran deeper into the forest until the cries disappeared in the forest canopy. When he felt safe, Iyapo stopped to rest against a thick tree. He closed his eyes, listened to his own breathing, the forest sounds, and the cool breeze that tickled his sweaty skin. The lulling sounds of the forest relaxed his muscles and he slumped onto the forest floor, drifting slowly to sleep.

HE HEARD A gun cock. Startled, Iyapo jumped up to face a small group of white men, rifles aimed at his head. Captain William Marsh pushed through, still carrying the javelin that had saved them from the *afiti*.

"This is the one," he said to his men.

"You ain't never said where John was," one man said.

"He got stupid. A lion killed him. C'mon back to the boat!" Captain William shoved Iyapo with the javelin. The other men grabbed his chains and kicked him forward. They mumbled that they had never seen a lion in this part of Africa.

Iyapo looked behind his shoulder. Captain Marsh walked fast, looking all around like a scared monkey. Iyapo knew, no matter what the Captain might say, that Lumo and his god would follow him and the white man to wherever they journeyed.

Regina Allen lives in upstate New York, where she is attending college full-time in a nursing program and works at a hospital as a patient care associate. When not studying or working, she writes speculative fiction, reads everything she can get her hands on and researches the strangest theories born out of her dreams. She is currently working on a science fiction short story and a novel.

The author speaks: Years ago, I researched American slavery and African kingdoms because I love history and was keenly interested in African mythologies and legends. The result was "City of Witches" and other short stories centered on the main character.

AHUIZOTL

NELLY GERALDINE GARCÍA-ROSAS

F URIOUS, THE SEA bellows, tearing the sails of the San Cristóbal, protests with roars of foam, yells like a woman in labour, cries like an abandoned child .... Those were the words I managed to make out in the last, demented babbles of a Moorish youth who, with eyes popping out, threw himself overboard during the storm that lashed the ship taking me to meet my brother's corpse.

Unlike the other passengers of the San Cristóbal, I did not embark for New Spain looking for fortune, but to stand face to face with misfortune and to bid goodbye to the last family member I had left. My brother, Fernando Villaplana, sailed in the year 1511 of Our Lord, being but a teenager. He had the fancy of becoming rich, gaining fame and possessing everything that our orphanhood had denied us. I remember seeing him, with eyes ablaze and hair uncombed, when he told me this before parting, as if the wind had already started flinging him towards those unknown lands full of wonder and danger, like the ones told in the *Amadís*. I knew from a letter of his that he had participated in the expedition commanded by Don Diego de Velázquez to the island of Cuba and that, a few years later, together with more than five hundred men, he joined the troops of Hernán Cortés to explore other lands and reclaim them in the name of His Majesty. After this, I had no news of him until, nearly thirty years after his parting, I received a letter from a friar named 'Juan de los Ángeles'.

With beautiful and tight lettering, the friar told me how they had found Fernando's corpse at the edge of the lake of Texcoco: "His skin was wet and slippery like that of a fish, but he did not squirm searching for the comfort of water; he remained still, as if asleep. He appeared to have no bruises or signs of violence. It was only up close that we realized his eyes, teeth and nails had been torn out with much care. *'Ahuizotl! Ahuizotl!'* cried an Indian who kept us company and, drooling like a rabid dog, refused to help us carry the deceased."

When I finished reading the epistle assuring me of a grave on sacred ground for my brother, I did not know if my unease sprang from the way in which events were narrated or the fact that I had read that name written by an unknown hand: 'Elena Villaplana'. Letter by letter, the maroon ink on the paper from New Spain returned me to the moment in which Fernando, dragged by the wind, had left me at the door of the convent of the Jerónimas so he could follow his dreams by the sea. From then on, I was Ágata de la Inmaculada Concepción; nevertheless, with the devastating news crumpling between my hands and tears in my eyes, the Elena inside me yelled, "*Ahuizotl! Ahuizotl!*" and forced me to head towards the murky waters of the New World.

The preparations for my departure happened in a mist, as in a dream, as though I were staring beneath the water. I remember little of what happened before I found myself kneeling next to the mast, praying and commending new souls to God during such a hard trial. It was then that the young Moor came running – drenched, he seemed black and slippery, and with his eyes so ominously open, he resembled a grotesque fish. He screamed strange words, perhaps in a strange tongue. I was only able to distinguish a few in Spanish before he threw himself overboard and disappeared amidst the foam.

A couple of weeks later, we arrived at the port of San Juan, which is also called 'Ulúa', for they say that the natives of the islet where the fortress-port is located howled at the sea, "*Chlúha! Chlúa!*" Words that the Spaniards understood as the actual name of the place. The crew was tired. It was agreed we would spend the night in an improvised camp on the beach and, at first light, would continue towards our destination, la Villa de la Veracruz. It was a relief to rest upon firm and warm sand, so that I fell asleep almost at once. Nevertheless, my sleep was restless; I dreamt that a huge figure emerged from the sea. On the shore, little animals the size of a dog greeted it, wagging their long tails that seemed to finish upon a hand. Waves crashed with strength and brought in their waters human corpses. Some seemed like abominations between man and fish, or seemed to have been turned inside out, and their guts were showing. The little creatures devoured, with much care, the eyes, teeth and nails of the corpses dragged by the sea for the satisfaction of the monstrous figure.

I awoke, bathed in sweat and trembling uncontrollably. I tried to commend myself to the Archangel Saint Michael, but the abominable images of the dream continued to haunt me in the darkness of moonless night. I don't know how long I was victim of this terror, but, still drenched with fear, I noticed suddenly that not far from me there were lights dancing in the palm trees. I approached them, thinking that it was a gathering of some of the mariners and it would do me well to sit before a fire. But no sailor was there: a group of strangely dressed Indians danced around a nest of palm leaves, inside which there stood a small stone figurine, no bigger than a fist. They sang in an odd tongue, but repeated constantly "*Chlúha! Chlúa! Dagoatl! Dagoatl!*" and howled like dogs, their cries increasing. The sailors from the San Cristóbal were awakened by the howling and, enraged, frightened them off by force. Soon, morning broke and I saw something shining amidst the sand removed by the dance of the Indians. It was a small stone figurine of a black-and-bright crystal, the obsidian stone they employ in the realm of the Indies to make knives. It represented the silhouette of a man with huge eyes and tiny, pointy ears. The hands, adhered to the body, resembled those of a frog and it might have had a tail that had broken off. I could not stop thinking about Fernando as I looked into the wide, large eyes of the figurine, so I took it with me.

The end of the trip was short and calm. We arrived at the Villa de la Veracruz at midday, thus I decided to leave immediately towards the city of México-Tenochtitlán, where, thanks to a letter from the Mother Superior, I would be received by the newly established convent of the Jerónimas of New Spain. The roads were tortuous and the mist did not allow me to see the mountains surrounding us. Sometimes, you could hear howls like the ones of the natives of the port of San Juan; the driver told us it was the coyotes from the mountain and that we should not be afraid. Nevertheless, I felt a drop of cold water stream down my side, until it reached the pocket of my habit, and it incremented the weight of the black figurine until I was slouching.

After I finally arrived at the convent and rested, I went to visit Friar Juan de los Ángeles at the Jesuit home. He was an old man and walked with difficulty. Even so, he wanted to take me to my brother's grave, which was far off, in the atrium of a small chapel. As we walked together, he once more related the story of the discovery of the corpse, going into detail on the missing eyes, teeth and nails. The friar's gaze seemed to grow empty every time he spoke of the appearance of Fernando's skin, "moist and slippery, like a fish". I tried to speak of something else, but he seemed engrossed, as though he did not know I was there. After a little while, we arrived at a small cemetery, where I prayed in silence. I carried no flowers to place next to the wooden cross, so I took out the figurine and decided to leave it by the grave, as a gift for my brother. Friar Juan de los Ángeles grew pale when he saw it, made the sign of the cross several times and began to scream, "The *Ahuizotl*! Have respect for the dead and take away from this sacred place the demon that murdered your brother. You, servant of the aquatic Satan, do not deserve to wear the habit with the figure of Our Lord!"

Not knowing what to do, I rushed away, disconcerted, through the cemetery.

Back at the convent I fell victim to feverish tremors, which kept me in bed for many days. I dreamt, over and over again, about the titanic figure emerging from the sea and on the beach, it was received with joy by the *ahuizotls*, who, imitating the screams of a birthing woman or the cry of an infant, devoured my brother over and over again, or made terrible necklaces of teeth and nails. One afternoon, when my fever seemed to have eased, a dark-skinned girl with black hair took me to walk by the edge of a river. The sun was sinking, revealing the intense brightness of a few stars, when the girl told me to wait, for she could hear something resembling a baby's cry. I could not stop her. A dark, scaly hand rose from beneath the murky waters, pulled her hair and everything went black.

Days later, they found the dead girl. A little child told me her corpse glinted, like a horrible fish at the market. I resolved then to abandon New Spain forever and with it, my brother's corpse and the terrible dreams.

I arrived at the port of Veracruz on a Thursday at dawn, the first rays from the sun greeting the sailors with hundreds of dead frogs and fish upon the sand. My ship was soon parting, but we managed to hear the screams from the coast; I felt a drop of cold water stream down my side, until it reached the pocket of my habit, and it incremented the weight of the black figurine until I was slouching. I held the figurine between my hands and, though I tried to pray, no words came out.

THE WAVES RISE until they resemble a mountain in the ocean that turns dark, like the skin of the *Ahuizotl*. Barely illuminated by the convulsive light of the candle, the obsidian figurine seems to glint by itself and I feel it coming: black, huge, stirring the ocean with its innumerable scales, its eyes eternally open. The scent of salt and blood drifts through the air. God help us.

Nelly Geraldine García-Rosas is a Mexican writer and a freelance copy editor. Her stories have been published in local independent magazines and small-press anthologies. When she's not dreaming about cats or Cthulhu, she updates her lovecraftian/astronomical blog, "Desde R'lyeh ..." (fascinante-mente-freak.blogspot.com), searching for scientific data about the time when the stars will be right.

The author speaks: I decided to set the plot of "Ahuizotl" in early New Spain (a couple of decades after the Spanish conquest of the Aztec Empire), because this period represented the primordial soup of the present Mexican idiosyncrasy. Aztec mythical creatures and gods, like the *ahuizotl*, were considered to be demons or diabolical beings by the Spaniards, so it was pretty interesting to "play" with the narrative, mixing that ancient lore with Lovecraftian Mythos and actual historical details.

AN IDOL FOR EMIKO

TRAVIS HEERMANN

I

WE ALL SUSPECTED that Emiko would give in soon. We had long pre-pared her "funeral" ceremony to signify her passage from this world to the other, but all these years, she had resisted.

The fishermen sometimes reported sighting her on her veranda, looking out over the Ariake Sea, a lone, hunched figure. They saw her waist-deep in surging froth, a bulwark against the tide, even in winter, head bowed under the weight of age and ugliness and stubbornness. She would have suffered less if she had listened to us.

Sometimes, the fishermen even claimed to see her out there, with her idiot son huddled next to her, his spindly arms and lumpen features like a pale, crumpled spider. Of course, that was impossible.

When Taro was alive, those two had kept to themselves, secluded in that decrepit house with the portion of once-resplendent tiled roof now collapsed in disrepair, that house which had once belonged to the proud Otomo clan. Before Taro's crimes, he would sometimes answer the door and gaze up at the visitor, all slack face and watery eyes, tongue licking absently at cracked lips. He would croak something to his mother and she would shout back from the depths of the house to send the visitor away.

The nail that sticks up must be pounded down, as the saying goes, and ever since the village had grown prosperous, Emiko had been like a jagged splinter hiding in a freshly polished floor.

Her grandfather came from old samurai blood, but after Tokugawa's rise to power, much of the Otomo clan had been scattered like leaves in an autumn wind. Emiko's grandfather had been one of those leaves. To proclaim his loyalty to the new Shogunate – and escape likely execution – he had given up his swords for the life of a *nori*-farmer, but he had kept the family's ancestral property. A farmer's livelihood had not been sufficient to maintain such a house.

When Emiko was little, her family weathered those starveling years like the rest of us. Fields blighted by war and drought. Fisheries disappearing like schools of smelt into the cerulean depths. Even the offshore crop of *nori* refused to grow. The village's *nori* was sought throughout the domain for its quality and even in lean times, the *nori*-farmers had always been able to sustain themselves. Then the Shogunate imposed crushing taxes to refill its coffers after decades of war. Small villages like ours staggered under the weight. Perhaps we had been cursed. The priest purified the village again and again, without improvement, until finally, he departed. We discussed bringing an augurer from Yedo, but there was no money to pay such a person. The *onmyouji* were all well-employed as the shogun and his samurai lords worked to consolidate their power. The tax collector, Takehisa, came and demanded more than we could give. He berated us, "Work harder! Fish more!" We could not, and he took his due anyway, and we starved.

Along with many of us, Emiko prayed to the gods and Buddhas for the village's survival. The old shrine to Fugen, reachable only by an arduous trek across treacherous tide pools, up the boulder-strewn cliff side, was too difficult for many of us, but Emiko went. A portion of the shrine was devoted to mothers praying for bountiful milk, festooned with cloth effigies of opulent breasts. She and her friend Haruka would pray together and sometimes, sit for hours and look out over the sea.

After Emiko's shame, the village women said, "What does *she* think she's doing up there? Her dugs are withered. Her womb is a shriveled persimmon." Even before the flower of her youth had decayed, they said, "No man will ever marry her again after what happened."

Even after Taro was gone, she offered *sake* and rice balls to the shrine. Even just before the end, a fisherman spoke of seeing her up there: a corpulent, hunched figure, nearly hairless, kneeling, pasty hands clasped against her forehead, as if her breasts would ever again swell with milk.

It had not always been so with Emiko. A precocious child, youngest of six who survived, inquisitive, thoughtful, bright-eyed, tousle-haired, giggling, a joy amidst the village during the hard times. She and Haruka. This adventurous duo had often left behind Emiko's younger sister, Yukiko, bereft and wailing, but that was the nature of children.

Yasuhiro had wept when he sent Haruka away with the hairy barbarians, but this father's selfless act saved us all.

Soon after that, the fish returned – strange though they were – and rains blew in from the sea to replenish the fields. The sea gave us gold and beautiful stones. The Portuguese came every year to trade for our fish and jewelry. But that was when Emiko's troubles started.

Only Emiko blamed Yasuhiro for what he had done; everyone else kept their reproach rightfully to themselves. Haruka's family, also of old samurai blood, was among the first to prosper. Their fishing boats rode low in the water, laden with catch, and their coffers brimmed with strange, golden *ryo* from the sea.

Emiko's family was also among the first. One day, her father flaunted a strange, golden coin in the marketplace. No one would accept it for payment – it was too much – so he just tucked it into his purse with a smug grin. He soon promised Emiko to Haruka's older brother, Ryuichi, but Emiko refused.

Her poor parents were frantic – afraid that she had been kidnapped by *ronin* brigands – the night she ran away to Omuta village. Word came back from Omuta a few days later that she had married a man named 'Kenta', a woodcrafter's son. She had met Kenta on the family's trips to Omuta to sell their *nori* and buy supplies with their newfound gold. Marriage to a trades-man was a decline in station that the son of a samurai would not accept. Takeyo and her other three brothers brought her home. The hearts of some went out to her, with her eyes bloodshot from weeping, downcast from shame, brow furrowed from anger, cheek swollen.

She would never speak of what they had done to her 'husband', but Kenta never came to claim her. In those days, she often was seen turning a yearning gaze down the road toward Omuta.

Later that year, the sea claimed the first of us, among them Emiko's parents and two of her brothers. It all happened so fast, we could only watch them go.

In spite of Emiko's shame, Ryuichi's family reasserted their proposal. In hopes of forcing her to submit, Takeyo agreed. Bruises on her arms and face bespoke a struggle of wills within the old Otomo house. Nevertheless, Emiko's stubborn refusal outraged Ryuichi and his family, and most of the vil-lage. Ryuichi's family had changed all of our fortunes. Who was she to be so selfish and disloyal? Takeyo could hardly be expected to support her forever. Emiko was still comely. Ryuichi swore he would one day take her to wife, even after the next shameful incident.

One evening, she ran through the village, gasping, eyes wide with mad-ness, babbling to everyone about what she had seen coming out of the sea. No one could believe – then – such a wild story, especially coming from her.

Two years passed, three, with Ryuichi pressing his fruitless pledge for Emiko's hand. It happened one midwinter night, with a cold rain that threat-ened snow. Takeyo and Ryuichi were drinking *shochu* in the *izakaya*, gorging themselves on the new kind of fish that had appeared in our nets in such abundance. Emiko was home alone; her younger sister Yukiko had just been married to Chiba, the fisherman Yoba's son. Ryuichi and Takeyo exchanged pointed glances, after which, Ryuichi politely excused himself.

Later that night, Ryuichi ran screaming through the village – even though his legs had gnarled and he had bloated somewhat by this time – as if an *oni* were snarling at his heels. Some said he clutched his trousers about his waist with one hand, the other wrist bleeding or broken. Others said that he strode through town like the well-to-do man he was.

Emiko sought solace with Yukiko, but Chiba scorned Emiko for having brought all this trouble on herself. He forbade Yukiko from seeing her. Yukiko had enough worries, a house to tend, a plentiful catch to cure for market, without troubling herself over so difficult and stubborn a person.

Ryuichi avoided Emiko, especially when she grew large with child. She never implied that he should claim the child. Taro's birth came in the hottest part of summer. Takeyo relegated her to a decrepit wing of the property to prevent the blood of the birth from tainting the rest of the house. The village children stole out there and peeked through decaying walls into Emiko's sequestered world, bringing back stories of the pale, blue-veined, croaking infant who suckled and slurped at her breast.

II

YEARS LATER, AFTER Taro was able to shamble beside her, she journeyed again to Omuta. When she returned, she faced from us a mix of disapproval and curiosity. Had she found Kenta? Would he be coming to join her? Did he still want her now that she had an idiot bastard to raise?

Only Yukiko would Emiko speak to. Emiko sobbed as she told of Kenta. The villagers in Omuta told her that he spoke often of Takeyo being "not right," of "some darkness behind Takeyo's eyes," something that had shaken Kenta to the depths of his belly. He wanted away from Omuta, from being too close to the sea. Worse, he ceased practicing his trade, drank up all the family's money, and drowned in his own vomit. Village gossip condemned his weakness. Why would any woman want such a spineless man? Why would any man want such a shamed woman?

Emiko stopped eating any fish and kept herself removed from her brothers, making her quarters with Taro in the decrepit wing of the house. Takeyo, even with his wealth of new gold, kept her in poverty.

Against this ocean of troubles, Emiko burned incense and supplicated herself at the feet of the cliff-top Fugen for hours a day, with little Taro picking at the detritus clinging to the cliff-top, gnawing at bits of lichen, leaping and gibbering at the gulls dipping in the sea breeze.

Yukiko had the village's new goldsmith fashion the idol for Emiko, a fine image of Fugen, with a translucent, oily-green stone embedded in its belly. The stone was found on the beach amidst a small scattering of other, brightly coloured stones that appeared one morning after the ebb of the tide.

But they were not just stones. Pearls, rubies, sapphires, and others none could identify. The children who found them divided them up as pretty trinkets and took them home, unsuspecting of their worth. Soon, many of us wore fine new clothes and built larger houses.

Emiko refused to share in this prosperity or take part in its celebration. The greater the size of the catch or the more plentiful the rain on the fields, the more she spurned our society.

Among the children, she became "Ugly Old Emiko", even though she was hardly old. They sometimes hid outside the house and taunted Taro when Emiko was away. When Taro charged them like an enraged monkey, they fled, and Taro withdrew and sulked, his yellow eyes scheming hatred. When Emiko was within, they clattered stones across the roof or lobbed them into the garden until she came out and raged at them. They left the carcasses of birds, fish, and small forest creatures near the house, or thrown onto the roof, or stuffed into crannies, cursing the place with the perpetual miasma of death. Some children, in their furtive peekings and lurkings, spoke of little Taro discovering these unpleasant gifts and hiding with them, devouring them, crunching the little bones and gnawing desiccated flesh and dry feathers and sunken eyes with his protuberant yellow teeth. Some called these tales unbelievable – what human being would do such a thing? – while others just shrugged, as if such behaviour were perfectly understandable from a boy of his lineage. His father had been among the first to embrace the changes.

The Shogun's tax collector, Takehisa, once encountered Taro on the path into the forest. The warrior's disdainful gaze must have soured at the sight of the boy's sallow, moist-looking skin, matted hair and soiled loincloth. Taro would have been about ten years old, then. Takehisa related later, over cups with the village constable in the *izakaya*, that the boy had reeked of death and shit and the sea. The boy's feral grin had unnerved Takehisa more than he would ever admit, especially after Taro approached tentatively and licked the samurai's hand. Tasting him. Takehisa spurned the boy with his foot, hand on his hilt to draw. Some mad, mute, animal look in the boy's eye, like a shark's, stayed the samurai's blade.

Emiko would sometimes venture from the house to retrieve her errant son, occasionally even apologizing for his behaviour. She dragged him back home with her iron grip, deaf to his bleating and mewling.

She encountered Takehisa once in the street, during one of her retrievals. The samurai demanded the year's taxes from her within the week and she faced him with wrath, heedless that he could cut her down with impunity, or have her thrown into the street, left to beg for the same scraps her son found. Her beleaguered face, waxy from lack of sunlight, furrowed with anger. "What taxes can you expect from me? I have nothing! The entire village is crawling with gold! Fish practically jump into the boats. Jewels enough to ransom ten emperors wash onto the beach as if a hundred treasure ships had sunk offshore! When I was a girl, there was barely a bowl of rice to share among the entire village! And now!" She rolled her watery eyes. "You, with your new, golden fittings on your scabbard and fine, silken clothes, brought all the way from Yedo. You can find more than my share of 'taxes' just by taking a walk across the sand on a morning. I'll have none of it!"

The samurai blustered and protested, but, with infinite rudeness, she turned her back without bowing, clenched her son's hand, and left Takehisa standing there in his fume.

Emiko wore the same threadbare *kimono* every day for years, bought the most meager supplies of cheap millet, and ate vegetables that only she would grow. To spite her stubbornness, Takeyo and his brother, when their time came, dragged their sack full of gold with them into the sea.

Yukiko tried to share some of her wealth with Emiko, to ease her poverty, but Emiko would not accept a single piece of gold. She shrilled at Yukiko, and at anyone else who would listen, that all of it was ill-gotten, corrupt. Yukiko discovered that Emiko had accumulated a substantial debt with the village merchant, in spite of the austerity of her life. The debt had accrued over many years. Yukiko paid this debt and even a sum forward, so that Emiko could feed herself and Taro. Yukiko's husband did not approve, but it was the woman's place to secure the house's financial dealings. When Emiko discovered what Yukiko had done, she never visited the merchant again.

Except for the blight that Emiko and her son became, the village was as happy as ever. We held festivals at the dark of every moon to thank the sea gods and Buddhas for our good fortune. We gorged ourselves on the new fish and *sake* and *shochu*.

Some of the lads hunted for boar in the hills and, on the occasions of their success, we feasted on meat. One of our young men, grown incredibly large and powerful thanks to his diet of new fish, felled a charging boar with a single blow of his fist.

Such tales made our bonfires livelier. Before long, most of the village was joining us out on the reef as we piled our bonfire high, and danced to the skin drum and raucous piping of the bamboo flute. Those who refused, like Emiko, we left to sulk in their decaying houses. Those nails eventually would be pounded down, as well. The old, ineffectual Shinto priest disappeared without a word, abandoning his temple on Clear Water Mountain. The new priest, with his golden headdress and strange shimmering robes, led our revelry.

Those were heady years. Forgetting about Emiko and Taro was easier with a warm *sake* jar in hand, the juicy taste of boar on the tongue, and golden *ryo* heavy in the purse.

III

THE HAIRY BARBARIANS in their strange ships came to the village every year to trade for supplies and jewelry, bringing exotic spices, silk from China, steel, spirits. The *gaijin* captain had learned to speak since that first meeting years ago. His interpreter had had a thick Nagasaki accent. The captain was impressed with how prosperous the village had become in the years since his first visit. Over *sake* and foreign *castella* cakes in the *izakaya* with the village leaders, the captain regaled us with his travels.

Ryuichi asked after his sister, Haruka, gone with the captain these many years.

The captain replied, "Unfortunate, but Haruka is dead. She sick and die last winter. She was good woman." He sucked his teeth and sighed. "That was good trade, yes? I give you gold charm. Your father throw into sea and say words. Magic work. Everything change. Everything here good now, yes?"

Ryuichi nodded, cradling in his lap the wrist that had never properly healed. He squatted like a round-eyed toad on the *tatami*. "Father was wise to trade her to you. We could not afford to feed her, anymore. I'm happy that you found her valuable." The flaps in his throat made his voice difficult by then.

The captain's bear-like face split into a gap-toothed grin. "Charm was good, yes? I need new wife, now. Have any more to trade?"

The village elders considered this and the following day, brought a handful of teenage girls to him. With a sour examination, he shook his head. "Ugly! What happened? I remember many girls beautiful here. Long ago time."

The elders could only shrug and shuffle their feet.

"Skin white. Bad hair. Buggy eyes." The disgust on the captain's face was plain. He never came back. We cursed him for a barbarian.

In spite of Emiko's perpetual stubbornness, Yukiko tried to keep good relations. Yukiko wanted Emiko to fit in with us. One day, not long after Yukiko's third son was born, Emiko came with a meager arrangement of flowers she had cut to celebrate the infant's birth. They walked through the village holding hands. Yukiko's older sons clung to their mother's legs. As they walked, we all listened.

Yukiko said, "Why must you live the way you do? My husband has grown wealthy. Let me share some of it with you. You need not starve. Give Taro some good fish and yourself some new clothes."

"I cannot."

"Why?"

"On the evening your son was born, it was nearly dark, the sun slipping into the sea. I saw Taro sitting in a tide pool, as he often does. The light was ... just so. When Taro stood up, he started to walk toward the reef with this strange walk."

"Strange?"

"Yes, not like a man."

"But he's a boy."

"No, like something *not a human being*. I was suddenly reminded of that night I saw it. That thing."

"Oh. That night." Yukiko sighed. We had all heard about it.

"I was digging clams in the evening and I had my bucket and father's shovel, digging, digging. And a man came out of the waves."

"A man? From the sea?"

"But not a man. Something else. As if a blowfish grew legs and arms, but didn't know how to walk on land. It saw me. Its eyes were like black *sake* bowls. I dropped my shovel and ran. Father beat me for leaving the bucket and shovel to be swept away by the tide."

"Yes, but he went out to retrieve it."

"Do you remember how frightened he was when he came back?" Yukiko cleared her throat.

"Do you remember the strange, square golden coin that father so adored?"

"Yes, with the strange writing, as big as my palm. Mother said he slept with it."

Emiko's face turned to stone. "There are far too many of such coins in the village now. He found that one in my clam bucket that night. I hadn't thought about that in years. Isn't it a strange thing to remember that just now?" Emiko's gaze went distant. "Isn't that strange ...."

"And Takeyo ...."

Emiko's face hardened again. "Takeyo found some of those coins in the bellies of those strange fish. Their fins are so odd, not like fins at all, like little fingers and legs ...."

"Ugly things, but they are so tasty!"

Emiko shuddered. "And the little faces in the net, not like fish faces. Like Ryuichi's face." She spat on the ground and looked hard at who Yukiko had become. "We shouldn't have eaten them. That is why I live as I do."

Yukiko wetly cleared her throat and patted Emiko's hand. "Please tell me you're not trekking all the way up to that Fugen shrine, anymore. It is such an arduous walk. Please tell me that you love the Fugen statue. I had it made just for you. I want to make your life easier, just a little."

Emiko sighed. "I keep it on the *kamidana*, next to grandfather's swords and mother's and father's funeral tablets. Sometimes, Taro stares at it for hours. He says it pulls at him, that the whorls in the stone change." She laughed to dispel the foolishness of the idea. "What's a mother to do?"

Yukiko laughed. Her two sons walked hand-in-hand with a still-normal, childlike gait. "Taro is 13 now? Such a fine boy. Especially now, he takes after his –" She froze. The hard-shouldered stiffness reappeared in Emiko's stance. Their walk was soon over.

The first trouble in many years came when the children began to disappear. First, the woodcutter's young daughter, then one of the *sake*-brewer's sons, five and six years old. Like Emiko, their families had also shunned the village's prosperity, allowing only as much as they needed to support themselves. They were adorable children, pink-cheeked and bright-eyed. They simply vanished. We searched the woods and seashore and caverns to the south, where the new priest left offerings to the sea gods.

The bones were discovered, half-buried under a thin carpet of bamboo leaves, cracked and gnawed, the marrow sucked out, as if devoured by a beast. We combed the forest for signs of bears and wolves, even though bears had never lived on Kyushu and no one had seen wolves in generations. Parents kept their children under close watch. If not for their precautions, Taro might have gotten away with more.

One moment, little Momoko was playing near one of the rice fields while her mother arranged some seedlings for planting and the next moment, the child was gone. A woman nearby spotted Taro scuttling into the bushes, dragging a limp little figure, like a monkey dragging a doll, except his strange gait suggested something other than monkey.

The women cried out in alarm. Several men charged after in pursuit, following a tenuous trail of blood to a hollow between some rocks at the skirts of Clear Water Mountain, near the old temple, abandoned and forgotten over a decade. We roared in horror and rage at the sight: Taro's hideous shape, bedraggled hair, red-rimmed eyes, his almost-snout, bloody lips and yellow teeth tearing into the soft flesh of the little girl's naked buttock. Her skull lay open, splattered on the rocks. We charged him, with our gaff hooks and rusty spears left over from the old wars, but he was faster than any monkey. With a snarl, a claw and a frog-like bounce, he tore out poor Bunta's throat and soared over our vengeful band, tearing off into the forest.

Some of us gave chase; some of us carried poor Momoko back to the village.

When we beat upon Emiko's door, she snarled as she came out, thinking to drive us off, but we would not be moved, in spite of the beginning changes in her. The idol was doing its work. Eyes grown larger and watery, skin sallow, body bloating. Such changes had spread throughout the village, faster in some than in others. We told her all of it and her face became a *Noh* mask. "I will find him," she said.

"He'll be punished!" we cried.

"Yes, he will." Her eyes did not blink.

Emiko went back into her house and we joined the others in the search.

Emiko later came to the constable and the headman, and announced that
Taro would never harm anyone again. The constable nearly arrested her,
but something in her demeanor gave him pause, a resignation and regret as
deep and solid as the basalt underlying a reef, as deep and sublime as the
cities of the sea gods. He let her go. As she shuffled away, she clutched the
golden idol of Fugen under her arm, with a tuft of bloody hair clinging to one
of the hard edges.

Decades later, a fisherman saw Emiko shuffling, hopping across the tide
pools toward the reef. Her remaining wisps of hair had gone stone-grey,
unkempt and sodden. By this time, the flabby wattles around her throat had
begun to form gills like those of the sea gods, her flesh grown pale, with the
ever-present moist sheen. Her webbed fingers clutched the idol made with
the strange, sickly green stone and gold given from the sea gods. Her shoulders hunched under the burden of silent tortures we could only imagine.
She waited as the tide came in around her, rising up to her waist, then her
chest. Then she lowered her head and disappeared under the waves.

When Yukiko and Chiba claimed the Otomo house by right of kinship,
they could barely walk on land anymore, themselves. They found a skeleton
carefully arranged near the *kamidana*, in the shadow of the Otomo swords
and family funeral tablets.

The sharp, protruding teeth and twisted limbs marked the skeleton as
Taro. A jagged cleft shattered the misshapen face. Yukiko made her husband
swear – until they went into the sea – that he would never utter a word of the
knife-and-tooth-marks on those bones.

Travis Heermann. Author, freelance writer, English instructor, poker player, biker, roustabout. His novel, *Heart of the Ronin*, is available now in trade
paperback and e-book from E-Reads. He has sold short fiction to *Cemetery
Dance*, *OG's Speculative Fiction*, the British Fantasy Society's Winter 2010
anthology, Library of Horror Press, and others. He taught English in Japan
for three years and stands out there like a space alien with his head on fire.

The author speaks: This story is set in early-17th-century Japan, right after
the rise of the Tokugawa Shogunate, before trade with "hairy barbarians"
was outlawed. The setting is the western coast of Kyushu, across the Ariake
Sea from Nagasaki, a major trading port with the Portuguese. When I heard
about this anthology, I knew I wanted to write a story set in Japan. An obvious direction was to explore Japan's deep connection to the sea, juxtaposed
with Lovecraft's sea-borne horrors, but I wasn't sure how to make it fresh.
Then I happened to read "A Rose for Emily" by William Faulkner (a fantas-
tic horror story in its own right) and I found my twist.

THE INFERNAL HISTORY OF THE IVYBRIDGE TWINS

MOLLY TANZER

for a number of people, whom, the author is certain, would not wish their names mentioned here

I

Concerning the life and death of St. John Fitzroy, Lord Calipash – the suffering of the Lady Calipash – the unsavory endeavors of Lord Calipash's cousin Mr. Villein – as well as an account of the curious circumstances surrounding the birth of the future Lord Calipash and his twin sister.

IN THE COUNTY of Devonshire, in the parish of Ivybridge, stood the ancestral home of the Lords Calipash. Calipash Manor was large, built sturdily of the local limestone, and had stood for many years without fire or other catastrophe marring its expanse. No one could impugn the size and an-tiquity of the house, yet often, one or another of those among Lord Calipash's acquaintance might be heard to comment that the Manor had a rather ram-bling, hodgepodge look to it and this could not be easily refuted without the peril of speaking a falsehood. The reason for this was that the Lords Calipash had always been the very essence of English patriotism and, rather than ever tearing down any part of the house and building anew, each Lord Calipash had chosen to make additions and improvements to older structures. Thus, though the prospect was somewhat sprawling, it served as a pleasant-enough reminder of the various styles of Devonian architecture and became some-thing of a local attraction.

St. John Fitzroy, Lord Calipash, was a handsome man: tall, fair-haired and blue-eyed. He had been bred up as any gentleman of rank and fortune might be, and therefore, the manner of his death was more singular than any aspect of his life. Now, given that this is, indeed, an *Infernal* History, the sad circumstances surrounding this good man's unexpected and early demise demand attention by the author, and they are inextricably linked with the Lord Calipash's cousin, a young scholar called 'Mr. Villein', who will figure more prominently in this narrative than his nobler relation.

Mr. Villein came to stay at Calipash Manor during the Seven Years' War, in order to prevent his being conscripted into the French army. Though indifference had previously characterized the relationship between Lord Calipash and Mr. Villein (Mr. Villein belonging to a significantly lower branch of the family tree), when Mr. Villein wrote to Lord Calipash to beg sanctuary, the good Lord would not deny his own flesh and blood. This was not to say, however, that Lord Calipash was above subtly encouraging his own flesh and blood to make his stay a short one and, to that end, he gave Mr. Villein the tower bedroom that had been built by one of the more eccentric Lords some generations prior to our tale, who so enjoyed pretending to be the Lady Jane Grey that he had the edifice constructed so his wife could dress up as a member of the privy council and keep him locked up there for as long as nine days at a stretch. But that was not the reason Lord Calipash bade his cousin reside there – the tower was a drafty place and given to damp, and thus seemed certain of securing a speedy departure. As it turns out, however, the two men were so unlike one another that what Lord Calipash thought was an insulting situation, Mr. Villein found entirely salubrious and so, happily, out of a case of simple misunderstanding grew an affection, founded on deepest admiration for Mr. Villein's part and, for Lord Calipash's, enjoyment of toadying.

All the long years of the international conflict Mr. Villein remained at Calipash Manor and, with the passing of each and every day, he came more into the confidence of Lord Calipash, until it was not an uncommon occurrence to hear members of Lord Calipash's circle using words like 'inseparable' to describe their relationship. Then, only six months before the signing of the Treaty of Paris, the possibility of continued fellowship between Lord Calipash and Mr. Villein was quite suddenly extinguished. A Mr. Fellingworth moved into the neighbourhood with his family, among them his daughter of fifteen years, Miss Alys Fellingworth. Dark of hair and eye but pale of cheek, her beauty did not go long unnoticed by the local swains. She had many suitors and many offers, but from among a nosegay of sparks, she chose as her favourite blossom the Lord Calipash.

Mr. Villein had also been among Miss Fellingworth's admirers and her decision wounded him – not so much that he refused to come to the wedding (He was very fond of cake), but certainly enough that all the love Mr. Villein had felt for Lord Calipash was instantly converted, as if by alchemy, to pure hatred. In his dolor, Mr. Villein managed to convince himself that Miss Fellingworth's father had pressured her to accept Lord Calipash's offer for the sake of his rank and income, against her true inclinations; that, had she been allowed to pick her heart's choice, she certainly would have accepted Mr. Villein's suit rather than his cousin's. Such notions occupied Mr. Villein's thoughts whenever he saw the happy couple together and every day, his mind became more and more inhospitable to any pleasure he might have otherwise felt on account of his friend's newfound felicity.

A reader of this history might well wonder why Mr. Villein did not quit Calipash Manor, given that his situation, previously so agreeable, he now found intolerable. Mr. Villein was, however, loath to leave England. He had received a letter from his sister informing him that, during his absence, his modest home had been commandeered by the army and thus, his furniture was in want of replacing, his lands trampled without hope of harvest, his stores pilfered. Perhaps worst of all, his wretched sister was with child by an Austrian soldier who had, it seemed, lied about his interest in playing the role of father beyond the few minutes required to grant him that status. It seemed prudent to Mr. Villein to keep apart from such appalling circumstances for as long as possible.

Then, one evening, from the window of his tower bedroom, Mr. Villein saw Lord Calipash partaking of certain marital pleasures with the new Lady Calipash against a tree in one of the gardens. Nauseated, Mr. Villein called for his servant and announced his determination to secretly leave Calipash Manor, once and for all, early the following morning. While the servant packed his bags and trunks, Mr. Villein penned a letter explaining his hasty departure to Lord Calipash and left it, along with a token of remembrance, in Lord Calipash's study.

Quite early the next morning, just as he was securing his cravat, Mr. Villein was treated to the unexpected-but-tantalizing sight of Lady Calipash in *deshabille*. She was beside herself with grief, but eventually, Mr. Villein, entirely sympathetic and eager to understand the source of her woe, coaxed the story from her fevered mind:

"I woke early, quite cold," gibbered Lady Calipash. "Lord Calipash had never come to bed, though he promised me when I went up that he should follow me after settling a few accounts. When I discovered him absent, I rose and sought him in his study only to find him – *dead*. Oh! It was too terrible! His eyes were open, wide and round and staring. At first, I thought it looked very much like he had been badly frightened, but then I thought he had almost a look of ... of *ecstasy* about him. I believe –"

Here the Lady Calipash faltered, and it took some minutes for Mr. Villein to get the rest of the story from her, for her agitated state required his fetching smelling salts from out of his valise. Eventually, she calmed enough to relate the following:

"I believe he might have done himself the injury that took him from me," she sobbed. "His wrists were slit and next to him lay his letter-opener. He ... he had used his own blood to scrawl a message on the skirtingboards ... Oh, Mr. Villein!"

"What did the message say?" asked Mr. Villein.

"It said, *He is calling, he is calling, I hear him*," she said and then she hesitated.

"What is it, Lady Calipash?" asked Mr. Villein.

"I cannot see its importance, but he had this in his other hand," said she and handed to Mr. Villein a small object wrapped in a handkerchief.

He took it from her and saw that it was an odd bit of ivory, wrought to look like a lad's head crowned with laurel. Mr. Villein put it in his pocket and smiled at the Lady Calipash.

"Likely it has nothing to do with your husband's tragic end," he said gently. "I purchased this whilst in Greece and the late Lord Calipash had often admired it. I gave it to him as a parting gift, for I had meant to withdraw from Calipash Manor this very morning."

"Oh, but you mustn't," begged Lady Calipash. "Not now, not after ... Lord Calipash would wish you to be here. You mustn't go just now, please! For my sake ...."

Mr. Villein would have been happy to remain on those terms, had the Lady Calipash finished speaking, but alas, there was one piece of information she had yet to relate.

" ... and for our child's sake, as well," she concluded.

While the Lord Calipash's final message was being scrubbed from the skirtingboards, and his death was being declared *an accident* by the constable in order that the departed Lord might be buried in the churchyard, Mr. Villein violently interrogated Lady Calipash's serving-maid. The story was true – the Lady was indeed expecting – and this intelligence displeased Mr. Villein so immensely that, even as he made himself pleasant and helpful with the hope that he might eventually win the Lady Calipash's affections, he sought to find a method of ridding her of her unborn child.

To Mr. Villein's mind, Lady Calipash could not but fall in love with her loyal confidant – believing as he did that she had always secretly admired him – but he knew that should she bear the late Lord Calipash's son, the estate would one day be entirely lost to Mr. Villein. Thus, he dosed the Lady with recipes born of his own researches, for while Mr. Villein's *current* profession was that of scholar, in his youth, he had pursued lines of study related to all manner of black magics and sorceries. For many years, he had put aside his wicked thaumaturgy, being too happy in the company of Lord Calipash to travel those paths that demand solitude, gloom and suffering, but, newly motivated, he returned to his former interests with a desperate passion.

Like the Wife of Bath, Mr. Villein knew all manner of remedies for love's mischances and he put wicked spells on the decoctions and tisanes that he prepared to help his cause. Yet, despite Mr. Villein's skill with infusion and incantation, Lady Calipash grew heavy with child; indeed, she had such a healthy maternal glow about her that the doctor exclaimed that for one so young to be brought to childbed, she was certain of a healthy *accouchement*. Mr. Villein, as canny an adept at lying as other arts, appeared to be thrilled by his Lady's prospects and was every day by her side. Though privately discouraged by her salutary condition, he was cheered by all manner of odd portents that he observed as her lying-in drew ever closer. First, a murder of large, evil-looking ravens took up residence upon the roof of Calipash Manor, cackling and cawing day and night. Then the ivy growing on Calipash Manor's aged walls turned from green to scarlet, a circumstance no naturalist in the area could satisfactorily explain. Though the Lady Calipash's delivery was expected in midwinter, a she-goat was found to be unexpectedly in the same delicate condition as her mistress and gave birth to a two-headed kid that was promptly beaten to death and buried far from the Manor.

Not long after that unhappy parturition, which had disturbed the residents of Calipash Manor so greatly that the news was kept from Lady Calipash for fear of doing her or her unborn child a mischief, the Lady began to feel the pangs of her own travail. At the very stroke of midnight, on the night of the dark of the moon, during a lightning storm that was as out of season as the she-goat's unusual kid, the Lady Calipash was happy to give birth to a healthy baby boy, the future Lord Calipash, and as surprised as the midwife when a second child followed, an equally plump and squalling girl. They were so alike that Lady Calipash named them Basil and Rosemary, and then promptly gave them over to the wet-nurse to be washed and fed.

The wet-nurse was a stout woman from the village, good-natured and well-intentioned, but a sounder sleeper than was wanted in that house. Though an infant's wail would rouse her in an instant, footfalls masked by thunder were too subtle for her country-bred ear and thus, she did not observe the solitary figure that stole silently into the nursery in the wee hours of that morning. For only a few moments did the individual linger, knowing well how restive infants can be in their first hours of life. By the eldritch glow of a lightning strike, Mr. Villein uncorked a phial containing the blood of the two-headed kid now buried and he smeared upon both of those rosy foreheads an unholy mark, which, before the next burst of thunder, sank without a trace into their soft and delicate skin.

II

*A brief account of the infancy, childhood, education, and adolescence of Basil
Vincent, the future Lord Calipash. and his sister Rosemary – as well as a
discussion of the effect that reputation has on the prospect of obtaining satisfactory friends and lovers.*

WHILE THE AUTHOR cannot offer an opinion on whether any person
deserves to suffer during his or her lifetime, the author *will* say with
utter certainty that Lady Calipash endured more on account of her Twins
than any good woman should expect when she finds herself in the happy
condition of mother. Their easy birth and her quick recovery were the end of
Lady Calipash's maternal bliss, for not long after she could sit up and cradle
her infant son in her arms, she was informed that a new wet-nurse must be
hired, as the old had quit the morning after the birth.

Lady Calipash was never told of the reason for the nurse's hasty departure, only that for a few days, her newborns had been nourished with goat's
milk, there being no suitable women in the neighbourhood to feed the hungry young lord and his equally rapacious sister. The truth of the matter was
that little Rosemary had bitten off the wet-nurse's nipple not an hour after
witnessing her first sunrise. When the poor woman ran out of the nursery,
clutching her bloody breast and screaming, the rest of the servants did not
much credit her account of the injury. When it was discovered that the new-
born was possessed of a set of thin, needle-sharp teeth behind her innocent
mouth, they would have drowned the girl in the well if not for Mr. Villein,
who scolded them for peasant superstition and told them to feed the babes
on the milk of the nanny goat who had borne the two-headed kid, until such
a time when a new wet nurse could be hired. That the wet-nurse's nipple was
never found became a source of ominous legend in the household, theories
swapped from servant to servant, until Mr. Villein heard two chambermaids
gossiping and beat them both dreadfully in order that they might serve as an
example of the consequences of idle chatter.

This incident was only the first of its kind, but alas, the chronicles of the
sufferings of those living in, or employed at, Calipash Manor after the birth
of the Infernal Twins (as they were called by servant, tenant farmer, villager
and gentleperson alike, well out of the hearing of either Lady Calipash or Mr.
Villein, of course) could comprise their own lengthy volume and thus, must
be abridged for the author's current purposes. Sufficient must be the following collection of vignettes:

From the first morning, Basil's cries sounded distinctly syllabic and when
the vicar came to baptize the Twins, he recognized the future Lord Calipash's

wailing as an ancient language known only to the most disreputable sort of cultist.

On the first dark of the moon after their birth, it was discovered that Rosemary had sprouted pale greenish webbing between her toes and fingers, as well as a set of pulsing gills just below her shell-pink earlobes. The next morning, the odd amphibious attributes were gone, but, to the distress of all, their appearance seemed inexorably linked to the lunar cycle, for they appeared every month thereafter.

Before either could speak a word, whenever a person stumbled or belched in their presence, one would laugh like a hyena then the other, and then they would both fall silent, staring at the individual until he or she fled the room.

One day after Basil began to teethe, Rosemary was discovered to be missing. No one could find her for several hours, but eventually, she reappeared in Basil's crib, apparently of her own volition. She was asleep and curled against her brother, who was contentedly gnawing on a bone that had been neatly and inexplicably removed from the lamb roast that was to have been Lady Calipash and Mr. Villein's supper that night.

Yet, such accounts are nothing to the constant uproar that ensued when, at last, Basil and Rosemary began to walk and speak. These accomplishments, usually met with celebration in most houses, were heralded by the staff formally petitioning for the Twins to be confined to certain areas of the house, but Mr. Villein, who had taken as much control of the business of Calipash Manor as he could, insisted that they be given as much freedom as they desired. This caused all manner of problems for the servants, but their complaints were met with cruel indifference by their new, if unofficial, master. It seemed to all that Mr. Villein actually delighted in making life difficult at Calipash Manor. It may be safely assumed that part of his wicked tyranny stemmed from the unwillingness of Lady Calipash to put aside her mourning and her being too constantly occupied with the unusual worries yielded by her motherhood to consider entering once again into a state of matrimony, despite his constant hints.

For the Twins, their newfound mobility was a source of constant joy. They were intelligent, inventive children, strong and active, and they managed to discover all manner of secret passageways and caches of treasure the Lady Calipash never knew of and Mr. Villein had not imagined existing, even in his wildest fancies of sustaining this period of living as a gentleman. The siblings were often found in all manner of places at odd times – after their being put to bed, it was not unusual to discover one or both in the library come midnight, claiming to be "looking at the pictures" in books that were only printed text. At cock-crow, one might encounter them in the attic, drawing be-tentacled things on the floorboards with bits of charcoal or less-pleasant substances.

Though the servants always secured the windows and triple-locked the nursery door come the dark of the moon, there was never a month that passed
without Rosemary escaping to do what she would in the lakes and ponds that
were part of the Calipash estate, the only indication of her black frolics bits
of fish-bones stuck between her teeth and pond-weed braided through her
midnight tresses.

Still, it was often easy to forget the Twins' wickedness between inci-
dents, for they appeared frequently to be mere children at play. They would
bring their mother natural oddities from the gardens, like a pretty stone or
a perfect pinecone, and beg to be allowed to help feed the hunting hounds
in the old Lord Calipash's now-neglected kennels. All the same, even when
they were sweet, it saddened Lady Calipash that Basil was, from the first, a
dark and sniveling creature and pretty Rosemary more likely to bite with her
sharp teeth than return an affectionate kiss. Even on good days, they had to
be prevented from entering the greenhouse or the kitchen – their presence
withered vegetation and, should one of them reach a hand into a cookie jar or
steal a nibble of carrot or potato from the night's dinner, the remaining food
would be found fouled with mold or ash upon their withdrawing.

Given the universal truth that servants will gossip, when stories like these
began to circulate throughout the neighbourhood, the once-steady stream of
visitors who had used to come to tour Calipash Manor decreased to a trickle
and no tutor could be hired at any salary. Lady Calipash thanked God that Mr.
Villein was there to conduct her children's education, but others were not so
sure this was such a boon. Surely, had Lady Calipash realized that Mr. Villein
viewed the Lady's request as an opportunity to teach the Twins, not only
Latin and Greek and English and Geography and Maths, but also his sorcer-
ous arts, she might have heeded the voices of dissent, instead of dismissing
their concerns as utter nonsense.

Though often cursed for their vileness, Basil and Rosemary grew up quite
happily in the company of Mr. Villein, their mother and the servants, until
they reached that age when children often begin to want for society. The
spring after they celebrated their eighth birthday, they pleaded with their
mother to be allowed to attend the May Day celebration in town. Against
her better judgment, Lady Calipash begged the favour of her father (who
was hosting the event); against *his* better judgment, Mr. Fellingworth, who
suffered perpetual and extraordinary dyspepsia as a result of worrying about
his decidedly odd grandchildren, said the Infernal Twins might come – if, and
only if they promised to behave themselves. After the incident the previous
month, at the birthday party of a young country gentleman, where the Twins
were accused to no resolution of somehow having put dead frogs under the

icing of the celebrant's towering cake, all were exceedingly cautious of allowing them to attend.

This caution was, regrettably, more deserved than the invitation. Rosemary arrived at the event in a costume of her own making, that of the
nymph Flora. When Mr. Villein was interrogated as to his reasoning for
such grotesque and ill-advised indulgence of childish fancy, he replied that
she had earlier proved her understanding that May Day had once been the
Roman festival of Floralia and it seemed a just reward for her attentiveness
in the schoolroom. This bit of pagan heresy might have been overlooked by
the other families, had not Mr. Villein later used the exact same justification
for Basil's behavior when the boy appeared at the celebration later on, clad
only in a bit of blue cloth wrapped about his slender body, and then staged
a reenactment for the children of Favonius' rape of Flora, Rosemary playing
her part with unbridled enthusiasm. Mr. Villein could not account for the resentment of the other parents, nor the ban placed on the Twins' presence at
any future public observances. For, as he told Lady Calipash, the pantomime
was accurate and thus, a rare educational moment during a day given over to
otherwise-pointless frivolity.

Unfortunately for the Twins, the result of that display was total social isolation – quite the opposite of their intention. From that day forward, they saw
no other children except for those of the staff, and the sense of rank instilled
in the future Lord Calipash and his sister from an early age forbade them
from playing with those humble urchins. Instead, they began to amuse themselves by trying out a few of the easier invocations taught to them by Mr. Villein and, in this manner, summoned two fiends: one an amorphous spirit who
would follow them about if it wasn't too windy a day, the other an eel with a
donkey's head who lived, much to the gardener's distress, in the pond at the
center of the rose garden. Rosemary also successfully reanimated an incredibly nasty, incredibly ancient goose, when it died of choking on a strawberry,
and the fell creature went about its former business of hissing at everyone
and shitting everywhere, until the stable boy hacked off its head with the
edge of a shovel and buried the remains at opposite ends of the estate.

Unfortunately, these childish amusements could not long entertain the
Twins once they reached an age when they should, by all accounts, have
been interfering with common girls (in Lord Calipash's case) or being court-
ed by the local boys (in Rosemary's). For his part, Basil could not be bothered with the fairer sex, so absorbed was he in mastering languages more
recherché than his indwelling R'lyehian or native English, or even the Latin,
Hebrew and Assyrian he had mastered before his tenth birthday (Greek he
never took to – that was Rosemary's province and the only foreign tongue
she ever mastered). Truth be told, even had Basil been interested in women,

his slouching posture, slight physique and petulant mouth would have likely ensured a series of speedy rejections. Contrariwise, Rosemary was a remarkably appealing creature, but there was something so frightening about her sharp-toothed smile and wicked gaze that no boy in the county could imagine comparing her lips to cherubs', or her eyes to the night sky, and thus, she, too, wanted for a lover.

Nature will, however, induce the most enlightened of us to act according to our animal inclinations and, to that end one night, just before their 15th birthday, Rosemary slipped into her brother's chambers after everyone else had gone to bed. She found Basil studying by himself. He did not look up at her to greet her, merely said, "*Fhtagn-e*," and ignored her. He had taught her a bit of his blood-tongue and their understanding of one another was so profound that she did not mind heeding the imperative and knelt patiently at his feet for him to come to the end of his work. Before the candle had burned too low, he looked down at her with a fond frown.

"What?" he asked.

"Brother," said she, with a serious expression, "I have no wish to die an old maid."

"What have I to do with that?" said he, wiping his eternally-drippy nose on his sleeve.

"No one will do it to me if you won't."

Basil considered this, realizing she spoke, not of matrimony, but of the act of love.

"Why should you want to?" asked he, at last. "From everything I've read, intercourse yields nothing but trouble for those who engage in libidinous sport."

Rosemary laughed.

"Would you like to come out with me, two nights hence?"

"On our birthday?"

"It's the dark of the moon," said she.

Basil straightened up and looked at her keenly. He nodded once, briskly, and that was enough for her. As she left him, she kissed his smooth cheek and, at her touch, he blushed for the first time in his life.

Before progressing to the following scene of depravity that the author finds it her sad duty to relate, let several things be said about this History. First, this is as true and accurate an account of the Infernal Twins of Ivybridge as anyone has yet attempted. Second, it is the duty of all historians to recount events with as much veracity as possible, never eliding over unpleasantness for propriety's sake. Had Suetonius shied away from his subject, we might never have known the true degeneracy of Caligula and no one could argue that Suetonius' dedication to his work has allowed mankind to learn from the mistakes made by the Twelve Caesars. Thus, the author moves on to her third point, that her own humble chronicle of the Ivybridge Twins is intended to be morally instructive rather than titillating. With this understanding, we must, unfortunately, press on.

The future Lord Calipash had never once attended his sister on her monthly jaunts and so, it must be said that, to his credit, it was curiosity rather than lust that comprised the bulk of his motivation that night. He dressed himself warmly, tiptoed to her door, and knocked very softly, only to find his sister standing beside him in a thin silk sheath, though her door had not yet been unlocked. He looked her up and down – there was snow on the ground outside; what was she about, dressing in such a nymphean manner? – but when she saw his alarm, given his own winter ensemble, she merely smiled. Basil was in that moment struck by how appealing were his sister's kitten-teeth, how her ebon tresses looked as soft as raven-down in the guttering candle-light. He swallowed nervously. She pinched out the candle, and then, holding a single slender finger to her lips, with gestures, Rosemary bid him follow her and they made their way down the hallway without a light. She knew the way and her moist palm gripped his dry one as they slipped downstairs, out the servant's door and into the cold, midwinter night.

Rosemary led her brother to one of the gardens – the pleasure-garden, full of little private grottoes – and there, against a tree already familiar with love's pleasures, she kissed him on the mouth. It was a clumsy kiss. The Twins had been well-tutored by the Greeks and Romans in the theory, but not the practice, of love – and theory can take one only so far. To their observer – for indeed they were observed – it seemed that both possessed an overabundance of carnal knowledge and thus, it was a longer encounter than most young people's inaugural attempts at amatory relations. Rosemary was eager and Basil shy, though when he kissed her neck and encountered her delicate sea-green gill pulsating against her ivory skin, gasping for something more substantial than air, he felt himself completely inflamed and pressed himself into the webbed hand that fumbled with his breeches buttons in the gloaming.

The Twins thought themselves invisible, that the location which they chose to celebrate their induction into Hymen's temple was completely obscure, and thus, they were too completely occupied with their personal concerns to notice something very interesting – that Calipash Manor was not completely dark, even at that early hour of the morning. A light shone dimly from the tower bedroom, where a lone figure, wracked with anger and jealousy and hatred, watched the Twins from the same window where he had observed two other individuals fornicate, perhaps somewhat less wantonly, almost sixteen years earlier.

III

*Containing more of the terrible wickedness of Mr. Villein – a record of the
circumstances surrounding the unhappy separation of the Ivybridge Twins –
how Rosemary became Mrs. Villein – concluding with the arrival of a curious
visitor to Calipash Manor and the results of his unexpected intrusion.*

MR. VILLEIN'S PURSUIT of the Lady Calipash had lasted for as many
years as Rosemary remained a child, but when the blood in her girl's
veins began to quicken and wrought those womanly changes upon her
youthful body so pleasing to the male eye, Mr. Villein found his lascivious
dreams to be newly occupied with daughter rather than mother. Since the
time, earlier in the year, when Rosemary had finally been allowed to dress
her hair and wear long skirts, Mr. Villein started paying her the sort of little
compliments that he assumed a young lady might find pleasing. Little did he
imagine that Rosemary thought him elderly, something less than handsome,
a dreary conversationalist, and one whose manners were not those of a true
gentleman. Thus, when he watched the virginal object of his affection sullied
enthusiastically by her ithyphallic brother, the indecent tableau came as a
substantial shock to Mr. Villein's mind.

The following day found Mr. Villein in a state of unwellness, plagued by a
fever and chills, but he appeared again the morning after that. The Infernal
Twins enquired kindly of his health. Mr. Villein gave them a warm smile and
assured them as to his feeling much better. He was, indeed, so very hale that
he should like to give them their birthday presents (a day or so late, but no
matter) if they might be compelled to attend him after breakfast? The Twins
agreed eagerly – both *loved* presents – and midmorning found the threesome
in Mr. Villein's private study, formerly that of St. John Fitzroy, Lord Calipash.

"Children," said he, "I bequeath unto you two priceless antiques, but,
unlike most of the gifts I have given you over the years, what is for one is not
to be used by the other. Rosemary, to you I give these – a set of tortoiseshell
combs carved into the likeness of Boubastos. To Basil, this bit of ivory. Careful with it, my dearest boy. It was the instrument of your father's undoing."

Basil, surprised, took the handkerchief-swaddled object and saw it was
the carven head of a young man, crowned with a wreath of laurel leaves. As
Rosemary cooed over her gift and vowed to wear the combs in her hair every
day thereafter, Basil looked up at his tutor inquisitively.

"How – what?" he asked, too surprised to speak more intelligently.

"The idol's head was given to me by a youth of remarkable beauty whilst I
was abroad in Greece," said Mr. Villein. "I have never touched it. The young
man said that one day, I should encounter the one for whom it was truly

intended, the new earthly manifestation of the ancient god which it represents, and that I must give it to him and him alone. Given your abilities, Basil,
I believe *you* are that manifestation. I made the mistake of showing it to your
father and he coveted it from the moment he saw it – but when he touched
the effigy, I believe the god drove him mad to punish him. I have never told
you this, but your father took his own life, likely for the heinous crime of – of
besmirching that which was always intended for other, wiser hands."

Basil clutched the fetish and nodded his deep thanks, too moved by Mr.
Villein's words to notice the agitated tone in which the last sentiment was
expressed. That he was the embodiment of a deity came as little surprise to
Basil – from an early age, he had sensed he was destined for greatness – but
he found it curious that Mr. Villein should have failed to tell him this until now.

The ivory figurine occupied his thoughts all during the day. Late that same
night, after a few hours spent in his sister's chambers, during which time they
successfully collaborated on a matter of urgent business, Basil unwrapped the
icon and touched it with his fingertips. To his great frustration, nothing at all
happened, not even after he held it in his palm for a full quarter of an hour.
Bitterly disappointed, Basil went unhappily to bed, only to experience strange
dreams during the night.

He saw a city of grand marble edifices, fathoms below the surface of
the sea and immemorially ancient. He saw that it was peopled by a shining,
dolphin-headed race, whose only profession seemed to be conducting the
hierophantic rites of a radiant god. He walked unseen among those people
and touched with his hands the columns of the temple which housed the god,
carved richly with scenes of worship. A voice called to him over and over, in
the language he had known since his birth, and he walked into the interior of
the fane to see the god for himself, only to realize the face was already known
to him, for it was the exact likeness of the ivory idol! Then the eyes of the
god, though wrought of a glowing stone, seemed to turn in their sockets and
meet his gaze. With that look, Basil understood many things beyond human
comprehension that both terrified and delighted him.

The future Lord Calipash awoke the next morning bleary-eyed and stupid,
to the alarm of both his sister and mother. He was irritable and shrewish
when interrogated as to the nature of his indisposition and his condition did
not improve the following day, nor the following, for his sleep was every night
disturbed by his seeking that which called to him. He would not speak to
anybody of his troubles and, when his ill humour still persisted after a week,
Rosemary and Lady Calipash agreed on the prudence of summoning the
doctor to attend the future Lord. Basil, however, turned away the physician,
claiming that he was merely tired. Annoyed, he left to take a long walk in the
woods that comprised a large part of the Calipash estate.

Let it be noted here that it was Mr. Villein who suggested that Basil's
room be searched in his absence. There, to the family's collective horror,
a ball of opium and a pipe were discovered among Basil's personal effects.
The doctor was quite alarmed by this, for, he said, while tincture of opium is
a well-regarded remedy, smoking it in its raw state was a foul practice only
undertaken by degenerates and Orientals. So, it was decided that Basil should
be confined to his room for as long as it took to rid him of the habit. Upon the
lad's return, there was a sort of ambush, comprised of stern words from the
doctor, disappointed head-shakes from Mr. Villein, tears from Lady Calipash,
and, for Rosemary's part, anger (She was, frankly, rather hurt that he hadn't
invited her to partake of the drug). Basil insisted he had no knowledge of how
the paraphernalia came to be in his room, but no rational person would much
heed the ravings of an opium-addict. He was locked in and all his meals were
sent up to his room.

A week later, Basil was not to be found within his chambers and a note in
his own hand lay upon his unmade bed. His maid found it, but, being illiterate,
she gave it over to Lady Calipash while the lady and her daughter were just
sitting down to table. Scanning the missive brought on such a fit of histrionics
in Lady Calipash that Mr. Villein came down to see what was the matter. He
could not get any sense out of the Lady and Rosemary had quit the breakfast-
ing room before he even arrived, too private a creature to show anyone the
depth of her distress. So, Mr. Villein snatched the letter away from the wailing
Lady Calipash and read it himself. He was as alarmed by its contents as she,
for it said only that Basil had found his confinement intolerable and had left
home to seek his fortune apart from those who would keep him imprisoned.

The author has heard it said that certain birds, like the canary or the
nightingale, cannot sing without their mate and suffer a decline when isolated. Similarly, upon Basil's unexpected flight from Calipash Manor, did
Rosemary enter a period of great melancholy, where no one and nothing
could lift her spirits. She could not account for Basil's behavior – not his
moodiness, nor his failure to take her with him – and so, she believed him
angry with her for her part in his quarantine, or, worse still, indifferent to her
entirely. Seasons passed without her smiling over the misfortunes of others or
raising up a single spirit of the damned to haunt the living. So, upon the year's
anniversary of Basil's absence, Mr. Villein sat down with Lady Calipash and
made a proposal.

"My lady," he said, "Rosemary has grown to a pretty age. I believe her
state of mind would be much improved by matrimony and, God willing, motherhood. To this end, I appeal to you to allow me to marry her, whereupon I
shall endeavor to provide for her as the most doting of husbands."

Lady Calipash was at first disturbed by this request, as she had long assumed that Mr. Villein's affections were settled upon her and not her daughter. But when Mr. Villein mentioned offhandedly that, with Basil absent, he was the only known male heir to the Calipash estate, and should he marry outside the family, neither Lady Calipash nor Rosemary would have any claim to the land or money beyond their annuities, the Lady found it prudent to accept Mr. Villein's suit on Rosemary's behalf.

Mr. Villein expected, and (It must be admitted) rather ghoulishly anticipated, Rosemary's disinclination to form such an alliance, but to the surprise of all, she accepted her fate with a degree of *insouciance* that might have worried a mother less invested in her own continued state of affluence. Without a single flicker of interest, Rosemary agreed to the union, took the requisite journey into town to buy her wedding clothes, said her vows, and lay down upon the marriage bed in order that Mr. Villein could defile her body with all manner of terrible perversions, a description of which will not be found in these pages, lest it inspire others to sink to such depths. The author will only say that Rosemary found herself subjected to iterations of Mr. Villein's profane attentions every night thereafter. If any good came out of these acts of wickedness performed upon her person, it was that it roused her out of her dysthymia and inspired her to once again care about her situation.

Not unexpectedly, Rosemary's emotional rejuvenation compelled her to journey down paths more corrupt than any the Twins had yet trod. Her nightly, nightmarish trysts with Mr. Vincent had driven her slightly mad, as well as made her violently aware that not all lovers are interested in their partner's pleasure. Remembering with fondness those occasions when her brother had conjured up from the depths of her body all manner of rapturous sensations, in her deep misery, Rosemary concocted a theory drawn as much from her own experience as from the works of the ancient physician Galen of Pergamon. As she accurately recalled, Galen had claimed that male and female reproductive systems are perfect inversions of one another. Thus, she deduced, the ecstasy she felt whilst coupling with her brother was likely due to their being twins and being the mirror image of one another.

To once again achieve satisfactory companionship, Rosemary therefore resolved upon creating a companion for herself out of the remains housed in the Calipash family crypt. By means of the necromancies learned in her youth, she stitched together a pleasure-golem made of the best-preserved parts of her ancestors, thanking whatever foul gods she was accustomed to petitioning for the unusually gelid temperature of that tomb. Taking a nose that looked like Basil's from this corpse, a pair of hands from that one, and her father's genitalia, she neatly managed the feat and, dressing the creature in Basil's clothing, slipped often into that frigid darkness to lie with it. Sadly,

her newfound happiness with her ersatz brother was, for two reasons, imperfect. The first was that none of the vocal chords she could obtain were capable
of reproducing Basil's distinctively nasal snarl, and thus the *doppelgänger*
remained mute, lest an unfamiliar moan ruin Rosemary's obscene delights.
The second trouble was more pernicious: she realized too late she had been
unable to entirely excise the putrefaction wrought by death upon the limbs of
her relations. Thus, she contracted a form of gangrene that began to slowly
rot of her once-pristine limbs.

For another year did this unhappy *status quo* persist, until one dreary
afternoon when Rosemary, returning from a long walk about the grounds, noticed a disreputable, slouching individual taking in the fine prospect offered
by the approach to Calipash Manor. Unafraid, Rosemary advanced on him,
noticing the burliness of the man's figure, the darkness of his skin, and the
shabby state of his long overcoat.

"Are you in want of something?" she called to the stranger and he looked
up at her, his face shaded by a mildewing tricorn. "There is scant comfort to
be found here at Calipash Manor, but if you require anything, it will be given
to you."

"To whom do I have the pleasure of speaking?" queried he in the rasping
accent of a white Creole, all the while stealing polite glances of her slightly
moldy countenance.

"I am the daughter of the lady of this house," answered Rosemary.

"Then thank you, my lady," said the man. "My name is Valentine, and I
have only just returned from Jamaica to find my family dead and my house
occupied by those with no obligation to provide for me."

"Have you no friends?"

"None, not being the sort of man who either makes or keeps them easily."

"Come with me, then," said Rosemary, admiring his honesty. She led Valentine up to the house and settled them in her private parlour, whereupon she
bid the servants bring him meat and drink. As he ate, he seemed to revive.
Rosemary saw a nasty flicker in his eyes that she quite liked and bid him tell
her more of himself. He laughed dryly and Rosemary had his tale:

"I'm afraid, Lady, that I owe you an apology, for I know one so fine as
yourself would never let me into such a house knowing my true history. I was
born into the world nothing more than the seventh son of a drunk cottar. We
were always in want, as there was never enough work to be had for all of us. I
killed my own brother over a bite of mutton, but, given that we were all starving, the magistrate saw it fitting that I should not be hanged, but impressed to
work as a common hand aboard a naval ship bound for the West Indies. I won't
distress you by relating the conditions I endured. Suffice it to say I survived.

"When I arrived at our destination, however, I found that it was not my fate to remain in the navy, for my sea captain promptly clapped me in irons and sold me as a white slave, likely due to my being an indifferent sailor and more likely to start riots among the men than help to settle them. I was bought by a plantation owner who went by the name of Thistlewood. This man got what labour he could out of me for several years, until I managed to escape to Port Royal with only the clothes on my back and a bit of food I'd stolen. There, I lived in a manner I shan't alarm you by describing, and only say that having done one murder, it was easy to repeat the crime for hire until I had enough coin to buy passage back to England – but, as I said earlier, when I returned home, I found every living person known to me dead or gone, except those with long memories who recalled enough of my character to kick me away from their doorsteps like a dog."

Rosemary could not but be profoundly moved by such a tale and she felt her dormant heart begin to warm anew with sympathy for this stranger. She assured him that he should have some work on her estate. Valentine was so overcome that he took Rosemary's hand in his – but their mutual felicity was interrupted by Mr. Villein, who chose that inopportune moment to enter Rosemary's chambers uninvited.

"What is the meaning of this treachery?" cried Mr. Villein, for though he often engaged in infidelities, the notion that his bride might do the same did not sit well with him, being that he was a jealous man by nature. "Release my wife, foul vagabond!"

"Wife!" exclaimed Valentine, his yellowish complexion turning grey. "How is it that I return home, only to find myself betrayed by one whom I thought harboured love for me?"

It would be impossible to guess whether Rosemary or Mr. Villein was more confused by this ejaculation, but neither had time to linger in a state of wonder for very long. The man withdrew a veritable cannon of a flintlock and cast off his wretched, threadbare overcoat to reveal that beneath it, he wore a rich, emerald-green brocade vest threaded through with designs wrought in gold and silver. His breeches were of the finest satin. When he looked down his nose at them like a lord, instead of lowering his eyes like a cottar's son, they saw he had all the bearing of a gentleman of high rank. Recognizing him at last, Rosemary shrieked. Mr. Villein paled and took a step back. Though strangely altered by time, the man was unmistakably Basil Vincent, Lord Calipash, returned at last to reclaim by force what should have been his by right of birth!

IV

The conclusion, detailing the reunion of the Ivybridge Twins – an account of the singular manner in which Rosemary defeated the gangrene that threatened her continued good health – what the author hopes the reader will take away from this Infernal History.

"YOU!" CRIED MR. Villein in alarm. "How *dare* you? How *can* you? They said the navy would keep you at least a decade in the service of this country!"

"*They?*" demanded Rosemary. "Who?"

"The press gang!" blustered Mr. Villein. "For the sum I paid them, I'll have them –"

But the Infernal Twins never discovered what Mr. Villein's intentions were regarding the unsatisfactory press gang, for Rosemary, overcome with grief and rage, snatched the flintlock pistol out of Basil's grasp and shot Mr. Villein through the throat. A fountain of blood gushed forth from just above Mr. Villein's cravat-pin, soaking his waistcoat and then the carpet, as he gasped his surprise and fell down on the ground.

"Basil," she said. "Basil, I'm so – I didn't –"

"You *married* him?"

"It was all Mother's doing," said Rosemary, rather hurt by his tone.

"But –"

"You were gone," she snapped, "and lest Mr. Villein marry some common slut and turn Mother and myself out of our house ...."

Even with such reasonable excuses, it was some time before Rosemary could adequately cajole Basil out of his peevish humor. Indeed, only when Rosemary asked if Basil had lived as a monk during the years of their estrangement did he glower at her as he had used to do and embraced her. They sat companionably together then and Basil gave her a truer account of his absence from Calipash Manor:

"The carven ivory head which our loathsome former tutor bequeathed unto me on the 15th anniversary of my birth was the instrument, strangely, of both my undoing and my salvation," said Basil. "Mr. Villein lied to me that I was the manifestation of the old god which it represents – indeed, I believe now that his intention was take me away from you so that he might have you for his own; that I, like my father before me, would be driven to suicide by the whispered secrets of that divine entity. Little did he know that, while I am not some sort of fleshly incarnation of that deity, I was born with the capacity to understand His whispered will and walk along the sacred paths that were more often trod when His worship was better known to our race.

"I believe once Mr. Villein saw that I was only mildly troubled by these new visions, he concocted a plot to be rid of me in a less arcane manner. The night before you discovered my absence, he let himself into my chambers and put a spell upon me while I slept that made me subject to his diabolical will. I awoke a prisoner of his desire, and he bade me rise and do as he wished. Dearest sister, I tell you now that you did not detect a forgery in my note, for it was written by none other than myself. After I had penned the false missive, Mr. Villein bade me follow him down to Ivybridge, whereupon he put a pint of ale before me and compelled me, via his fell hold upon me, to act in the manner of a drunken commoner, brawling with the local boys until the constable was called and I was thrown in jail. Not recognizing me, due to my long isolation, my sentence was as I told you – that of forced conscription into the navy.

"To a certain point, my tale as I told it to you whilst in the character of the scoundrel Valentine was true – I suffered much on my voyage to Jamaica and was subsequently sold as a slave. What I did not tell you was the astonishing manner of my escape from that abominable plantation. My master hated me, likely because he instinctively sensed his inferiority to my person. My manners mark me as a noble individual, even when clad in rags, and being that he was a low sort who was considered a gentleman due to his profession rather than his birth, my master gave to me the most dangerous and disgusting tasks. One of his favourite degradations was to station me at the small dock where the little coracles were tied up, so that I could be given the catches of fish to clean them, constantly subjected to wasp stings and cuts and other indignities of that sort.

"Yet, it was this task that liberated me, for one afternoon, I arrived at the dock to see the fishermen in a tizzy, as one had the good fortune of catching a dolphin. The creature was still alive, incredibly, and I heard its voice in my mind as clearly as I heard their celebration. *Save me and I shall save you*, it said unto me in that language that has always marked me as bacchant to the god of which I earlier spoke. I picked up a large stick to use as a cudgel and beat the fisherfolk away from their catch, telling them to get back to work, as the cetacean was of no use to our master. He should want snapper or jackfish for his dinner rather than oily porpoise flesh. They heeded me, for they were a little afraid of me – often, as you might imagine, dear sister, bad things would happen to those who chose to cross me in some way – and I heaved the dolphin back into the sea. At first, I thought it swam away and that it had merely been sun-madness that had earlier made me hear its voice, but then, after the fishermen had paddled out of sight, the dolphin surfaced with a bulging leather satchel clutched in its beak. It contained gold and jewels that my new friend told me were gathered from shipwrecks on the ocean floor, and that I should use this wealth to outfit myself as a gentleman and buy passage back to England. The creature's only caveat was that, upon my arrival, I must once again visit the sea and return to one of its kin the ivory head, as our tutor had not, as it turns out, been given the object. Rather, it seems that Mr. Villein defiled an ancient holy place near Delphi during his travels in Greece by stealing the artifact away from its proper alcove.

"I agreed to these terms and, after waiting at the docks for a little longer so I might poison the fish it was my duty to clean, and thus enact a paltry revenge upon my tyrannical master, hastened back to Devonshire. I knew nothing of your situation, but feared much. Upon returning home, I assumed the persona of Valentine as a way of ascertaining if, in my absence, your sentiments had changed toward your long-absent brother and the manner in which we were accustomed to living with one another. Seeing your heart go out to such a picaroon assured me of your constancy and I regret very much that I earlier so impugned your honour. But sister, now that you know of my distresses, you must tell me of yours – pray, how did you come to be married to Mr. Villein and so afflicted by the disease that I see nibbles away at your perfect flesh?"

Rosemary then recounted what has already been recorded here, and she and Basil resolved upon a course of action that shall comprise the *denouement* of this chronicle. Both were determined that the gangrenous affliction should not claim Rosemary, but until Lady Calipash, wondering why her daughter did not come down to dinner, intruded into the parlour where the siblings colluded, they could not see how. The idea occurred to the Twins when Lady Calipash's alarm at seeing Mr. Villein's corpse upon the carpet was so tremendous that she began to scream. Basil, fearing they should be overheard and the murder discovered before they had concocted an adequate reason for his unfortunate death, caught Lady Calipash by the neck when she would not calm herself. As he wrapped his fingers about her throat, Basil noticed the softness of his mother's skin, and, looking deeply into her fearful eyes, saw that she was still a handsome creature of not five-and-thirty.

"Sister," he began, but Rosemary had already anticipated his mind and agreed that she should immediately switch her consciousness with Lady Calipash's by means of witchcraft she and Basil had long ago learned (and occasionally utilized in their youthful lovemaking) from the donkey-headed eel-creature they had conjured, and henceforth inhabit her own mother's skin. This was done directly. After securely locking Rosemary's former body (now occupied by their terrified mother) into the family crypt, along with Mr. Villein's corpse, mother and prodigal son, rather than brother and sister, had the carriage made ready and they drove to the head of the River Plym, whereupon Basil summoned one of the aquatic priests of his god and handed over the relic that has figured so prominently in their narrative.

To conclude, the author hopes that readers of this History will find this account entirely mortifying and disgusting, and seek to avoid modeling any part of his or her behaviour upon that of the Infernal Ivybridge Twins – though, to be fair, it must be recorded that, for all the duration of their cacodemoniacal lives, the Twins preserved the tenderest affection for each other. Still, there has never been found anywhere in the world a less-worthy man or woman than they and, until the moonless night when the Twins decided to join the ranks of the cetaceous worshipers of their unholy deity – Lord Calipash being called thence, his sister long-missing her former amphibious wanderings – there was not a neighbour, a tenant, or a servant who did not rue the day they came into the company of Basil and Rosemary.

Molly Tanzer is the managing editor of *Lightspeed* and *Fantasy Magazine*. Her fiction has been published in *Running with the Pack*, *Crossed Genres*, and *Palimpsest*. The account of her adventures going minigolfing with zombie polka band The Widow's Bane appeared in the September 2010 issue of *Strange Horizons*. Please visit her any time at her website, http://mollytanzer.com

The author speaks: I wish I had a better story about how I came to write "The Infernal History of the Ivybridge Twins", but basically, I was watching *Barry Lyndon* and thought to myself, "I would really like to write a picaresque but about incestuous twin necromancers." Later that evening, I got out my copy of *Tom Jones* to peruse for a bit for inspiration and right there on the first page, there's this line: "The Tortoise ... besides the delicious *Calipash* and *Calipee*, contains many different kinds of Food ...." The explanatory note told me that *calipash* was "[A] gelatinous, greenish substance lying beneath the upper shell of a turtle" and it seemed an appropriately disgusting family name, with nice, aquatic resonance for the Lovecraftian element I knew I wanted to incorporate. I desired the story to have a similar feel to many of the 18th century novels I studied while getting my Master's degree; setting the action in that time period led me to think of Neoclassicism, which led me to consider the bizarre, Apollonian elements of "The Temple", and somehow, in the end, all that randomness became "The Infernal History of the Ivybridge Twins". Let this serve as a cautionary tale to all considering a degree in the Humanities ....

BLACK LEAVES

MASON IAN BUNDSCHUH

I N 1838, LARS Levi Læstadius went among the Sami to record the legends
and myths of the last indigenous people of northern Europe. Their memory stretched back five thousand years, into a time when science was not the
god of the age; when what was in the darkness of night and in the mists of
the deep forests was not tame or mindless Nature; when things walked that
now are called 'superstitions'.

In his travels, Læstadius teased out from the secretive Sami all that he
could and, when he returned, fevered and hollowed out, like a man who had
been stranded alone on a ship adrift, he presented his findings as a series
of treaties. But cold logic and the scientific method were already solving all
mysteries; what use had anyone for the mad ramblings of savages? Those
who had commissioned it quietly hid his manuscript.

Over the next 159 years, a piece was lost here, or sold to a private collector there, until in 1997, the last remaining known portions were published.
But it did not contain all that Læstadius recorded during his cold years in the
land of the Sami.

*These words come from the darkness carried by the reciting of the elders and
were taught to me by Etuva, who heard it from Pathu Sharp-Nose.*

WE WERE ON the hunt, swift and silent through the trees, our prey quickly
losing ground. But it escaped us in a gorge where no escape should be
found. Our spears came up empty. Beyond the brambles where it disappeared, there was a dark passageway in the mountain where a hidden spring
had carved a tunnel deep through the stone.

Into it we went, sharpened ash before us, moss-wet rocks on either side.
We followed a winding path so narrow even the women among us could not
walk abreast. Long we walked; the light waned and grew dim. When the sun
had almost been forgotten, we came out once again into the daylight. This
was a great joy.

We stood in a vast bowl surrounded by unbroken cliffs footed by tumbled scree, our way hard in the loose stone. In the center grew a great forest, old and strong. We marked our passageway with a cairn and put red blood-palms to the capstone to seal it.

Into the mirk we went, our hearts were filled with curiosity and daring. This place was surely a place of power, a place to find one's destiny. We came at length to the center of the forest, as best we could tell. It was a clearing on a low hill, empty and barren but for eight dead trees standing in the dusty center – a circle of ancient grey wood twisted into gruesome shapes. None of us would touch these trees, for each had the feel of a tortured thing.

The day had grown long. Not one of us wished to be close to this profane ground at nightfall. We went back into the forest and grew excited at the sudden smell of cook-smoke. Ash-needles at the ready, we advanced through the woods, winding closer to the smoke of man. We came to a small clearing, in the midst of which stood a rundown cabin of strange angles. It had many doors, but few windows, and seemed mostly to be made of corridors. Not a soul we found. The house was still and empty. But the fading smell of a cook fire would not leave us, so we made camp.

There was a dread in the air that increased with the darkening dusk. Even we would not risk a night outside under the strange trees. Into the house that was not a house we moved. Choosing a room where we could build a fire and guard the door, we dared to sleep with only a single watch.

In the morning, we saw that we had not been left alone. Our man Pitu was dead in the doorway. Teeth had been laid into him. Of the red water that is life to men, there was none left. His axe was in his hand; a strange muddy ichor smeared it. We knew it would mean death to stay in that valley any longer. Its curse lay over us like a shadow on our hearts.

Back through the forest we rushed to find the cairn that marked our way, but of the marked pile there was no trace. We circled the steep cliffs of the valley, looking for our narrow entrance, but the wall was unbroken, the cairn gone.

Our empty stomachs forced us to cut into the forest for game. Birds and deer were plentiful. Passing through the forest, we came across several more ruins. Some were mere stone jumbles with long-rotted timber. It was not long before we found ourselves back in the clearing at the center of the forest. Though none of us knew we'd gone so far into the woods. We had been brought back to this place against our will.

The stunted trees still stood in the clearing, though in the lowering sunlight there seemed a ghastly tinge to their limbs. There were now wilted, dark, leaves creeping from the repulsive branches. On one branch, a fresh axe-cut gleamed pale against the grey bark.

The sun was in its last watch and we knew that we had to flee. Into the silent woods we rushed, to circle the towering stone wall and find our way home. But we grew disoriented – I know not how. We could not find the edge of the forest and night was now upon us. Whatever thing hunted in this place, it had surely set its face against us. We made a ring of fire, the center well-stocked with tinder. We would make our stand and shake our spears at whatever appeared.

The night came on us with terror. The woods were not empty; we were not alone. Dark shapes passed under the eaves beyond the firelight. May we all face death in battle instead of the cold, stalking dread that we faced that night.

No star flew in the sky, no moon, or even the silvery outlines of the edges of clouds. All was rustling, restless dark. We kept the fire high, but knew its protection was as thin as stalks of dried grass. If we made it through this night, we'd not last another.

Then the singing started, cold and cruel – as if it were the maddening moon herself given voice. No words we could understand, but the song struck us dumb. We all felt the pull, the call of the empty hunger from beyond the fire. Each of us fought to stay within the protecting circle of flames. Our woman Ela yielded. Out of the ring of her clan she passed, though we called and shouted after her. Her eyes were already dead. The singing stopped. Now we heard only a slow, wet rattling and then nothing. The silence was worse.

Morning came and we still stood at our dwindling fires, spears still raised, though our hearts were grim. The sun could not warm us. Once again, we headed to the circling cliffs, searching for our cairn and the way out. But the stone wall remained unbroken. The trap was set and closed.

Sleep could not be kept from us any longer if we were to survive another night. Our man Melethu took the watch and we laid down our heads.

To us came troubled dreams – an image of a little girl who sat on a stool against the heavy doorway of a dirty hut. She sang softly at the night beyond. The night wanted to get in, but the girl sang so that it could not pass. The girl turned to us, stared at us and pointed towards the door. Her mouth opened, but only song came out. Eventually, she took a breath and said in a strange tongue, "They want blood and warmth, for they have none of their own." The sulking silence of the hungry night beyond the door erupted in a noise too terrible to describe. Hurriedly, the girl began singing again, but it was too late.

We were now awake and the terrible noises had not stopped; nor was it still the hours of the day. The darkness of dusk had long since filled the whole sky.

Our man Melethu was beyond raising alarm. Our woman Hma rushed towards the knot of rags that had been Melethu, spear down. But to us it appeared that long limbs reached down from the very trees above and snatched her from our sight. Only her bodiless screams drifted down over us.

Madness came over us as dark shapes rushed among us. Our spears struck blindly. It was only the accidental stumbling into the near-dead fire by our woman Hallaf that spared us. Sparks and light flared over the scene of blood and carnage, there was a rush, and we were once again alone. There were only the two of us now: man and woman, as it was in the beginning. But Hallaf was wounded direly.

Piling wood and brush high on the fire, we sang songs over the dead then waited grimly for the dawn, back to back. Death was impatient to devour us. We would hold off for several hours more. The sun finally rose in the East, filling the bowl of the valley with sanity again. We were but two, but we were two of the battle clan. We would seek out death for a fight.

Pushing into the underbrush, we headed deeper into the woods. Finally we came to that accursed clearing where stood the ancient withered trees. Full terrible they drank from the fresh-dug earth; dark-red sap oozed from gouges in their grey trunks, gouges made by spears. Crows perched on the wormy branches. Their wilted leaves trembled in the midmorning light. We had no doubt of what lay buried at the feet of these terrible trees.

Apart from the cries of battle and shouts of war, none of us had spoken for days. None of us had dared to break the silence of the hunt. But now, the horror of this place washed over us: we were no longer on the hunt; we were the hunted.

Our woman Hallaf, the last besides the teller of this tale, lifted her spear to the gnarled wood of the cursed tree. The vile boughs skittered as though a bitter wind blew through them. A memory of a dream brought forth words of dread: "They want blood and warmth, for they have none of their own."

We took our hand-axes from our belts.

The sap ran thick and red from wounds, as blade bit into wood. We raised our hands swiftly, hewing the rotting trunks unceasingly. The branches shuddered; the crows screamed as with the voices of the damned, but still, our iron bit deep into the splintering flesh. One by one, we toppled the awful trees. The stench of gore rose over the stony clearing.

Our work was not done.

Stacking the stinking wood over the bleeding stumps, we piled the pyre high, that not even the roots would escape the fire. Every fallen branch on the edge of the ring of trees, every swath of dry grass, was added to the heap till the sun was well past its zenith. With flint and iron, we made a spark. With breath and tinder, it turned to a flame. With stacks of wood, it burned in a blaze. The bubbling limbs hissed and steamed – a thousand voices of pain. Fire licked at the devil's bark, blackened the vile branches.

Our grim task done, we stumbled back through the cool woods away from the carnage of that cursed grove. Our stiffening wounds slowed us. Breaking through the outer trees, we faced the tall, circling wall of stone. Here, our woman Hallaf could go no further. Her wounds were very great. She died there in the sunlight of the stony slope, out from under the deceiving shade of that place. Falling softly, without a word, she died.

Now there is no more we; there is only I. The last left of those who passed into this valley. I am now alone.

It was almost evening when I found the passage in the stone. We had passed this place several times. Each time, it had been hidden from us. I did not dare stay in that place one more night. I would rather pass through the narrow tunnel in darkness than see the cold stars from within the valley again.

I alone left that grove. I alone returned. We were broken apart there and I shall never go back, even to bury Hallaf, whom I loved.

Novelist and short-story writer Mason Ian Bundschuh was raised in Hawaii, educated in England and dwells in Las Vegas, where he occupies his time messing with helicopters, reading Old English and rocking with his band Atlas Takes Aim. He also jams a mean ukulele and surfs ... but not in Las Vegas. You can find him at www.MasonBundschuh.com

The author speaks: The Sami were the last hunter and gatherers of Europe, an archaic anomaly left over from the Ice Age; but very little is known of them, and their primitive mythology and religion. I'd been reading the *Kalevala* (which were Finnish oral traditions collected in the 19th century) and was intrigued by the description of the Sami as an alien, mysterious and somewhat fantastical race who worked strange rites in the inhospitable wilderness of the north. One man had gone among the Sami to preserve their secrets – that part of my tale is true, as is the strange fact that his manuscript was suppressed and then lost. My imagination took over when I asked myself what the Sami may have known that was so horrible that scientific and enlightened men would hide it from the world.

THE SECOND THEFT OF ALHAZRED'S MANUSCRIPT

BRADLEY H. SINOR

"WATSON, WOULD IT surprise you to know that there is an organization that once rejected me for membership, but also has declined my offers of assistance on no less than two other occasions?"

I looked up at my friend, Sherlock Holmes, who had been standing silently at the window of our Baker Street quarters for nearly a quarter-hour. It was now two months since he had "returned to life," as the tabloid London newspapers had proclaimed it.

"Are you perhaps referring to the Diogenes Club?" I asked, as I set down the copy of the *Times* that I had been reading. Holmes had mentioned, a few months after I first learned of his brother, Mycroft, and the queerest club in London, that he had chosen not to seek membership in the organization.

"I would not want to give Mycroft the pleasure of blackballing his own brother," he had told me. "No, the group I am referring to is far less well-known than the Diogenes Club and, in fact, has no name."

I must admit that I was puzzled, given that beyond its membership, there were few people who knew of the Diogenes Club and certainly fewer that knew of its connections with the British government.

Since Holmes was not one to dwell overmuch on the past, save where it concerned information he needed in order to deal with one of his cases, there had to be another reason for his bringing up this subject. That was when I heard the familiar squeaking on the stairway, which meant that someone was approaching our door.

"So, why would someone from that group be coming now to call on you, Holmes?" I asked.

"Watson!" Holmes laughed. "You amaze me. I go away for three years and then I find that you have taken over the mantle of the consulting detective. I suppose now I will find myself taking up my pen to chronicle your cases."

I would be lying if I said that this sudden praise did not inflate my ego more than a little bit. "I take it my little deduction was correct?" I said, trying to inject a note of commonplaceness into my voice.

"Indeed, I saw the man in question getting out of a hansom cab not three minutes ago. He and his companion seemed quite agitated," Holmes said.

As if on cue, there was a knocking on the door and the page boy stepped into the room.

"Two gentlemen to see you, sir." He held out a tray with the visitors' card on it.

Holmes walked across the room and picked up his clay pipe from its place on the mantel. After examining the tobacco in it, he plucked a thin ember from the fire place and lit the bowl.

"You may show them in," he said.

One of our visitors was an exceptionally plain-looking man, the sort whose face you might forget a few seconds after he walked away from you, while the other was a big fellow reaching up to six foot three or four inches, if not more.

"Good evening, Mr. Holmes. I 'm sure you are quite surprised that we have crossed your threshold on this day." The first stranger removed his silk top hat. He lifted the ebony walking stick and held it under his arm.

"Your presence is not surprising."

"Is that your ego speaking?" From their words and Holmes' earlier statement, I felt there was obviously history between them.

"Ego? Hardly! If you think that, then you do not truly understand either me or my methods." Holmes gestured toward his chair, where a pile of clippings from the last several days' newspapers lay. "I have eyes, sir, and a mind. When I see that there have been three robberies in the past two weeks, all unsolved, two of them the homes of men I know to be members of your organization and at one at the office of your brother-in-law, I know that something is afoot regarding your group."

"I see that your powers of observation are as sharp as they ever were, in spite of, or perhaps because of, your recent 'extended holiday'," the plain-faced man said.

The words were obviously intended to injure Holmes' ego, but the man did not know my friend, or he would have understood that he was wasting his breath.

"Oh, where are my manners?" said Holmes, making a point of ignoring our visitor's last words. "My 'extended holiday', as it has just been called, has atrophied my manners. Watson, allow me to introduce you to Sir James Marsden, Baronet, who also is the leader of the organization that I mentioned to you earlier."

"It's a pleasure, Sir James," I said. The man had a firm, dry handshake, but it his eyes struck me the most. They were hard, dark and distant, reminding me of some of our men who had ventured into the tribal areas of the mountains and seen things that had ripped into their souls.

"The pleasure is mine, Doctor. I read of the passing of your wife some months ago. My condolences," he said, nodding toward the other man, who nodded but said nothing. "My companion and bodyguard, Davis St. John."

Mention of Mary brought a feeling of sadness to the pit of my stomach. It was a feeling that I embraced, but had learned to put aside, with memories of our all-too-brief happiness together.

"So, Sir James, the facts, if you will," Holmes said casually.

Sir James sank into the plush chair at the far corner of the fireplace. "It has been stolen," he said.

"What has been stolen?" Holmes voice was even and unemotional, though I suspect it had the exact sound he wanted.

"The manuscript, as you predicted so many years ago that it would be, although we had taken every step within our power to prevent this. I will say that there have been at least a dozen attempts over the years and this is the only one that has succeeded," said our visitor.

"It matters not how many, just that there was one who managed to pull it off. I warned you years ago that it perhaps would have been better had the thing been burned and the ashes scattered to the four winds," said Holmes. I had never heard such vehemence in my friend's voice.

"You may have been right in your idea. I admit that, now," said Sir James.

"When did this happen?" asked Holmes.

"As best we can tell, some four days ago. The vault that it was being kept in is only opened when something is being added to its contents," said Sir James. "We had come into possession of some small, star-shaped stones that could be used to command certain situations." Our visitor glanced over at me, as if weighing what – and how much – to say.

"Please continue, Sir James. Simply be aware that anything you can tell me, you can tell Dr. Watson, and know that if you insist on his not being present, I will terminate this interview at once," said Holmes.

"Of course," Sir James said. "Watson's trustworthiness is well known."

Holmes began to pace slowly across the room, puffing on his pipe as he went. It was as if the three years of his absence had melted away. I could tell he was mulling over possibilities.

"Then you will accept the case?" asked Sir James.

"No, because I suspect that you will find it is one of your own who has 'liberated' the manuscript, a book collector who decided that it would make a fine addition to his personal collection," said Holmes, looking toward me.

"You will find, Watson, that the Machiavellian doings of some bibliophiles almost put them on a level with the late Professor Moriarty. I believe that this was the tale that you spun me when you asked me to get involved in the first matter."

I had to admit that Holmes was right. In my life, I have known several bibliophiles who were, to say the least, willing to go to any extent to add a lusted-after first edition, or a rare volume, to their collection.

"You seem to forget the events of ten years ago. You saw what happened." Sir James' voice had grown louder to emphasize his words.

"I saw a number of things; many of them had explanations that could be traced back to hysteria, rather than reality," said Holmes. That last remark was enough to cause the Baronet to leap to his feet and be out of our door in less than a minute, his companion close behind him.

I turned toward my friend and said, "Holmes, you were a bit ru...." However, I did not get to finish the sentence. Holmes had doffed his dressing gown and was grabbing his coat from the rack. His attitude had turned from that of disdain to one of intensity.

"Quick, Watson, the window. Make sure you are not seen."

I didn't understand, but knew that Holmes had reasons, good reasons. From the edge of the window, I could see Sir James and his companion standing on the edge of the street.

"He's hailing a hansom, from down the street."

"That would be Bisang. He always hangs about there when he is waiting for a fare. That gives us just the time we need. Bring your revolver; this may be a nasty business."

Since I had only just cleaned my pistol, not out of need from having fired it recently, but simply out of habit in caring for one's weapon, I had no trouble in laying my hands on it.

Holmes was already standing at the street door, which he had opened just a crack. He motioned me to wait as I came down the stairs.

A moment later, we were out the door. A tall, thin boy, one of Holmes' band of street Arabs, appeared at our side. "Anything I can do, Mr. Holmes?"

"Indeed, Wiggins, your timing is excellent. Get yourself and several of the others after that cab that just pulled out," Holmes said.

"The one with the green stripe? I can follow that one on me own.".

"Nevertheless, take help. Waverly is always good. I want to know where the men in the cab go and then, wherever that is, watched."

The young fellow nodded and then vanished into the crowd.

"We have much to do and, I suspect, not all that much time to do it in," said Holmes, as he waved another cab to us, to which he gave an address that I did not recognize.

Once we were *en route*, my friend did not say anything for nearly ten minutes. I had seen him in this mood before, so I waited. There were times when he could be forthcoming with answers; there were times when getting the slightest information from him would be like pulling teeth.

"I imagine you are somewhat confused," he said finally.

"It's obvious that you are not turning your back on this case, in spite of what you told Sir James," I said.

"You yourself have noted in your rather florid chronicles of my cases that there have been a number of matters for which the world is not yet ready. This would qualify as one of those," he said. "It happened some six months before young Stamford brought you to the laboratory at Bart's. The organisation that Sir James represents claims to have been in existence for centuries, protecting the world from things of a dark and possibly supernatural nature. Of course, I did not know it at the time. He approached me through young Musgrave; apparently, he was a friend of the family, wanting my assistance in finding a book that had been stolen.

"The book in question was actually only a portion of an Arabic manuscript called the *Al-Azif*, dated from around 730 A.D. It was written by a man who used the name 'Abdul Alhazred'. Since that is not an Arabic name, I suspect it was a *nom de plume*. It purports to be a spell book and history of ancient gods called 'The Great Old Ones', who seem intent on taking command of this world."

"'Ancient gods'?" I hoped that Holmes could hear the tone of sneering in my voice. This hardly seemed the domain of my friend. I must confess that some part of me wondered if it was all part of some elaborate practical joke on Holmes' part. But that would be so unlike him that I ruled that possibility out at once.

"'Gods', hardly. I did not rule out the possibility that the author and many of those who read his work were completely insane. I do not believe in ghosts, vampires or such creatures as that. Everything can be explained rationally and within the realm of logical thought."

"Sir James said you had seen things," I continued.

"Indeed, the recovery of the manuscript brought me into an occult under-world that was bloody and without mercy, and that stretches from even the lowliest East End hovel to the highest drawing rooms in the land. I suspect that even the late Professor Moriarty would have found himself repulsed by it. I did see things that, quite honestly, I could not explain, but I am certain, even to this day, that there are valid scientific explanations for them. I told that to the members of Sir James' organization when I applied for member-ship. It was one of the reasons, I suspect, that they blackballed me. They claimed it was because that their 'psychic' members had foreseen my rise to fame and I would bring too much notice to their little group. I crossed paths with them, on two additional occasions during cases, and both times they refused my assistance."

I chuckled. I did not believe in any of the spiritualist occult nonsense and had been in many an argument with Doyle over the matter, but at least in this one case, these so-called psychics had been right: if anything, he was more famous now since he had "returned from the dead".

"The problem, Watson, is that, regardless of what you or I might believe, there are people who think that possession of that manuscript might give them power beyond belief and are not adverse to harming a great number of people in the process. That is why it is imperative that it be retrieved from whatever hands that those pages have fallen into. If they are the same ones with whom I crossed swords a dozen years ago, this is not a matter that I can ignore."

"But you told Sir James that this was not a matter of any consequence." I paused for a moment. "Are you being a bit petty over that blackballing they gave you?"

"Say simply that I don't completely trust Sir James and his compatriots. Just as there are people who would do anything, including murder, for power, there are also those who would protect us from them that can be tempted to the dark side." I could have sworn I saw a slight smile pass over Holmes' face as he added, "Besides, when have you ever known me to be petty?"

A HALF-HOUR LATER, Holmes and I found ourselves standing in front of a large grey building with dozens of people moving in and out. Several were loading boxes onto a wagon; it looked as if one of them had a large animal skull under one arm.

"And this place is...?" I asked.

"One of the most unique and unknown places in all of London. It is one of a number of additional storage areas operated by the British Museum," said Holmes. "I stumbled on the place many years ago, and, thanks to the kindness of several of the directors of the Museum, have been permitted to visit here on occasion."

Given the size of the British Museum, I could well understand that they would have far more in their collection than could either be displayed or stored at their main building. I had a sudden vision of unending streams of items marching from the four corners of the empire to find their new homes in the British Museum.

It was obvious Holmes had been to the place a number of times; he wound his way through the maze of shelves and stacked boxes with ease. Everywhere I looked, I could see Greek statues, South African masks and black stone monoliths inscribed in some unknown tongue, standing next to each other.

"Ah, here we are," said Holmes. He gestured at a door that stood flanked by a strange black statue of an octopus-headed creature and a pure-white polar bear, which reared up to its full height. It was one of those places that, if you didn't know it was there, ninety-nine times out of a hundred, you would never notice it.

"This is the domain of Professor Richard Chadbourn Sanderson, perhaps one of the foremost experts in the world on the folkloric roots of civilization as we know it," said Holmes. "But this is most unusual...."

"How so?"

"He generally keeps his door bolted." As we stepped into the room, I noticed the heavy-duty lock below the door handle, as well as several others along the door's frame. The workroom on the other side was only about ten feet long and half that wide, but it was crowded with an eclectic collection of items so that it felt more like a closet.

"I gather he likes his privacy."

"More that he dislikes people. Were he more outgoing, I would have said he might be an ideal candidate for the Diogenes Club."

With that introduction, I expected to find an aged, stooped little man with white hair and inch-thick spectacles. That was definitely not what Professor Sanderson turned out to be. He was six feet tall, with blonde hair, an eye patch and a scar that ran half the length of his face, definitely not your typical academic and definitely not what I expected to see. Of course, I had not expected to find him very dead, impaled on a spear. I knew before I reached the body that the man was dead, but checked for a pulse, anyway.

"He's gone, Holmes," I said. Since rigor was not fully set in the body, that meant that he had been killed just over three to four hours ago. The large amount of blood that had dried on the floor indicated that the body had not been moved since the attack.

Holmes knelt next to me to examine the spear with his small magnifying glass. The weapon was a good five feet long and at least two inches thick.

"There was something freshly painted on the shaft," said Holmes. Looking over his shoulder, I could see nothing but the streaks of blood and bits of flesh that were clinging to the carved surface of the weapon. "Additionally, this weapon should not be here."

"I'm sure Sanderson would agree with you on that point," I said.

"Of that I have no doubt, but what I was referring to was the fact that this is a South American spear, from a tribe along the upper Amazon. This warehouse is devoted to Africa and eastern Europe; South American artifacts are kept at another location. So, whoever the killer was brought this weapon with him." Not that anyone would have thought it odd to bring a spear into the British Museum; people were no doubt highly used to seeing odd items coming and going and would have made no comment at all.

Holmes turned his attention to the area around the corpse. In the chaos, I had to wonder how he would discern any evidence of the killer. Although I suspected that, had Sanderson been alive, he would have been able to immediately lay his hands on any required material. I had to admit that at times, my study had been like that and Mary had frequently remonstrated with me, with that gentle stare of hers. I would have given anything right then to hear that disapproving sigh of hers even one more time.

Holmes worked his way from one end of the room to the other, picking up one item here and another there, plucking at something with a pair of tweezers he took from a table and staring intently through his magnifying glass at other things.

"It is not often that we have been the first on the scene at a crime, Watson. Were it not an old acquaintance now lying dead, I would say it was a most refreshing and enjoyable experience. I have seen all I need to and now know that the killer was a big man who moved with an economy of skill. He was acquainted with Sanderson and did not find what he was looking for."

"Should I bother to ask how you know all this?"

"You know my methods, Watson. Given what I have said, what would you say I have seen?"

I pursed my lips for a moment. "Given the man's preference for solitude that you described, unless there is a back door, I would say that the Professor let the person in the door."

"Excellent, Watson. There is a side door to the room, but it is still locked, and from the inside. Go on," said Holmes with a smile.

I scanned the room again, trying to see the most minute detail, but everything seemed to be drowned in the overabundance of things in the area. I shrugged my shoulders and admitted defeat.

"Worry not, old friend. The clues are there It is just a matter of knowing what you are observing. In some cases, however, it is not what is there, but what is not there. That spear is big and heavy; it would take a large man to have the strength to drive it through another man. That, along with a half-footprint in the blood, gives us his size. That there is not a large number of broken items in the area indicates that our killer could move with some dexterity."

"And the fact that he did not obtain what he was looking for?" I asked.

At that point, Holmes dramatically picked up a leather portfolio that I had noticed him looking at earlier. "Because I have it," he said, passing his prize over to me. "After dealing with Sir Charles the first time, I discovered that the

Professor had apparently acquired a page of the manuscript. I spoke with him about it several times, but got no satisfactory answers."

There were several designs drawn on the page and line after line of cramped Arabic writing. I touched the paper and it felt odd to my finger, like something I did not want in close proximity to me. "This was worth killing over?"

"There are those who would swear on their immortal souls that it is," said Holmes.

WE LEFT QUICKLY, using the side door, and were away from the building in only a matter of minutes. Holmes knew the maze-like passages like the back of his hand, a fact that, given this was Sherlock Holmes, did not surprise me in the slightest.

"But shouldn't we notify the police?" I said.

"Under normal circumstances I would not have hesitated in doing just that, but these are not normal circumstances. While much was smeared, I could make out several symbols that had been painted on the shaft of the spear, similar to ones I glimpsed in the *Necronomicon*."

"*Necronomicon*?" I said.

"My apologies, Watson. That is the English title for the *Al-Azif*."

The two of us walked quickly along the street in front of the Museum warehouse, each one watching and listening for some sign that the murder had been discovered. I would have preferred to be in a cab racing away from the area, but the very act of walking helped dispel any nervousness that the last few minutes had caused.

Yet, as we walked, I could not shake the feeling that we were being followed. It was more a feeling in the pit of my stomach, rather than anything else, but it was the same that I had had on more than one occasion during my days in Afghanistan. I tried to casually look over my shoulder, catch reflections in windows, but there was nothing, or else, it was that I did not recognize whoever it was that was following us.

"Holmes ...."

"Yes, we are being followed, Watson, by two small men in sailor's jackets, with caps pulled down low on their faces. They have been dogging our trail since we left the warehouse."

"Police?"

Holmes chuckled, "The Metropolitan Police may at times scrape the bottom of the barrel when it comes to recruiting, but these fellows are far below that level."

We were several blocks from the warehouse and the evening had spread quickly, especially since what gas lights there were in this area that were not broken had yet to feel the lamplighter's touch. What businesses we passed had been locked up and shuttered, or had been long since abandoned by their owners.

"We are just a few blocks from a pub called 'The Long John'. I propose we stop in there and see if our companions are willing to come into the light," Holmes said.

"What is to prevent them from simply lingering outside until we leave?" I said.

"Let them ," Holmes said. "There is a smugglers' tunnel in the back that we will make use of."

However, they say that even the best laid plans go astray, which applied on occasion to even the ones that were developed by Holmes. The two of us had turned into an alley that would lead to the pub on the next street, our earlier companions hanging back half a block, when three other figures appeared out of the shadows and came at us. One, a big man, had a crooked-looking knife in his hand, while the other two were unarmed. All of them were wrapped in ragged coats, with mufflers and hats masking their faces.

Holmes charged toward one of them, grabbing his left arm and throwing the man to the ground in a single swift movement. He followed it with two swift kicks to the fellow's torso. I had my revolver out and drove the butt hard against the second one's skull, the sound being enough to know that I had done some damage. He tottered for a moment and went over onto the cobblestones of the street.

The third one, the big man who had the knife, had held back, but now he moved toward us, brandishing the weapon and jabbing it into the air. Holmes stared at him, matching his movements to the other man. The dance between them went on for several seconds before Holmes acted. He feinted in one direction then whirled around and launched a drop-kick that impacted hard in the center of the man's chest; a quick two-handed smash put his attacker unmoving on the ground.

"Was that last an example of Baritsu?" I asked. That Japanese style of wrestling had, according to Holmes, saved his life at the Reichenbach Falls.

"Hardly. Merely something I picked up," said Holmes.

I looked back along the street, but our other pursuers were nowhere to be seen. If they were allied with these men, then they had presumably retreated when they saw their comrades go down, no doubt now *en route* to report on the outcome of the battle.

My opponent had not moved from where he had gone down and I could not at first be certain that he was even breathing. When I touched his wrist to check for a pulse, the skin under my fingers felt slimy, almost like that of a fish. I pulled the scarf and hat away from his face and found myself staring at something I was hard-pressed to be sure was not an hallucination. The face of this, I hesitate to even call him a 'man', looked like some cruel cross between a human and a fish. On the side of the neck were what might even be gills. I have seen strange things in my life, in places that ranged from the battlefields to the darker places that my career with Holmes had taken me, but this ranked as the strangest.

"Holmes, this is not right," I said, in a voice that sounded strained to my ear.

"How so, Doctor?" he said coming to my side. His face was impassive, even in the darkness, as he studied the being.

"Given what I found, this does not bode well," he said, and gestured toward the other man. Holmes had stripped him of his facial coverings and I knew at whom I was looking. It was Davis St. John, Sir Charles' companion of this morning.

"IT ALL MAKES sense," was all that Holmes would say, *en route* back to Baker Street. I had long ago learned that asking for details from him, until that moment when he was ready, was a waste of time. The most I could expect would be vague words and half-muttered statements, which were exactly what I seemed to be getting. So, as we drove, I satisfied myself with lighting my pipe and watching the city roll by.

The cab had barely pulled to a halt in front of our quarters before Wiggins' lanky figure had appeared out of the shadows and leaped up onto the cab, clinging to the edge by his long thin fingers."We have him, Mr. Holmes!" said the young Irregular. "It's a house, eight blocks from Condign Square," he said, spouting out the address so quickly it sounded like a single word.

"Good man, Wiggins. Get in!" The youth clamored inside, without bothering to open the door, squeezing in between the two of us. Since our cab was a smaller one, the fit was tight, but that did not matter at the moment.

"I know the area: private homes, a few shops. Not the best part of town, but certainly not the worst. Hardly the area in which I would have expected to find Sir Charles residing," I said.

"I imagine that, officially, he doesn't," said Holmes.

Again, he would say no more until we had arrived at our goal, having walked the last few blocks, since it would not do to announce our presence. We found the other Irregular in an alley a half-block from the house; the view was an excellent one of the front and side of our goal.

"Well, Alexander, what have you to report?" said Holmes.

"Sir Charles went inside two hours ago and hasn't left," the second Irregular replied.

"Excellent job, boys," said Holmes. "It's time for you to be elsewhere. Things might get a little dangerous in the next few hours." He extracted two coins and tossed them over to Wiggins and Alexander; both were gone with a nod.

"So I take it it's time for a bit of burglary?" I said. This wouldn't be the first time that Holmes and I had violated the law in pursuit of a case.

"I think not; I feel an urge to go in the front door."

So, that was exactly what we did: walked right up to the front door and pounded on it. It occurred to me, as we were standing there, that the night seemed darker and even here, in the center of London, there was a silence that until now had only been in the background. I felt a strange chill; if I were a superstitious man, I would have said that someone had just walked on my grave.

"Sometimes, the direct approach is the best, but you do have to be prepared to keep demanding attention," said Holmes. He was about to knock again when the door opened and we found ourselves facing, not Sir Charles but a woman in her thirties, dressed in dark colors that seemed to shift with the light around her.

"Please come in, gentlemen," she said.

"I presume we are expected," said my companion.

"Indeed you are, Mr. Holmes. My uncle will be with you in just a few minutes. There is brandy on the sideboard and you will find cigars in the humidor near the fireplace."

This was not what, fifteen minutes before, I would have predicted happening. We were escorted into a room filled from floor to ceiling with bookshelves that were overflowing with books, scrolls, and portfolios. In the center of the room was a huge carved wooden desk, one of the most ornate that I had ever seen. Lying dead-center on it was a pile of parchment pages covered with drawings and words in what I was certain was Arabic.

"Holmes! The *Al-Azif*!" I stepped over to the desk and reached out toward the manuscript, but could not bring myself to touch the papers.

The woman reappeared without a sound, lit the lamps and stoked the fire in the fireplace at one end of the room, and then was gone, all without a word.

The dark wood of the walls, which seemed almost black in places, was covered in a strange, inlaid design that seemed to make it hard to focus on any specific part for more than a few seconds.

"What is it about this place?" I muttered. For a few moments, I had the same sensations in the pit of my stomach that I had had on those few times when I had been intoxicated to the point of almost passing out.

"I see it now, Watson. This whole room has been prepared for this moment," Holmes said.

That was when the voice started. I wasn't even sure if I heard it at first; there was just a slight churning sound, an echo in the distance that might or might not have been there. Only gradually, over a space of a few minutes, did the sound become words and a voice that we could hear. The words made no sense, yet they grew louder and clearer.

"It's Sir Charles. He obviously has some kind of tube system to carry his voice here from another part of the house," said Holmes.

The door that we had entered was locked. I banged my shoulder twice against it, but it did not move and I doubted that even the two of us combined could batter it down. The gaslights flared as the chanting continued, wrapping the room in twisted shadows. As I looked around, the very angles of the room, the bookcases, the furniture, everything seemed wrong, as if they were just slightly out of focus.

"Sir Charles!" yelled Holmes. "You are destroying a tradition that goes back centuries. You are one of the protectors of this realm."

The chanting continued. If Sir Charles heard Holmes, he was ignoring him. I had my revolver out, but I realized that I had no target at which to fire.

From inside his jacket, Holmes pulled out the loose parchment page then threw it straight into the fire. The heat caused the paper to dance in the air for a moment before being engulfed in flames. Holmes threw himself against me and dragged the two of us down behind the desk.

I'm a little unclear about what happened next. I do remember the flames roaring through the whole room then fading away. The next thing I knew, we were running through billowing smoke; this time, the study door gave way and we were free. In the distance, I could hear the sound of warnings of fire and people rushing around us.

"I don't know about you, Watson, but I, for one, could use a stiff drink," said Holmes.

"Several," I said.

"I WAS A fool, Watson. I let my own hubris at my treatment by this organization blind me to some obvious facts," said Holmes.

It was two days after the fire and the reports of it had only been a minor event in the London papers, quickly fading for the far-more-sensational tales of a killer who seemed to be using a strange-looking black sword. The papers had reported finding the body of Sir Charles and the woman who owned the house. There was, of course, speculation that she was his mistress.

"How so? You are not a mind-reader; there was no reason you should have suspected Sir Charles as the thief," I said. "After all, he was the one who came to recruit you to find the criminal – i.e., himself."

"Yes, obviously, he realized that I had not returned all of the manuscript to them those ten years ago and felt this was the only way flush it out."

"But why? Was it simply the value of such a historical curiosity?"

"I think that Sir Charles felt that it was real and could summon these creatures. He realized that I had retained some part of the manuscript and he needed it. The burglaries were designed to flush the remaining page out into the open. I cannot explain everything we saw that night. I suspect that there was a hallucinogenic of some sort pumped into the room via the gas outlets."

Before I could say anything, Mrs. Hudson came in the door, an envelope in her hand.

"I found this in the kitchen," she said. "I just turned around and this was lying in the center of my cutting board. No one but myself was there."

Holmes arched an eyebrow and accepted the envelope. "Expensive paper, goes for at least a shilling a box. The handwriting shows a sure, steady hand," he said. On the front were the words: "To be delivered to the hand of Sherlock Holmes." He opened it, stared at the page, then passed it over to me.

It was two words, written in the same hand that had addressed the envelope. "Thank you."

Bradley H. Sinor has seen his short stories published in numerous science fiction, fantasy and horror anthologies such as *The Improbable Adventures of Sherlock Holmes; Tales of the Shadowmen, Vol. 6: Grand Guignol; Ring of Fire 2*; and *The Grantville Gazette*. Three collections of his short fiction have been released by Yard Dog Press: *Dark and Stormy Nights*, *In the Shadows*, and *Playing with Secrets* (along with stories by his wife Sue Sinor). His newest collection of stories, *Echoes from the Darkness*, is from Arctic Wolf Press. His non-fiction work has appeared in a variety of magazines and anthologies.

The author speaks: "The Second Theft of Alhazred's Manuscript" is set in 1894, some months after Sir Arthur Conan Doyle's "The Adventure of the Empty House", which featured Sherlock Holmes' return from his apparent death. Since Holmes was known to frequent the British Museum when he first came to London, I had always wondered if he knew about the manuscripts in parts of the building that were not open to the public.

NGIRI'S CATCH

AARON POLSON

O LD MEN SAY the River breathes and throbs and eats just like a man, but the River is no man. The River is older and infinitely larger. Being so, its hunger aches more than that of a man; its experience of the world stretches from a highland jungle dawn to the fat delta at the rim of an Atlantic sunset. The River knows. The River suffers barges and smaller dugout boats on its skin, mere gnats to the Baobab, because it knows a time before man and its patience reaches beyond mankind's twilight. It has seen black skies burning with ice and waits for the fire-capped end. The River is home to myth, and legends play in its current.

ON THE DECK of a crowded barge, Ngiri crouches with pinched, focused eyes. He has become sick of the dance of the boat – the stench of the animals, the constant cackle of voices during the long daylight hours, the steady jostling for position – and wishes for a quiet moment in the forest near his village. But the Force Publique came a month ago with their bayonets and rifles, and there would be no peace in the village or quiet moment in the forest. Ngiri fled with his mother in the night and now, they are stuck on the barge bound for Leopoldville. Perhaps there, she hopes, they will find a life other than the disease and murder of the village.

Ngiri creeps forward, leaning on his toes, part-curious boy, part-predatory animal, part-war-displaced orphan. His prey, a tiny black-and-green beetle, scuttles across the grey-brown planks of the barge deck, skirting a line of shadow without breaking the invisible wall into the sun. Ngiri's fingers stretch. He wets his lips with his tongue. For a few moments, he is oblivious to the bustle of livestock and other passengers, the bleating of goats, bartering of old men over a half-basket of fish, and rumours.

There are rumours of a missing man and murder.

Ngiri falls backward as a sandal comes down, crushing the beetle. A woman's voice rumbles, washing over the cacophony of the boat.

"What is it now, little boy? Lost something?"

Her dress is bright, blue and red, so bright Ngiri squints at the brilliance of it. He lowers his face and frowns at the dirt caked on his bare feet. With his daydream burst, he shakes his head. "No. No. Just ...."

"Best be off. Find your mother, boy. The barge isn't safe to wander alone. Stay close to your mother." The woman turns away.

Ngiri swipes at the air with his balled fist. His eyes drop to the squashed bug. A shadow covers his back.

"Hello."

Ngiri flinches at the sight of the old man.

The stranger's voice rumbles like spring storm clouds. He kneels. "You're quite the insect-lover."

Even Ngiri's grandfather, the oldest man he'd ever met, didn't have a face so wrinkled and deep-set. In the stranger's face, Ngiri finds the deep grooves of bark on a wattle tree. Wrinkles, Grandfather had always said, were marks of wisdom. Ngiri can't help but imagine the near-black lines as strange tattoos, almost a map of rivers.

"I said, 'Hello.'" The stranger smiles, showing the boy his mouth of teeth, impossibly white for a man of his age.

"Hello."

"What's your name, son?"

Ngiri shoos a fly from his neck. "Ngiri Mebengue," he says.

"Ah, Ngiri. Hello. I am Amadi. Just Amadi." The old man winks. "You are a fine collector of insects. I've been watching you all morning."

The boy glances at his feet, again, then back to the old man. "Yes, sir. I was bored."

"I'm an old man, Ngiri. Old and often bored, myself. I should thank you for the entertainment. In fact, I collect insects. Or I did, before ...." He holds up his left arm. Where a hand should be, only a stump remains.

"I – I'm sorry."

"No need. I'm sure they've done as much in your village, too. The white devils. Their army. We are not safe in our own land ...."

"Yes. They ...." Ngiri's voice is tiny and afraid. He glances over his shoulder, searching the river for one of the European steamers. "... killed my father."

"We are under a dark cloud. A plague." The old man's eyes brighten. "Maybe you can help."

Ngiri's stomach knots. He feels a dryness in his mouth. On the barge, he is trapped. Ngiri looks past the old man. The woman in bright blue-and-red talks with other women. She places her hands against her hips, lets her head droop, and frowns.

"They're talking about Martin Mwebe," Amadi says, nodding his head slowly. His remaining hand points to the crushed insect. "Poor Martin."

"Martin?"

"The man who vanished from the boat. He worked for the government. For the Belgians." Amadi's shoulders rise and fall, and a small breath escapes his lips. He reaches into the canvas bag hanging at his side and produces three small glass jars, each no bigger than a baby's fist. He holds the jars toward Ngiri. "Would you help me, Ngiri?"

"Help? How can I help you?"

"With the beetles." Amadi's eyes flash as black as a beetle carapace. He holds out the jars for Ngiri. "I am an old man. A simple man. How many white devils are in your village?"

Ngiri tilts his head. "Ten, I think. Along with at least a hundred Africans. Soldiers."

"It's not our countrymen who worry me. Do you think you can find at least ten beetles on this boat?"

Ngiri reaches out with one tentative hand. He glances at the old man's eyes and then down at the jars. Each has a dark, cork stopper. Each is clean and free of scratches, fine little baubles of glass. Ngiri's fingertips touch the smooth, cool surface of one vial. "Beetles?"

"Yes."

The boy looks at the jars and back to Amadi's lined face. "How ... how will this help my village?"

"First, the beetles. Then I'll explain."

Ngiri sets his lips and nods.

RUMOURS SPREAD ON the barge. Martin Mwebe, a lithe man of twenty from Koiekoie, can't be found. Several men insist they heard him cry out in the night. Others claim the night watch would have seen something. Ngiri hears only snippets of the gossip, suggestions that the man must have fallen overboard. Other rumours circulate, whispers of foul play because Mwebe sold out his own people to the white men.

Ngiri fills the jars with a dozen black, green and red beetles.

Once his jars are full, Ngiri picks his way through the maze of baskets, past the heavy odours of fish stew and green onions cooking over charcoal stoves. He climbs over several mountains of goods covered with dingy tarpaulins, tied down with yellowed rope. He avoids the eyes of the other passengers, clutching his small treasures close to his side until he finds the old man, Amadi, waiting under a mosquito net in a quiet corner near the back of the barge.

"Amadi," he says.

The old man's eyes open. "Ah, Ngiri. My hunter." He studies the glass containers in the boy's hands. "And a good day's catch."

"I brought twelve. You said ten, but –"

"It's good. Better, just in case. You did this on your own?"

"Yes."

"Good. Good." Amadi digs in a pouch hanging from his waist and holds out a few coins. "What was the name of your village?"

The boy hesitates. "'T'nutu'. North of the big lake."

"Yes. I know where it is. Your pay. You've earned it."

Ngiri's hand reaches out and takes the money. He examines it, screwing up his face. "I don't recognize the language."

"Very old," Amadi says.

The boy nibbles his lower lip. He would have collected the insects for nothing but something to do, something to keep his fingers occupied and his brain away from the crowds and swaying of the barge. The coins feel strangely heavy; the tip of a thumb runs across the ridged edge of one, tracing each groove and indentation. "Thank you." The boy doesn't move.

"Is there something else, Ngiri?"

The boy's fingers pull at the hem of his shirt. "Did Martin really fall from the boat?"

The old man scratches the side of his face with his gnarled fingers. "Martin Mwebe?"

Ngiri nods.

Amadi holds up a jar of beetles. The tiny occupants claw and scratch against the glass. Amadi leans forward, whispering. "Martin Mwebe is gone." The word "gone" falls like a stone into the river.

Ngiri feels the heat in his face. His stomach drops.

"Have you heard of M'basui Gwandu? These Belgian dogs stirred M'basui from his sleep with gunpowder and blood. Do you know what that means, Ngiri?"

The boy shakes his head. Doubt hangs on his shoulders like a damp cloth. The old men of the village talk and tell stories, and Ngiri remembers bits and broken pieces of the name. *M'basui Gwandu*. The broken pieces force a shiver through his bones.

Amadi smiles. "Just as well. M'basui is hungry. We've known each other for a long time. He can help us purge our country of this European plague."

Ngiri backs away, turning toward the sound of his mother's calling voice.

"Stay safe, little one," Amadi says. "Stay safe and stay with your mother tonight."

THE BARGE HUMS with the snores of sleepers. Ngiri wriggles from under his mother's arm. Amadi planted a seed in the boy's imagination, a seed which sprouted with the coming of twilight. Death, on a barge, is not unheard of. Men drown on occasion. He tries to paint the river abomination M'basui Gwandu in his mind, but doubt cools his fear. Ngiri rides on the cusp between childhood and adulthood, between believing and disbelieving. There surely could be no monster in the river, no ancient one as Amadi said. But, when he wakes, curiosity pricks him.

He waits, eyes open, as a river patrol passes. A white soldier calls out to the barge in French. Amadi's voice answers, not the night watch. "All is clear," he says. Ngiri's muscles tense, as the patrol steamer chugs away to the north, and then he rises from his bed.

The old man stands at the front of the barge. The night watchman lies at his feet. Ngiri feels the push of blood through his excited heart. Amadi holds his arms out to each side, curved slightly toward the star-filled sky. The man whistles, slow and low, as if calling to a friend in the darkness. Ngiri lingers behind a stack of wooden crates, watching. The surface of the river glints with fragments of the moon and stars. Save for the snores and low whistles, the world is quiet. Even the river listens.

A sound rises like a dull knife sawing through a shawl. No, this noise is more than a dull rumble, more than a strange, incorporeal sound. Ngiri's flesh puckers. The cold wraps him in its arms. The noise breaks into recognizable phrases, a rhythm. Words. Chanting from deep under the water. The pattern of the chanting falls in line with Amadi's whistles. A dark shape rises from the river.

It is a night shape, an imagined monster of shadows and childhood fear, the brush of branches against the thatched roof of a hut, the strange shifting of light and dark in the quiet hours. Long, jointed legs push through the water's surface. Ngiri draws a few steps closer, stumbling. He stops no more than twenty feet from the outstretched shape of the old man. The night watchman doesn't stir.

The monster rises higher and moonlight flickers in its eyes, rows of them like a spider, black and glistening. A mouth opens. The barge jars and sways. Enormous wings blot the stars.

Amadi grunts.

The rumble starts again, this time like laughter, this time unbated by the depth of the river below Ngiri's feet. The head of the thing bends lower. Unblinking eyes glitter like glass fragments in mud. Amadi grunts again, but this time, the guttural sound shapes into a word. No word Ngiri would recognize; only, the boy knows it must be a word. Shadows take the old man, pulling him into the maw of the river monster, and Ngiri feels the rush

in his head, the dizzying pound of blood through his small body. Before he
faints, he imagines a great winged thing, crossing the pale disk of moon. He
crumples to the deck.

TRAVELERS BUSTLE FROM the barge, streaming down the dock into
Leopoldville while white officers lead patrols of Force Publique through the
throng. Ngiri clamps his fingers on his mother's hand. The buildings press
against them, brightly painted and gay, but close. Clotted with people, hand-
carts, and livestock, the city is much more claustrophobic than the open air
on the barge.

The boy sees a memory shimmer in the crowd. He drops his mother's
hand and runs. She turns and shouts, but the boy is gone, woven into the
human fabric.

The man walks away from Ngiri, but the boy runs faster and catches his
shirttail. Amadi turns. A moment passes, dense with humidity and sweat
from Ngiri's forehead.

"Amadi," he pants.

The old man kneels. "Yes?"

"You ... disappeared ...." The words float beyond the reach of Ngiri's
tongue. His memory dances with imagination, and he can't cut the dream
from reality. "I thought you'd been ... killed."

Amadi holds up his good hand. The other arm is now severed above the
elbow. The pink stump protrudes from his shirt cuff.

"Your arm –"

"Oh ... yes. M'basui Gwandu asks such a little price, don't you think?"
Amadi's good hand slips into his pocket and takes out one jar at a time,
handing them to Ngiri. "You were right. There were only ten." The old man
smiles.

"Ten?"

"In your village."

Ngiri counts the tiny occupants of the jars. Ten beetles.

The old man's face slackens. He nods slowly. "Yes. The beetles. Do with
them what you will. M'basui enjoyed the taste of Belgian flesh, I daresay
more than our African brother Martin. Now the beetles are yours." His black
eyes blink.

"The beetles ... I don't understand."

"M'basui took their bodies, but I saved the rest for you. Their souls."

A strong hand wraps Ngiri's arm.

"I'm sorry if my son is bothering you," his mother says. "We were walking –"

Amadi holds up a hand. "No bother. He is a good boy. A faithful boy." The old man starts to turn away.

"Amadi?"

"All M'basui asks is a small sacrifice. A promise with more to come." Amadi rubs the stump of his shortened arm. "Not all wars are fought with spears and guns. You can fill those jars as often as you like. Fill them and call to the river when the moon is full." With that, the man turns into the busy street and its current carries him away.

Aaron Polson currently lives in Lawrence, Kansas with his wife, two sons and a tattooed rabbit. His stories have featured magic goldfish, monstrous beetles and a book of lullabies for baby vampires. His work has seen print in *Shock Totem, Blood Lite II* and *Monstrous,* with several new stories forthcoming in *Shimmer, Space and Time* and other publications. *The Saints are Dead*, a collection of weird fiction, magical realism and the kitchen sink, is due from Aqueous Press in 2011. You can visit Aaron on the web at www.aaronpolson.net.

The author speaks: "Ngiri's Catch" was influenced by a recent radio diary from journalist Ofeibea Quist-Arcton, as she traveled the Congo River, and my memory of both Joseph Conrad's *Heart of Darkness* and Chinua Achebe's *Things Fall Apart*. The tension between Africans and white, European colonists has haunted the continent for centuries; all I did was imagine dark forces in the ancient river and the story flowed from there. I chose a child for the protagonist, as I often do, to share a sense of wonder (and, at times, dread) with the reader, as the strangeness of that child's world is revealed to him. The Force Publique mentioned in the story was a historic entity and they committed horrible atrocities against their fellow Africans under Belgian command.

WHAT HIDES AND WHAT RETURNS

BRYAN THAO WORRA

When the water rises, the fish eat the ants; when the water falls, the ants eat the fish.

— Traditional Lao Proverb

CALL ME 'SAENG'. The raucous chaos of the age drew all manner of ambitious men to Laos. These *falang* arrived from all over: Mostly French, a few British and Indians, some Ottomans, Chinese traders, avaricious souls from almost every corner I ever heard described. Fortune hunters calling themselves 'explorers' and 'civilizers'. They were men at the end of their century, their revolutions of industry and empire. And they needed guides in our realm of a million elephants.

But know we are also a land of a million secrets. Some of our truths? They are best undisturbed.

Because I have an almost unnatural gift with languages and possess the slight build to traverse spaces otherwise beyond my employers in our jungles, it is never too long between opportunities. I have always been happy to oblige them in what small ways I can. Guide or confidant, whatever role required, I can procure many amazing things for you if you have the means to afford them.

Today, I am abashed to disclose what we, in our *naiveté*, would do for a paltry pittance of *piastres*. Thirty pieces of silver bought you the world.

"Saeng, come with us," they ask.

"Saeng, we need you," they say.

"Saeng, you must join us," they insist.

I'm not inclined to boast of my accomplishments, but am most satisfied with my work return. My popularity draws criticism. Some don't believe it proper to work with a *falang*. Others are jealous and want to be rivals, such as my sulky cousin Khampha.

He, older than I, is more drawn to the prospect of wealth than the delight of discovery. Brutish and sullen, he has physical strength that gives him a

confidence undermined by his impatience and miserly heart. Family propriety obliges me to recommend him to my employers. We share risks and
reward. Without fail, he will protest I have not given him a fair share. In our
last argument, he caused me great distress by telling our employers I was
cheating them and withholding finds I led them to.

Someone could have been shot over that, if I weren't a quick thinker. So
foolish.

I'm not interested in the accumulation of wealth. Money beyond what
is needed brings problems, not happiness, especially in Laos. A sentiment
Khampha thoroughly disagrees with. He cannot see how quickly he spends
what he acquires without attaining happiness, a boar without self-control. But
family is family.

My parents tend a modest farm just a few hours northeast of the capitol
of Luang Prabang, but I prefer to live in the city near the river because that is
easiest for my employers to find me.

I am simple in my negotiations: "More danger, more money." This is
direct. I learned from many others the French never respect you unless you
negotiate fiercely. But there is still an art to it, one Khampha never mastered.

Negotiation is essential. For every exquisite orchid or quaint patch of
dwarf bamboo, creeping vines and mangrove swamps hide crocodiles or
voracious tigers. Lurking all across our countryside, aggressive cobras the
length of many men strike from the tall grass. There is a particular tragedy
to hapless souls paralyzed in the brush as their last breath escapes them.
With their reckless tread, my employers easily encounter giant pythons or
deadly bamboo pit-vipers, thin as a sliver. Reptiles, scorpions, spiders, para-
sites, and leeches are all abundant and pitiless. Our wilderness is constantly
devouring; a carcass is stripped within a day by predators and scavengers.
Little is left to decay.

Lao custom maintains we return and live many lives, but I assure you
there are better ways to come and go than others.

I hold no illusions about my relationship to the *falang*. They prize my
company for my intelligence, my youthful daring and my utter expendability.
I am becoming more cautious with each successive venture. My employers
demonstrate well that wealth is of little consequence if you are dead.

And this is as dangerous a time as we have ever known. Laos has recently fallen under full occupation by France. To the south, they clash with
troops from Siam, who employ fighting techniques gleaned from European
mercenaries. It was not so long ago the ambitious Black Flag bandits were
a menace across the countryside after the Haw Wars. The French spent
months hunting the last defiant remnants of their vicious forces. There were
few cities that had not been set to torch and plundered for our wealth. Our

mountains are filled with many who do not appreciate the order of cities and *falang*, and there, they practice rites unknown beyond our borders that have not changed since their first fire thousands of years ago.

In the West, they like to believe things change. They like to talk about monkeys who turn into humans. They laugh when I tell similar stories about strange fish Yunnanese traders say turn into dragons. We all have our myths of reality we treasure.

I was surprised when Khampha came to me in my home almost a year ago. We had gone to great lengths to avoid each other in Luang Prabang. Khampha was hasty and it seemed as if he had forgotten all the animosity between us of recent months.

He presented his purpose brusquely: He wanted my aid acquiring a rare palm-leaf manuscript we had seen together as children, a copy of the epic *Thao Cheuang*. I reminded him that the copy he was referring to had been seized and taken to Siam almost a decade before, when the French began consolidating their power. It was beyond our reach.

Khampha corrected me that our revered Ajan Somnung at Wat Wisunalat had made several copies and that these included unique additions to the original. Alas, Ajan Somnung was beheaded by Black Flag bandits when they razed Wat Wisunalat. The library was lost in the flames. Khampha could not accept that and insisted with a snort that a copy of the manuscript must be somewhere.

He paced the room, agitated. He insisted it was utterly important. The book contained clues to a temple of great holy power from well before the recorded ages of Lane Xang, the whispered Wat Bhunboutdham no living human had ever seen. I had to stifle an incredulous laugh at the absurdity of his inquiries.

I reminded him that no one really understood the texts. Even Ajan Somnung confessed that his commentaries were humble efforts to add some clarity to the rambling ancient verse. Khampha interrupted me testily.

"Your mistake is you always think I'm some *ban nok* bumpkin who knows nothing. You forget I was there with you in our classes. I was paying attention, too. It's not respectful of you to dismiss me so poorly."

I was embarrassed by his accusation and, to regain my composure, I changed the subject to the practical.

"So, who is this for? Father Boreau? Monsieur Dupin, perhaps? I'm excited for you, cousin. I hope this will lead to many more opportunities for you."

Khampha smiled smugly as he pried nosily among my curios in my home. "It's none of the usual people I work for. This man knows our culture, even more than Dupin. And he is not afraid to spend money to acquire what he wants."

I thought of all of the new people who had come to Luang Prabang in recent months. It was very difficult not to become known if you were a wealthy
falang. Besides Lao, my cousin only spoke rudimentary French. I knew he
and his friends preferred to carouse drunkenly near Wat Xieng Thong. That
it should be one who knew Lao culture allowed me to deduce at least seven
possible candidates.

"Oh!" I blurted. "Is it Monsieur Guillaume of Maison Ducornet? He seems
generous if you have his favour."

Khampha scowled. I smiled at my cousin.

"Don't abuse your intelligence. Guillaume has many wealthy clients in
Paris of indescribable hunger. I don't think he likes much of our country. He
seeks something more unusual and ancient."

"If he comes with a closed mind, he will find many closed doors, cousin," I
remarked. "But why go to so much trouble for him? Many *falang* pay well for
far less risk."

"It's not just for him."

"How did he even hear of Wat Bhunboutdham? Few in our own country
know about it," I asked.

"You remember my parents' talk of the *falang* who died here, Henri
Mouhot? He was buried nearby, but his belongings were sent to Europe.
Guillaume found a journal of Mouhot's years ago that spoke of Wat Bhun-
boutdham."

Everyone knew the story of how the famed explorer died screaming-mad
in malarial fever in the jungle nearby.

"To discover examples of ancient Lao the world has never seen before?
Falang should learn to live in the present moment and appreciate what is
here, already."

"They pay well for a stranger's pasts," Khampha laughed with a sly smile.

"I suppose it is the civilized thing to do."

"He is very particular about who participates, but if you want, I'll mention
you," Khampha offered. "I'll ensure your fair share."

I promised to look for what Khampha wanted and would ask friends all
over to find a surviving copy of Ajan Somnung's manuscript. I warned him it
might take some time and he would need to be patient.

Satisfied, Khampha took his leave, muttering vaguely that Ajan Somnung
knew and could have proven the truth of the old legends any time he wanted.

I shook my head at his parting. Lao tradition believes that unhealthy
desire leads to suffering. You might spend your afterlife as some pitiable
wandering minor spirit with a mouth smaller than a grain of rice but a belly
the size of a rotting cask, insatiably hungry. Or worse.

Khampha's visit troubled me, but I had made a sincere promise to him in good faith. I was also intrigued, ultimately rewarded for my diligence within a few months, thanks to a good friend in Savannakhet. Their father had helped Ajan Somnung make copies of the *Thao Cheuang*. With the fighting down in the south, it was not easy to arrange for its safe arrival in Luang Prabang, but I found myself overjoyed to see the familiar text once more.

Ajan Somnung had sternly encouraged us not to look too closely for some secrets, but to turn our eyes to the lessons of the Buddha. The search for Nirvana should supersede any attachments to this illusory world and all its perilous entanglements. He had taught us that death was impermanent, a great dreaming slumber, and one day, we could break free of our eternal returns because, after a time, even death would die.

I had to take care unfurling the aged palm leaves. Many were in terrible condition, crumbling at my gentlest touch, and I could see already many sections were missing or beyond legibility. Ajan Somnung's version still seemed indecipherable, but I tried to take some notes of my own in the chance it would prove useful for another occasion.

I soon notified Khampha of the manuscript's arrival and he came immediately, eyes burning with singular intensity, as I'd never seen before in my cousin. As a good host, I offered him some food, but he did not take any. He did not waste time poring over the manuscript, except the section outlining the capture of Muang Pakan and the division of their territories. His fingers quivered like a shrew when he turned to me and exclaimed: "Listen!" And he proceeded to read to me a passage that spoke of an old, old temple where a strange god was worshiped by a race of giant creatures before humans came to be. Preposterous, but Ajang Somnung wrote the note with deep conviction.

"Tomorrow I talk to Guillaume. Lend me the manuscript; I need it. We'll go and find whatever secrets are there. It must be an amazing treasure of jewels and gold." His delight was irrepressible.

So saying, Khampha scurried out into the evening. I reviewed the notes I'd copied from Ajan Somnung, and realized they were far stranger and provocative than I would have believed our gentle teacher capable of. What I now knew of Wat Bhunboutdham disturbed me and troubled my dreams that night. As much as my cousin and I might disagree, I felt compelled to speak with him before he left. But in the morning, it was already too late.

I learned from a friend serving the Guillaumes that they had all left with great excitement – my cousin Khampha ecstatic, while the hardy Monsieur Guillaume gave strict instruction to the others not to disclose the location, lest rivals beat them to their glittering prize. There were 13 in all.

By karma, that week, I met Madame Guillaume and easily earned her
confidence. It helped that Khampha was my cousin. We shared a deep mutual
concern for everyone who had departed by his lead.

In our first moments, she looked about constantly, as if some foreign
thing were coming from beyond to break into her world. Some world where
she made everything seem petty and trivial against a vast, galactic backdrop
only she could perceive.

The Guillaumes lived in a two-story villa that exuded an alien-but-re-
fined intellect in its arrangement. The broad windows had mahogany shut-
ters that they rarely opened, to keep out the day's heat. As she showed me
around their home, my curiosity was piqued by Monsieur Guillaume's study
and the great lengths he had undertaken to bring his library to Laos. The
design was elegant, yet its geometry puzzled me, the harmonies decidedly
distinct from other homes I had visited. Their villa was densely furnished
with designs almost out of a different time, a different aesthetic, both commanding and esoteric.

Madame Guillaume was a dark-eyed woman, her heavy jet tresses coiled
atop her head. Her face was sharp and angular, but the rest of her reminded
me of the lush, flowing Khmer sandstone statuary of antiquity that the *falang*
ardently admired. She was a sufficiently pious woman, who did not dress
lavishly but within the prim basics of the Parisian style. She wore a curious, antique copper brooch composed of geometric tendrils wriggling and
intertwining around a most fearsome eye – a bauble from another life, she
claimed. She offered me tea. I did not refuse.

She was evasive about how she had first met her husband, but she readily
discussed her other journeys with him.

I learned that, in her travels, she had conversed with the communal
cenobites in India, who followed the model of Mar Awgin, and she had also
consulted the aging mystic Helena Blavatsky on theosophy. She'd had meet-
ings with many remarkable men and women abroad, emerging with a sense
of the cosmos not so far removed from the rigid, austere faith she'd grown
up with. She admired the discipline of our ascetic hermits, but I confessed I
found them repellent in their relentless mortification of the body, their denial
of their humanity to transcend our petty failings.

Some would say it was an inappropriate gathering, but if you learn from it,
how can it be wrong? Our worlds are not some fragile bits of glass that shatter at the encounter with the Other. Our ability to inquire surely defines our
humanity; it sets us above hounds and mere rutting beasts of the field, all jaw
and genital.

To my delight, she found my curiosity charming and invited me to come
back if I had occasion.

One morning, I brought her a selection of fresh fruit from my family's farm and some uncommon examples from the deeper jungle that I had retrieved with no small effort. Their succulence is an indescribable temptation. I am sure *falang* have never seen such delicacies in their own homelands. It would have been unfitting and inhospitable for me not to introduce her to them during her time among us.

She received them graciously and, as we sat at the table, we conversed of many things, the merits of good and evil, the need for order to triumph over chaos, the journeys of empire and the wisdom of civilization.

"Centuries ago, Ashoka the Great conquered the realm of Kalinga, but he was overcome with sorrow at the lives he destroyed and the karmic weight he had taken upon himself," I told her, to explain the beliefs of our homeland. "He sought to atone by dispatching holy wise men around the world to teach the *dharma* and the truths of the Buddha."

As I reflected on the carnage of the *falang* of the last decade, I wondered whom they will send someday. She seemed lost in thought, distracted by something as if I were an insignificant fly. She poured a cup of tea. I could hear clocks ticking around the room. Occasionally, they would chime.

She inquired about my cousin Khampha. "Is he steadfast?"

I smiled. "As long as I have known him, he knows whom to protect and he will do so unfailingly. He has great strength and instincts."

She seemed pleased to learn she was a perceptive judge of character.

Idly, she revealed her belief in a lost continent of Lemuria, drunk by a pitiless ocean eons ago. They were peopled by mindless-yet-spiritual giants, prone to degeneracy and horrid acts. Madame Guillaume suggested that not all of the Lemurians sank with their homeland in the cataclysm.

In turn, I shared the story of the loathsome Old Ones of Laos, ancient elder things who once terrorized humanity, such as treacherous Raphana-suan, a nefarious giant fiend who devoured mortals, affronting the heavens with his lust and malice. It was clear she found my account as quaint as children's tales.

THERE WAS A commotion one day near Wat Xieng Thong, with many men rushing back and forth, gathering supplies and making frantic preparations, seeking blessings from the monks for their task.

"What is it?" Madame Guillaume inquired. "What has them so excited?" She watched their efforts with intense curiosity. I asked the men and returned to her.

"They are getting ready to hunt a tiger," I told her. "It has been seen running wild for many months now and it is clear nothing can appease it. It has killed many in the hills and deep forest."

"A tiger has them so distressed?" she asked, with clear disbelief on her face.

"They do not believe it is an ordinary tiger, but one of the spirits who take the shape of tigers. Sometimes, they appear as a beautiful, bathing woman with long, dark hair, sometimes as a meditating monk by a tree," I told her. "But they are all dangerous."

I knew of a time when such a spirit appeared as a baby. They then tore you to pieces when your guard was down. "They use the souls of their victims to give them power. It is dangerous for men to hunt them, because they will eventually be killed and turned into tigers, themselves, by vengeful spirits."

She laughed dismissively at my account. A *falang* will only believe so much in our nation. They forget their own words about 'when in Rome'. Perhaps it is better that way.

"How dangerous is it, truly?" she asked. "In the wilderness of your people?"

I knew she wanted a 'rational' answer. I did not wish to worry her and, instead, regaled her with tales of gentle creatures and inspired sights that rewarded the patient traveler. "But haste in Laos can be lethal and you cannot take what is on the surface for granted. What is tranquil to the eye can have a storm in the heart," I conceded. "The most dangerous of all are other humans. A human is hardest of all to be certain of. If Khampha has any weakness, it is that he does not know the ways of others as well as I," I explained. "Even when he can speak to the villagers in the mountains, he does not understand their beliefs, their customs. He thinks they should just do things as the Lao do and make it easier for themselves."

"He seems very good with the French," Madame Guillaume reminded me. "He is very obedient and quick to please us."

"I suppose that is enough," I replied.

On another morning, we strolled leisurely through the streets of the city in the early hours, while it was still cool. I deigned to show her the gilded spires and temples we'd erected over the centuries. She thought the elaborate giant serpents on the balustrades of our temples horrific and heathen, but I explained their comforting significance as our guardians in such a world as ours. But to her, the serpent was forever some symbol of paradise lost, a fallen humanity estranged from the divine truth and good words.

The *falang* are curious creatures to me, insistent on the written, as if one's spoken word is insufficient. They found a thousand ways to complicate time, enchanting our neighbours with trinkets and clockworks in exchange for poppies and silk, a bit of spice and teas. A strange bargain.

What a bleak world they come from.

One afternoon, in the villa, she presented me with a book of poetry by Lautreamont, *Chansons de Maldoror*. I cannot claim to fully appreciate its cryptic fantasies and the misanthropic verse she read to me. But she was enamoured with his language and the florid poems of Baudelaire. I gave her an antique Buddha I had kept from one of my many travels. She told me it would fetch an excellent price in Paris.

It has not always been easy for me to make my way among people. When I was young, and so quickly apprehended the words of strangers, some soon accused me of dark magic and I dared not stay long among the highlanders, whose elders were a grim, suspicious and superstitious lot. When the *falang* arrived and I began to practice their language with ease, many dismissed me as some mere parrot, a mimic incapable of original thought or a sense of history. But I was useful and amusing as a guide. Word spread, little by little.

Madame Guillaume entertained me with the theories of Pasteur and his vaccines, but many who arrived from foreign shores were still unprepared for the pitiless crucible of our tropics. They fell to malaria, dengue fever and other horrific diseases that left them dying, miserable and delirious in our sun.

I came to appreciate Madame Guillaume's extensive knowledge of *les petites morts*, the little deaths of the world. I shudder to recall them and the way a human screams in their throes. Humanity is filled with many forbidden moments, memories they lock away, lest they be undone by truths, or the writhing chaos that may destroy them and bring total oblivion.

"Your jungles remind us of lost worlds, their raw beauty a reminder of a pure humanity before we tamed nature, shackling her intensity to our mortal, time-bound whims," she said wistfully, as we stood atop holy Mount Phu Si, watching for some sign of Monsieur Guillaume's return. For nearly a month, we returned there each sunset. I began to think of the Annamite legend of Nui Vong Phu, a tragic beauty who turned to stone, awaiting her husband's return from the sea near Lang Son.

There is a Russian writer who said we must not lie to ourselves, because we may come to believe our own lies and be unable to distinguish between the truths in ourselves and the world around us.

I think he is not very far from being a Buddhist.

Time passes strangely in Laos, where the *falang* call us 'lotus-eaters', as each day seems little different than the last to them. News travels of melancholy Legionnaires, suicides who've fallen to *la cafard*, a peculiar malaise exacerbated by the heat and depression from viewing the vast stretches of jade leaves and peaks of our realm. Monsieur Masie, a French consul in the city, had been among the more prominent men to meet such an end. The *falang* priests called for more faith.

There was a day when I intended to come to the Guillaumes' villa to discuss the ancient legends that Monsieur Guillaume was so driven to unearth, but Madame Guillaume's gardener informed me that she had disappeared without a word in the night. There wasn't a trace, a hint, a single clue that might explain her departure. I asked among the boatmen, the merchants of the morning market. No one had seen her. She had not taken a thing with her, but, as if she were a phantasm, it was as if she had never been here at all. I was questioned, but no one openly accused me of anything. After a few weeks, an official declared she had wandered into the forest and doubtless been devoured by some savage beast, or run afoul of Black Flag bandits. There is no evidence to support any of these explanations.

The servants kept the villa in order for several weeks before they grew bored. With no sense of their masters' returns, they scavenged what they could and sold the valuables discretely among their compatriots, discarding the rest, particularly the library of the Guillaumes, left in a sad disarray of tattered pages upon the floor. I, too, salvaged what I could.

My recent dreams occasionally figured a strange, howling woman, and images of blood and flight across space like some bird or fiend. But I do not believe there was any message from beyond, any cryptic signal to bring to the fortunetellers of the city.

Months passed and the villa was still abandoned. It was in a state of disrepair from unscrupulous vandals and a rumour of inauspicious spirits pervading the space. Accounts of a 'presence' spooked the neighbors, who did their best to ignore the house and move on with their affairs. But there was a night I felt compelled to go. I found the door ajar and heard something rustling within. I entered.

I saw a shadow fumbling, squatting, shifting about, but not wholly panicked. It sensed me and called out, "Who are you?"

"It is only I, Saeng," I replied. The shadow moved partially into the moonlight. It was a *falang*, with a long, disheveled beard, and I soon realized it was a very changed Monsieur Guillaume. He had a glint in his eyes like some savage creature. But he smiled.

"You know of our journey?"

I answered in the affirmative.

"No one else has returned?"

"No. No one." It was the truth, turning into a legend here.

"Not even Khampha?"

"Not even my cousin," I said. "What happened, monsieur?"

"He fled when we needed him most," the man answered. I asked him to give me a full account.

He shuffled towards a far wall and slumped down before he began. I could still feel his eyes on me. The room was fragrant, like the deep jungle.

"All of my life, they have mistaken me for something I am not," he began. "They think me a fool; they think me a rogue or some dilettante. Don't think I don't hear the whispers in the darkness, the snickering, the chortles and sneers, young man. But I have always sought true wisdom. It is true I traffic in objects for eclectic tastes, for those who could not bear the travails of retrieving their shiny, little baubles themselves. But I always recover the true valuables. Here, around the world. It sustains me."We are animals. We are meant to sweat and, for millennia, every day was a challenge of life and death for humans. To explore and civilize, in this, we must send those who can still deal with uncertainty and risk, and emerge undaunted. You live in your world of demons and fear, but there is such light to apprehend. You fall so short of what you can be. Of what you can change."

"Did you find the temple?" I asked, fearing for his sanity.

"The mystery is fundamental, you know. Most people are nothing but zombies – somnambulists stumbling through life in some sad, dreaming haze – but if we can wake up a soul, we have accomplished something. I don't know if we found the temple we sought. We found a temple – far, far from where Khampha believed we would. Our bearings were lost and the journey was arduous.

"We came, prepared as civilized men. Thirteen of us in all. For the last several kilometers, we'd finally had a breakthrough from clambering over all of that brush and stone. We were following an ancient trail of unknown origin, barely anything at all. The centuries had done a profound job of reclaiming it. What we found had the logic of a human trail, moving with obvious purpose; it was not some meandering animal track. We were heading for a steep ravine."

It is difficult to describe his breathing. It was as if it no longer came naturally to him. He cocked his head curiously at me, as if to see if I was still listening to him. His voice lowered.

"Khampha told us that the people ascribed death and savagery to forest spirits among these hills. The narrow trail walled us in by brush. All of us noticed that the jungle, always overflowing with the sounds of life, was distressingly silent. There was a presence in the brush that we could not hear or see. It was merely felt. If only you could have seen it. It was all so primordial. This was surely untouched Laos. The leaves were thick on every side, the trees grown close together over centuries. An occasional breeze pushed past us down the remnants of the ancient trail, making the leaves whisper. It was haunting. The stones were slick and we had to be careful with our footing.

But at last, there it was before us. It was beautiful. How could the living have left it behind? There, something beyond words.

"We found the temple, the '*wat*', as you call it. It was built against a sheer stone cliff, in a valley no one has ever mapped, an enigmatic range thought inaccessible to explorers. Truly, it was crafted from stones we'd never seen before, not even on the Plaines Des Jarres. The structure was overgrown and it was so weathered I could not reliably guess its age." He coughed violently.

"There were ruined cyclopean blocks, that conformed to where we might expect to find the *kuti*, and a primitive, crude structure equal to a massive *thaat*. Who knows how high the *thaat* must have originally been, but it would have loomed over us. I calculate it may have been at least four hundred and forty-seven meters tall, from its base to its pinnacle, when it was pristine," he recounted with awe.

"We found columns near the facade, jutting like shattered tree stumps scattered by some gargantuan terror. You could almost imagine them grinning at those of us who remained, like some withered hag. But, though the exterior was in such a sad state, we found it easy enough to remove the brush sealing the massive doors of the central hall. We lit our lanterns and proceeded forward, pressing into the massive main chamber. What a space it was. The floor was made of great squares of dark stone. At the end of the chamber, there was merely a huge, curiously carved block of the same stone. There was a massive door, and we pried it open."

From this point, his narrative became so vague that I had difficulty following him. I speculated that the tropic sun had affected his mind.

He told me that he had opened the door, but in its opening, induced a bad effect on the men in his employ. They refused point-blank to follow him any further through that gaping opening. Something shook even the strongest among them, except Khampha. So, the two entered alone, Monsieur Guillaume with his pistol and flickering lantern, finding a massive, rough-hewn stair that wound its way down into the innards of the earth, apparently. He followed this and came into a broad corridor, in the shadows of which his tiny flame was utterly engulfed. As he told me this, he spoke with strange annoyance of a crimson serpent which slithered ahead of him, just beyond the circle of light, all the time he was below ground.

Making his way along dank passages that were wells of unearthly blackness, he at last came to a heavy door fantastically carved, which he felt must be where the worshipers hid the riches of the ancients. He pressed against the door and it fell open to them. Even Khampha fled then, but it was of no matter.

"The treasure?" I interrupted eagerly.

Monsieur Guillaume laughed ruefully.

"*Rien*. Nothing. Not a flake, not a stone or gem – nothing at all." He paused reflectively. "Nothing I alone could bear away."

He broke again into a terrible, ragged-sounding cough. Again, his tale lapsed into vagueness. I gathered that he had left the temple hurriedly, without searching any further. The men had fled into the darkness and he could not catch up with them. It took all of this time to return.

"You have your life," I reminded him. "Surely, it is valuable." I could not bring myself to tell him of the disappearance of his wife.

He shook his head. He seemed lost in thought for some moments.

"*Alors*, sleeping things we are," he muttered, "What is life but reconciliations with regrets? We should have shut the door when we left …." He began to snore strangely, so I took my leave.

When I returned to my home, I was troubled by the conversation and intended to return in the morning to speak with him of these matters with more clarity. I was startled to discover my cousin Khampha in my home, his clothes torn and ripped, his eyes fearful. He signaled me to be quiet, whispering angrily, "Where have you been?"

"I went to visit the Guillaumes," I replied quietly. A panic overtook him. He pounded his fists fiercely against his body and shook his head.

"What did you see?" he asked accusingly. "What did you see?"

I told him of what I had seen, and what I had been told. He again shook his head, fear within his eyes.

"That's nothing even close to what happened, cousin. Nothing at all. Never return there! Never return! Forget any jewels, any gold you think you might find there. It's nothing."

He was almost frothing, incomprehensible, as I pressed him to explain. He glanced again and again at my doorway, before finally intimating the truth as he saw it. A journey plagued by misfortune and lost bearings, as he'd never endured.

"He didn't need me. Not really. He didn't need any of us. It was as if something unnamable called him, summoned him from some distant, monstrous shore to complete his terrible work."

"You exaggerate," I protested.

"I do not! At every turn, he countered my words, ignored my advice, forsook me as if I were some ant. He stared instead at his devices, things I'd never seen before in the hands of any *falang*. He pointed and barked at us, demanded we obey him at the most impossible turns."

"We took two boats a certain length up the river and disembarked with our equipment. We had to cross a particularly treacherous ridge. Guillaume's man, Etienne, lost his footing, plummeting nearly one hundred meters down, shredded apart by the jagged limestone jutting below us. Guillaume made no remark, no request to recover the equipment or his companion. He grunted and ordered us to be more careful.

"The weather? Miserable. I was no more than a slave to his ravenous quest. I saw his eyes and I knew my place in his world. But I found the manuscript! I did. But we weren't partners. We weren't equals in any respect. We found ourselves among a fierce people, bold as any. But none would come with us. Another of our men fell into a pit of bamboo stakes the villagers said were meant for tigers and we were down to 11. One of my friends suggested we kill Guillaume and the remaining *falang* – we'd blame Black Flag bandits – but I think he heard us. We had walked no more than a half-hour when my friend was bitten by a viper the colour of a bright ruby, as I'd never seen before. It slithered away before I could avenge him. I'll never forget his scream and you know we've seen many die. This was like no death we've seen, Saeng.

"It's impossible to reach the clearing Ajan Somnung spoke of without us getting bloody and tangled up in thorn and brush. We cut our hands and back and heads, so much of our flesh left on the vines. We were all in such misery that it was as if we were entering a gate of Hell."

He spoke fearfully of the sinister carvings in the temple, of strange creatures the carvings suggested had crafted the complex and abandoned it, the horrifying dreams that plagued the men in their time there.

"Is it true you abandoned Monsieur Guillaume?" I asked, trying to restore rationality to the conversation.

"It is," Khampha said. "But I stayed as long as I could. I swear. More than any reasonable soul would stay. But we're forbidden there. This was a place for legends to die – to remain forgotten, perhaps. I don't really know, anymore. Humans were not meant to be there. But he insisted on opening every passage and I followed his descent into the very bowels of the world, until that last, terrible door.

"When he opened it, not a ray of light could penetrate beyond it into the room ahead. And when he touched the shadowy edge of the darkness, something touched back and stepped forth like a reflection, a perfect reflection that devoured him for his curiosity. Whoever or whatever is in the villa is NOT Guillaume as I left him in that temple ...."

A bird shrieked from my roof. Khampha screamed and fled into the night, eyes wild with terror.

On my floor, I saw the last tatters of the manuscript of Ajan Somnung, broken past restoration.

Perhaps it was only my imagination that heard a scream, a howl, a laugh outside.

Now I hear something scratching, rustling restlessly beyond my thin door. I know it remembers why some things were meant to stay forgotten ....

Bryan Thao Worra is an award-winning Lao American writer based in Minneapolis. An NEA Fellow in literature, his work appears internationally in numerous anthologies, magazines and newspapers, including *Tales of the Unanticipated, Innsmouth Free Press, Astropoetica, Illumen, Outsiders Within, Dark Wisdom* and *Mad Poets of Terra*. He is the author of two books of speculative poetry, *On the Other Side of the Eye* and *BARROW*. You can visit him online at: http://thaoworra.blogspot.com

The author chortles: Set in the mid 1890s in northern Laos, "What Hides and What Remains" draws from the history and supernatural traditions of Southeast Asia, during an era of French colonialism and a global thirst for the industrial and the exotic. Much of the setting remains today, little changed from over a century ago in many areas.

BLACK HILL

ORRIN GRAY

THAT PLACE WAS still called 'Black Hill' when I come there, though it was as flat as a plate and nothing stood taller'n a man's shoulder far as the eye could see, 'cept the shacks and the derricks. Not a tree nor a lick of grass to be seen, everything stomped dead by the men and the horses and the trucks.

My first day there, I asked Burke why they called it 'Black Hill' and he laughed and stamped his foot on the bare, brown dirt. "The hill's unner there," he said. "Not a lake nor a river, like they say it, but sure enough a hill, all piled up an' waitin', pressin' up on th' ground, clawin' ta get out. Nothin' but the dirt 'tween it an' us. We poke a hole in th' dirt an' up it jumps!"

Burke had been out there from the beginning. He was there when they drove the Stapleton #1, and he saw the black gold just well up from the ground and come pouring out. Enough, it seemed, to make any man rich.

He bought up a parcel of land out west of El Dorado with the money he made and started the Black Hill Oil Company. By the time he sent for me, the Black Hill field was already putting up more'n three hundred thousand barrels a day.

I didn't know why he needed me and I said as much, though I was thankful for the work. He just shook his head. "This here's only th' beginnin'," he said. "There's another world down there, Smith. Things the like-a-which Man ain't never dreamed, let alone seen. If all I wanted was ta be rich, I coulda quit by now, but there's somethin' more down there. Somethin' else. I cain't say what, exactly, but I aim ta find it."

Burke and I had worked together in Iowa for a spell, years back. I wasn't nothing but an amateur geologist. I'd delivered the mail, 'fore I ruint my leg, and I'd taught a bit of school. I had a wife and two girls back in Iowa, but there weren't no work for a man like me in those days anywhere but in the fields, so the fields was where I worked. And when Burke called for me, I came because the money was good and I knew him for a man I could put my back against.

I lived in the shacks, like most everyone else who worked the fields. As field geologist, I had one to myself, but it still weren't much more'n four walls and a bed. There was a desk against the wall, under the one window, and I sat there and wrote letters to Matilda and the girls when I could.

Burke worked the men hard but fair. He strode about the field, barking orders and working with 'em side-by-side. He was as tall and rudely constructed as a derrick hisself, and his hair and beard were as bristly and red as an oil fire. He was missing two-and-a-half fingers on his right hand, lost to one of the walking boards. His left ear was gone and half his face a mess of scars, owing to a mishap with some nitroglycerine.

He'd been married back when I knew him, but his wife had since passed and left him with a pretty little dark-eyed girl who, I gathered, lived with some spinster aunt at the hotel in town. Whenever I rode in with Burke on one errand or another, he'd always insist we stop by the hotel so he could buy her a root beer or an ice cream, and pick her up in his long arms and spin her above his head. It was a sweet sight, seeing how he doted on her. The only thing it made me regret was my own girls being so far away, and how I was missing watching them grow up.

I'D BEEN AT the field three weeks when Burke rode up with a pair of horses, told me to mount up and follow him. We rode out past the edge of the field, past the last of the derricks, to a spot where a copse of trees once stood, 'fore they were all dragged down and sawed up for timber. The ground was swept as smooth and flat as if it was the floor of some fella's house.

"This here," Burke said, "is what I bought this land fer. There was somethin' here when I come out, a wheel a stones like them the Injuns set aside, though I could'n find nobody from 'round here could say which tribe mighta put 'em up. I come out 'fore the men, moved them stones myself, by hand. Didn' want nobody gettin' spooked off. They's a wild mix a folks works th' fields, as you well know, an' some of 'em are too superstitious fer their own good. But look here; I don' think this was no burial ground nor nothin' of th' sort. I think them Injuns, whichever ones they was, *knowed* they was somethin' unner this ground an' they marked th' spot."

"You mean oil?" I asked. I knew some folks believed oil was medicinal, that they'd set up shacks and stagecoach stops around tar springs and drunk the black stuff that bubbled up to cure everything from gout to infertility. And I knew the Indians were better geologists than anybody'd ever given 'em credit for, better able to find the flow of underground rivers and stratas of good rock than they'd any right to be. So, I didn't suppose it was unreasonable to think they mighta known there was oil down there, or marked the place to find it.

Burke just shrugged at me, didn't answer my question straight. Instead, he said, "Gonna build me a derrick here. Gonna dig deep, deeper'n any well we dug so far. I want you on it, 'cause I know I kin count by you."

And I didn't think nothing more of it, save that I was proud to be trusted, to be depended on. The next day, we started digging.

THE DIGGING DIDN'T go easy. It seemed like every day, there was something new went wrong. A storm come up and dropped bucketfuls of hail on the whole field, blew a derrick over. Two of the men got into it over something, and one pulled a knife and killed the other. Three of the men took sick and couldn't work. Four more vanished over the course of a week and weren't never found. And, through it all, the pipe went down and down and down.

We passed over several promising-looking strikes, 'cause they weren't whatever Burke was looking for, and the men working the towers got restless. Still we went down and down, until finally we hit something else.

There was a sound come up from the hole, like a gasp. The men figured we'd hit a pocket of gas and everyone backed off in case it was like to burn. Then the derrick shook all the way up and the ground seemed to slide a little under our feet. There come a noise from the hole like I ain't never heard the ground make in all my years. When I was a boy, my pa'd known a man who worked a whaling ship and he said that whales *sang* to one another. He'd put his hands together over his mouth and blown a call that he said was as close as he could do to what they sounded like. This sounded like that call.

All the men went back another pace, not knowing if maybe we'd hit a sinkhole, or God knows what. There was another groan, then an old cave stink, and then the black stuff started coming up around the pipe like a tide. I'd seen gushers in my day, the pressurized wells that blew the tops off the derricks, but this weren't the same. This weren't no geyser; this were a flood, the oil *pouring* up from under the ground like a barrel that's been overturned. Everybody was silent for another minute and then the men gathered 'round all cheered, 'cause they knowed we'd finally hit whatever it was we'd been aiming at.

I'D EXPECTED BURKE to be blown over by our success, but when he come out to look at the well, his smile didn't touch his eyes none.

That night, he invited me to eat dinner with him in his shack, which weren't really much better'n mine, though it had a coupla rooms. I remembered his wife and little girl had lived in it with him when he started the field, back before his wife got carried off by whatever it was carried her off.

Burke served me a dinner of baked beans and set out a bottle of whiskey on the table between us. He seemed distracted, thoughtful. 'Pensive', as they say. He told me I'd done a good job on the well, but didn't seem to want to talk much more about it.

"I got no need ta tell you what oil is," he finally said, after we'd drained most of the bottle. "Dead stuff. Rotted a thousand years, pressed down by th' dirt. You know who th' first wildcatters in this country consulted 'fore diggin'? Not geologists. Mediums. Spiritualists. They knowed, even then. Hell, mebbe they knowed better. Mebbe it's us has forgot."

He stopped and raised his glass, only to find it empty. He sat it back down and continued, without refilling it, "Somethin' dies an' you put it down in th' dirt; it' don' disappear. It stays, forever. They's not a place on this earth somethin' ain't died, where somethin' don' lay buried. All this world's a boneyard an' us just ghouls crouched on top, breakin' open tombs. I made my peace wi' it. A man does, ta live th' life we live. But here ...." He reached over to a sideboard and took up an old, worn black Bible and opened it up. From the back, he took out a scrap of paper, brown and worn smooth by years of handling, and passed it to me. "Kin you read that?" he asked.

I could, but only just. The handwriting was careful but uneven, like it'd been copied down slow by a palsied hand. It was just one line: *THAT IS NOT DEAD WHICH CAN ETERNAL LIE.*

"Took that off a feller came ta shut down th' field," Burke said. "Fancied hisself some kinda preacher, though nota-th' Word a God. He said all sortsa things, crazy things, 'bout there bein' somethin' underneath us, somethin' that dreamed though it was dead. He had a gun. Managed to light a buncha th' place on fire. Took an ax ta one-a-th' derricks, 'fore I shot him wi' my rifle. He had that in his pocket. Can't rightly say why I kept it, but I thought about it a lot since. An' damned if it ain't right, just a bit. Oil, right? It's dead, jus' dead stuff crammed down there in its tomb, but it can lay there forever, cain't it? An' when we dig it up, there it is, waitin' to come out, fulla heat an' fire an' life. What does that tell ya?"

I didn't get a chance to answer him and I don't rightly know what I'd've said if I had, because right then, he noticed the flicker of the shadows against the wall. "Fire," he breathed and my heart jumped up, 'cause fire's the worst curse there is when you're in the field.

Burke rushed out, already barking orders, and I followed him. If the doubtful and morbid thoughts of a few minutes before were still in him, as they must've been, then he kept 'em well hid. He shouted to the men and they jumped to, fighting to keep the fires away from the pipes and the nitroglycerine trucks.

I was a few paces behind Burke and when the ground shivered under my feet, I stopped and swung my eyes across the field. The fires seemed like they was burning everywhere, like they'd sprung up from every corner of the place at once. I could see the whole field, it seemed like, all licked with curling orange tongues, the derricks that wasn't yet burning standing like the silhouettes of ships' masts before the flames.

The ground gave another shake under me, like the flank of a horse shivering to throw off flies. Through the smoke, I saw my derrick sway. I ran toward it. The fire hadn't reached it yet and I was prob'ly needed someplace else, but I somehow had a feeling that the derrick was where I had to be.

As I got right up to it, I heard that same sound, the one I remembered from earlier in the day, and I saw the derrick start to topple. At the same time, a crack opened up below me like a mouth in the dirt. I felt my feet going out from under me and saw that big skeleton of wood and metal coming down toward my head. The next thing I remember, I was hanging from the derrick where it laid across an empty black chasm, a pit that seemed like it went down all the way to the center of the earth. Down in that darkness, I saw something move.

In the years that've intervened since that night, the doctors have tried their best to convince me that I misremember some of what come next, but I know they're wrong. I remember it clear as day. There was something down in the dark below me, something that heaved itself up toward the surface, toward the light, toward me. I remembered suddenly why that place was called 'Black Hill'. I saw that great bulk heave and slop toward me in the dark. I saw what looked like golden eyes opening and closing, and hungry mouths smacking. I smelt a smell like what sometimes comes up from caves and holes that've been closed away fer too long. I heard a hiss and a groan, and I believe I closed my eyes. Then I heard Burke's voice.

He was shouting, but there was something different about the sound. It was ragged and hoarse, but that wasn't it. It was like he was talking straight at a feller, not like he was yelling all around as he had been before.

I opened my eyes up again and I saw him, standing by the edge of the crack in the ground, looking like some heathen god with the fires burning behind him. He was shouting down into the pit.

"What more kin you take from me?" he demanded. "What more could you want? You took ma hand, ma face, ma wife! I done give you ever'thin' I got, damn you, ever'thin' I am. I ain't got nothin' left you kin take, nothin' but her, an' her y'll not have! I'll see you in hell myself, first."

And then he stepped into the hole. Other men in the field heard Burke shout and saw me hanging there on the tipped-over derrick. But if anyone else saw what happened to him, they pretended not to. They said they saw him standing there, and that they saw him fall, but that's it. I know, though, that he didn't fall. That he went down there to spite the Devil, or whatever it was he saw down there, and something came up to meet him, something black and old and putrid as a rotted log that's set for months at the bottom of a pond. I saw him go down into that blackness like a mammoth being pulled down into a tar pit. That's the last thing I saw 'fore I blacked out.

BY THE TIME I come to, the fires had been put out. The men told me that, even though I'd been unconscious, it'd taken three of them to pry my arms off the derrick's supports.

Soon as I was able to walk again, I made a man take me out to survey the field. The damage was bad: nearly half the derricks lost, barrels of oil burned up, and one of the nitroglycerine trucks had exploded. My derrick still lay on its side, but there was little enough to show that the crack had ever been beneath it. I asked the man with me. He said that the ground had shaken again and the crack sealed up. There was just a scar to mark its passing, an uneven place where one lip of the ground was higher'n the other.

Burke had a business partner, a banker from Wichita, who took over his interest in the Black Hill Oil Company and sold it off to one of the other concerns. In his will, Burke had left a stipulation that his daughter never have a stake in it. By the time she was of an age to marry, she was provided fer nicely by the investment of Burke's money into other ventures.

I never worked the fields again. When my wife died, I come here to the sanitarium, where I've stayed ever since. My two girls are grown and married now, but they take turns coming to visit me. They've taken such good care of me since the incident.

There're days when I think I could leave this place, move in with one of them and have a life outside these walls, long as I stayed out of automobiles and away from oil fields. And maybe I would, were it not fer the dreams.

I dream, not of the world, but of the future. The future that Burke and I helped to bring about and that I'm powerless to prevent. I see a country crisscrossed with roads where thousands of automobiles drive every day. I see ships as big as whales, plying the sea with bellies full of black blood. I see a world of perpetual light and motion, powered by the unquiet dead.

Orrin Gray is a skeleton who likes monsters. His stories of cursed books, mad monks, and ominous paintings have appeared in *Bound for Evil, Delicate Toxins*, and, of course, at Innsmouth Free Press, among other places. He can be found online at www.orringrey.com.

The author speaks: I actually spent a lot of my formative years right near where "Black Hill" was set. The real place was called 'Oil Hill'. It was long gone by the time I lived there, its passing only marked by the occasional pump jack out in someone's pasture. But there were photographs up here and there that showed what the fields had looked like back in their heyday. I always wanted to set a weird story in those old oil fields. When I started thinking about all that oil down there, made up mostly of ancient organic matter, dead but not inert, well, that sounded pretty Lovecraftian to me.

AMUNDSEN'S LAST RUN

NATHALIE BOISARD-BEUDIN

AMUNDSEN TAPPED ON his pilot's shoulder, indicating to Rene Guilbaud where they should attempt their sea-landing – a small, canal-like harbour in the huge iceberg below them. The Frenchman shook his head. Too narrow. Too short. Unable to hear his own voice over the noise of the motors, he made wide gestures to emphasize his meaning, tapping the sheet with the coordinates, as well. They were still too far from their planned destination yet. The *Italia* had foundered much farther to the east.

Roald Amundsen stamped his foot. Guilbaud raised his arms in anger. The explorer leaned over his shoulder and brought the drive stick sharply down. The seaplane did a mad dive as Guilbaud scrambled, screaming, to regain control of the aircraft. Then, all of the sudden, both engines stopped. Like that, while they glided into the iceberg.

Amundsen regained consciousness, his body's pain a welcome indicator that he was alive. His first estimate told him his right leg was broken and a few of his ribs might be in the same state. The crushed-up cabin of the Latham 47 was obscenely embedded in the ice, making it unlikely that Guilbaud and Leif Dietrichson, his co-pilot, might have survived the impact. Amundsen had only managed that by racing to the back of the plane at the last minute, flinging himself down just before the impact. It infuriated him to think they could have floated to a stop in the small inner canal he had indicated to Guilbaud. But the Frenchman's obstinate refusal had put them all in jeopardy, forcing him to desperate measures.

He dared not disobey the humming.

DURING HIS EXPEDITION of 1925 to the North Pole, he had encountered this giant iceberg and experienced technical difficulties in its presence. A radio breakdown, followed by sudden motor extinction, had nearly killed them all. By an incredible fluke, they had saved themselves, but lost a plane. While the team was clearing the ice for one of the two remaining planes to fly off, they had heard a slow, whining hum rising from the ice, like a chant, in particular at night. A commanding chant. Back then, and for awhile after their return to safety, they had dismissed the experience as a collective hal-lucination. They had existed on very little food in critical temperatures for a long time, after all. And icebergs do have their own noises, as they creak and float and melt.

However, back home, images of the massive, 'S'-shaped iceberg, its hum-ming calling to him in tones he thought he could understand, invaded his dreams. He woke in the mornings disorientated and passed his days look-ing for clues he did not recognize in books, newspapers and the odd film. Icebergs were not charted, as they tended to drift, but this one had a singular shape: tapering in its middle from an almost-square basis, with sinusoid lower banks forming what looked like natural harbours, with fairly shallow, under-water quay-like banks, possibly carved by a spinning current. The damaged seaplane had neatly severed one such quay and the iceberg's course would have been affected by the loss of symmetry.

Night after night, the dreams had plagued him with urgent-yet-undeci-pherable messages, until one day, he had stumbled upon an article recalling the so-called "Curse of the Pharaohs" that had afflicted the team of Carter and Carnarvon, fully illustrated with strange god-figures and a picture of the Pyramids. Amundsen immediately recognised the tapering pattern at the center of the iceberg in that picture, a realization that had sent him racing to unearth the history of such cold giants. A geologist from Oslo had confirmed that the huge ice mountains were very old, indeed – possibly as old as the earth – and must, perforce, like any mountain, contain many trapped organ-isms and skeletons inside their folds, remnants of ancient earth creations

Could the iceberg be some sort of grave? The idea had taken root in his mind and refused to budge, despite his stern, realistic upbringing. His dreams became more vivid, vague forms oscillating in time with the hum-ming against a pyramidal background, with the noise level rising to a thump-ing rhythm, as of a heartbeat. A ruler was waiting for him, said the chanting dreams; a ruler was waiting in the mountain's heart to rise again.

During the day, the explorer was able to dismiss the visions as ridiculous, a product of hysteria, but each night, they came back to haunt him until they became an obsession. Amundsen was nothing if not driven by a scientific mind and curiosity. It was all tosh, he told himself. He would find out the truth and be rid of this nonsense, once and for all. He therefore put together a plan for investigating the iceberg and its reality. However, the following year, he had been drawn into another run for the North Pole race and had to postpone his plans. He found that the exertion of that quest had calmed him, somehow – a point for the hysteria theory – and that his dreams were not so frequent then, or during the series of talks and conferences he had found himself propelled into by his victory.

THE ICE CRACKED under his weight and the pain caused by the slight movement flashed, sobering him greatly. What had he done?

It had taken him almost two years to come back. Two years, during which the dreams had returned, scaling the walls of his sanity, eroding his nights until he had driven his whole crew to their deaths. All in pursuit of a chimera! He attempted to stand up, helping himself with a bent part of fuselage. He should survey the plane, see if there were any other survivors. His first attempt to move was unsuccessful, the metal folding under his weight, his ribs screaming with pain. Crawling, then ….

He went over to the mangled debris of the seaplane, calling. Only silence answered. Silence and … creaking? Sharper. Something more metallic like … overheated motors. Cracking. Cracking ice cubes. He spun as fast as he could, to find himself facing a crystal-like pyramid. One of its sides had been breached by the crashing aircraft and it gaped open, slowly breaking down under the weight of the cabin. Had the iceberg been rock-solid, it should not have been affected, but the impact showed the structure to be hollow, as indeed, it had been in Amundsen's dreams, minus the humming or fantastic-looking creatures. Peeking inside a crack, he could make out an inner wall, about a meter deep inside the pyramid. In the uncertain gloom of the never-quite-night of June, Amundsen could only guess at its volume, which – like the outer shell itself – looked man-made. Was it some kind of inner chamber?

He crawled closer to the plane, trying to see if he could salvage some food, some covers or others means to keep warm. Holding onto the shafts that supported the wings, he was finally able to stand and get his hands on two broken pieces of rod. He wrapped these with a piece of cloth to hold his leg stiff. Another piece would serve well as a cane, but as he was searching the wreck, a thick layer of clouds obscured the horizon, makeshift night for the Arctic Circle, and his lighter proved a feeble and insufficient alternative light source. He moved closer to the breached ice wall, which would serve as windbreaker for the night. If he survived the cold, he would be in a better position to start looking for valuables in the morning. A broken wing floater might serve as a makeshift boat to carry him away – possibly ….

Dropping a handful of papers on the ground, Amundsen sat as close as he could to the wall. It did not feel any colder than the walls of his rooms as a boy back in Borge and far less rough than the wood panelling he had nestled against then. He should not sleep. Without anyone to wake him, slumber in icy conditions might mean he would not ever wake up. Unfortunately, his broken limbs ensured he could not walk, or dance and stamp, or just keep himself busy, as he would normally have done in such circumstances, as he had done in the tremendous ordeal that had been the rescue of 1925. But then they had been a whole team, working night and day to clear a path on the ice so a plane could take off. They had kept moving in sub-freezing conditions and had taken turns to sleep. Yet, lack of food and rest had created this ludicrous hallucination that had brought him back here today. That had preyed on his mind for three years, nearly driving him mad, in the process. Humming, vibrating through his brain, though his bones, a plaintive chant with dark edges, where sacrifice was expected and exacted. He reflected that, in the present case, sacrifice had indeed been performed. Five men had died in the impact and he, himself, wasn't in too brilliant a shape. His head felt warm, much too warm to be healthy, melting the ice next to him. His body shook slightly, pulsating softly with pain. And a rhythm. Startled, he straightened up, trying to decipher the new vibrations in his body. Yes, something was sending waves through the ice, a dull throbbing like bells calling servants to church. A summons, gathering speed in the gloom. Amundsen's eyes had become used to the darkness and he could now see some light oozing from the pyramid, dark against dark, and fine pin-points of light dancing in time with the thrumming. Was he hallucinating, again? Maybe the light was an effect of concussion, from the shock?

Straining to get up, he turned his eyes again to the breach in the wall. The inner volume was luminous! He could clearly see it now, an obviously man-made structure carved with designs he could not quite discern. The pinpoints were more active there and their chanting – could it be that they were the source of the chanting? – more vehement, more insidious. He wanted to go inside the pyramid and join them. He could tell they were angry at his delay, but at the same time, his body had frozen, the hair at the back of his neck risen in clear warning. His head felt like a spinning top, tossed between emotions, his teeth chattering and his eyes too-widely opened. He called out, a muffled cry smothered by biting his own tongue.

The humming had stopped, the lights frozen in their ballet. A second, two, three. And then they rushed to the breach, pushing him aside on their way out. They twirled angrily into the absent night, furious wasps looking for a target, and went straight to the seaplane. Amundsen saw them disappear into the cockpit and immediately heard the metal complain. He felt warmth on his face. His hands touching his cheek felt sticky. Blood? The lights had come so close; could they have cut him? It certainly sounded like they were wreaking havoc in the shattered aircraft, which was whining and moaning against their assault. He dared not get any closer to see what was happening. Not that he needed to. After a few minutes of furious activity, the broken plane lit up in a brief flash and disappeared, shimmering dust falling slowly to the ice where the huge, metal carcass had been moments before. The lights were still there, forming some sort of spiral that shot up straight towards the sky before coming back down just as quickly, zooming past Amundsen into the pyramid. Inside, their dance took on a savage rhythm, a frenzy illuminating the whole structure. The explorer could nearly make out the patterns on the inner building, twirling designs like flowers or tentacles. Or the diaphragm shutter on a camera. Meanwhile the lights seemed ready to swarm again, gathering in a spearhead formation, their buzz strong and urgent, attacking the whole structure in waves. An aperture slowly unfolded on the inner structure, letting darkness seep into the chamber, absorbing the noise and light in slow, oily ripples as Amundsen looked on, frozen into place. Something darker than night moved into the room, advancing in tentacle-like movements from the opening, smothering the lights, one-by-one, slowly coming closer to the breach. Viscous gloom reached out from the crack, feeling its way upward.

Amundsen felt it brush against its face and flung himself backwards. He fell heavily onto his back, his leg sending agonizing pain through his body. His mind was solely focused on escaping, as fast and as far as he could. Crawling backwards, his eyes fixed on the fissure, he searched for the broken wing-float he had found earlier and pulled aside, finding the structure just as darkness began oozing from the pyramid towards him. Pushing the fragile vessel into the water canal, he pulled himself on board just in time. But he had nothing to paddle with and his hands were of little help in pushing him farther out to sea. Gloom reached the water's edge and pooled on the surface, rising into a large, murky wave that lapped at the floating shell, seized it and flung it back hard against the wall of the pyramid.

With his back broken, but still alive, Amundsen looked on as darkness retreated to the inner temple, passing over his supine body. For a moment, he entertained the illusion that he was safe. Crippled and cold, yet saved somehow. Then the pyramid started pulsing into the night, humming once more in a stern rhythm, lighting up once again. Suddenly, it dissolved in a chanting blizzard of light and ice shards, tearing at the feeble night, tearing at him, tearing at the universe, until there was nothing left and everything once again fell silent.

Nathalie Boisard-Beudin is a middle-aged French woman living in Rome, Italy. She has more hobbies than spare time, alas – reading, cooking, writing, painting, and photography – so hopes that her technical colleagues at the European Space Agency will soon come up with a solution to that problem by stretching the fabric of time. Either that or send her up to write about the travels and trials of the International Space Station, the way this was done for the exploratory missions of old. Clearly, the woman is a dreamer.

The author speaks: Icebergs are mountains created from water that might be as old as the Earth or beyond; who knows what secret of our ancestry they might contain in their folds? Is this what makes the white-and-blue giants creak and moan about like heavy ghosts? On the other hand, on the 18 of June 1928, Antarctic explorer Roald Amundsen disappeared without a trace as he was out on a rescue mission. His body has never been recovered. In such absence blooms a story.

RED STAR, YELLOW SIGN

LEIGH KIMMEL

THE HALLS OF the Smolny Institute, Leningrad's Communist Party headquarters, were quiet at such a late hour. A couple of NKVD guards maintained a bored watch at the security checkpoint. Little challenge to a man determined to avenge his honour upon that cuckold, the City's mayor.

The sound of footsteps brought Leonid Nikolaev to full alertness. Yes, here was the man who'd made free with his wife, walking down the corridor like he had a right to everything he set his sloe eyes upon. Damnation, but the memory still stung, the humiliation of being mocked by colleagues as the rumours spread about how eagerly Milda had spread her thighs –

Nikolaev's breath became rapid and his vision blurred. His skin crawled with filth and, although he tried to tell himself it was just because he hadn't been able to afford to visit the bathhouse in weeks, he knew he was just whistling in the dark.

No time for distractions. Nikolaev tightened his grip on the pistol concealed in his briefcase. The cold metal focused his thoughts. He shut out memories of strange symbols and stranger creatures, of the darkness that had begun calling to him during the impossible brightness of the White Nights six months earlier.

Mayor Kirov turned the corner, still walking as if he hadn't a care in the world. Watching the back of his rival's neck, Nikolaev studied the pink flesh of a well-fed senior Party official. The pistol snapped up, as if of its own volition. Nikolaev hardly felt his own hand squeeze the trigger.

His clarity shattered, pistol in hand, Nikolaev stared down at the floor. Sergei Kirov, First Secretary of the Leningrad Communist Party, lay sprawled there, a thin line of blood leaking from his mouth.

"What have I done?" Nikolaev's voice sounded weak and thin in his ears, and not just from being stunned by the pistol's report. "Oh, what *have* I done?"

One thing he knew for certain: his life wouldn't be worth a plugged *kopek* when the NKVD found him and nobody was going to believe he'd done it solely out of sexual jealousy. He wasn't even sure he believed it himself.

What to do now? If he was going to end up dead anyway, wouldn't it be better to take his own life than wait for the non-existent mercies of the NKVD? Within his mind echoed memories of voices chanting in languages he'd never learned, yet understood perfectly, telling of the joys of offering oneself and one's victim up to Their Supremacies the Great Old Ones in an act of murder-suicide.

Nikolaev put his pistol to his own head, but before he could complete the deed, an object struck his hand and the shot went awry. Drained, physically and emotionally, Nikolaev sank bonelessly to the floor beside Kirov.

To: Leningrad Operational Center
From: R'lyeh
Date: December 1, 1934

THEIR SUPREMACIES WISH to remind their operatives of the absolute necessity of maintaining plausible deniability at all times. Although the growing popularity and evident ability of the Kirov human posed a long-term threat to the utility of Communism as a self-limiting tyranny to socially neuter the humans and render them harmless to the purposes of the Great Old Ones, in the short term, the careless manner in which its elimination was achieved poses a far greater risk that our activities will be exposed.

THE HASTILY-ORGANIZED TRIP from Moscow to Leningrad had been particularly unpleasant. As a responsible Party and government officer, Nikolai Yezhov was familiar with dropping everything to respond to a crisis.

Never had he made such a trip while grieving, furious and helpless over the murder of an admired colleague. It would've been an exaggeration to call Sergei Kirov a friend – the gap in their respective ages and backgrounds was simply too great to bridge at that level. But in the time that they'd worked together in the Central Committee, Yezhov had come to deeply respect Kirov. Cheerful and unassuming, the older man had never looked down upon Yezhov for his short stature or meager education, but had treated him as a comrade in every way.

And now Kirov lay dead, gunned down from behind. When the news reached Moscow, Stalin had wasted no time in calling his key staffers together for an emergency meeting. And when Stalin called, you came, even if you were just sitting down for supper with your family.

Now here Yezhov and his colleagues were in Leningrad, packed into Kirov's office, which Stalin had made his emergency headquarters. The fury fairly rolled off Stalin in waves as he cursed the city's NKVD chief for failing to protect Kirov, the first and finest of the Leader's friends. Never mind that

Russian was not Stalin's native language; he showed a fine and subtle mastery of the exquisite art of Russian malediction.

And now, with a wave of Stalin's hand, the disgraced city chief was dismissed. His colleagues didn't even watch as he slunk away. They'd already brought the assassin forward.

The man they brought in hardly looked like a dangerous killer. Scarcely taller than Yezhov himself, Nikolaev more closely resembled a homeless person swept up from the gutter by the *militsia* for parasitism. Sunken eyes stared from an ashen, haggard face. When the city chiefs released his arms, he collapsed on his knees. Blinking like a sunstruck owl, the man stared up at Stalin.

"Wh-who are you?"

Stalin scowled. Around the room, Party officials tensed, expecting an explosion of outrage. Yezhov recalled his own first meeting with the Leader. Then he realized that Nikolaev, as a lowly functionary, would never have seen the pockmarked Georgian behind Stalin's official image.

Yezhov grabbed Stalin's portrait from the wall and held it before Nikolaev. "This is Comrade Stalin. He has come to investigate what has happened to Comrade Kirov."

Nikolaev's wailed tearfully, "What have I done? What have I done?"

Stalin leaned forward, his fierce hazel eyes fixing Nikolaev like those of a hunting tiger. "I am told that you fired the shot which killed Kirov."

Nikolaev gulped audibly and nodded, his lips trembling too much to form words.

However, his visible distress didn't keep Stalin from pressing the issue. "So, why did you do it?"

Nikolaev murmured, "They needed it removed." Then he suddenly shook his head as if clearing it and spoke again, louder. "What is a man supposed to do when another man puts the horns on him?"

The second was a line fairly guaranteed to prick Stalin's Georgian sense of familial honour. It might have actually worked, except that Stalin's hearing was sharp enough to pick up that first, half-mumbled reply.

"Who needed what 'removed'?" Stalin grasped Nikolaev by the front of his threadbare shirt, pulled him up to better examine him. "Was this someone in the Party, perhaps a Trotskyite or a Zinovievite mole, working on orders to do the Party harm?"

Yezhov braced for an outburst of Stalin's notorious anti-Semitism. Having a Jewish wife had made Yezhov acutely aware of that particular hot button of Stalin's.

But no, Stalin didn't get a chance, for Nikolaev pointed directly at Leningrad's deputy NKVD chief. "Why are you asking me? Ask him."

Stalin's swarthy features darkened as the blood went to his face. "Don't get smart with me, you worthless little pipsqueak. Now, tell me who put you up to this crime."

Nikolaev nodded slowly, as if unable to keep his head upright. "You yourself said –"

Stalin slapped Nikolaev across the mouth, so hard the little wretch went sprawling across the floor. "Get him out of here, now."

The Chekists were particularly rough in dragging Nikolaev away. One of them even landed him a few blows on particularly painful places. Yet, he remained oddly insensate, as if something were not connecting properly within his mind.

Yezhov looked around at the other senior Party officials who filled the room. Had any of them noticed the peculiarity of the assassin's behavior, the sense that he was not only not in his right mind, but that his mind might well have been tampered with in some way?

But Stalin was already calling for Nikolaev's wife to be brought in. Interrupting the Leader was not exactly conducive to good health and long life.

To: R'lyeh
From: Leningrad Operational Center
Date: December 2, 1934

MAY WE REMIND Their Supremacies that we took the normal precautions of implanting our tool with a compulsion that would ensure its self-destruction when it completed its assignment? We could not have foreseen that this compulsion would have been interrupted in its execution.

However, it appears that we will be able to divert attention to local divisions within the humans. The Stalin human is particularly obsessed with personal enmities and will pursue them beyond all rational limits. With proper direction, we will be able to use it to prune out certain problematic elements in the organization.

EVEN THROUGH A crackly telephone line, there was something wonderful about hearing, "I love you, Papa," in the soft lisp of a child's still-growing mouth. Yezhov smiled, imagining he could smell his daughter's milk-scented hair. "I love you too, Natashenka."

His attention interrupted, Yezhov looked up to see Agranov just outside the office door. Better get off the phone.

Agranov wasn't quite frowning, but it was hard to miss the tightness at the corners of his lips as he said, "A little *personal* conversation, Comrade Yezhov?"

Yezhov smiled, although he doubted it really covered his embarrassment at having been found out. "I suppose it could be considered an abuse of government resources, but our daughter's just settling in –"

"I hadn't heard Yevgenia Solomonovna was expecting –"

Yezhov's cheeks burned. "She wasn't. She didn't want her literary salon interrupted, so I took her to one of the orphanages around Moscow and we adopted a little girl." He clamped down on the rush of words, annoyed that he'd let himself get caught by surprise. It wouldn't do at all to blurt out how he'd picked that particular orphanage because a girlfriend of his had left a baby there a few years earlier and his wife's desire for a child provided perfect cover to retrieve his own. Though he pointedly ignored how often Yevgenia's literary lion-hunting ended in her bed, Yezhov avoided drawing attention to his own affairs.

Yevgenia had been a bit nonplussed that little Natasha was turning out to be quite the daddy's girl, but was rapidly reconciling herself to this unexpected turn of affections. She'd even convinced herself that she had picked Natasha because the girl's eyes reminded her of his own.

But there was no time to dwell upon it, not when he needed to get Agranov's attention away from the whole matter. He made a show of brushing his hands off. "Right now, we've got work to do, so let's be about it."

Together, they walked down to the official car that waited in front of the reclaimed Smolny Institute to take them to Leningrad NKVD headquarters, where Nikolaev was being held in the investigative prison. In spite of the early hour, it was already dark. Yezhov remembered Leningrad's winter darkness well from his own childhood, but Agranov seemed unsettled.

At least the Northern Lights were reasonably bright in compensation. Yezhov grinned at Agranov, pointing out the fact.

Except that the NKVD officer just looked up and frowned. "I don't see them. Some skyglow from the city lights, but nothing like the stories I've heard about the Leningrad auroras."

Yezhov looked up. Far overhead, titanic streamers of terrible, deep purple light shimmered, writhing into loops that reminded him of an octopus' tentacles.

When Agranov insisted that he saw nothing except some faint wisps of cloud, Yezhov decided not to push the matter. They had orders from Stalin, to squeeze all possible information from the pathetic Nikolaev. Standing here arguing about the Northern Lights would accomplish nothing.

Still, they made the trip to NKVD headquarters in awkward silence, punctuated from time to time with uneasy attempts to discuss the case. Yezhov was actually somewhat relieved to arrive, even if it did mean having to descend into the prison levels to get to the interrogation room.

As the NKVD representative, Agranov handled the actual interrogation. Yezhov observed, his presence required because Nikolaev's actions had reflected badly on the Party Control Commission.

It still didn't make dealing with Nikolaev any more pleasant. When brought in, the man shook so badly he couldn't walk without support. Nikolaev sagged into the chair like a sack of meat and bones, bereft of any animating spirit. Agranov had been pushing him hard for the last three days. Tonight, Yezhov thought the prisoner close to hysterics and more babbling nonsense.

There is definitely something wrong with that man's mind. Trying to distract himself from what was about to unfold yet again, Yezhov looked through some of the evidence for the case.

A battered, much-handled book was supposed to be a diary found in Nikolaev's apartment. It detailed his developing plans for a grand political act. A blow against those he perceived as having betrayed the October Revolution? Thumbing through it, Yezhov noted the progressively-sloppier handwriting. It seemed much more a mirror of Nikolaev's mental disintegration.

At a sudden sharp cry, Yezhov looked up and gave Agranov a frown of disapproval: *Not so hard, Comrade – Stalin wants us to squeeze him for information, not smash him to pieces.* Satisfied his message had been received, he returned his attention to the diary.

Oddly, the vocabulary changed along with the handwriting. Nikolaev was supposed to be of humble origins and minimal schooling, a former metalworker. Yezhov himself had been a voracious reader, trying to mitigate his own truncated education. But, over the last year, Nikolaev's diary entries had begun using elevated words and phrases, difficult for Yezhov to parse without a dictionary. Why would an obsessive traitor wish to better himself through schooling. Or was it schooling?

Was this evidence the man's mind had been tampered with? Yezhov was reluctant to mention it to Agranov, after the latter's blind scorn about the Northern Lights. No, better to do some investigating on his own, starting with Nikolaev's apartment. When he had incontrovertible evidence of his suspicions, facts that couldn't be dismissed because of his personal shortcomings, then he would present it to the Party leadership.

To: Leningrad Operational Center
From: R'lyeh
Date: December 5, 1934

HOW CAN YOU have been so incompetent as to have allowed the humans' investigative agencies to locate materials which your ill-chosen and poorly-conditioned tool produced? Already, one of these insufferable creatures has become suspicious and is beginning to look in directions difficult to conceal.

It is absolutely essential that this Yezhov human be neutralized in such a way that involves no mental manipulation, nothing that might arouse further suspicion. It is not sufficient to kill it. Its reputation among its kind must be completely and irrevocably demolished to the point that no one will dare question its fate.

YEZHOV KNEW HIS old hometown well enough to navigate it in the middle of the night. The Party might look dimly upon a respected member investigating the icy streets and dim buildings without a bodyguard. Especially now, given Kirov's death and fears of other assassins. But Yezhov suspected his search would be impossible with a strong official escort.

The building housing Nikolaev's apartment wasn't that different from the ones Yezhov recalled from his own childhood. Though the city had been the Imperial capital then, the air still reeked of boiled cabbage. The same domestic quarrels still filtered through the closed doors.

The Nikolaevs' apartment was quiet. The adults were in custody, as suspected accomplices, and the children in one of the special orphanages for children of Enemies of the People. Though the NKVD had hastily searched the place, the officers would've been looking for mundane conspiracy clues. Not hints of interference from mysterious entities that could turn a Party man into whimpering mush.

Removing the NKVD wax seal from the door wasn't precisely normal procedure. But a senior official of the Party Control Commission had wide operational latitude, especially within such an investigation: the murder of the Leningrad Party chief by a disgraced Party member. Still, Yezhov lifted the seal without damaging it. It would be far easier to replace it later, than to acquire another one.

With a creak, the door opened into profound darkness. When Yezhov's eyes adjusted, he located a light switch. A single bulb cast only a meager reddish glow upon the chambers within. More evidence of the financial turmoil mentioned in Nikolaev's dairy, amid his confused ramblings about noble heroes and grand blows against the Revolution's betrayers.

Still, it was sufficient to allow Yezhov to navigate his way through the battered furniture, to look in the various cupboards and drawers for anything out of place. To be sure, the place was somewhat better furnished than those of his childhood, simply because its occupants had been Party members and thus, able to avail themselves of such luxuries as shelves on which to put the volumes of instructional materials they'd accumulated.

He was so busy looking behind and through all those bound volumes for hidden papers that he almost didn't notice the figurine which had fallen behind the shelving unit. He put his hand down to steady himself while looking at the bottom shelf and suddenly felt something hard and knobby under his fingers. Startled, he pulled it out to take a closer look and immediately wondered what could have possibly struck Nikolaev as attractive about this grotesque creature, like a bat-winged man with staring eyes and a beard of squidlike tentacles.

Unless it was placed here by whoever had tampered with his mind, perhaps as a reminder of their power. No doubt, the NKVD would have seen nothing significant about it and probably never even noticed they had knocked it off its perch during their investigations.

Examining it more closely, Yezhov noticed a peculiar design repeated around its base, a symbol like a twisting, writhing trefoil picked out in yellow paint. Just looking at it made his stomach nauseous and his eyes twitch away. Yes, most definitely some kind of tool of control, but of whom and from where?

Whom could he consult about it, let alone entrust with further investigation? Not Agranov, who clearly despised him. Had Agranov not seen the Northern Lights? Or was Agranov part of a larger plot, one connecting this nasty little figurine with the mysterious and unearthly display in the sky?

Yezhov dropped the figurine into his pocket. Yes, he'd been right to carry out his own investigation. He'd track this filth to its source, reveal to the Party an infection of unimaginable horror and scope. The Party would act to save itself, and reveal its true heroism to the human race.

He barely remembered to replace the NKVD's wax seal on the apartment door before he left, taking the steps down to the street two at a time in his haste. Overhead, the sky was alive with light. Rising from the neon gloom of Leningrad's sky-glow, the great streamers of light flashed with frantic intensity like some unearthly creature signalling a desperate message across the sky.

That disturbing light forced Yezhov to avert his eyes from the sky. Looking down, he noticed a mark on a storm-drain grating. The faint mark seemed scratched into the metal, but he was certain the same symbol twisted around the figurine's base.

Some people liked to claim that the city's sewer system went all the way back to its founding by Peter the Great, but Yezhov had clear memories of districts without proper sewer service when he'd been growing up. If something unearthly had infiltrated the USSR and was using Party members for its own nefarious purposes, the construction of Leningrad's modern sewer system would have afforded a perfect cover for the establishment of its base of operations.

Getting the grate pried up without attracting attention to himself wasn't easy, but he still remembered some tricks from his youth. However, he soon realized he wasn't as young as he felt. Things that had come easy to a junior metalworker weren't so trivial to a senior official softened by a decade of Party privilege.

The stench made Yezhov wrinkle his nose. Comfortable living had weakened him in other ways, as well. Only resolve enabled him to push his way in. This business could not be left to fester.

The sound of his footsteps on the access ledge echoed and re-echoed, mixing with the babble of effluent flowing and hitting splashblocks, creating a confusing tangle of noise. More than once, he had to stop and just listen, trying to sort out the various sounds, to recognize anything that didn't belong.

Yezhov was beginning to wonder if he'd come on a fool's errand when something he half-saw in the corner of his eye tickled at his awareness. He turned to get a better look, yet found it oddly difficult to focus upon it.

Just like the symbol repeated endlessly upon the figurine in Nikolaev's apartment. Yezhov focused directly on the bricks and, by force of will, closely examined the delicate lines traced there in yellow paint. By examining only a portion at a time, he was able to see enough to feel confident that yes, he was looking at that same symbol.

At the knowledge that he had to be very close to his quarry's lair, Yezhov's heart began to pound. He had to pause to calm himself, to think clearly. He had to think of a way to reliably locate that mysterious yellow sign when it was all he could do to look at it.

It took a little trial and error to discover that his peripheral vision was actually a more reliable way of detecting a sign. Each time he got that twitchy feeling, he would look just enough to confirm that yes, the yellow sign was indeed painted there, and then move forward in search of the next one.

Ahead came a sharp sound, not a splash but a sucking, like something soft being pushed or drawn through an opening too narrow for it to pass easily. The back of his neck prickled and he flattened himself against the filthy wall, looking ahead for whatever had made it.

In the dim light of the purplish fungi that clustered on the walls, Yezhov was able to get only a confused impression of vast eyes like glowing saucers, surrounded by a mass of squirming tentacles patterned in colours that shifted and shimmered before his eyes. He unholstered his pistol. *Aim at the eyes. The brain should be right behind it.*

The first shot went wild, ricocheting off the wall with a shower of sparks astonishingly bright to his dark-adapted eyes. He advanced the next chamber, fired. The monster emitted a horrific scream that brought bile to the back of Yezhov's throat and the thing thrashed its tentacles, sending raw sewage spraying in all directions.

Yezhov fought the urge to flinch, forced himself to keep firing until the hammer clicked onto an empty chamber. He'd failed to bring additional rounds, a lapse that would now cost him his life.

Filled with dread, Yezhov slowly realized he heard human voices now, instead of the keening of that hideous monstrosity. His knees went weak with relief.

Yezhov shouted over his shoulder, "It's down here. I think I've wounded it."

And then he was joined by two young NKVD men, both armed. When the first one's pistol shots located the creature, the second raised a tube to his shoulder and fired a device that filled the tunnel with a trail of brilliant light. Its projectile slammed into the tentacled nightmare, which dissolved into a ball of fire. Moments later, there was nothing left but a foul, burning stench.

One of the NKVD men looked at him. "Comrade Yezhov, that was very foolish of you, trying to take on a Lloigor by yourself."

They believe. They understand. "So, that's what that thing was. I presume it left that symbol." Yezhov gestured vaguely in the direction of the Yellow Sign marked upon the nearby wall.

The NKVD officer nodded. "Yes, it's one of servants of the Ancient Power Beyond the Stars."

"And it's what was controlling Nikolaev, setting him on Kirov?"

That got an even more energetic nod from the NKVD man, whose eyes seemed unnaturally bright in the stygian gloom. "Exactly. We've destroyed the puppet master, but its dupes and servants are scattered throughout the USSR. Nobody can be safe until we've rooted out all of them, everywhere."

Yezhov gestured back the way they had come. "Then there's no further purpose in remaining down here. We've got work to do, and we'd best be about it."

To: R'lyeh
From: Leningrad Operational Center
Date: December 6, 1934

INFORM THEIR SUPREMACIES the matter has been successfully resolved. The attention of the Yezhov human, which had apprehended at least some part of our true nature, has been deflected, albeit with the sacrifice of one of our number. It will now be a simple matter to convince the Yezhov human to take command of the punitive organs of the USSR and carry out a vast extermination program, believing that it is thus eliminating the remaining agents of Their Supremacies. Because it will act of its own free will, based upon our disinformation and not from any compulsion on our part, it will be remembered for a thousand years as one of the greatest monsters of history. Any human who may uncover any hint of our involvement in the matter will not dare to speak of the matter, lest it, too, be condemned by its fellows as an apologist for mass murder, a moral monster of the worst sort.

NIKOLAEV WENT TO his death in the same squalid, pitiful manner he'd lived his life, protesting a confused innocence. Yezhov noted the number of senior officials, tasked with the investigation, who found convenient ways to absent themselves from the execution.

Yezhov himself wanted to be elsewhere. Only a substantial bracer of strong drink let him endure the sight of that pathetic little man being led to his doom. There could be no other way. Yezhov wanted his daughter to grow up proud of a father who did not shirk even the unpleasant parts of duty to Party and State.

Now it was time to complete what had been started here, to extirpate, root and branch, the foul influence of the tentacled nightmare he'd encountered beneath the streets of Leningrad. Of course, nobody would ever believe a story about an ancient monstrosity from beyond the stars, so it must be phrased in terms that Stalin and the other senior officials of Party and government would understand, of a Trotskyite-Zinovievite conspiracy of wreckers and assassins. But, in the end, the effect would be the same: the cleansing of the sacred Motherland of a power that could destroy it.

Leigh Kimmel lives in Indianapolis, Indiana, where she is a bookseller and web designer. She has degrees in history and in Russian language and literature. Her stories have been published in *Black October, Beyond the Last Star* and *Every Day Fiction*. Leigh is working on a novel.

The author speaks: "Red Star, Yellow Sign" was inspired by my study of Russian history. Historians have called the Kirov murder "the mystery of the century" because of the many questions surrounding it: Did Stalin order the killing? Did Nikolaev have protection at high levels? Did Nikolaev even pull the trigger, or was he a patsy for an NKVD assassin? Thus, it seemed natural to ask, *What if ancient eldritch entities had interfered in this critical moment of history?*

Found in a Trunk from Extremadura

MEDDY LIGNER

T HE MAN ENTERED the central aisle where he found, at the end, the reception desk. Some columns, ornate from capital to base, gave the room an ambiance both austere and academic, an impression reinforced by the photos of ancient *savants* hanging on the walls. Everything in this place he breathed in; the knowing and that sum of knowledge seemed to crush anyone who entered there. He began the passage with difficulty, handicapped by a right leg that made him limp. Advancing, he systematically threw glances at the ranges of stacks, where were crammed books by the thousands. Astronomy, history, geography, law, philosophy, studies filed in order before his eyes as he approached the end of the aisle. On each side, students worked, installed at tables lighted by weak lamps; they murmured among themselves, so as not to disturb the others. In addition, there reigned over that place a sense of calm and studiousness, even as he noticed two men engaged in active discussion. One of the two, with a wan complexion, stared in a fashion almost inappropriate. In return, the man lanced him with a rapid look then superbly ignored him. He finally achieved his objective:

– Good morning. Can you help me, please? he asked the librarian.

There was a pause before the librarian lifted his nose from his magazine. Over a pair of glasses, two yellow globes twitched:

– Of course. What can I do for you, *Monsieur*?

– I understand that you have archives concerning the riches of the world and I have heard that you possess an example of the *Voyage of Don Ignacio de Arroyo*. Would it be possible to consult it?

ALL IS BLURRED inside my head ... A fog thicker than the London smog ... the void ... I remember almost nothing. Only images, of which others tell me nothing that helps. Scattered dots, with no lines between them.

It's the interior chaos. I'm very afraid that I have a failing memory. Why am I in this bar and how could I have landed here?

Good God. I haven't the faintest idea!

And these men who fix me with an evil eye ... I must look awful to get such glances ... What could have happened?

Wait ... something's coming back ... his head tells me something ... I have the impression that he knows me ... and ... and me him, also, apparently ... he's motioning to me with his hand ... one could say that he's inviting me to sit at his table ....

MY NAME IS Ignacio de Arroyo and if, in the evening of my life, I take up my pen to write these lines, it is to lighten my spirit of a most heavy burden. I have never spoken of any of these events and– as God is my witness, praise Him and His Blessed Mother– I adjure to tell the entire truth of that which I have seen during my journey in the New World. I was present; I have seen and heard all.

Everything began in the month of April, in the Year of Grace 1539. Some months before, I had taken a caravel from the port of Seville to traverse the Great Ocean in the hope of making a fortune. Mythical Peru attracted every lust. There, in a tavern in Lima, I met Don Santiago de López. Originally from Cádiz, the cadet member of a family of ruined nobility, this Andalusian gentleman sought to recruit men for his new expedition. Gold fascinated him and, to obtain this precious metal, Don Santiago de López was ready for anything. Like the rest of us, the Conquistadors of the New World. All of us dreamed of walking in the steps of Cortés , who put his hand on the fabulous treasures of opulent Tenochtitlan. We all wished to imitate Pizarro, who had captured the phenomenal riches of the Inca. So, when Don Santiago proposed to me that I become his second in discovering the legendary El Dorado, I accepted without hesitation.

I RESPOND TO his invitation and sit facing him. The man is a giant of two meters, of a strapping build. One could say an athlete or a rugby player, who must weigh ninety kilos. Next to him, I feel like a shrimp. With tan skin and blue eyes, he wears a grey suit, very sober. He smiles as if he's known me a long time. We sit there for several moments, looking at each other. Without a word. And then, finally, it's he who speaks. His voice is grave, calm and he articulates perfectly each syllable:

– I know that you have some big problems. I can help you. Meet me in two hours in the Main Library. Don't be late.

He's getting ready to leave me, already?

– Wait ... wait ... what's your name?

– Call me 'Bob'.

– Why all the mystery, Bob? Do you know some things about me? I ….

– Until then.

I can't believe my eyes! This guy has some nerve! I take pains to join him and he's already leaving! And then, as if it's the most normal thing in the world, he tranquilly finishes his glass before standing and saluting me. I don't stop him for further explanation. Everything is all so confused in my head.

I begin to remember pieces, but good God, this is complicated … since Bob the Giant left me, the memories rise to the surface like bubbles of air in water.

Howard Phillips Lovecraft was born on August 20, 1895 and died March 15, 1937 from cancer of the intestine. And me? I think I remember that I was born barely a century after him. On the other hand, I don't believe that I've lived as long as the Magus of Providence.

Lovecraft … it's bizarre that the guy had the word 'love' in his name, yet he was never a specialist on the subject … a failed marriage, a hermit's life … It's said that his best friends were his cats … strange ….

I've seen in his biography that in April 1917, Lovecraft enlisted in the National Guard of Rhode Island after the declaration of war by the United States on Germany. It was his mother, in reporting that he was in bad health, who succeeded in making him return. And if she had not succeeded? If she had failed in her attempt? Her son might have been able to depart for the European trenches. Might he have returned? If yes, what influence would this traumatic experience have had on the solitary man from Providence? Would he have become the legendary author that we know?

WE WERE 24 conquistadors embarking on the quest to find El Dorado. We had all been doughty warriors for many years. We had fought on the fields of battle in Italy or against the Saracens. Under the conditions of our en-comienda *[commission], we had requisitioned 20 Indians who, aided by some mules, carried our rations and equipment. Two among them served to guide and interpret for us. Three horses were also on the voyage and our convoy also counted one cannon. Finally, our ranks harboured Brother Hernando, originally with me in Cáceres, who represented our Most Holy Church and had the mission of evangelizing any pagans that we would eventually encounter.*

The entire baggage train set out on the road on April 14, in the Year of Grace 1539, heading northeast toward the dense and impenetrable forest. It was, according to Don Santiago de López, in this region yet unexplored that we would find El Dorado. Our captain had information from the Indians that he had encountered during previous expeditions. They had told him of a mythical city hidden in the depths of the forest and had indicated how to reach it.

At the hour of departure, Brother Hernando blessed all of our troop: "In Nomine Patris, et Filii, et Spiritu Sancti. Amen." Then we started out on the road.

LOVECRAFT ... HOWARD Phillips ... this man has always fascinated me ... It could be because I have read so many books that I have actually forgotten the titles ... the myth of Cthulhu ... a cosmogony complete, a universe entire ... with forbidden books ... the *Necronomicon*, the Pnakotic Manuscripts, the *Book of Dzyan* ... Where does reality stop? Where does fiction begin? It's like an old bit of parchment. After the death of my grandfather, I found it while going through his affairs ... it was at the bottom of an old trunk, covered in dust ... the text was written in Old Spanish ... I tried very hard to translate it, but I quickly gave up ... I have never been any good at languages ... How was my grandfather able to procure the document? ... That I don't know ... I know only that he dabbled with junk and antiquities ....

BY FOLLOWING THE Incan roads, we rapidly crossed the Andes and arrived on foot without encumbrance in dense forest. There, progress became much more problematical. The overpowering heat forced us to drop our armour and our coats of mail, even our faithful morions *[helmets]. Because of the extreme heat, the powder in our arquebuses compacted and quickly became useless. Happily, we still had our arbalests and our swords. The latter were a great help in hacking a way through the abundant vegetation. The forest was not the only thing hostile to us: the mosquitoes made life disagreeable and the snakes could, at any moment, make us lose our lives. Sadly, this happened to one of our companions. The punishing conditions had wicked repercussions for the morale of our troop: the men complained often and, in two or three instances, the tension resulted in fights. Our beasts also suffered under the circumstances and they became a drag on our advance. They became so dispirited that we were forced to abandon them. We had to do the same with the cannon.*

I JUST LEFT that beknighted bar. Outside, it's cold and the streets are deserted. Is it dusk or dawn? No idea.

I walk toward the Main Library. I must meet with Bob because I have the feeling that it is he who can give me the keys to leaving this infernal spiral ... in any case, what do I have to lose?

I am completely lost ....

A black cat just cut in front of me. An evil omen? I'm not very superstitious, but under the current circumstances, I'm wary ... in fact, I've never really liked animals ... I remember when I was a kid ... I must have been ten or eleven, with my friends; we captured an old tomcat who regularly wandered the neighbourhood ... I still dream about him: he was a fat, grey tiger ... To amuse ourselves, we attached a big stone to his neck. We wanted to dunk him in the pond behind my house ... The cat fought like a devil, but we wouldn't let him escape, though he scratched us a lot. Of course, once in the water, he sank. The stupid things we do at that age!

LIKE ALL THE others, I profoundly hated this virgin forest, but, at the same time, she exerted a powerful fascination on me. The profusion of life particularly impressed me and, at night, I stopped often to listen to the birdsong, the buzzing of insects and the howling of monkeys. An original, inhabited paradise. Since we had left the Andean plateau, we had not encountered a living soul. No trace of indigenous people.

After six days on the march in this green hell, we finally found the river we were looking for. Snaking through the middle of the forest, the water's course was at least twice as large as our Guadalquivir and its waters carried a sort of red mud. According to the information that Don Santiago had, it was necessary to continue for two days. For this purpose, we constructed with haste three great rafts that we immediately launched on the water. The prospect of gold increased our strength ten-fold.

We stayed for a while near the banks of the river, where the current was weakest, then advanced at a fast rate, faster than we had through the forest. On the second day, toward noon, in the winding of the river, we saw in the middle of the trees an immense megalith of stone, erected at the foot of the bank. It looked like one of the ancient menhirs found in certain countries of the Old Continent. Don Santiago ordered us to disembark at the foot of this colossal stone. As tall as five men, at least, this block possessed a surface perfectly smooth and polished. Judging this to be a pagan idol, Brother Hernando demanded in the name of our Most Holy Church that we throw it down, but Don Santiago firmly refused. It was necessary to save our strength. El Dorado was now very close by.

I HAVE READ somewhere that Lovecraft felt ill at ease in his time, that he would have preferred to live in the 18th century. A little like me ... I would have lived in Antiquity, walking the streets of Imperial Rome or the Greece of Pericles ... Ah! There is the entrance to the Main Library. I climb the steps ... hop, here I am in the main lecture hall ... Kids work at the study tables and there, at the end, I see Bob the Giant ... I stand in front of him.

– Here I am. Am I late?

– Sit there and wait, he says, indicating the chair next to him.

– I'd like an explanation, at least. You can't tell me why you had me come here? Whom are we waiting for?

– 'Patience is the mother of all virtues.'

– Okay, but I'm a little bemused by all this mystery, and –

– Wait, look over there, he says, pointing to the entrance I have just entered through moments before.

– That man is your key.

A man wearing a macintosh advances down the center aisle. I notice immediately that he limps, that his right leg hurts him. He comes closer and I begin to see his face … more and more clearly … the oval face … the fine and regular features … the almond eyes with a glassy look … the skinny profile … the sallow skin … no … no … It's not possible … this man … He just looked at me and I know him … This cannot be who I think it is … I swim in delirium … He is now some meters from me … There is no longer any possible doubt … It is indeed Howard Phillips Lovecraft … I am afraid.

– Good morning. Can you help me, please? he asks the librarian.

The other takes some time to respond then Lovecraft continues:

– I understand that you have archives concerning the riches of the world and I have heard that you possess an example of the *Voyage of Don Ignacio de Arroyo*. Would it be possible to consult it?

I feel as if a lance of brilliant light just pierced me through and through and searched my heart. I'm two fingers away from fainting. Everything around me pitches about, but bit by bit, I master myself. This *Voyage of Don Ignacio de Arroyo* … the trunk of my grandfather … I had thought to be in possession of the only copy of the manuscript and yet, here before my very eyes, the Master of Arkham asks to see the manuscript. The employee answers him with all the courtesy of the world:

– *Monsieur*, I'm very sorry. In fact, we did possess a copy of this rarest of manuscripts, but unhappily, last week, someone stole the document from us. It is an inestimable loss and I sincerely hope that we will once again lay our hands on it. Hmm … hmm … it's too bad …."

This is the moment. I must attempt something, try to enter into contact. As Bob the Giant said, Lovecraft is my key.

– If you might permit me, sir, I say. Mr. Howard Phillips Lovecraft, isn't it? He turns his head toward me. A shiver goes through me.

– How do you know my name, lad? I don't know you.

– I'm one of your biggest fans. I've read all of your works. I recognized you and ….

– What? What are you talking about?

– I … I … Listen. This manuscript, as bizarre as it may sound to you, I have it at my house … I know that may seem incredible, but right now, everything's topsy-turvy … My Spanish grandfather left it to me … more or less … Let's say I discovered it one of his old trunks after his death … would you like to have a glance at it?

His black and piercing eyes fix me with insistence. I get the nauseating impression that he is visiting my mind and searching my soul ... An urge to vomit mounts ... I continue:

– So, what do you say?

– Very well, lad. When can we go there?

– Right now, if you wish. You have only to follow me. But first, I'd like to ask you a question.

– Say what you wish.

– All right ... What happened to your leg that you walk like that?

– A souvenir of war. In 1917, I left for France to fight the Germans. I knew the hell of the trenches: the assaults, the bombardments, the death, the mustard gas, the mud, the rats. In July 1918, in Champagne, during an enemy offensive, I took a piece of shrapnel in the knee. A dirty wound. The war was finished for me. I was even decorated ... a beautiful bullshit!

The world is collapsing around me. I have the distinct impression that I just dove into the abyss of time. Should I believe what I just heard? If this man is truly Lovecraft and if what he just told me is true, I must frankly be turning into a lunatic. I have to cling to something. Quick, Bob the Giant! I turn toward him. But he's not there. Disappeared! Vanished! I look around me. The librarian has also disappeared. No one is there. Not even a cat. The library is deserted, dark. I'm alone. Alone with He who whispers in the shadows.

THE OBJECT OF our quest was close by the megalith. The mythical city was located not far from the banks of the river, but the luxuriant vegetation prevented anyone from seeing it from the water. Once upon a time, this city must have been rich and powerful. Its walls were composed of blocks of cyclopean stone, more impressive than those I had seen at Cuzco, the Incan capital. There had been there gigantic palaces, temples with colossal walls and even a battlement that supported an observatory for studying the course of the stars. In times past, this metropolis must have been the capital of a prosperous empire. Who had been able to erect these monumental constructs? Who had lived in them? However, these questions remained unanswered because, unhappily, this city appeared to have been abandoned for an eternity and nature had taken back its rights, invading the place anew. In discovering this sad spectacle, I confess that I almost cried in vexation. By the Most Holy Cross, we had accomplished all these efforts to fall on the steps of ruins! What an injustice! Mad with rage, Don Santiago ordered us to dig in every nook and cranny of every room, every palace, every temple. He screamed loudly that these accursed natives must have buried their treasure, or hidden it in a secret place. We searched with the energy of despair.

I MUST HAVE been dreaming. If I ever tell anyone this story, it'll be the psych hospital right then and there. Brace yourself! I'm there in my house in the company of Howard Phillips Lovecraft! My barracks, let's say. It's the only thing my parents left me. An old, dilapidated shack, located on the edge of the city park. The only good thing my parents owned before sinking into the shadow of madness ... for good.

While I try to find my grandfather's manuscript, the creator of the myth of Cthulhu, faithful to his reputation for erudition, is in the process of examining the books that line the dusty shelves of my library.

There it is, finally! I just put my hand on a piece of yellowing paper, lurking at the bottom of a drawer. I hesitate for a moment – is any of this real? I hand the object to my host, who automatically sits on my sofa and begins to scan the lines of the precious work. He speaks no word to me, captivated as he is by his reading. He seems jubilant before this bibliophile's feast, but gradually, his features harden, shrivel. A glow of madness begins to agitate his look. Then he finally gets up, the manuscript in his hand, standing immobile in front of the window of my room. I call him, but he doesn't answer me. Now, his face expresses dementia, eyes bulging, his face twisted into a rictus. And suddenly, the Mage of Providence begins to speak in a stentorian voice, ageless words, psalms that seem to go back to the beginning of time:

– *Hxulu it bakal puk ti joggot belem! Râamma het palixli toatl!*

All at once, I plunge into a bottomless spiral.

Did I lose consciousness? Am I trapped in a dream? All is black, invisible.

I smell a pestilential odour that spreads around me, that envelops and sickens me. I still can't see, but other senses guide me. All at once, the window of my room breaks into a million pieces and from the outside, a Siberian wind blasts into my house. The cold air stings me. I feel my body stiffen. Then I hear a beating of wings, heavy and massive, entering my house. Footsteps echo on the floor. This *thing* that has entered ... suddenly, a human cry rends the air, strident, unbearable. It is the scream of someone who is about to die. A cry that freezes my blood. A terrible crash follows. They fight. They shred a body; they dismember it; they grind it savagely amid deafening groans ... Whoever makes these sounds isn't human. What follows only lasts a moment ... and then no more. The thing returns to the window. I hear again the sound of wings taking flight ... silence ... and this time, I slide completely into the shadows ....

So, kid, you've got quite the hangover, eh? Your guts are on fire, right? As if they were eating you from within, as if a pernicious evil emptied you of your strength? That's why you look like a skeleton, old friend. You've only got skin on your bones and, behind your eyes, one can see death dance ... you're not far from the end. I know something about it; you can well imagine! I know that's me, too … 'Cancer of the intestine,' that's what they say! No cure! It only remains to die slowly ….

Oh, no! Let's change a little! Obviously, lad, you and the cats, that's not joy! Vengeance is a plate that's served cold. These charming animals will look after you. You know, they have a wisdom of many centuries. They were present at the Pharaohs' sides when the last ones ruled over rich Egypt. Remember Ulthar! They will repast on your flesh! They will make a feast of your entrails. They will delight in your eyes. They will clean your bones until they are as white as ivory ….

Stop it! Change the scene! Lad, here you are now in a good old trench! Ah, listen! It's the signal to attack! Fix bayonets! You must bring the hill to the enemy! Cannon thunder, balls whistle, shells burst in a marvelous cacophony. Gas alarm! You must put on this devilish mask that makes it difficult to breathe! You have just enough time to see that the sky is grey and as low as if in Hell! Your comrades fall like flies. Some call for their mothers; others hold their entrails in their hands. Are you afraid? You see the one there who is bawling like a baby? And yes! That's good old Bob the Giant! He's lost an arm. And wham! This time, it's for you! Excruciating pain twists your leg. Unbearable, no? A piece of shrapnel tears into your knee.

ACCOMPANIED BY ONE of the guides, with whom I has struck up a friendship, I entered a large room located in the cellar of one of the ruined temples. The place had been plunged into shadow and, in order for us to see, we had to burn torches. And there, we were surprised to see our shadows dance on a myriad of multicoloured frescoes! We observed them for a while and the things they represented terrified us. These frescoes evoked pagan scenes with winged monsters, resembling griffons or dragons. Obviously, these creatures of Satan came here to be offered human sacrifices. A diabolical rite of black magic, I don't know what it was, but I was afraid and crossed myself, repeatedly kissing the crucifix that hung around my neck. In observing attentively every detail of these paintings, my guide fell into a kind of prayer that had been burned several times in these walls. My companion informed me that he was able to decipher the sounds and began to recite the evil verses in a monotone. Evil took him; let God forgive him! I do not know what, exactly, these words triggered, but outside, a great evil befell our men. An odour sharp and mephitic then invaded the atmosphere outside and it seemed that a battle raged. Human cries mixed with the growls of infernal creatures.

The monsters. The monsters had been awakened and massacred my companions to the last man. Paralyzed, the guide and I hid in our hole, praying to escape the griffons and demons.

I lack the words to describe what I heard and even now, my old age does not give me any more courage. Even today, I am still terrified. Even though the inhuman uproar lasted only a few moments.

Many hours later, we made the decision to come out and we discovered that our companions, without exception, had been killed. Their bodies, atrociously mutilated, littered the ground in the middle of immense pools of blood. It was obvious: we were the only two left, the guide and I, in the middle of those accursed ruins. Therefore, we decided to leave that malefic place, to rejoin the civilized world and forget these events.

By the Grace of God, may He be praised, Him and His Most Blessed Mother, we came back to civilization. But being hunted by these baleful memories was not easy. That is why, sometime later, I resigned myself to return for good to our dear Spain. And is there, in my city of Cáceres, that I decided humbly to end my days. Without ever speaking to anyone about this singular adventure.

For my greater sorrow, the words of that satanic prayer remain engraved on my spirit, and I do not know by what witchcraft I could ever get rid of it. So, I have reproduced it verbatim at the bottom of this manuscript. A way to exorcize my anguish. I have never tried to verify if the formula was correct, but I invite those who read my work to greater prudence.

God help you!

MY HOUSE IS in a pitiable state. As if an orangutan had passed through here. Traces of blood maculate my floor. What happened? I find ... I search my memories, but ... I don't remember anything ... I go outside ... There is a cat prowling ... I walk straight ahead, without aim ...

All is blurred inside my head ... A fog thicker than the London smog ... the void ... I remember almost nothing. Only images, of which others tell me nothing that helps. Scattered dots, with no lines between them.

It's the interior chaos. I'm very afraid that I have a failing memory. Why am I in this bar and how could I have landed here?

Good God. I haven't the faintest idea!

And these men who fix me with an evil eye ... I must look awful to get such glances ... What could have happened?

Wait ... something's coming back ... his head tells me something ... I have the impression that he knows me ... and ... and me him, also, apparently ... he's motioning to me with his hand ... one could say that he's inviting me to sit at his table ....

Meddy Ligner was born in 1974 in Bressuire, a small town in the western part of France. He spent his first 18 years there. He goes back frequently to see his family and to play baseball with the famous Garocheurs. He studied history and afterwards, he taught French abroad in Finland, Russia and China. Since 2003, he has worked as a teacher of history and geography in Poitiers, France, where he lives with his wife, his daughter and his son. His website is: http://meddyligner.blogspot.com

The author speaks: "I discovered Lovecraft late, thanks to one of my room-mates during military service. According to him, it was very good. So, I fol-lowed his advice and I started with "The Call of Cthulhu". I liked it and I read other stories. My favourite one is "The Case of Charles Dexter Ward".
Lovecraft fascinated me through his stories, his mythology, his gods coming from the dawn of time. This whole cosmology is very thrilling. Furthermore, the personality of HPL is mysterious: a hermit living isolated, surrounded by books. He is a kind of accursed writer (Alive, he had no success) and a guru for several generations of authors.
I did not want to write a linear story. I am interested in narrative techniques and I tried to experiment with this text.

CPSIA information can be obtained at www.ICGtesting.com
224867LV00002B/17/P